"Suspenseful and cathartic, the engrossing novel *What Was Lost* follows a healing woman as she reflects upon the damaged fragments of her past to reclaim her rightful future path."

—*Foreword Reviews*, 5/5 STARS

"A strong sense of humanity and compassion powers the novel."

—*Publishers Weekly*

"*What Was Lost* operates like a delicate nesting doll of secrets and confessions hidden within each other in a seemingly peaceful small town, the idealized neighborhood family, and childhood traumas. Each doll shatters the lies of the one before. Connelly writes tenderly as if releasing a long-held whisper that her protagonist, Marti, has been holding in all her life. The changes in time and POV deftly reveal the way the past is always present."

—Melissa Acquino Coss, author of *Carmen and Grace*

"Connelly combines a heavy fist with a light touch, and she knows when to use each. *What Was Lost* is a searing narrative of sexual abuse, artistic sabotage, and their aftermaths. At the same time, it's an uncommonly compassionate tracing of the webs of confusion and insight that connect parent to child, child to parent, and generation to generation. Reading Marti's story made me tingle and ache."

—James L. May, author of *The Body Outside of the Kremlin*

"Stunningly written, unerringly human, and deeply felt, Melissa Connelly's *What Was Lost* is everything I yearn for in a novel, a story about people that I love in all of their flawed messiness, trying to make sense of and move through the murk and ache of their pasts, to discover and assert who and what else they might be."

—LYNN STEGER STRONG, author of *Flight, Want* and *Hold Still*

WHAT WAS LOST

A Novel

MELISSA CONNELLY

SHE WRITES PRESS

Published 2024
Printed in the United States of America

Print ISBN: 978-1-64742-784-9
E-ISBN: 978-1-64742-785-6
Library of Congress Control Number: 2024913201

For information, address:
She Writes Press
1569 Solano Ave #546
Berkeley, CA 94707

Interior design and typeset by Katherine Lloyd, The DESK

She Writes Press is a division of SparkPoint Studio, LLC.

Dedicated to the memory of Forrest Holloway

1951–2004

For everything, and so much more

I came to see the damage that was done
and the treasures that prevail.

—Adrienne Rich

Part I

SKIN

1

E ver since Jan mentioned hearing Mrs. Colgan still lived in her house in Chatham, Marti became a scurrying rat searching for a way out of a maze. All exits led to Connie Colgan. Marti was troubled by the casual way Jan dropped this information, yet how could her sister understand? Jan didn't know Marti's secrets. The only one who did was Peter Colgan.

Marti struggled to wedge suitcases into the car trunk, both the trunk and her head were jammed too full—*The lights, the garbage, what am I forgetting?* The avoidance of the real question—*What am I doing?*—was causing her head to implode with minutiae. Her nerves were lit matches as she steadied herself against the car contemplating what she needed.

Courage. No wizard selling any.

It was happening so fast that she could scarcely believe she was returning to Chatham, Vermont, the hometown she'd run from almost thirty years ago. She put in for family leave at work, fabricating a dying aunt, undaunted by the paperwork on which she documented details of this nonexistent aunt. For nine years she'd worked at this children's hospital, passionately throwing herself into the lives of children and families she worked with, rarely absent, never vacationing longer than a week, and yet now, suddenly, she'd be gone for two months. Some of the children would die before she returned. Marisol, her closest work friend, puzzled by the suddenness of this leave, quizzed Marti on the

3

aunt she'd never heard of and Marti spun Marisol tales of Aunt Connie Colgan. This further increased her feelings of isolation on the eve of this journey. It made no sense: this compulsion to see Mrs. Colgan in order to correct past lies, all while creating new falsehoods.

Her dream was, that after confessing all to Mrs. Colgan, time would bend and stretch in a way to let her reestablish the relationship she'd had with Mrs. Colgan—*closer than an aunt!* The absence of that relationship had left her with a deep gulf, and now as Tess, Marti's daughter, was entering a more difficult age, Marti needed Mrs. Colgan's guidance more than ever.

She'd told Tess her job was making her use up old vacation time. "Don't want to waste it, so we might as well get away for the whole summer, right?" she said, trying to spin it, knowing it was upending her daughter's eagerly anticipated summer in Brooklyn.

Recently they'd had a blowup after Tess stayed out late and lied about where she'd been. Marti knew Tess thought this was the reason for the trip. *Isn't everything about her?* She *was* glad to get Tess away, yet that wasn't why they were going, and Marti couldn't share the reason (she wasn't clear herself). Her daughter's fury was a festering undercurrent dragging them both down.

Tess was sitting on the stoop, headphones on, swaying to the music of her CD player. When calling her name produced no response, Marti walked over and shook her shoulder. "Huh?" Tess removed one bud from her ear—just one.

"Did you pack the animals' bowls?"

Tess shuffled—deliberately slow, Marti suspected—into the house, came out and sat again, the bowls clattering beside her. "In the car, Tess, they belong in the car." Marti exaggeratedly gestured the motion.

"All right, Your Majesty!" Tess took a bow as she opened the door and threw the bowls onto the seat, pausing to untangle her hair from the headphone wires. They shared the same frizzy thick blonde hair, although, at forty-three, Marti's was already turning a silver white.

It would have been easier to get the bowls herself, but weren't parents supposed to instill responsibility in children? Wasn't that the endless busywork of parenthood? She'd envisioned parenthood to be exploring the universe with them and helping them find their place in it; instead, it was *brush your teeth, do your homework.*

Well, Marti thought, *every job has drudge work; even a midwife has the afterbirth to clean up.*

Will I finally clean up the mess I made?

"I'll get Caliban and Precious, and we'll be off."

Tess nodded without removing her headphones.

Marti put a can of tuna fish in the cat carrier to lure the cat; Precious only glared while Caliban poked his big dog head in. Marti yanked him out, tuna oil dribbling from his mouth. He'd be fine for the car ride; Precious, however, would climb and claw if not caged. Tess came inside complaining that Marti was taking too long. Marti pointed, and the two of them chased the cat, trying to corner her. Precious outmaneuvered them at every turn. Eventually, they plopped down on the couch, laughing. "God, she's psychic," Marti said. "She can tell which direction we're going before we've even decided."

"We need something unexpected." Tess sprang up and swung her arm behind the sofa, scooping the cat high into the air with one hand while Precious raised her orange fur and pedaled her legs, a cartoon character in midair. Tess placed the cat in the cage and snapped it shut. "Easy as pie. See, Mom?" Tess took the carrier outside, placed it in the back seat, and climbed in next to Precious. Marti followed with Caliban.

"The front, Tess."

"Why?"

Marti sighed her mother sigh.

"I know you're not a chauffeur, but it's not like we'll be talking;

I'm gonna have my music on." Still, Tess changed seats. Precious shrieked as Caliban jumped in. He barked in response.

Marti hesitated while the sullen daughter, excited dog, and caterwauling cat all looked at her expectantly. "Okay, let's go." She tried to sound confident. "No time like the present." *If you faked an emotion long enough, didn't you begin to feel it?* She turned the car on, half hoping it wouldn't start.

It was a very reliable car.

Everything was lush and green once they crossed the Vermont border, and she was glad the law against billboards still held. Whenever someone learned where Marti was from, they said: *What a great place to grow up! You're lucky!*

Marti glanced over at a sleeping Tess. Her cheeks still held a trace of baby fat, while her forehead was dotted with pimples and her facial features were evolving at different rates. Awkward and beautiful in equal measure, it smacked of that teetering bridge between girl and woman. She thought about Lucas, the boy Tess had been spending time with. Was he a boyfriend? Sex at fourteen?

Fourteen.

Beg, Martha, beg.

Winding onto Chatham's Main Street, she was relieved that it wasn't quite the same small town, yet inexplicably, she also felt an ache of loss, for even the recognizable seemed out of place, as if what was imprinted on her brain was deceiving her.

Tess awoke. "We're here? Hey—where's your house?"

"Not now."

"Aren't you curious, Mom?"

The lake cottage they'd rented was stuck in time where even the mildew seemed of another era. The next morning, they went for a swim off their dock and invented a game where they'd create scenarios in which a character was unaware of the dock's edge.

"Mom, look. A woman walks with her friend. 'Do you see my new dress? Pure silk, the finest in the world!'" Tess pranced about, an exaggeration of a runway model. "You may feel it only if your hands are completely dry—no water can ever touch my precious dress. Oh, oh! Help! My dress!" Tess shouted as she deliberately fell off the dock. Marti applauded.

Marti used Caliban in her routine. "Silly dog, why are you barking? What do you think you see? There's nothing, I tell you, nothing on that side of the street! I'll show you!" She stomped across the deck, falling in and shouting, "You dreadful dog! You tricked me!" Caliban was a large brown mutt, with a head that seemed enormous, almost like a cow's—one ear perpetually stuck straight up while the other flopped down. Caliban followed her in, his jump anything but graceful, wagging his tail proudly as if aware of his part in the performance.

Returning to the cabin, they rummaged through closets, finding games and toys—Sorry, badminton rackets, and jigsaw puzzles. Tess hadn't even put her music on since arriving. There was a TV, and Tess agreed Marti could put it away.

As Marti carried the TV to the back of a closet, a scarf fell on her head, battering her senses with a musty familiarity. Scent, that instant transporter, was at work. Unguarded, she couldn't hold the memory back of another closet; her limp body banging against the closet wall. She yanked the scarf off as she remembered the sound of her whimpers. *No, no, no.* Had she spoken aloud? Never quite sure, for in those long moments the disembodied feeling was strong . . . If she had no bones, did she have a voice box? The sliding door rattled back and forth as she rested unsteadily against it. Now that she was back in Chatham, would she relive it all? The closet was a terrible kind of home she'd never left.

"Mom, what are you doing?"

Marti picked up the scarf hoping to inhale the smell again,

but the scent was gone. Memory and smell, you couldn't hold them off, both elusive pranksters; they'd reel you in, fill you up, and then leave you nothing to grasp on to.

Tess was spending time at the lake beach, having made friends with a girl named Emily whose family was staying in the same cluster of cabins. Marti met Emily's mother, Linda, who was eager to chat, seemingly bored trailing behind her three-year-old daughter, while her husband and nine-year-old son were fishing. The family was from Connecticut and would also be here all summer. Linda invited them for dinner. "And bring your husband." At Marti's explanation of divorce, Linda's face contorted into surprise. *Did she think everyone had a husband off fishing?*

Linda opened the door, makeup on, dressed in a colorful sundress. Marti was wearing her frayed shorts, her wet hair an uncombed mess. She feebly handed Linda the obligatory bottle of wine.

"Come around the back deck, Art's grilling below. Hope you like chicken, although you'd think we'd have fish with all that time fishing." Linda said this last part loudly in Art's direction. She led Marti to the deck and poured wine. "Right back." Marti offered to help, but Linda waved her off so Marti sat, sipping, trying not to gulp, until Linda returned carrying a salad. "Sorry for that mistake about your husband. I didn't realize—" She patted Marti's arm, and Marti wanted to swat Linda's hand away. *Maybe I'm glad not to be part of a perfect two-parent family.*

She pushed her hair back; it was beginning to dry and curl into its usual wild state, and she hadn't remembered a clip. "The divorce was a long time ago."

In her marriage, Marti had felt suffocated. She'd been on her own since age fifteen and still thought of herself as a drifter despite a husband and baby. She resisted buying the house in Brooklyn. Rob pushed the idea and Marti felt like fleeing.

She didn't flee, at least not physically. Trapped as she felt, it was nothing compared to what came next: Rob was the one who left. *Careful what you wish for.* The most terrifying part was that Marti wasn't alone: a small child depended upon her. Rob generously gave Marti the house she'd never wanted, compensation for an uncertain future. Tess grew into a confident teenager, life swirling around an inert Marti.

"Marti, do you work?" Linda asked.

"I'm an art therapist at a children's hospital."

"How interesting! I must hear more after I take this platter to Art." Linda's heels clattered as she went down the steps.

The girls were whispering in the woods, hiding from Emily's brother, Matthew. Little Rose ran to her daddy and hugged his legs. Marti stood and called to Linda as she came up the steps, "Don't you think Rose is too close to the grill?"

"Art's right there." Linda topped off Marti's wine glass while Marti's eyes remained fixed below. "*Relax*, Marti." Linda raised her glass. "To vacations! How did you get so much time off in the summer?" Linda scooped up a pile of silverware and napkins that lay on the table and began setting them. Marti felt foolish for having not noticed and set the table herself. Instead she'd sat waiting uselessly.

"I had vacation owed me."

"I imagine you need time off from your job. Are the kids very sick?"

"Yes, they—"

"Oh, let's not talk about that. *So depressing.*" Linda stood up, studying the table, and when satisfied that everything was in place, she sat back down. "Lovely here, isn't it? Our first time, and fine with Art, because of the fishing."

"Don't talk about my fishing!" Art shouted up from below.

Linda laughed. "Well, where are the fish?"

"Mom, I like fishing," Matthew said, coming up the deck

stairs with the girls following. He grabbed a handful of chips and some fell back into the bowl.

"Matthew, gross. Stop being a pig," Emily said as they all swarmed around the chip bowl.

"Mommy, Matthew's taking all the chips," Rose whined, stuffing a pile into the dip where she left them, chips poking out like shark fins.

"Talk about gross," Matthew sneered.

"All right, animals—I mean children—back away." Linda turned to Marti. "How did you find this lake?"

"Mom grew up here," Tess answered.

"Really? You haven't mentioned. You must have lots of people to catch up with, and yet you're here with us. What about family?"

"My parents passed away, and my sister lives in Burlington."

"Yeah, Mom, when are we going to see Aunt Jan?"

"When Megan's back from her camp job. My niece," Marti said, eager to shift the conversation.

"Still," Linda persisted, "you must have old pals. Hard to keep up with after graduation. It'll be exciting to see them, won't it?"

"I left before high school ended."

"Your family moved?"

"Yes," Marti answered cautiously. It was hard to be questioned about your history when it didn't match anyone else's.

"Mom, there's that lady you want to see, right? The mother of your old boyfriend?"

She could hear Mrs. Colgan's voice now, that slight Irish lilt you had to listen carefully for to be sure it was there, and when you heard it, it seemed like a gift just for you. The gift Marti wanted to hear was: *A terrible lie you told, I understand, poor child, you were scared. All's forgiven.*

"Ah," Art said, coming up the stairs, "an old boyfriend! Scouting out the mother first, ingenious plan."

"Not a boyfriend, just a neighbor."

"That's not what Aunt Jan said." Tess giggled.

Marti drank her wine. Why had she come to this dinner? She'd been using any excuse to avoid the inevitable: Mrs. Colgan, the reason she was here.

The perfect opportunity came a few days later when Tess left at dawn to go rafting with Emily's family. Marti chose not to go, and yet at this early hour, she felt abandoned. *Left out of the living.* Caliban was watching her, tentatively thumping his tail, anticipating their morning swim. She grabbed their towels, and he yelped gleefully at the sign. Marti didn't bother with a suit as the sun was only just beginning to brush the water and there'd be no one to observe her. She dived in; the water felt glorious on her naked skin. Caliban followed, paddling steadily, his long tail swishing back and forth like a sprinkler spraying water. Every few minutes he'd return to shore and shake off, only to swim again, aiming in Marti's direction. She was his destination, the center of his world, devotion beyond any human one, and it never ceased to move her.

Thoughts of procrastination crept in, but no, today was her chance. The swimming had strengthened her. She put on the skirt she'd bought for this occasion and dabbed powder on her face, a futile attempt to conceal her scars—some things can't be hidden.

After Marti made it right with Mrs. Colgan, Tess would meet her. She pictured Tess playing with the grandchildren while Mrs. Colgan fussed over them, doling out snacks—especially the jar of M&M's she always kept close at hand and passed around to defuse any quarrels. Tess would almost *be* one of those grandchildren.

Could there be a more forgiving woman? Why has it taken me so long?

The grandchildren Marti pictured weren't Peter's but rather any of the other seven Colgans. She didn't know whether Peter had a family; all she'd heard was that he lived in Boston. Didn't she need forgiveness from him too?

When she got to Hemlock Street, she parked by her old house, which looked surprisingly cheerful now that the somber blue siding had been painted a bright white. The enormous dark trees in front were gone, replaced by dogwoods still blooming with welcoming white flowers. Peering around the back, she spied a bicycle, asleep on its side. *Does a happy family live here?*

Her father had taught her to ride a bike just before he suddenly died from a brain aneurysm. Everyone referred to him by his name, Ed Farrell. *Daddy* was a myth only Marti clung to.

"You didn't miss much," was what her mother, Peg, said.

"You were *lucky* you didn't know him," Jan, five years older, hissed.

Apparently, Ed had a drinking problem that led to late night belligerence, although Marti knew nothing of that, having slept through it all. She remembered only his charms—the laughter, jokes, and fun—all the things that went missing afterward.

Her most vivid memory was of riding on his back in the lake. He'd swim steady and strong, propelling them farther in the water as she tightly gripped his wide shoulders, never afraid, only thrilled, believing nothing could hurt her if she was with Daddy. She never shared this memory with Jan or her mother, imagining what they'd say to deflate it:

"Sure, he'd take you swimming while I toiled away."

"You were too young. You don't know. *I do.*"

In the years following his death, Peg and Jan developed a bond almost as if they were a couple, and Marti couldn't jockey her way in. Her ally had been Daddy. Daddy, who picked Marti's dolly up and danced, pretending to be in love with Dolly while an enchanted Marti watched. Daddy, who treasured the drawings she made for him. Daddy, who reached in his pocket each morning just before leaving for work, Marti wiggling in anticipation until he said, "What have we here?" and handed her the end of a Life Savers roll, a few pieces remaining. She'd wait to suck them until he was out the door, a consolation prize for his absence. She could still taste the tangy peppermints and evoke the pleasure of rolling them in circles with her tongue. Daddy, who made her feel loved and cherished until he vanished abruptly and completely. Marti never stopped hoping his ghost would appear.

She walked on to view the entire yard and saw the big oak tree was still there. She'd spent hours beneath this tree playing with stick dolls she made. The tree trunk was their home, and Marti set up different rooms between the coiled roots, roots that always looked like dinosaur feet to her. Moss grew on one side, creating a cozy carpet floor. She'd gather leaves and vines to make clothes for the dolls. Pine cones, bark, and acorns became their furniture. She created scenarios for them: picnics, parades, and carnivals, anything to give joy to her forest family. She named the stick dolls: Twig, Fern, Acorn, Leaf, with Forest as their last name. They all had distinct personalities yet loved one another and celebrated each other's triumphs. At the end of each day, she put them snugly in their shared bed, more like a nest, knowing they'd rest, perfectly content. Staring at the tree, Marti felt the presence of that lonely girl who'd wanted to be a member of that forest family. She yearned to sit and comfort that girl, yet wasn't at all sure she'd be a comfort.

Across was the Colgan house, the yellow color faded, and still the house looked inviting. Once Marti had lain on their kitchen floor writhing in pain, yet what flooded back was the feeling of love she found there. *Will Mrs. Colgan recognize me? You don't forget someone who wrecks your world.*

She approached their front door and rang. (As a kid she used the back door, but that felt presumptuous now.) It seemed like she was waiting a long time. *She's old. Maybe she walks slowly. Maybe she can't hear the bell. Maybe it's not a long time.* She shifted her hands in and out of her skirt pockets. A small Asian boy opened the door, and she asked if it was the Colgan house.

"Uh-huh."

"Is Mrs. Colgan home?"

The boy shook his head. Marti smiled—the concreteness of children—question answered, nothing more.

"Do you know when she'll be back?"

"She won't." He shook his head again. Marti waited for more. "Granny died. You don't get to come back when you die."

She struggled to comprehend . . . Wasn't it just weeks ago that Jan told her? She wanted to ask him to repeat it, but no, she couldn't. "I can't believe—" she whispered, not wanting the words to sink in. She leaned against the doorframe. The boy was staring. She forced herself to look up. "Your grandmother? I'm so sorry."

"Me too. Granny Colgan was nice."

"The nicest ever."

What now—should she leave? That would be skulking away; she had to face whichever Colgan this boy belonged to—and say what? *Sorry for your loss.* She'd need to be respectful and leave it at that. They wouldn't want to hear Marti's confession now; she'd have to find redemption on her own.

2

Marti's first seven years were spent playing at the Colgans', but that ended abruptly and she filled her lonely times with sketching images of the beautiful girl she longed to be. When tired of that impossible fantasy, she moved on to drawing dream houses and creating them out of shoeboxes, homes for her beloved forest family. Her favorite part was making teeny, tiny things. Matchboxes became beds, stamps pasted together might be quilts or pictures for the cardboard walls, bottle caps were mirrors or tabletops supported at the bottom by cinnamon sticks. Paper clips were twisted into trombones or bars on a jungle gym. She never tired of ideas and worked relentlessly. Her mother and Jan gave her miniatures as holiday gifts. The gesture was nice, although they clearly didn't understand: she *wanted* to make her own.

Her junior high art teacher, Miss Jarvis, liked Marti's sketches and asked her lots of questions. When Marti told her about the houses, she encouraged Marti to bring them in to show the class. The students were impressed. Miss Jarvis told her the box worlds were called *dioramas*; Marti liked the name but continued calling them box worlds. Instead, she named one of the figures inside Diorama.

After class a girl asked if she could come to Marti's house to learn how to make the box worlds. Marti was incredulous: no peer had befriended her since that last day at the Colgans'. No one. Didn't this girl know what a pariah Marti was? Sure, Brooke moved to Chatham only recently, but she had eyes, didn't she? Afraid it was a trap, Marti stood silent. Brooke ran her hands through her long black hair, her silver bracelets clanking as she did so, and confidently asked again. Marti felt like a cat who knows she needs rescuing from the lonely tree but is suspicious to accept the waiting arms. She nodded slowly, tentatively, and let Brooke enter the world of her beloved creations.

And so she began high school, feeling buffered by this new friend. Brooke didn't smoke Marlboros like other kids; instead, she rolled hers in brown rolling papers and kept them in a silver case. She was always running out of cigarettes and bumming off everyone else, and no one minded because she was Brooke. She had a unique clothing style, wearing long dresses, chains, and ribbons tied at her waist with little toys dangling off the ribbons. Marti began sewing clothes for both of them. She made halter tops out of bandannas. After gathering piles of men's ties, Marti sewed them vertically together into skirts that widened from the waist down.

The rumor was Brooke's family left the last town they'd lived in because Brooke's older brother got into trouble and was now in military school.

Brooke had an interesting gait, a lopsided saunter, almost— but not quite—dragging one foot behind her. It matched her voice, a slight slur or lisp that made her seem nonchalant, with a disinterested laziness—you were the one who had to do the work of listening. Brooke told tales of what a great horseback rider she'd been before a horse fell on her. She said she'd spent months in the hospital and it had affected *everything*. Her emphasis on *everything* made it clear that that was the explanation for the walk and the voice, and her survival gave her a tough-girl air. She walked tall into a room swinging her long hair, knowing she'd be noticed. Following behind her, Marti tried fruitlessly to imitate that slinky walk. Marti's curly hair was kept in tight braids, a few strands loose to cover her face with no swinging it about, ever. Hoping to go unseen, she was the perfect companion for Brooke.

Brooke surrounded herself with an entourage who defined themselves by their proximity to Brooke. Marti was elated and grateful to be a member of this group. Peter Colgan was a friend of Brooke's, and Marti chose to overlook this. Brooke usually had two boyfriends orbiting her in chorus, and they'd roam about together as a threesome—the admission price you had to pay if you wanted Brooke. Marti didn't want boys looking at her. None were.

They all signed up for art class. "Well, now, who have we here?" the art teacher began, snaking his way through the rows of desks, looking boldly into each student's eyes. "Myself, I have two first names or two last names, depending on how you look at it, which is what art is all about: more than one way of viewing the world. You could call me Mr. Douglas or Mr. Spencer, though it seems silly and arbitrary, doesn't it? Why not just call me Spencer, like my friends do."

The kids liked this. Spencer Douglas, with his flannel shirts and jeans, seemed like one of them, only way cooler. He even told them his age—twenty-seven. His dark hair, parted in the middle, fell straight to his shoulders, much longer than the boys were allowed. Brooke whispered to Marti, "I think he looks like James Taylor. Or maybe George Harrison?"

"What's that buzz?" Spencer turned to them. "Your name!" he demanded, banging on Brooke's desk.

"Brooke."

"Stream, nice to meet you." The class laughed.

"What," Spencer questioned, "is a brook not a stream? And you," he said, considering Marti, "are the little fish following the stream, hoping it leads to an ocean."

Spencer assigned them self-portraits. Not wanting to draw her face, Marti sketched her hands. Working hard, she detailed her large writer's bump and the lines around her knuckles.

"Now, here is an original portrait. Marti Farrell, lovely as her face is—" Students sniggered and Marti couldn't blame them. "*Lovely as her face is,*" Spencer emphasized, and no one laughed this time, "has chosen to draw her hands. Original thinking. Although"—he walked over to Marti—"how fascinating this face is! These lines tell a story." He held Marti's chin, running his finger along her cheek, tracing the scars. She couldn't turn away, as he was holding tight. She stared down at his arm where she noticed black hair sprouting around a woven bracelet on his wrist. She closed her eyes, a feeble effort to ward off a hot tear trickling down her reddened cheek.

"Ah, no need to be embarrassed. The point is, you must embrace your individuality—that which belongs only to you." Spencer used one finger to wipe the tear before moving on. Marti let her breath out slowly between clenched teeth and tried to quiet her heartbeat until the bell finally rang, releasing her. She quickly made for the door, but Spencer blocked it. "Marti, I have some books that might interest you."

"I have to get to class."

Spencer raised his eyebrows. "Another time. I'm quite sure another time."

Never.

Each student was asked to talk about an artist they were inspired by. Alison Quint, a girl whose work Marti admired, raised her hand. "I like Andrew Wyeth."

"What about him?" Spencer asked.

"*Christina's World* makes you wonder about the young girl,

Christina. Is she paralyzed? It's this pretty world and she's not part of it." Marti remembered the painting yet couldn't have named the artist or talked about it the way Alison did.

"In truth," Spencer said, "she was fifty-five and a polio survivor, an illness everyone feared at that time, and that fear launched Wyeth's career. He was technically proficient—like you, quaint Alice." (The students cackled at the way Spencer continually crafted nicknames.) "Yet he has nothing to say—a bit of wonderland, Alice, though good of you to have an answer, and I'm not surprised you like him."

Peter said he liked Henri Rousseau, describing the painting *Sleeping Gypsy*. "Interesting," Spencer said, leaning over Peter's desk. "Rousseau painted big, dramatic pictures of fierce animals yet was ultimately limited by his own weak nature. An unsurprising choice for you, Petey." Spencer looked straight into his face, and Peter blushed.

Weaving his way through the room, stopping randomly, he'd bang on a desk and declare, "Your turn!" Marti tried to think. Picasso? Van Gogh? No, they'd already been used. Was there any other artist she could even name? Rembrandt? Michelangelo? She knew nothing about them and didn't think Spencer would like those answers. "Let me guess," Spencer said, tapping on a boy's desk. "Salvador Dalí?"

The boy flashed a smile. "How did you know?"

"Oh, Brandon, something about the dripping eyeball in your last painting gave me a small clue. Another artist you might want to check out is René Magritte, also a surrealist, one who painted ordinary objects and, by placing them in unusual contexts, made you question the ordinary and, therefore, reality itself. Come by after school, sir, and I'll show you some of his work." The class stirred and Brandon beamed, for it was the first time a freshman had been invited into Spencer's privileged group of the talented and chosen who hung around him after school.

"And you, Desirée?" Spencer asked a girl named Denise.

"Paul Klee," she answered eagerly.

"It's pronounced *clay*; he's not a member of the glee club."

Students laughed and, uncharacteristically, Spencer hushed them. "Never mind—how would you know? I'm glad to see you're a fan of abstract expressionism. I hope that means your work will open up more. You've great promise."

Delight showed on Denise's face, but Spencer didn't wait to see, as he'd already moved on to Brooke. "Um, I don't have any artist I like. I mean, I like paintings when I see them. I couldn't tell you why I like what I like, I just do."

Spencer laughed. "Good answer. Your unfiltered emotions are why you, Babbling Brooke, make the perfect muse. Doesn't she, boys?"

Next, an unfortunate boy answered, "Norman Rockwell."

Marti, frantically scrolling the book titles on Spencer's shelves, was pleased to find a woman's name. "Joan Miró," she blurted out when her turn came.

"Really? Why?"

"I just like the way she makes me, um, feel things."

"What things?" Spencer leaned closer.

"I can't name them."

"Hmm—I wouldn't have taken you for a Dadaist. However, you should know it's a man making you feel things, not a woman. I'll show you some of his work after class." Marti didn't stay after class but looked Miró up in the library, wanting to be prepared in case Spencer asked her to elaborate. She didn't understand the pictures or truly comprehend words like *Dada*.

Spencer frequently praised Marti's work, yet she remained vigilant for any mention of her scars. Why was he interested? Most people, Marti included, recoiled from them. He *touched* them. "Look at Marti's picture. Such depth. The hungry pigeon sifting through garbage, art created by someone who's suffered."

While Marti cringed at the word *suffered*, she felt drawn to Spencer's praise. She was talented, wasn't she? And she had suffered, hadn't she?

Eventually, she brought her box worlds into class wanting Spencer to see another side to her work—these were happier than her sketches. He leaned over them, his face blank. Confronted by his silence, she scooped them up. She couldn't have him sneer words like *child's play* at her beloved, intimate creations. "How long have you been toiling on these alone in your garret?" he asked, cocking his head into a question while keeping his eyes steadily focused on the boxes she clutched. "They're astonishing, wonderful. Leave these, so we can examine them further after school." He rested his hand on the top of one of the boxes, grazing her fingers as if about to wrestle the boxes away from her. She shook her head. "Ah, I understand—you can't part with them. Another time, you can't deprive me forever." He removed his hand and smiled, revealing a small dimple in one cheek, a crescent moon. When his mouth was still, there was only a faint line, as if the dimple were a secret between them.

Brooke had joined the realm of Spencer's exclusive after-school club. She brought her friends along and urged Marti to come. "It's a blast, isn't it?" she said, nudging Peter.

"Spencer always talks about liking your work." Peter was relentlessly nice to her, constantly carrying his guilt, and Marti missed the boy who had snatched her toys. Sometimes she balked at Peter's presence, not that she couldn't forgive him—she had a long time ago; her mother's barrage of contempt for the Colgans had ironically eased any anger Marti felt—but she was striving for a future, and Peter reminded her of the sorrowful past.

Brooke continued, "We can tell him *anything*. It's cool, he plays really good music, Dylan, the Doors and stuff."

"Velvet Underground," Trey, one of Brooke's current boyfriends, muttered. "They're the best."

They persisted in inviting her. Coming up with excuses was tricky because she wouldn't reveal how much Spencer touching her scars upset her. Eventually, Marti decided to go to his room, just once, casually, as if it were no big deal. When she arrived, there were several students, all juniors and seniors except for Brooke's group and Brandon. Bobby Jasko, known as the barefoot boy, was there. Going barefoot was, of course, against school rules, yet no teacher ever challenged him. Winter was coming—would he walk barefoot in the snow? Or take his shoes off after he got to school? The more Marti thought about it, the sillier it seemed. She leaned against the doorframe, hesitating.

"Come in," Spencer called, "we're listening to Frank Zappa, one of the geniuses of our time, mothers of invention, what we're all doing, giving birth to our creativity." Marti slid into a seat next to Peter. Everyone's eyes were on Spencer, and his were on Marti. "You've joined us at last; I knew you would. Marti, a true artist, bares her soul in her work." This kind of talk she feared yet secretly savored. "We're looking at the work of Edvard Munch, another brave soul. Marti, do you know his paintings?" She nodded a barely perceptible nod, as in fact, she'd never heard of him.

"Sweetie Petey, get the lights. I'll show some slides."

Spencer talked, students asked questions, and music played. Brooke and Trey hung onto each other, making out a few times right in the classroom, as did Bobby and a girl whose name Marti didn't know. Introductions were considered unnecessary for the smug members of Spencer's elite clique.

When she told her mother how well she was doing in art, Peg admonished Marti to focus on other subjects, particularly French, which she was doing poorly in. French was the graduate degree Peg was working toward. At home Jan and Peg conversed in French, encouraging Marti to join in, but she never did. Now Jan was away at college, returning only occasionally, and Peg was preoccupied with completing her graduate thesis while teaching at the local college.

Just like her friends, Marti began going to Spencer's most afternoons. She was shocked the first time he lit a joint and passed it around. She'd smoked before in Brooke's dark basement, but this was in daylight and with a teacher in school. Joints didn't happen every day, only when the school was empty, and it was an unspoken rule that it had to be Spencer's initiative.

Often Marti walked home with Peter. Apprehensive as she was of boys, she knew Peter would never try anything with her because of their history. He worshipped Spencer, and this made Marti a little queasy, as she could see Spencer took advantage of him. *Peter, get us this. Petey, do this*, and Peter would jump, an eager puppy. She couldn't help seeing the parallels to her own friendship with Brooke.

One afternoon Peter invited her to his house. Marti dithered; she hadn't been there in seven years and knew her mother wouldn't approve, and yet Peg was aware that Peter and Marti were friends again and hadn't forbidden it. *It's just a house. Why not? I have the memory anyway.*

Walking into the Colgan whirl of activity, she felt a rush of aching joy, realizing how much she'd missed this ever since it was snatched away. "Marti, how lovely to see you!" Mrs. Colgan gave her a hug, looking just as Marti remembered, her hair swept up in an old-fashioned bun, wearing sensible shoes and a floral dress with an apron over it. Styles would come and go, but Mrs. Colgan remained as consistent as a humble spring dandelion. "Would you children like a snack? I made popcorn for the younger ones." Marti glanced at the dining room table where Richie, Marybeth, and two kids Marti vaguely recognized from the neighborhood were playing Monopoly.

"Let me see." Peter pulled a chair up to the table and straddled it backward. "Who has the green ones?"

A boy nodded proudly. "Me."

"Way to go, Jimmy!" Peter slapped his back and Marybeth scowled. "Well, you have two red ones, Marybeth. You've got to do a trade for the third, a trade at any cost. Do it, sis."

"Interference!" Richie shouted.

"Yeah, interference!" echoed Jimmy. Marti laughed, remembering this code word the Colgans always used in their squabbles, and how everyone else, feeling so at home, used the word as if it were their own.

"Make Peter stop," Richie said to Mrs. Colgan as she entered, holding a jar of M&M's.

"Ah, I've what's needed—happy pills. Everyone may have one, but if they don't make you happy, you'll get no more." She offered them around the table. "And now that everyone is happy, I'm off to Mass. Keep an eye on the younger ones, Peter, but no interference. Marti will be a good referee, I'm sure." She winked at Marti. Marti watched as Mrs. Colgan put on her coat, tied a scarf around her head, and lifted rosary beads from a hook by the door. She knew Mrs. Colgan went to Mass every day, having often observed her leaving at this time. The whole family went on Sundays and sometimes on a Friday or Saturday evening. Marti's family rarely attended Mass after her father died.

She was struck by what a different Peter this was, confident and relaxed, charismatic to the younger kids. Soon the kids begged Marti to play and argued over the privilege of sitting with her, and she loved this adoration. Was this how Spencer felt around his students?

In Spencer's room she was guarded, needing to both prove and protect herself. This feeling magnified when she was stoned, and going to the Colgans' afterward became the release. It was fun playing with the little kids and having Mrs. Colgan (who never noticed that they were high) feed them, especially her homemade honey cakes, which Marti had never forgotten.

Her mother was pleased that Marti was busy, and didn't keep close tabs on her. One day she remarked, "That Brooke is something, overcoming her handicap the way she does. She makes it work for her. A good lesson for you."

Marti was incensed; a horse falling on you was a much better story than her own.

Charcoal broiled. Railroad tracks. Craters of the moon.

And Brooke didn't have to take gym, Marti's most hated class. Marti wondered why, popping the question as casually as she could. "Oh," Brooke said with a toss of her hair, "they said I don't need gym. Personally, I think it's because they don't want the other girls to see my gorgeous body in the locker room and feel bad." Her roguish grin flashed across her face.

One day Brooke skipped school with Brandon, her new conquest. Peter asked Marti if she'd be at Spencer's and she wavered, as she'd never gone without Brooke and wasn't sure the group accepted her. However, she knew Spencer wanted her there. When she arrived, there was no Peter, only a few older kids she barely knew. Everyone asked for Brooke, Marti being only an extension of Brooke. She wished she hadn't come, yet now felt she had no choice but to slink into a chair and accept the joint each time it came her way. Not really listening to the conversation, she looked out the window where a light snow had begun, the first of the season. This was usually a seminal, much talked about event, as snow would be with them for many months, and yet no one mentioned it. Marti felt mournful for the unappreciated snow. The students were chattering about a party and eventually everyone got up to go to it, everyone except Marti. She didn't know whether she was included and waited to be asked, but they departed quickly, leaving only Spencer and Marti.

Spencer took a last inhale of a joint and started putting the pot away. Marti gathered her things slowly, wanting to be sure the others were safely out of the building before leaving, lest they think she was following them. "Hang on," Spencer said, looking down at the marijuana he was carefully scooping into a film canister, "I didn't mean you should leave. You weren't interested in the party?" Marti shrugged. "Of course not." Spencer moved to a chair closer to her. "You've been watching the snow."

"It's beautiful."

"How so?"

"How? Don't you think—" Marti stopped, bewildered. This cool, cynical new world was devoid of magic.

"I'm asking *what* you see. I want to see the snow as you see it."

"The way it falls, so careful and precise. Like it *matters*. So delicate with no two alike, I love thinking about that. It's hard to believe white isn't a color when it's so bright."

"White is all colors. Black is the absence of color."

Marti felt foolish. She'd been trying to show off what she'd learned in science, bungling it instead. Spencer got up and rummaged around on a bookshelf. "Of course when you're mixing a paint palette, black *is* all colors." He turned back and smiled as if reassuring her she hadn't made a mistake. "What we see is light. Color is light, and white, having all of it, is the full spectrum."

Marti nodded, thinking before she spoke. "The snow is a perfect white. Maybe it's perfect because it's everything."

Spencer laid a book on her desk. "Wilson Bentley, otherwise known as Snowflake Bentley. He's from Vermont. Have you heard of him?" She shook her head. "Take a look, you're in for a treat. He spent his life photographing snowflakes." Spencer stood directly in front of her, his long belt strap dangling in her view.

Marti flipped through plates of individual snowflakes. "They're wonderful." She handed the book back.

"No, it's yours." He pushed the book against her chest.

Marti stood, trying to break the chain of body, book, hand. "I'll bring it back in a few days so others can look."

"They won't appreciate it. I want you to have it. It'll make me feel good knowing that book is next to you at night.

"Marti, you do know nothing is perfect? Snowflake Bentley thought snow was, so much so that it killed him. He caught pneumonia after photographing in a blizzard."

"How sad."

"Not really, he died in service to what he loved."

Marti bent down and put the book in her bag. She felt a sensation on her scalp and realized Spencer was touching one of the curls that had fallen out of her braids. She remained still. "Not even the purest snow is perfect, yet the golden shine of your hair defies my logic." He twirled a curl around his finger. Once he released it, she straightened up and lifted her book bag to her chest, a shield in front of her. "There's so much light and beauty in your artwork, and it's mixed with pain. The way you merge the contrast . . . I'm in awe of your talent."

"Thanks."

"Don't thank me, I should be thanking you for sharing from such a deep place. It's brave of you. The pain—it comes from these?" Spencer brushed his fingers across the scars on her face. Marti bristled. "Don't be ashamed. Tell me what happened."

"I had an accident."

"Did someone burn you?"

"No, no. Not like that." *What did Spencer think? Some evil mother torturing her?* "We were playing; Pe—he didn't know. Some hot water fell on me." Spencer sat and gestured to Marti to do the same. She slid back into her seat. He moved his chair farther away as if to see her more completely, sticking his legs straight out and folding his arms, waiting. His jeans had a worn spot on the thigh, and she could see a pink shadow of skin. *He really wants to know what happened. He wants to know me.*

Still, she couldn't talk about the accident, or its aftermath, so she talked of other things, pictures she'd drawn in elementary school and how different they were from everyone else's. She thought Spencer would find this boring, yet he listened intently. "They laughed at your pictures because you didn't put the sun in the middle with a blue sky around it. They couldn't understand. Your teachers should have recognized your gift. Teachers can be the worst conformists, such a paradox: a teacher should free a student's mind, not narrow it. Cruel, really, to let your work be teased instead of nurturing and protecting you, yet you survived because you're strong. And so, so beautiful. Do you know that?"

She shook her head. "You are. And your scars"—Spencer reached out, grazing his fingers along them—"are beautiful." She jerked away.

"Poor Marti, you don't believe me. I believe in you. Why else would I single you out in class? You've wondered, haven't you? Of course you have. It's your talent and beauty. Your beauty haunts me."

He let that sentence linger. Leaning forward, cupping her head in his hands, he slowly kissed her lips. Marti was immobile. Then tentatively she began to respond. At that, Spencer pulled away and kissed her forehead before standing up. "We are like souls, Marti. But it's late."

She stumbled out of the room. It continued snowing on the walk home. She took the book out of her bag because holding it was the only way she could believe what had happened. Besides, Snowflake Bentley wouldn't mind snow on his book, would he? She reached one bare palm up, an offering to the snow. She counted each flake as they landed softly on her hand before dissolving.

Clasping the book tight under her covers that night, Marti tossed and turned, trying to reconstruct the feeling of the kiss and the sound of Spencer's voice saying, "Your beauty haunts me." *Did he really say that?* She couldn't sleep, for she was awaiting the next day.

3

"Daddy, somebody's at the door. Ned's talking to a lady."

"Okay, Pearl, I'm coming."

Marti tried to convince herself it might be Tom or Richie or Andy, but oh, she knew that voice, melodious like his mother's, only deeper now, and this depth startled her, realizing what children they'd been; Peter's voice had still carried traces of a boy's voice the last time she'd heard it. He came around the corner carrying a basket of laundry. "Hello, I'll be with you in a minute." He didn't look at her as he placed the basket down on the hall table. Some clothes spilled out, and he stooped for them, saying quietly to Ned, "You know better than to open the door without me."

"I told him, Daddy," the girl crowed, running into the hall. She looked like the boy, maybe even the same age.

"Leave it alone, Pearl. I have to talk to the realtor." While he was distracted by the kids and overflowing basket, Marti had a chance to observe him. He was a man of forty-three, slender, although not quite a toothpick anymore. What was left of his hair was still red, only now it was a horseshoe around a bald head. *Bozo*, Spencer would have called him, yet it wouldn't have been an accurate nickname, as there was an alluring quality about Peter, simultaneously boyish and mature.

"Not the realtor. It's—it's me, Peter. Marti—Marti Farrell." He whirled around, a pair of red leggings in his hands, staring.

29

Without speaking, he carefully placed the leggings in the basket. "Sorry to startle you, I—"

"Marti, my god! What are you doing here?"

"I—I wanted to visit your mother. I'm so sorry to hear . . ." Her voice faded.

"You came all this way to see Ma? You live in New York, right? That's what I'd heard anyway."

"No, I mean, yes, I live in New York. I'm here on vacation, staying at the lake. Peter, I don't know what to say. When did she—"

"Daddy." Pearl tugged on her father's arm. "Invite her in. I'm Pearl and this is my brother, Ned." Marti shook Pearl's stuck-out hand and held hers out to a suddenly shy Ned, standing behind his father's back. He tentatively accepted her hand. She was conscious of no physical greeting from Peter.

As if sensing her thought, Peter said, "Sorry, I'm just stunned. Come in the kitchen—would you like water, coffee?" He carried the laundry basket and gestured awkwardly for her to follow. She was amazed at how little the house had changed—all of it familiar: the upright piano with music books stacked on one end, board games on the other, and the walls covered with family photos— although there were many new faces. She slid into the vinyl booth that curved in a semicircle around the kitchen table, remembering that game the Colgan kids used to play where they'd push each other all the way around to one end, and whoever was at the end would pretend to fall off and run to the other end, the game continuing until all of them fell off. Peter put the laundry basket on the table, handed her water, sat across from her with the laundry basket between them. He said, "I can't visit long. I'm expecting a realtor."

Pearl plopped down next to Marti, and Ned followed. "I'm four," Pearl said, holding up four fingers. "So is Ned, but I'm older. By how much, Daddy?"

Marti appreciated the diversion. There was too much to say; she couldn't begin.

"Six minutes."

"Six minutes," Pearl repeated solemnly.

"I was four when I met your daddy," Marti said, looking at Peter, trying to crack his wooden demeanor. He was folding a pair of overalls.

"Really?" Ned leaned across his sister for a closer look.

"So these are my nosy beasts. Twins, double trouble." Peter laughed, and Marti recognized the wide-open innocent quality in his face.

"I'm trying to take in the shock—all these years. I can't believe you came back. You look good, really good."

Marti touched her face and then dropped her hand. "Jan told me she ran into Betty, and it got me thinking about your mother, and I—I just wanted to—" Marti's voice came to a standstill, and after a pause, she asked, "When did she die?"

"Two weeks ago. A stroke."

So recent. If only . . .

"It's strange being here without her." The kids slid out of the booth and left the room.

"Your house looks the same," Marti said, gesturing with her hands.

"Yeah, Ma saved *everything*, our report cards, art projects. Look at this." He stood and lifted a ceramic tile off the counter. Two figures suspended in midair were painted on it, dressed alike in red suits with purple ties, yellow polka dots on their black shoes, their arms and legs wide, signifying movement. Written above them: *Tap Dancers*. He laughed. "My third-grade artwork. I'd seen Sammy Davis Jr. on TV and was sure I wanted to be a tap dancer—that week."

"Nice to know it meant so much to her. I have nothing from my childhood. Although, to be fair, I didn't want reminders; I'd have burned them." Peter flinched at the word *burned* and turned back to the counter.

Marti stood. "I'll go now. I don't want to intrude. Again, I'm sorry." She twisted her hands tightly together before continuing, "Your mother, she didn't deserve what I did—" Seeing Peter's hunched figure stiffen, she stopped.

Pearl and Ned burst through the swinging door. "Daddy, look what we found." Pearl held out an old shoebox full of little plastic figures. "What are they?"

"TV Tinykins," Peter and Marti answered in near unison. They were cartoon characters not much larger than a thumbnail.

"Wow," Peter said, picking up a miniature Fred Flintstone. "Remember these?"

"Sure. We played with them endlessly."

"Who are they?" Ned asked. "We don't know anybody."

"No, you wouldn't." Peter laughed as he and Marti stood close, combing through the box. Picking up each piece, Peter named them until stumped by the members of Top Cat's gang. "If he's Fancy-Fancy, who's this?"

"That's Spook. He had the black tie. Fancy-Fancy had the white one. I'd know because you always had Top Cat and made me be everyone else." Marti turned the figure over. "You can even see where I chewed it."

"You *were* the chewer—I knew it. You always denied it." Peter pointed at Marti.

"Of course I denied. Stupid, I wasn't. Well, maybe sometimes—"

"Wait!" Pearl held up her hands. "You played with these?" She stared at Marti.

"Yes," Peter answered. "Enough now, we're supposed to be cleaning, not making a new mess. People are coming to see the house, remember?" He dropped the figurines back into the box, and they rattled as if in protest.

Pearl tugged on Marti's arm. "Daddy and you were little together?"

"I lived across the street."

Peter walked toward the front door.

"Where's your house? Can we play there?" Pearl asked.

"I don't live there anymore. Come, I'll show you." She motioned for them to follow outside.

"Are you going to stay with us? Please?"

Peter whirled around. "Pearl, don't be silly. Marti just came to say hi."

"Do you have kids?" Pearl asked.

"Stop, Pearl. She has to go."

"I have a daughter, bigger than you. That was my house," Marti said, pointing. The children weren't really looking; they were whispering among themselves.

"Would you like a Popsicle?" Ned asked.

"Who said anything about Popsicles? Nice try, Ned. She's *leaving*." Peter didn't look at Marti.

"Peter, how long are you here for?"

"Don't know. It's going to take a while to get this house ready to sell." His voice sounded far away and sad. Marti struggled to think of what to say beyond *sorry*. Before she could speak, he continued in a different tone, "It's a nice place to spend the summer—for them." He gestured to the kids who were chasing each other on the lawn.

"They're sweet, Peter. I'm happy for you."

"Thanks." He half smiled, showing the subtle gap between his front teeth.

"I'm here for the summer too."

"That long? Why?"

"Told you, I'm vacationing here. Maybe we could get together—"

Peter had already turned away.

Marti belatedly realized she'd skipped a stop sign. *That went well, idiot.* She continued driving fast, zooming past familiar sites full of wounds she wasn't ready to open. Abruptly she pulled over, turned off the car, and banged her hands against the steering wheel, sobbing. *Dead. All these years I could've talked to her. Fucking coward. Two weeks, two weeks. Peter must have told his parents the truth. Surely, she died with that peace of mind? Oh, let's be honest— my wanting to tell Mrs. Colgan was about exonerating me, not easing her. Me, me, me.*

She thought of Peter's children, knowing Mrs. Colgan must have doted on them, picturing her hiding little surprises each visit. The world felt wrong without her.

When she got back to the cottage, Marti patted Caliban's head. "Hey, good boy. Let's swim." At the word *swim*, he ran down to the dock. Marti changed quickly, dove in and swam vigorously.

Peter appeared happy. Why shouldn't he? The Colgans were a real family, and his had been a happy childhood—despite Marti. Why would he want to see her? He had a mother to grieve, two beautiful children to raise, and a sweet wife somewhere (where was she?).

Caliban felt secure going only a short distance, and usually Marti heeded this by staying nearby, but today she felt vexed by his timidity and swam swiftly across the lake. She was too scared to tell Peter what she needed: *I can't bury the past deep enough. It keeps clawing its way out. Help me.*

Reaching the opposite shore, she turned and looked at all the docks bobbing slightly and swam from dock to dock tapping each of them like it was a relay race. When she finally headed back, she could hear Caliban sputtering toward her. She greeted him, grateful for his love.

On the dock, she lay back, closed her eyes, and rubbed her hand along her faded scars. *How much do they show?* She remained scarred on the inside and needed the scars as evidence: *This is what happened to me. It explains almost everything.*

She knew this was a lie.

Dinner was waiting in case Tess came home hungry, and maybe if it wasn't too late, they could play a game of Sorry. The days when Tess went everywhere with Marti were long gone, and Marti missed the sense of legitimacy it gave her in the world. Linda never had to justify herself; with three children she could easily play the busy card, being busy having become a marker of success. Without Tess, what could Marti use to fill the void?

Tess went straight to bed, and the next day she walked sleepily onto the back porch where Marti was eating lunch. Marti asked about the rafting trip. "It was fun, Mom, and not too scary."

"What you call *not too scary* would terrify me."

"Maybe. Emily's mom got scared. She yelled at Emily's dad to stop the boat like he was powering it or something."

"A raft?"

"Crazy, right?" Tess laughed, swinging her legs over the chair arm. Tess was already taller than Marti with her father's long loose limbs, whereas Marti sometimes thought she'd stunted her own growth by willing invisibility.

"Trust me, I'd have been worse."

"Totally," Tess agreed. "I remember horseback riding with you. They said *trot* and you had a total freak-out." Accurate, Marti remembered. Tess went into the kitchen. Marti looked out at the mountains beyond the lake, recalling all the landscapes she'd painted in Miss Jarvis's class—and initially in Spencer's. "So did you see who you wanted?" Marti winced; the word *wanted* cast a harsh light on Marti's memories. "Well? That lady?" Tess said between bites of granola.

"No. Mrs. Colgan died a few weeks ago." Marti pushed her plate away.

"Sorry. How did you find out?"

"One of her children told me. She had a stroke."

"I know you really wanted to see her."

"I wish you could have met her; you'd have loved her. She could have been a grandmother to you."

"A grandmother? What a weird thing to say. I have Nanna, and Grandma is still my grandma, even though she's gone. Why would I want another?" Tess was close to Rob's mother, and Peg had been a good grandmother, warm and kind. Marti had been jealous of her daughter receiving the unconditional love she'd coveted, because even after Tess was born, Peg remained critical of Marti, and Marti still felt like an outsider, only now it was Tess, not Jan, garnering all the attention.

When the divorce happened, Peg acted as if it were all Marti's fault. *I knew you wouldn't let it work.* Marti had wanted more children, a big happy family like the Colgans. Peg knew she'd been trying for more, yet she never acknowledged Marti's loss. It was, *Poor Tess, all alone with just her mama,* the implication being that Marti was surely the short end of the stick. Marti changed the subject. "I saw my house. It's a different color."

"Worse, huh?"

"No, way better." Marti laughed. "Friendlier. Lighter." Tess looked mystified. Marti found it hard to communicate the loneliness of her past to Tess. By letting your child know your childhood wasn't perfect, weren't you inadvertently shattering any illusions they held about their own?

"Are you going to see the Colgans again?" Tess asked.

"I doubt it."

"Why not? You're so antisocial. You never date. Whoever you saw could give you Peter's address; maybe he lives near."

"I saw Peter."

"What?" Tess put her bowl down and stared at Marti.

"Why do you want me to date Peter? Because you have a boyfriend?"

Tess carried her bowl to the kitchen sink and dropped it with a loud clang. "Lucas is a friend. *Friend*, you know that word? I try talking about you and you shut down." She began mimicking Marti. "*Oh, I saw one of the Colgans.* You didn't say Peter."

"Because I went to see his mother and, for your information, he's married."

"You met his wife?"

"I met his kids."

Tess sat back down. She picked up the cat and scratched her ears. "Maybe he's divorced."

"His kids are little; I doubt he'd be divorced already."

"Oh, that never happens! Really? Do you hear yourself?"

Precious leapt off Tess's lap and hissed at Marti. Tess laughed. Marti moved her chair back, muttering, "Why do you hate me so?"

"Because she knows you're scared. And there you go changing the subject."

"Sorry. Stupid thing I said about divorce. I know, *really* stupid. But I'm not interested in Peter. He never was a boyfriend."

"Why does Aunt Jan think he is?"

"Because, well, it makes it easier."

"Makes what easier?"

"She doesn't know what really happened."

"You mean the accident? Peter caused your accident, right?"

"He was a kid. Not his fault."

"Why do you get so uptight when I mention him?"

"My mother and Jan blamed Peter, so they couldn't understand why we were friends." Marti was aware she was altering the truth. *Do I owe Tess the truth or a mother's protection? I did this with my mother too. Don't trouble the people you love. Have I taught*

Tess to do the same? It's inevitable: loving someone means we burden them.

"Like Lucas is my friend."

"Touché."

"If I had a boyfriend, would that be so bad?"

"It just complicates things. You're so young. Even a good kid can lose their way. It can happen easily, before you even realize—"

"Did you, Mom? Lose your way?"

Marti carried her plate back to the kitchen. "Have you had enough to eat?"

"Wow, you're slick, deflect everything. Forget it, I'm going to the lake. Emily and I are checking out the public beach. You didn't tell me there's a bigger beach."

The beach they'd been going to was the small renters-only beach. Chatham was a town divided between tourists and locals, and Marti had chosen to be incognito, a tourist.

After Tess left, Marti felt the paradox: she didn't want to be alone or with anyone. She drove slowly through town, this time looking at familiar places. Passing Brooke's house, she pulled over and dredged up the memory of her first visit. Brooke's mother with a drink in one hand and a cigarette dangling from a holder in the other, a bit of a Cruella de Vil look about her, as she sized Marti up. "Well, well, my, oh my, what have you brought in out of the rain, Brooke? Yes, indeed, indeed, my daughter does like to pick up strays, doesn't she?" She slurred the words, laughing, boozy with confidence, knowing how this truth would land. Their dog approached, sniffing Marti intently. Brooke's father walked over seemingly in an effort to shoo the dog away and tripped on the edge of the carpet. He used Marti's body to steady himself while his hand roamed along her backside. Mr. Davies lurched, almost falling, as Brooke yanked Marti away ushering her through a door, down the stairs to the basement. They went into a small room. Brooke locked the door behind them. The room was half-finished, mostly concrete. Cushions were scattered in a circle on an orange shag rug. A turntable sat in the middle, records strewn everywhere in and out of their covers. Windowless and dark with only a dim overhead flickering light. As unwelcoming as the room was, it was obviously Brooke's sanctuary. Posters and Brooke's artwork hung on the walls. Candles were carefully placed on an old army trunk, almost like an altar, with two photos behind the candles, one of a toddler girl and the other of an older boy. Marti asked about them.

"My older brother and baby sister. I haven't seen my sister in years. She's in an institution. A *home*, Mom calls it, but I know it isn't. If it was a home, why wouldn't she be home with us? And why can't I see her? Raven was super sweet. It's a good thing Mom never comes down here, she'd *hate* that I have that picture. We're supposed to pretend Raven never existed—how fucked up is that?" Marti looked closely at the picture; Raven looked a bit like Brooke except she didn't have Brooke's wide eyes. Her eyes were small and close together, beady, truly like a raven, an odd look.

"And Johnny, my brother, he used to get in trouble so they sent him to military school, and now, get this: he's joining the navy when he graduates. Hell, he'd rather go to Vietnam and get killed than be here. I don't blame him." Brooke smiled a grim smile. "But it leaves me alone"—she pointed up with her finger—"with the loonies."

Marti drove off. *Enough nostalgia.* Why did one always long for the past, even when it was a sad and ugly past?

In the center of town, Marti spotted an art store. It had been a long time since she'd created any artwork. Her job was helping children use art as a refuge, but where was hers? The store was bigger than Marti expected with rows and rows of brushes, paints, paper, charcoal, clay, and beads. What attracted her were the bins of brightly colored tiles, each tile unique, a world unto itself. She enjoyed the smooth, slippery feel in her hands and the steady drum of sound as she dropped tiles, one by one, back into the bin. The shopkeeper approached. "Beautiful, aren't they? Do you do mosaics?"

"I never have."

"It's not hard. I could start you off if you're interested." She explained the process and showed Marti how to use the tile cutter. Marti enjoyed the sharp, definitive sound of the tiles breaking apart. She handed Marti a book to choose a picture from, lots of birds and ancient Egyptians in profile. Marti flipped the pages back and forth, dissatisfied. One of a mermaid caught her eye, not because she liked mermaids—she didn't—it was the water surrounding the mermaid that drew her. She realized the picture she wanted was not in a book but in her head, and she slammed the book shut. The shopkeeper tried to talk Marti out of this, stating it would be difficult for a beginner. Determined, Marti left the store with a sketchbook, pencils, board, glue, tile cutter, and bags of tile.

Dumping the tiles on the porch table, she luxuriated in running her hands through them, lining them up like bright slithering snakes. Each time she decided on a favorite color, she'd spot another and change her mind.

Over the next few days, Marti sat on the dock sketching the lake, paying careful attention to the twirling light and shadow on the water. Tess went to the public beach each day where she'd met a whole new group of kids. Mother and daughter were spending little time together and while this saddened Marti, conversely, she appreciated having time, feeling invigorated by her artwork.

Why did I lose this?

Fall 1971

n class Spencer was lavishing attention on Brandon and none on Marti. Brooke was smug with her new status, muse to the anointed one. Marti continued going to Spencer's room after school each day, unable to decide if he was truly avoiding her or if she was just too, too desperate. One day Spencer brought in some of his paintings, big canvases with bold dark colors intersecting in elaborate intertwining shapes. He said he was creating something new, taking the art world in a different direction, and the students nodded in awe.

Curiously, joints stopped being circulated and Marti asked Peter about it. He explained that the janitor warned Spencer to be careful because people could still smell it in the morning. How could Peter be privy to something Marti didn't know? She was always there, hanging onto Spencer's every utterance. She tried asking when Spencer had said this, but Peter, clueless to Marti's need, paid no attention to the question. Later, alone with Brooke, she asked.

"Don't worry, we're not in trouble." Brooke didn't look up from the cigarette she was rolling.

"I just wondered, when did he say that?"

"Miss the weed, huh? Probably he told us at his house, remember?" She lit her cigarette and took a long drag.

"His house? I've never been there! When—"

"Whoa—easy. What's the big deal? I forgot you weren't there." Marti shrugged, trying for nonchalance, while Brooke explained that Spencer wanted to show Brandon some paintings that were too large to bring in.

"What's his house like?"

"Ooh, Marti, look at you! You got a thing for him."

"I don't." Marti looked down and twirled the fringe on her suede belt.

"You know he's taken."

"Uh, of course."

"Women don't steal each other's men. I'll let you have him when I'm done." Brooke flicked her ash for emphasis.

"Brooke—you and Spencer?"

"Spencer! What are you talking about? I meant Brandon." Brooke watched as Marti's face shifted. "Ha, got you." She pointed her cigarette at Marti. "I knew it! You've got a thing for Spencer. That's cool. Friday night there's a party at his house. We're invited."

Marti spent hours deciding what to wear. She had one outfit she wore almost every day, her carpenter jeans, blue work shirt with a man's suit vest over it. Not just any vest, but one she'd found in an old trunk of her father's clothes. It was huge on her, yet she didn't care since it was his. Besides, she liked wearing baggy layers, feeling exposed without them. Tonight, however, she'd try for something more sophisticated. She wore a red turtleneck and a skirt she'd sewn out of a pair of jeans, splitting the jeans along their inside seam and adding fabric to the middle of the front and back. She'd been wearing her toothbrush around her neck on a piece of leather, thinking it seemed like a cool Brooke thing until Trey called it gross. She cast about for something else, deciding on a little purple velvet pouch and tied that on the leather string. What to put inside? It was stupid to have an empty pouch. She put in her keys and money. She unraveled her braids and brushed her hair, but seeing her thick wild curls in the mirror, she braided them again.

Her mother looked up from the schoolwork she was doing at the kitchen table. "No toothbrush around your neck, that's a better look. Have fun," she said, turning back to her notes, which were scattered across all available surfaces these days as Peg was scrambling to write her dissertation. Marti walked across the street and rang Peter's bell. She'd avoided going with Brooke, as she didn't want teasing. Peter told her about how his sister Marybeth was planning a circus in their backyard for the next day.

"You won't believe it; she's gone all over the neighborhood selling tickets. At twenty-five cents, she's already made five bucks."

"Five twenty-five now." Marti reached in her pouch and handed Peter a quarter.

"You want to come?"

"Sure. Tell Marybeth. Where's my ticket?" Marti playfully shoved Peter. "What a scam! Take my hard-earned money and no ticket?"

Peter laughed. "You know Marybeth, she's crazy about you. Come to think of it, she'll let you in for free and I can keep your quarter." Marti wrestled to get it back. "Hey, stop. We're here."

She was startled, having momentarily forgotten their destination. They were only four blocks from her house. *How can he live this close?* She'd pictured Spencer living in a cabin on a dirt road, not right in town. Peter pointed to a wooden gray house with peeling paint, one that any local would recognize as a rental, usually to college students. Peter ran up the steps and knocked; Marti slowly followed.

Spencer was dressed in ripped jeans with a white T-shirt hanging loose outside his pants. "You two are early. When you're older, you'll learn an eight o'clock party rarely starts before ten." Marti hesitated, embarrassed. "Come in, come in. Don't just stand there. Anyway, I could have guessed"—he looked at Marti—"that you'd be first."

Blushing, she checked whether Peter noticed, but he was busy looking at the artwork covering the walls, larger versions of the pictures Spencer brought into class. Boldly colored squares and circles layered on top of each other. The colors were jarring to

Marti, red, purple, black, orange, and pink all densely packed into the canvases, leaving nowhere calm for the eyes to rest.

"Spencer, these are great."

"Thank you, Peter; however, could you use a more descriptive adjective? Words like *great* and *nice* mean nothing. What would you say to describe them, Marti?"

"I wouldn't say nice." She laughed nervously. "I mean, they aren't nice. Not that I don't like them . . . but they're kind of . . . not calm."

"How interesting that my pictures unsettle you."

"I mean the colors aren't . . . peaceful. That's the point, right? They're supposed to be that way."

"Astute, Marti. Yes, unlike, say, those boring landscapes insipid Alice Wonderland paints in soothing pastels." Marti nodded, although she felt uncomfortable with Spencer demeaning Alison's work. The bell rang and three people entered, two women and a man. They all looked around Spencer's age. "This is Doug, Jenny, and Nadine."

Nadine was tall with wispy red ringlets almost to her waist. She wore a long turquoise dress. Turning to Marti, she said, "How groovy having Spencer for a teacher. I never had teachers like that. You, Jenny?"

"Hell no. I had nuns who spanked."

"I might have to give Marti a spanking. She says my work isn't pleasing."

"I didn't mean—"

"Yes, you did and besides, let the thought of a spanking dangle out there . . ." Spencer twirled his hand in the air. There were no chairs, only a few cushions on the floor. Doug sat down, forgoing a cushion, and placed a big bag of marijuana on the long table. It technically wasn't a table, rather an old door propped on cinder blocks with the doorknob still attached. Doug began rolling joints.

The bell rang again. It was Brooke, Brandon, and Trey with two senior boys whose names Marti didn't know trailing behind. Once inside, Brooke turned to the senior boys and asked for a cigarette. They each handed her one; Brooke tucked one cigarette behind her ear and rested the other between her lips, waiting. Both boys quickly held up lit matches and Brooke made a joke of pretending she needed two lights.

Marti sat at the table, fidgeting with the doorknob. It was loose and she could spin it all the way around. She watched Doug clean the pot. Was it the leaves or sticks he rolled? Spencer put a record on. The music was loud and Marti didn't recognize it.

Nadine sat next to Marti. "Doug, so slow. Too methodical. We don't care if every seed is out. Who minds a pop or two?" Nadine drummed her fingers on the table. She wore a ring on each finger including her thumb. She took a match from a box in the center of the table, snapped it lit with her finger, and held it in front of Doug. "Ready whenever you are." Marti was intrigued by these kinds of matches having previously watched with admiration while Brooke lit them with her teeth. Marti was still working on the finger light.

"Queen Nadine, always the jittery one," Spencer said, running his fingers through Nadine's hair. He buried his head in her hair and whispered something in her ear that made Nadine laugh. Doug finished rolling three joints and handed them to Spencer, muttering, "Soothe the beast first."

Spencer took his time laying them out in a triangle in front of Nadine. "You choose. Begin at the beginning. Or the middle or the end if you must." Nadine picked one up and lit it, taking a long, steady drag. Spencer was the only one still standing. He turned to Marti. "Marti, Marti, quite contrary, why do you keep your golden hair in braids?"

"Yeah, Marti, your hair's pretty, so curly," Peter said.

Brooke giggled. "Like a bird's nest."

"An apt metaphor," Spencer said, leaning into Marti as he removed another joint from the triangle. He took a match and lit it on his jean zipper. Hearing the sound of the metal and the whoosh of the flame right next to her ear, Marti jerked her head away. Spencer continued, "An apt metaphor because Marti is our little bird singing her song all alone in her tree. Marti, may we join you?" He inhaled, passing the joint to Marti. Some people held joints nonchalantly like cigarettes, while others held them deliberately, sucking with effort. Maybe it depended on whether one was a smoker? Wanting the right look, Marti, a non-smoker, tried taking it casually, lightly sucking the smoke into her mouth and holding it until she needed to breathe. She didn't know how to inhale into her lungs. The joints circled the room, and everyone had some except Doug who shrugged it off while continuing to roll.

Marti looked around at the artwork. How satisfying to live in a house that was full of your work. At Peter's house the walls were covered with kids' art, and at Marti's the walls were perfectly arranged with prints painted by strangers. The kitchen bulletin board held her mother's papers. *Good that Mom has her work*, Jan said to her once. *We wouldn't want her to be a widow too wrapped up in her children.*

No danger of that.

She was startled out of her thoughts by Spencer lightly unraveling one of her braids. He kneaded her hair in his hands and spread it out before beginning on the next braid. Marti was aware of the little hairs on the back of her neck standing up in attention. She remained perfectly still, unsure of what response was expected. When he finished the second braid, he scooped up her hair and held it momentarily suspended before letting it fall. "There," he whispered. Conversation continued among the group, Marti conscious only of Spencer hovering behind her. Quite stoned, she felt obliged to toke each time a joint came her way.

"Don't you love her?" Nadine said, nudging Marti.

"Who?" Marti managed.

"Janis, of course," Nadine said, "the music."

"Oh, sure," Marti answered. She'd lost awareness of the music in the background. Janis—did she know who that was? It didn't sound like Janis Ian. It was that other one, the one everyone talked about who died. What was the group she sang with—Jefferson Airplane? No, that was somebody else. She didn't think she could bluff this conversation and so decided to move away, but before she could stand, Spencer leaned over her, opened the pouch around her neck, and looked inside. Without commenting, he crossed to the other side of the table.

Brandon gave Brooke a shotgun, carefully inhaling the smoke before putting his lips to hers and blowing it into her mouth. They took their time, slowly, sensuously. Marti had seen Brooke do this with Trey before. When she saw Spencer give one to Nadine, she assumed they must be lovers until Nadine turned and offered Brooke one. Marti was shocked to see Brooke accept and next give Spencer one, winking at Marti as she did. Eventually, the only people not doing shotguns were Peter, Marti, and Doug (still rolling). Peter got up and walked around the room, looking at the artwork. Putting on his coat, he said he was going to check out the sky. Marti stood up to follow, but Spencer nudged her back down.

"Want one?" he asked. After inhaling he lowered himself to his knees and blew the smoke into her mouth while passing the joint to someone behind her back. He reached his hand under her hair, cradling her head. After a moment, he leaned away from her, saying, "Marti, you let the smoke out too fast, try again. *R-e-l-a-x.*" As he drew the word out, he tapped his fingers on her neck, emphasizing the letters. Marti heard someone snigger and her face grew warm.

Spencer reached for another joint. "Practice makes perfect." He leaned forward and held her head still with his hand while he blew smoke into her open mouth. She tried keeping it in, aware it was in her mouth, not her lungs. Spencer moved back, not releasing his hand. After the smoke gave her away by curling out of her mouth, Spencer leaned forward and pressed his lips hard against hers. Relenting to the insistent pressure, Marti parted her lips. Spencer's tongue inched forward, and just as quickly he stopped, stood up, and moved to the other side of the table. He leaned into Jenny, whispering.

Marti lifted her eyes and looked warily around the room. The senior boys were in the corner pulling records out of a wooden milk crate, excitedly exclaiming over each one. Brandon and Brooke were making out while Trey, sitting on the other side of Brooke, stared down at his legs where one of Brooke's hands rested on his thigh, palm side up, her fingers occasionally twitching like half worms dying after they'd been severed by a child's curiosity. Doug was steadily rolling. Nadine was stacking the joints into a pyramid. Jenny and Spencer were talking and laughing in low voices. Marti stood up and walked out onto the porch. "Can you see stars, Peter?"

"Nah, kind of cloudy. Think it's going to snow. Listen, Marti," he said, turning to her, "I've got to get going. Do you want to stay or go?"

Oh, I'm staying, she'd say with a flip of her hair. *I'm staying, most definitely staying.*

4

Spencer invited Marti to another party at his house. She asked Peter if he was going, but no, he'd be with his family celebrating Marybeth's birthday. Marti felt a twinge of guilt, as she'd said she'd be at the birthday, yet there was no way she'd miss Spencer's; she could think of nothing else.

Uneasy, knowing that Peter, her crutch, wouldn't be there, she conversely was excited for what that might mean. She rang Spencer's bell, shifting her feet back and forth, waiting and debating how soon to ring again. Rang again. Waited. Rang again. Waited.

"Marti, I forgot how punctual you are. I was sleeping." Spencer spoke as he pulled a black T-shirt over his head. He had a line of dark hair that stretched down his chest to his belly button. His pants hung loose without a belt, revealing his hips protruding from the sides of his stomach.

"Err, sorry. No one else is here? I can come back later." Marti turned to leave.

Spencer pulled her hand. "Don't be silly." Inside she stood until he motioned for her to sit. She opted to sit on the same floor cushion as last time so she'd have the doorknob on the table to fiddle with. She spun it. "That again," Spencer said. She was pleased he'd noticed. "Would you like wine?"

"Uh, okay." She'd tasted wine only a few times and didn't like it. Spencer sat cross-legged on the cushion next to her, his knee poking out through a rip in his jeans. They were silent until she asked, "Who else is coming?"

"Don't know. I invited a few people. You, however, are very early."

"Sorry."

"Stop"—Spencer put a finger on her lip—"saying you're sorry."

"Sor—" They both laughed; Marti continued fiddling with the doorknob.

"Are you nervous?"

"No."

"Don't be coy."

"Um, I just wondered, are your friends coming? I, uh, like your friends."

"Really? I didn't think you noticed them." Spencer laughed and poured himself some wine. He added more to Marti's glass although it was still full. She gulped the wine, and some dribbled down her neck as the glass was too full not to spill. She was embarrassed, but Spencer paid no notice. "Ah, tell the truth, Marti, the thought of us is why you're here." It was true; every moment she spent in his presence thrilled her. Spencer began unraveling her braids. "Am I going to have to do this every time? You know I like your hair down."

"Sor—" Spencer stopped her this time by leaning over and kissing her. It was so light she wasn't even clear he was kissing, yet his mouth was near and she could feel his breath. More insistent were his fingers caressing the side of her face.

"You're lovely with your secret Mona Lisa smile, and your scars. They tell your story." Marti jerked away, realizing his finger was tracing the scar lines. "Don't. They're beautiful. They give you depth unusual at your age; never be ashamed. A badge of honor, they celebrate you: a survivor. I want to know the story. Tell me, tell me." He whispered this last part in her ear while holding the glass up to her lips.

Marti remembered the nurses holding up water glasses in the hospital: *Drink. Drink.* She felt that same insistence now. She drank and Spencer kept the glass suspended in the air. It was intoxicating the way he was serving her, taking care of her. Not speaking, he occasionally caressed her with his fingers while the wine whirled inside her, washing away her tension.

He was waiting, waiting for her story. Had anyone ever wanted to hear it before?

And so she told him . . .

Summer 1964

We'd been out buying new school shoes, that sure sign summer was ending and there'd be no way of stopping it. Jan kept chattering about her new school and I didn't want to think about school, so as soon as we got home I asked Mommy if I could go to Peter's. "Sure," Mommy said, turning toward Jan. "She loves being a big girl, walking across the street by herself."

This annoyed me. True, I went to the Colgans' every day but not because of something babyish like crossing the street. I went because I loved everything about the Colgans. There were eight Colgan kids, and we'd all play together, games like Spud, Kick the Can, and Capture the Flag. Mrs. Colgan was interested in whatever we were doing and always complimented me: *How clever you are at that game!*

If Peter rang my bell, Mommy would say, "I'm working. You'll have to play outside." My house was always tidy and it felt empty, whereas Peter's was full of toys, games, and noise bursting everywhere. All the kids in the neighborhood played there. I would have been jealous except I knew, without it ever being said, that Peter and I had a secret bond, and, maybe because of this, Mrs. Colgan always made me feel special—a side smile, a wink, an extra marshmallow in my hot chocolate. When I grew up, I wasn't going to be like my mother with such a lonely home; I'd have lots of kids and smile all the time like Mrs. Colgan.

I wanted summer to go on and on and on because in the summer, it was as if I *were* a Colgan, and when fall came, I'd lose that. The Colgan kids would saunter home from school, laughing, playing all the way, while I'd be with Mrs. Thomas, the babysitter, shushing and pulling me. I wouldn't even have Jan because Jan would be at junior high, where she'd be a member of after-school clubs. I'd be stuck, a member of nothing.

I found Peter, Tom, Andy, and Richie in the backyard. Tom suggested we go to the playground. Peter and I silently colluded to stay behind, as the best times were when we played alone and could be as silly as we wanted; no playground could compare. We went onto the screen porch and pulled out a box full of troll dolls. Their odd faces, both friendly and smug and all the same, were so very satisfying. We dressed the trolls, made up names, and gave them voices. Cozy Rosie wore the flowered dress. I started twisting her hair. "Oh, Marti, please make my hair look like a rose," Peter demanded in Rosie's high, squeaky voice.

Candy Mandy wore the dress with lollipops on it, and Natty-Bratty Baby wouldn't wear any clothes. "Waah! Waah!" I cried, being Natty-Bratty Baby. "Leave me alone! Don't comb my hair, it hurts!" I was loud enough to draw Mrs. Colgan to the porch.

"Oh, I see what's going on. You two are at the trolls again. Who do we have here?"

"Natty-Bratty Baby won't let us do her hair," Peter said.

"Maybe I can help." Mrs. Colgan reached for the troll and brush. "You have to be gentle and start from the bottom. Is that better, Natty-Bratty Baby?" We laughed watching as Mrs. Colgan brushed the coarse purple hair, cooing, pretending the troll was delighted. "Perhaps if you changed her name she'd behave better."

"We like her bad," Peter said.

"Hmm, I'd have guessed. Better the troll than you two," Mrs. Colgan said, handing her back to me.

"Oh, Mama," Peter asked, "can I have a rose from the garden? For Cozy Rosie?"

"One of your father's prize roses, would you now? And who's this?" Mrs. Colgan picked up Candy Mandy.

"Candy Mandy," I answered. "She loves candy."

"A bit like some children I know. I'll be back with your rose." A moment later, she offered up a tiny yellow rosebud. "And here—left over from your sister's birthday, you think Candy Mandy might enjoy wearing this?" She held out a candy necklace. I wrapped it all around the troll. In a few minutes, Peter and I were both bent over, eating the little candies off the troll.

Mrs. Colgan returned with watermelon slices. "Your father called. He's going to be late, so dinner will wait. Have a snack to tide you over, though I see you devoured the poor child's clothes. I've turned the oven low to keep the potatoes and meatloaf warm, and I'll turn off the water for the cauliflower. Remember, the oven is hot. Don't touch it. I'll be upstairs taking a little catnap. And Marti, dear, of course you're welcome for dinner. I'm glad we'll be seeing so much of you now that you'll be walking home from school with Peter and the brood." I was puzzled. "Ah, child, did your ma not tell you? When I heard she was hiring Mrs. Thomas, I thought what a pity, when you could just come home with us, if you like."

"Yes! Oh, yes!" I shouted eagerly, then blushed.

Mrs. Colgan smiled. "Settled then, I'm glad. Eat your watermelon outside so you don't drip in the porch."

We excitedly planned what we'd do every day after school. I envisioned Mrs. Colgan greeting us at the door with a plate of homemade cookies. Peter spit his watermelon seeds as far as he could across the lawn. "Try it," he said, "it's fun." Soon we were spitting seeds at each other and got all sticky, so Peter suggested a squirt gun fight. He filled two guns with the hose, and we chased each other.

"No fair!" I yelled because my gun leaked. I stopped to fill it while Peter continued squirting. "Time out! You can't shoot me while I'm filling mine."

"Yes, I can!" Peter gloated, still shooting.

I was mad because I knew Peter deliberately gave me the leaky gun. I lifted the hose and squirted it in his face. "Take that!"

"You can't do that! You have to use a gun." Peter wrenched the hose from my hand.

I ran into the house. "Nah! Nah! You can't get me!" I shouted from the kitchen as Peter struggled to follow, pulling the hose, only it wouldn't reach inside. I waved my arms and stuck out my tongue. Peter dropped the hose and ran into the kitchen.

"Oh yeah?" Peter sneered. "Take that!" He grabbed the metal pot off the stove and threw the water at me. He dropped the pot, and it landed with a loud clatter. Next came the sound of a scream; I heard it before I understood it came from me.

Mommy was yelling at Mrs. Colgan, and I was on the kitchen floor. *When did she get here? And why is she yelling?* I didn't want to hear that, so I concentrated on pulling the white milk scab off my arm. Peter was crying in the corner. I turned toward him. "Why did you pour milk on me?" He cried louder.

"Milk, is that what it is?" Mommy asked.

"No, no," Mrs. Colgan said, "boiled water, for cauliflower. I thought I turned it off . . . I don't know why her skin is white . . . The burn . . ."

Cauliflower? Is that the white stuff? I pulled more off my face. *So rubbery.* I could hear the other Colgan children behind a door in another room, whispering anxiously; Betty, the oldest, was trying to hush them for some reason.

"Oh, my god!" Mommy shrieked, pulling my arm away. "It's her skin, that's what the white is! She's pulling off her skin! When will the ambulance get here?"

Mrs. Colgan bent down and put a pack of frozen peas on my face. I pushed it off. I hated peas. "Marti, dear, leave it. The cold will make you feel better." It was too cold; it hurt, it burned. *How could cold burn?* I closed my eyes.

This is what I remember: Mrs. Colgan beside me steadying the frozen peas, holding my hand and murmuring, *There, there.* Mrs. Colgan, not Mommy. Over the years I've wondered at that. Didn't Mommy kneel down too? And yet, even in the ambulance, it was the ambulance man who held my hand and told me it would be all right. Then he poked needles into me. Everything hurt and I wanted to cry out for Mommy, which didn't make sense because Mommy was right there sitting silently across from me, so I cried for Daddy and heard the man ask if he'd been called. "My husband passed away," Mommy said, and I cried louder, as if it were the first time I'd heard.

"Ma'am, sorry. Recent then?" Not answering, Mommy moved closer and stroked my hair. Suddenly, it wasn't hurting anymore. I laughed, thinking it was funny that the man thought Daddy had just died when now it was such a long, long time ago.

I don't remember getting out of the ambulance or entering the hospital. A time gap that I hate having, a piece of life lost, a crucial clue to something and I don't even know what.

I awoke to darkness, unable to move. One of my arms was strapped tight to a wooden board, palm side up with a needle in my arm. My other arm was tied to the side rail of the bed. One elevated leg was also tied to a board. I was a marionette, all moving parts that needed string, wood, and hinges to function. I didn't know if anyone else was there, and it didn't matter as I couldn't move anyway. This narrow darkness was my world. I stared up at nothing and felt strangely comforted as the silence and darkness matched my numbness. *I feel dead. Am I?*

Next came a loud sound, an odd grating noise. It was a zipper opening. *I'm in a bag?* Light burst in like fireworks in a night sky. I could see someone's eyes, only their eyes, a person wearing a mask. They untied my arms and propped the puppet up. "I'm Miss Anton, your nurse. What do you think of the tent? Kind of like camping, isn't it? Only this tent is special. It gives you oxygen and keeps the air clean." Her gloved hand placed a straw in my mouth. "Drink," she said, holding the glass while I struggled to remember how to move my mouth.

Everyone in gowns, eyes, only eyes, everyone blurring into a swirl of eyes, Mommy and Jan included. The eyes said: *Drink your water. Drink your water.* My right arm, right leg, and right side of my face were all bandaged. Sometimes a whole crowd of eyes came, doctor eyes. They'd talk to each other while pulling off the bandages, prodding at the wounds as if I weren't there; only the pain reminded me that I existed.

After some time—it could have been a day or a month—the tent was removed and my limbs freed, except for the needle arm still tied to the board. At least now I could lift the board. "Careful with that," a nurse warned. "Don't wave it around. You could dislodge the needle, and we wouldn't want to have to stick you again."

Sometimes there were lots of people poking and other times long periods with no one. Random, I could never brace for what was to come. Often I'd awaken to see Mommy dozing in a chair, slumped down, her hospital gown disheveled and her hair sloppily spilling out of the cap. It scared me: Mommy was never sloppy. I wanted my perfectly pressed, all-powerful stone mother.

Again, crowds of doctors examining under the bandages and nurses commanding: *Drink your water.* I didn't like to drink because it hurt to swallow, but then again, everything hurt. I wanted to scratch the hurt away. Just as I started getting under a bandage to scratch, a swarm of doctor eyes came into the room. "Whoa there, missy." A doctor held my arm firmly. "What do you think you're doing?"

Another doctor took out some scissors and cut away the dressings on my leg and arm. I tried sitting up to see, but someone held me down. "Curious, eh? Let us take care of this. You just rest." A doctor took out a metal ruler and measured each of the burns, comparing the color and size of each one. Holding my head tight, they ripped the face bandage off to measure. I started crying. The first salty tear trickled down my face, landing on the wound, making it feel like it was burning all over again. I tried to stop, but a few tears had already spilled out and I had to wait as each one hit its target—salt in the wound. By the fourth tear, it was a detail I was anticipating from afar: the slow, steady journey down my cheek until *X* marked the spot. I imagined a tiny witch there, stirring a brew of salt, tears, and fire. Ignoring me, the doctors talked as they applied fresh bandages. "We have to debride soon. Schedule that. Oh, and get a nurse in here for restraints." They left without a backward glance.

When the nurse came, it was Miss Anton. She began wrapping a roll of gauze around my free arm, attaching it to the side rail. "No," I moaned, "please don't tie me."

"Honey, I have to. It'll be okay."

I stared at the arm, not my arm anymore. And without my arm, I couldn't suck my thumb, the only thing I knew to do for comfort. "Don't put me in the tent." I thrashed around as if the tent had already swallowed me.

"Hush, you're not going in the tent now. They just want you to leave the bandages alone. Show us what a good girl you are and we'll take these off in a few days, okay?" Miss Anton was leaving, and I tried stifling my tears unsuccessfully. She turned back at the sound. "Oh, hon, you're crying? You're going to be okay. *Really.* I've got a joke for you: What's the most famous fruit in history?"

"I don't know."

"A date." I laughed because I liked Miss Anton trying. She took a tissue and wiped my eyes. This made me cry again. "There, there, how about a drink, a little sip of water?" She held it to my lips and I drank. "You're getting better, Marti, I promise. Here, I'll loosen the straps a bit because I trust you won't touch the wounds."

I wanted sleep. There was nothing else.

Each day the doctors came in to debride the burns. They put medicine in my IV before unwrapping the bandages and scraping with a metal tool along the burns, removing scabs. The medicine made me sleepy, yet still I could feel my skin being pulled and my nerves screaming in alarm. I closed my eyes and that only heightened the sound. Underneath there was a softer, scarier sound: skin cracking.

Finished, they'd put me in the tent. Before I hated it, but now it meant they were done scraping for the day. The tent became my home, and I kept it closed even when I didn't have to. That way, I could bend my head to my thumb and suck with no one telling me not to.

I wasn't supposed to have any toys because they weren't sanitary. When Jan visited, she'd slip into the tent and hand me presents, small toys she snuck from home, and she'd play games with me.

5

Describing these games to Spencer, Marti laughed. Had she *ever* laughed thinking of the hospital? She couldn't believe what she was telling Spencer—even about sucking her thumb. Spencer murmured in her ear, "How much fun it would be playing games under a tent with you."

She stopped talking, thinking he would kiss her, and when he didn't, she was relieved. She'd thought she came here because of the kiss but now understood, no, it was this: he *wanted* to know her story. By telling it, she could give away a small piece of her sorrow. In the middle of this realization, Spencer began suddenly tickling her, a sensation she hadn't experienced in years, not since her father. She began to squirm and laugh, and Spencer laughed also. She pushed him, rolled away, and banged into the side of the door table. "Ouch," she said, and they paused a moment before the tickling and laughing resumed. "Stop, oh stop, stop! I can't stop laughing!"

"Okay, then," Spencer said, abruptly still, which made Marti burst out in a fresh round of giggles. They tussled several more minutes before slowly coming to a natural cessation. Sitting quietly, Marti wondered what would come next. "There," he said, "that's better. You needed a break. Still, there's more. Go on, Marti, I want to hear it all."

His eyes were fixed on her, waiting.

Fall 1964

I wanted my favorite stuffed animal, Papa Bear. Jan said, "No, he's too big. If they find him, they'll throw him away." Papa Bear had a big round stomach, and I always thought it was big because it was meant to hold all my tears. I did my best crying on his soft belly. Maybe my toys had already been thrown away. I pictured Papa Bear lying in a dump with dirty paper plates covering him and rats climbing over him to lick the plates. *No point crying anymore.*

I kept expecting the Colgans to visit. When I asked Mommy, she didn't answer. Instead, a lady came to see me. "I'm Miss Hegman, your second grade teacher." She held out her gloved hand and I tried moving mine, having momentarily forgotten I was tied. "Don't trouble yourself." Miss Hegman patted my arm. "I wanted to visit and tell you how much we miss you. The children made cards." She leaned forward, whispering, "Your mom helped me sneak them in."

She turned a bag over, and construction paper cards of many colors spilled out. There were pictures of flowers and suns; most had names printed in pencil, and some had messages: *Get well soon. We miss you.* There was one that had only black crayon scrawled across a gray piece of construction paper and the signature was so small, Marti almost didn't notice it: *Peter.* Miss Hegman held up each card. I looked at Mommy. *School started already? How long have I been here?*

Miss Hegman came back several times and told me what was going on in class. I felt queasy thinking of walking into the class-room—the new kid, only creepier, because I wouldn't really be new. I liked Miss Hegman and that only made it worse.

One day Mommy told me I'd have an operation. "They will take some skin from your behind and attach it to places where your skin is damaged, to your face, arm, and leg. It's called a skin graft."

I didn't know why she'd joke like this. *Ha ha, butt face.* She kept talking, telling me I'd be asleep, it wouldn't hurt. "Your skin will look much better, almost like nothing happened."

But how bad did my skin look? How could being a butt face be better?

Later I asked Miss Anton for a mirror. "Sweetheart, don't trouble yourself. You can't see anyway because of the bandages. You can't remove the bandages; only doctors and nurses can. Imagine, even your mother can't take the bandages off!"

"Can you?"

"Sweetie, be patient."

I asked Jan what I looked like, and she didn't answer.

"Get me a mirror."

"I can't do that, Marti. You can't take them off."

"Please? One of Mom's little mirrors? One peek, that's all." Looking away, she shook her head. I shouted, "I'm telling everyone you brought me toys and came in the tent. You'll be in trouble!"

"You little brat, I was being nice!" Jan swung her feet off the bed and left. Now I wouldn't get a mirror or toys. I felt mean. I was mean. I *wanted* to be mean.

Mommy came when it was time for the operation. As soon as she said *operation*, I started crying. I'd played that game at Peter's house. We'd use tweezers to remove plastic pieces out of a cardboard person, and if you bumped, there was a horrible zapping noise.

A doctor put a needle into the IV, saying I'd fall asleep soon. I cried louder and tried to pull my arm loose from the board. I mustn't sleep; that was the only way I could stop them. Mommy took my hand. "Marti, look at my dress. I remember it's your favorite." I did love her white shirtwaist dress with colored pictures stamped all over it.

Mommy pointed at a picture. "See this one? A lady is walking her dog. All of a sudden, a flock of birds fly overhead." Mommy's fingers twirled to another picture. "What do you think happened next?" She nudged me and I shrugged. "I'll tell you. The dog ran after the birds. The lady chased the dog and couldn't catch up. So she hopped onto a bicycle." She spun her finger until it landed on a man riding a bicycle.

"Mommy, that's a man."

"Yes, in this country a person could change from a girl to a boy, quick as a flash." Mommy snapped her fingers. "Oh, it's a splendid, magical country, isn't it?" She stroked my hair. "Lots of wonderful things. See those balloons there? Everywhere balloons. In fact, that was what the birds were chasing in the first place . . ."

The story lulled along, and each time I opened my eyes, I'd hear Mommy telling me about balloons, umbrellas, and apple trees. I've always treasured that memory of being lulled to sleep by the caress of her hands and the cadence of her voice. The dress story is my proof: I've been loved.

The days continued in a blur of doctors removing bandages, scraping skin, replacing bandages, the routine repeating again and again. When they took the tent away for good, I missed it and started sleeping with the covers pulled tightly over my head. I still sleep that way.

Sometimes now they left my door open. I was shocked to discover other children going past. My hospital room had become my whole world, and I hadn't ever wondered what was on the other side of the door. A boy whizzed back and forth, riding his IV pole, sneaking peeks at me. Finally he stopped and asked why I never came out. I didn't know the answer. I didn't want to leave my room, yet I was happy he was talking to me. The nurses started taking me for walks, always when the corridor was empty.

After the bandages were removed, Miss Anton gave me a mirror, assuring me the scars would fade. My once smooth skin was now interrupted by raised tracks and swirls, looking like a picture of the moon's craters. *This is who I am now.* I was going home, not knowing the hardest part was just beginning.

It might have been easier to hide behind bandages when I finally entered second grade. Miss Hegman told the children not to stare. A girl started crying when I was assigned the seat next to her, so Miss Hegman switched her with a boy, Larry. "Boo-hoo, I'm so scared. Miss Hegman, please change my seat." The class laughed and Larry smirked, having simultaneously made fun of me and the crying girl—a double triumph.

I still hadn't seen any of the Colgans, and Mommy finally told me the Colgan house and Peter were now forbidden. Peter was in my class. He was always watching me. If I returned the look, he'd avert his eyes. When our paths directly crossed, he was overly solicitous: "Marti, you can have my place in line," or "Do you need help finding a reading book?" Once he asked, "Does it hurt?" I pretended not to hear him, as he was now just a nuisance, a reminder.

He offered to sharpen my pencil and I snapped, "Go away. I'm not a retard. You are." He stopped trying to talk to me after that. Still, I could feel his gawking eyes.

Alone in my room, I'd stare at my face in the mirror and run my hand across smooth skin until I hit bumps. If only I could get to a smooth layer underneath. Wasn't that why they scraped me? I pulled at the skin on my thighs until it bled. *Yes! Now I can remove the burn.* A new scab always formed, and once it healed, the scar remained unchanged. This astonished me—didn't I dig deep enough? I'd try over and over, only on my thigh where no one could discover my secret and tie me down again.

6

"Sometimes I—I still do that, even though I know it won't change anything, just a habit now." Marti took a long drink of wine.

"Where?" Spencer asked. "May I see?" Shocked by the question, Marti nonetheless began slowly rolling up the hem of her long patchwork skirt. Spencer moved her hand away and pushed the skirt up. When he got to her thigh where scars—and some scabs—were evident, he leaned down and kissed them.

She quickly pulled her skirt back down to her ankles, hugging her knees up to her chest, contorting herself into a tight ball with her head tucked in. "I didn't mean . . . Those are gross."

"No, no, Marti, they're you, and you are beautiful, every part of you. Please don't go back into your shell." Placing one hand on her chin and the other cradling the back of her head, he lifted her head carefully. As he turned her face towards him, the trembling in her legs ceased and instead she felt the beginning of a great release. "All of it, Marti, let it all out." And she began to cry softly at first, and then it turned into sobs and wails until at last, one long flat moan that seemed to have no end. Spencer brought her tissues, and he wiped the snot that covered her face. After her crying finally subsided, he told her it was time for her to leave.

Of course he wanted her to go (where was the party anyway?). He wouldn't kiss her now—the snotty, moaning, scabby mess. She stood unsteadily on her feet. "Will you be okay getting home?" he asked. She nodded and started for the door. He stopped her and held her shoulders gently before kissing her forehead softly. She was reminded of a joke her father had often played of pretending to wipe dirt off her forehead before kissing it.

"You have more to tell me, Marti. Come tomorrow, okay?" He said the last word quietly, bending to look in her face as if he was asking for permission.

Marti slept a long time and felt perfectly rested in the morning as she lay in bed, thinking of that fatherly kiss, and how she'd misconstrued both of their motives. Of course he didn't want to fool around with her; she was a kid he wanted to help. He'd even tickled her, just like she was a little child. Yes, he was handsome, and yes, she felt it, but no, she wasn't ready for *that*. There'd be no sex. It was a relief because what she'd been seeking wasn't sexual at all—she understood that now—and what had terrified her wasn't that: it was Spencer's exploration of her pain. Yet it turned out he knew that this was just what she needed. And in the process, he carted away some of her burden.

Her mother questioned her going out on a Sunday evening and was pleased when she said she'd be doing homework, studying with Alison. "Such a nice girl, that Alison." Her mother's remarks were never innocent; she was always undercutting someone, this time, Brooke and Peter.

Again Spencer took a long time answering the door and when he finally did, he was clearly ready, having already poured wine. Marti talked of the kids who teased and the ones who didn't. "That was almost worse."

"How so?" Spencer leaned forward, listening intently.

"Because I knew they felt sorry for me. I was their charity case; they could tell their Sunday school teachers how kind they were. They thought they were helping *me*, but really, I was helping *them* feel better about themselves. Some teachers, too, they used my pain to boost themselves." Marti hadn't comprehended that she felt this until she voiced it aloud.

Spencer shook his head. "You have extraordinary insight." He held the wine glass to her lips. His attention never wavered as he listened.

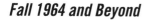

Fall 1964 and Beyond

The boys at school developed special taunts. *Charcoal broiled face. Railroad tracks, where do your trains go?* The girls were worse, giggling behind the boys, and it continued this way, year after year. In fifth grade, a group of girls pulled me aside in the schoolyard. "Glen wants to ask you out."

I moved away until a girl yanked my arm. "You don't believe us? Go over there—go." She shoved me toward a group of waiting boys. "Glen wants to give you his ID bracelet."

The boys surrounded me. "Marti, oh Marti, will you please go steady with me?" Glen dangled his shimmering silver bracelet with *Glen* engraved upon it. "*Please, please*, be my girlfriend." He got down on one knee. I scratched my head and looked away, trying to pretend I was thinking about something else or, even better, was someplace else. I saw Peter on the other side of the playground leaning against the fence, hunched over with his hands in his jean pockets.

One of the girls said, "Marti, he's serious. *Really.* He means it."

Another piped in, "Don't you know it's rude not to answer?"

I pushed my hair over my face and folded my arms across my chest, waiting for what I always called *made it till the bell time.* Everyone else called it recess.

As sixth-grade graduation approached, the teacher passed out autograph books and gave the students time to look through them. I was excited, as I'd been prepping for this moment by studying Jan's book, reading the clever and funny sayings. I eagerly unzipped my book and flipped through the colored pages, deciding to save the last two for Jan and Mom.

There was a list inside to be completed: most popular, prettiest, and wittiest student. Maybe, after I wrote all the clever sayings I'd memorized from Jan's book, someone would name me wittiest.

I felt a tap on my shoulder: Larry, the sniggering boy from second grade. "Can I sign your book?" I was surprised and pleased, thinking maybe now that we were graduating, things were different. He didn't offer his and returned mine with a rail-road track drawn inside.

That afternoon Mom asked to see the book, and I quickly ripped Larry's page out. "No one signed your book yet?"

"I wanted you and Jan to be first."

"How sweet! I'm sure you'll get lots of signatures. Jan got from everyone in her class, and you must ask the principal and all your teachers."

Each afternoon I practiced different signatures, morphing my handwriting into new styles, filling the book with rhymes and slogans culled from Jan's book. *To a good kid, from a better one (just kidding), Suzy Johnson.* I copied about five rhymes and signatures each day and showed them to Jan and Mom; neither suspected the ruse.

I did ask a couple of teachers, and they scrawled their names and quickly wrote, *Good Luck.* I asked Miss Hegman, still my favorite teacher because of the bond we formed in those hospital days. When I saw what she wrote, *To thine own self be true*, I felt she knew what I'd done with the false signatures. I vowed some-day I would be true—after I buried my charcoal-broiled self.

7

"Drink," Spencer said softly, holding the glass up to her lips, and this made Marti cry. "No more sadness," he whispered, placing the glass back on the table. He began kissing the tears as they streamed down her face, making an exaggerated motion as if racing to capture them all. "Slow down, I can't catch that quickly!"

Marti laughed while still crying. "Whew," Spencer said, "let's check that I've got them all." He tenderly encircled her face with kisses, moving on to her neck, saying, "Oh, I missed a few, they landed down here."

"Sorry."

"See, there you go, using that word. Surely you can see how ridiculous *sorry* is? Never, never, say it." He kissed her insistently this time, his tongue pushing deep into her mouth, his hands sliding along her body. "Marti, Marti, let's heal you with love," he murmured, moving his hands faster, touching her in an ever-changing pattern. "I'll check for tears here," he said, unbuttoning her blouse one button at a time, slowly kissing each space before moving on to the next button.

It was happening fast—not what she expected. Still, it felt good, exciting, dangerous, and terrifying all at the same time. Did she want it?

He reached behind and released her bra. "I'm surprised you wear one," he said abruptly, changing the mood.

Marti tensed, wondering what he meant. Was it because she was too small? "I, uh, sor—"

Spencer pressed his hand to her lips. "Don't say it again. You said it before and I let you get away with it, but now, now you owe me." He pushed her back onto the cushions, and as if he could read her mind, flung the bra in the air, saying, "Never mind, you silly serious girl." He kissed her, cupping his hands over her breasts, making them tingle in a way she didn't know they could. He twirled her nipples; it hurt, yet she liked it. He licked her nipples, and Marti shuddered and pressed against him, hoping to make him stop or not stop. Pushing her skirt up, Spencer reached between her legs and next pulled his pants off. She felt a jolt of fear, closed her legs, and started pulling her skirt down.

No, he isn't. Not really. He can't be. Not that.

"Sweet Martha, relax. I won't hurt you. You trust me, don't you?" Spencer rose up on one elbow looking kindly at her.

She had already trusted him with everything.

"Does anyone else call you Martha?"

"No." She liked her full name, the old-fashioned quality of it. She felt more like a Martha than a Marti, although strangely, no one, not teachers or even her family, ever called her that.

"Good. Then it belongs to me. And when I use it in school, you'll know I'm thinking of you in a special way and your body will come alive at the thought." As he spoke, his hands stroked her body, touching her where no one ever had. Marti felt he was stirring something deep inside her, exposing her truest self.

He put her hand on his penis. It was stiff. She'd never seen one, was curious to see it, yet didn't want to. Her hand fell away.

Closing her eyes, she let Spencer open her legs. He pushed into her and she stifled a cry. Despite that silent cry, her body was eager everywhere he touched. She never knew it was possible to feel such pain and pleasure simultaneously. She wanted it to end, not end. He pushed harder and harder in rhythm until he moaned and shuddered to a slow stillness.

They lay in silence. Unsure what to do next, Marti was waiting for a cue from Spencer when there was a knock at the door. No one had come yesterday when he said there was a party. Surely not today? "Hang on," Spencer called out casually. He laughed as he pulled his pants on and leaned over to help Marti with her bra and blouse. She thought he'd give her a last kiss. He didn't.

It was Nadine, Doug, and another man, Paul. "Hey, little sister." Nadine hugged her and scanned the room. "Where are your pals?"

"They didn't come."

"No, they didn't *come*, didn't *come*." Spencer chuckled, lighting up the joint Doug handed him. Marti sat and began spinning the door knob. Spencer put a record on, the Rolling Stones, and placed the album cover in front of her. It had a zipper you could actually pull up and down along the crotch of a man's black jeans.

Nadine sat next to Marti and tapped the album cover, "Fantastic, isn't it? Andy Warhol's a genius."

Andy Warhol? Spencer had talked about him and Marti assumed he was a painter. Now she deduced she'd gotten it wrong: he's a member of the Rolling Stones. She'd file that away.

Doug, who was not rolling joints, sat and started to talk about Nixon and the bombing in Cambodia. "Immoral," Nadine said, shifting her body away from Marti as they all nodded in agreement. The song "Wild Horses" played, and Marti understood the feeling: nothing, nothing, could drag her away.

Marti didn't know where Cambodia was. *Was it part of Vietnam?* Only recently she'd deciphered which side the US supported, South Vietnam, yet she still didn't understand enough to follow any discussion about the war. *Who were the Viet Cong? Which side were they on?* The more Marti read the newspapers, the more confused she grew, as if it were a movie she'd walked in on the middle of. She wouldn't display her ignorance by asking since she wasn't even sure which questions to ask, so she nodded her head and stayed quiet hoping they wouldn't spot her lack of knowledge. She needn't have worried; no one seemed to notice her at all.

Soon Doug and Paul said they had to leave and offered Marti a ride. She looked at Spencer, busy whispering to Nadine, who clearly wasn't leaving. He barely nodded goodbye, didn't even reach for the hand she held out. She sat in the back of Doug's Jeep while Paul and Doug talked of more things she didn't understand.

In her bedroom, she sat on the pink bedspread, mystified as she surveyed her possessions. The box worlds and miniatures were carefully arranged on a shelf, along with comic books and piggy banks, relics from a life that didn't exist anymore, or one that certainly no longer belonged to her. She was an intruder in this bedroom. Clothes she'd frantically tried on and abandoned in anticipation of this evening lay strewn about in piles. Papa Bear was smothered underneath a bunch of them as he sat in his little red rocking chair. She picked him up and examined him. His fur had worn away in spots, and Marti had replaced it over the years with patches of childhood castoffs: a favorite nightgown with baby lambs on it, a lacy pink birthday dress for turning six, the skirt from her Annie Oakley costume with whirling lassos on it.

Her clothes still on, she climbed into bed, clutching Papa Bear. She noticed how saggy his head was becoming; it wouldn't stay upright and flopped back and forth. *I'll fix that soon*, she whispered, promising. She was aware that there were drops of blood on her flowered underwear.

Part II

BLOOD

8

Winter/Spring 1972

On Monday Marti wore her hair down, but Spencer barely glanced in her direction. No one was going to his room after school, and without a sign from Spencer she couldn't go alone. The same unnerving scenario happened Tuesday.

Trying to distract herself, she went shopping for a birthday present for Marybeth and decided on a plastic circus set with a tent, acrobats, lions, elephants, hoops for animals to jump through, and a lady to ride the elephant. She wondered if the toy was too young for a turning-eight Marybeth but got it anyway. Marti elaborately wrapped the present, sneaking a piece of her mother's expensive wrapping paper and carefully tying a fancy bow. She painted a card with circus images. Mrs. Colgan answered the door, informing her Peter wasn't home. "I came to give Marybeth a present. Sorry I missed the party." She held out the gift and Mrs. Colgan led her to the den, all the while exclaiming over her card. Marybeth and Nancy were sitting on the rug, playing with a pulley they'd attached to a window. Tied at the end of the rope was a silver pail holding two dolls dangling in front of a dollhouse.

"Help! We're stuck!" shouted Marybeth before noticing Marti. Embarrassed, she dropped the rope and stood up, looking quizzically at her mother. The dolls fell out of the bucket and bounced on the floor.

"Marti came to see you. I'll leave you girls alone, now." The den was full of light from windows on three sides. The other wall was covered in kids' artwork and family photos, even one of Marti and Peter, age four, all caked in mud. Beneath the windows were cabinets, half-closed, full of toys and games.

Nancy started opening the present, but Marybeth snatched it back. "Mine, remember?" Marybeth unwrapped it carefully, preserving the paper in a neat pile, and after thanking Marti, ran to show her mother.

"Want to play with us?" she asked upon returning.

"Sure," Marti answered, enthused and grateful. "We can take the dolls to the circus."

"Yes, they can ride the pulley to get there. My doll's name is Valerie."

"Mine's Tabitha," Nancy said. "You can have this one. Sorry, it's a boy, that's all we have left."

"That's okay. What's a good name for a boy?" Marti thought about saying Spencer but pushed this silly thought aside, realizing she'd rather not think of him at all. "How about Alexander? Sounds kind of like a prince."

"Very good," Nancy said, nodding. They set up the circus, and Marti became so engrossed in playing that she didn't hear someone enter.

Marybeth jumped up. "Peter, look what Marti gave me."

"Wicked!" Peter grinned at Marti. "Been here long?"

"A while—having fun."

"Play with us." Nancy yanked Peter to the floor, and they played until Mrs. Colgan called the girls away for chores.

"Nice of you," Peter said, still fiddling with an elephant. "Marybeth missed you Saturday, but this definitely makes up for that. How was Spencer's?"

Reluctantly pulled away from the make-believe, she didn't know how to answer. *How was it?* Sometimes she thought it was the most wonderful thing that ever happened, and other times, the worst. She didn't feel allowed to have an opinion; it was all up to Spencer, and he hadn't given her any clues.

"Who was there?"

"Just those friends of his, you know, Nadine and Doug."

"Uh-huh. I think tomorrow we can go to his room."

The next morning, Marti brushed her hair one hundred strokes and wore the same patchwork skirt she'd worn Saturday—maybe he'd notice. Ignored in class, she still tagged along after school. Spencer announced that Principal Jacques had given permission for them to paint a mural. "We can paint the whole hallway, around the corner, up to the music room, and past the bathrooms."

The art room was the last room around a corner at the end of a long corridor. The mural was a good idea, Marti thought, as it was a particularly barren hall. The other hallways had bulletin boards with students' work posted on brightly colored paper, yet ironically, the walls outside the art room were bare. Early in the year, both Peter and Alison had inquired about this and Spencer responded, "Do you want me to display your pretty pictures like you're trained seals? Think about it. We're in the *process* of creating; it's not a stagnant thing. You can't just hang art on a wall for show-and-tell." He dismissed any further discussion with a sardonic wave of his hand.

"I think Mr. Jacques has in mind for you to paint sunsets, or maybe a montage of students diligently studying, but I give you permission to use your free minds to paint whatever you like. Think about it—or don't think about it, be spontaneous. We'll start tomorrow."

Marti understood "paint whatever you like" didn't mean a picturesque hillside, and she was beginning to grasp the contradiction: they were free to express themselves only if it matched Spencer's concept of liberation. He wanted them to paint abstractly, but that wasn't what interested Marti. Her mind wandered to playing with Marybeth and Nancy; she'd love to paint circus animals, but could envision Spencer's contempt. She considered playing on this with a mockery of her own: trained seals performing for their ring master.

Thinking more about that afternoon in the Colgans' den, she had her idea. The next day, she chose a far end of the wall. This was partly because she needed room for what she wanted to create and also because she hoped Spencer would approach her. She didn't start painting right away as others did; instead, she sat on the floor sketching. She quickly grew absorbed, and this was a useful reprieve for forgetting both Spencer and her forlorn self. Only the sketching mattered. She felt a hand on her spine and flinched, unaware that Spencer had come up behind her. *How could I not have known?* "Martha, whatever could make you jump like that?"

Her face reddened, a mix of embarrassment and arousal: *Martha.* He squatted, touched her knee, and asked what she was sketching. She tried explaining her idea, but was distracted by his feather-like fingers insistently tapping her knee. All the new sensations flooded back, her body alert with expectation—especially down there. She wanted to be with him. *With him* was how she thought of it, not knowing what to call it. *Making love? Fucking? Balling?* None of the terms seemed accurate.

Spencer stood up. "People, look over here. Martha Washington"—students cackled at the name—"is sketching a window with sunlight pouring in." His voice dripped with disdain. Students stopped to look, their brushes poised in midair away from the abstract swirls they were painting. Several hooted, Trey loudest of all. Brooke playfully reached her hand out to shush him, yet her own laughter wasn't fully disguised.

"Now, ye of little faith." Spencer paused triumphantly, arching his eyebrows, having gotten the predicted reaction. "Remember Marti's work in class? I think this must be leading somewhere not quite so obvious."

Marti did have something more in mind; she wasn't sure it would impress Spencer, yet it was what she wanted to do. After she finished the Colgans' window, she sketched the dollhouse and suspended the doll family on the roof. They were clinging on, desperation showing on their faces; the sunlight pouring in from the window highlighted this danger. She worked hard, inspired, and grateful to have something occupying her mind other than Spencer. *What did touching her knee mean? What had the weekend meant to Spencer?* She was dying to tell someone, Brooke or even Peter. She'd listened admiringly to Brooke's tales of boyfriends. Wasn't it her turn? Spencer's evasive eyes answered that.

Days passed while she sat on the hallway floor sketching, Spencer only glancing indifferently a few times. He didn't touch or even speak to her, and she tried to stop hoping for something, concluding it was futile. At the end of the week, he suddenly bent down and whispered in her ear, "My house, five o'clock." He moved on, not waiting for an answer.

Spencer told the students to wrap it up and Marti hurried home, without waiting to walk with anyone. She took a shower and changed out of her overalls, deciding to wear her black leotard, thinking this made her look older—maybe even sexy? Trying on several skirts, she settled on a burgundy velvet India Import with little mirrors sewn into it. It seemed like something Nadine might wear.

Her mother wasn't home and wouldn't be back from teaching until at least seven thirty. She started to leave a note but changed her mind because she never left notes. If it got late, she'd call and say she was at Brooke's. How long would she be at Spencer's?

She knocked softly on the door; no sound came from inside. Knocking louder, she tried peering through the window but couldn't see anything, as it was dark. She continued knocking until finally giving up and turning to retreat down the steps.

The door opened, and Spencer pulled her inside. "Was that

you scratching like a mouse? I should've known." After closing the door, he pushed her against a wall and began kissing her hard. Her mouth hurt and she stiffened. Spencer laughed. "Martha, what's wrong? Isn't this why you're here? Ah, I forget—you're such a shy bird. I don't mean to frighten you, but you must know you're sexy in your tight, slinky black."

He led her to his bedroom, which she hadn't seen before. There was a mattress on the floor, books and newspapers scattered about. "Wait here, I'll get wine." The only place to sit was the bed, so Marti stood until Spencer returned.

"Sit." She sat cross-legged on the floor, next to a pile of clothes; interspersed with the jeans and T-shirts were balls of white underwear. Spencer sat on the bed, held out a glass of wine, and patted the space beside him. "Let's have no games. The bed is, after all, where you want to be." The sheets lay creased, expectant. Marti crawled across the floor and accepted the glass. She sat on the bed, leaving a gap between them.

"Drink your wine. It'll calm you, Nervous Nelly. Don't forget: I've seen your passion. Maybe no one else has, but I know it's there." He put his wine glass down and began gently pushing wisps of hair away from her face and circling it with kisses. "Such beautiful skin. Luminous, like your art." *Beautiful skin? Luminous? Did he really say these things?* "I am liking your sketches. I didn't mean to embarrass you the other day."

"I wasn't."

"Liar. Your blush betrays you." He laughed. "I do relish seeing that blush, then I know I've got you." Marti quickly drank her wine. "I noticed your work developing today. I don't know what it will be. I never know with you, and I'm always intrigued." He kissed Marti on the mouth, softer this time, and she responded. He lowered her down on the bed and began kissing her neck. Marti squirmed, a mixture of pleasure and fear. "Ah, good, you're ready." He took off his shirt and pants.

Marti was uncertain—was she supposed to take her clothes off? In the movies didn't the man usually do it? Spencer reached around her waist and unbuttoned her skirt and pulled it down. "Damn, you've got one of those silly attached things. I was afraid of that." Marti hurried to remove her leotard.

"Never mind, this could be fun." He moved his head down toward her legs and parted the leotard to one side. He coiled her pubic hair around his fingers. Marti worried—did she have too much hair? It seemed so when she saw other girls changing. Spencer gently licked her leg. He ran his tongue around the hair touching her crack, and she shuddered. He looked up. "Too much for you, Martha? All in good time." He pulled at her leotard, motioning for her to remove it. She did and next unsnapped her bra.

He frowned. "Most liberated women don't wear bras, don't you know? If you must, at least get rid of this dreadful white and get a sexy black lace one." Marti nodded. "On second thought, no, that might arouse Mommy's suspicions and we mustn't do that, you understand? Where does Mommy think you are?"

"She's at work. She teaches a class till seven."

"A working mother, good for you. You can grow up without her constant scrutiny. And growing up is what you're doing. A wonderful experience for you, Martha, you can learn all about sex from a man who treats you right, not some foolish boy quick to get his rocks off. I'll take my time pleasuring you." He leaned forward, whispering in her ear, "Do you want that?" She nodded. "Don't nod like a mute. Say it: I want you, Spencer."

"I want you, Spencer," Marti repeated, reaching one arm out to him.

"That's better, Martha." Spencer rolled on top of her and kissed her hard, then licked her nipples, round and round in circles. It felt so good she never wanted him to stop. He entered her, and it didn't hurt like last time. When he was done, he whispered for her to come back the next afternoon and closed his eyes. She was sad he wanted her to leave but thrilled that he wanted her to come back. She tiptoed out the door.

Two or three times a week became the routine, although Marti could never predict it. Spencer might tell her when to come back while she was at his house; other times he'd say nothing and she'd have to wait until he approached her at school, whispering in her ear: *Today*. It was all up to Spencer. He never asked what she wanted. Of course, even if he had, she'd never say no. It meant everything, and so this casual, random way he arranged it left her teetering on edge.

She understood she'd been foolish to think they'd be a couple out in public, and Spencer, she was realizing, reveled in this stealth. He'd quickly place a furtive hand down her pants when no one was looking. It made her feel dirty and shameful, but she pretended things were otherwise. She wrote *Mrs. Spencer Douglas*, *Marti Douglas*, *Spencer and Marti* on bits of paper she'd rip up afterward. She tried writing *Martha and Spencer*, but it seemed the name Martha belonged only to him. She'd speak these words out loud when she was alone, just to hear the sound of their names together. One day she wrote *Spencer and Marti* on a gum wrapper and folded it into the gum wrapper chain she'd begun making years ago. She added more wrappers after that one, so no one would discover it. She hooked the chain around her window frame and memorized which wrapper held her secret. She'd lie in bed staring at it.

When she arrived at Spencer's, he'd often be uncommunicative and quickly lead her into the bedroom for sex. She disliked this rush. After Spencer finished, he'd sit up, light a joint, and begin talking. He'd talk about concepts she knew nothing of: psychology, philosophy, and politics. Often she hadn't the slightest comprehension of what he was saying, but it didn't seem to matter; Spencer was satisfied with her silent nodding head.

"You're so wise, Marti. Many people, even older than I, can't discourse on these subjects, not with the depths you can." She didn't question this; she took it to mean their connection was so powerful that he could see inside her soul. She hung onto every fact he revealed about himself. He'd moved from Boston to Chatham to teach in an experimental school the college was creating, and when this failed to materialize, he ended up at Chatham High. He said he was miserable and talked of leaving soon to backpack around the world.

"Just think of it, Martha, we could travel through Europe, Africa, and Asia. Wait till you try the hashish in Morocco! In India, an enlightened person like yourself would find community." She wasn't sure what *enlightened* meant yet was thrilled to think, someday, they'd be a real couple. He must love her if he wanted to show her the world through his eyes. Would they run away together? *Elope.* Marti imagined him coming for her late at night, throwing a stone at her window. She'd creep out, and they'd walk hand and hand into the unfolding dawn's light. (Sometimes she pictured him arriving on a horse. She'd climb on back, wrap her arms tightly around his waist, and they'd gallop into the sunrise. She knew that fantasy was silly.)

Spencer loaned her books by Nietzsche, Jung, and R.D. Laing. He carefully crossed his name out from the inside of each book. She'd casually pull these books out and soak up the admiration Brooke's boyfriends gave her for possessing these. Mao's *Little Red Book* became the badge of honor she carried everywhere.

She was reading Abbie Hoffman's *Steal This Book* in the school cafeteria when Bobby, the barefoot boy, ran up and grabbed it, saying he wanted to read it. Marti shook her head and Bobby laughed. "Marti, it says *steal this book*, and I always do what I'm told." She reached for it but he walked off, holding it high over his head, waving it triumphantly.

Marti was petrified Spencer would be angry. How carefully

had he crossed out his name? She waited to tell him until after they had sex, waited until Spencer was talking ideas, smoking joints while she drank wine. Spencer rarely drank the wine himself but encouraged her, *It will relax you.* She accepted this as just criticism: she was too uptight. After taking several sips, she told him about the book. He laughed and said, "Touché, Bobby, excellent! I wanted him to read it, and you should still read it, Marti. The college bookstore has it—and of course—don't pay for it."

After Spencer finished talking, often they'd have sex again and he'd focus on her. He'd place his fingers inside her, moving them, commanding her to tell him what she liked. "Women have certain points that bring them pleasure. Martha, you must discover them and tell your lover."

Your lover. She liked the sound of that. She wriggled toward his fingers. "Don't move, Martha, not at all. Let me do it." He spread her legs apart and held them down with one arm. His other hand teased her pubic hair, and his fingers probed up and down, inside and outside of her. She started to shift position, but he stopped her. "I told you, no. Just feel my touch. You're moving right to the center of your pleasure, but did you know women can have more than one orgasm?" She wasn't sure she knew what an orgasm was. "Play a little, slow down, savor the feeling—it will be more fully realized, and you'll find new ways to enjoy yourself. Tell me where you want me to touch, and we'll let you have a fun ride."

"Here," she said shyly.

"Good, good."

"Oh, and there and here," she added, as his fingers explored.

Spencer laughed and removed his hand. "You're moving, Martha. Stay still."

"I-I can't help it. I'll try."

"Don't be so serious. It's a *game*, Martha. Are you having fun?" She nodded. "You want me, don't you?" She nodded again.

"Say it, Martha, or I'll stop." He twisted his fingers in her pubic hair and pulled hard on the word *stop*.

"Oh, please don't stop. I-I want you, Spencer, I want you."

"You want it bad? Say it."

"I want it bad."

"Then you can have it . . . whatever you want . . . you can have . . . for as long as you want."

She wondered about birth control. Brooke was on the pill, but Marti didn't know where she got it. How could she ask? There were other things, weren't there? Maybe Spencer was already taking care of it, given how he never asked. Was he putting a condom on at the last minute without her knowing? He must be.

Spencer began telling her to come to his house more frequently, and he was rarely having kids to his room after school. The work on the mural slowed to a standstill and students were grumbling, although Peter defended Spencer, saying he must be busy painting. Marti's friends retreated to Brooke's basement, their fallback hangout, and Marti continually made excuses as to why she couldn't join them.

Spencer talked her through what he wanted her to do. "Martha, hold me tight, move your hands up and down—you know, a hand job—surely some schoolboys have asked you to do this?" Marti shook her head, ashamed that no boy had ever asked anything, not even to hold hands. She thought this would disappoint Spencer, but he smiled. "Ah, I should have known. You're too smart to waste your time. Don't worry, I'll teach you everything."

And he did. Every day there seemed to be something new. The first time he performed oral sex on her, slowly, rhythmically, she found the excitement almost unbearable. He kissed her thighs and looked up at her face. "You like this, Marti?"

Embarrassed at liking it so much and thinking he must be disgusted, she said, "Uh, no, you don't have to."

"That's not what I asked. I'd *like* to do this if you want it."

"Um, yes, please."

"Um, yes, please? Are you ordering ice cream?" He laughed. "I won't continue until you beg me, Martha." He kissed her pubic hair and licked her gently along her crack. "Beg."

"Please, Spencer. I want you." He licked her harder, faster, in a deep penetrating circle. Her excitement grew and grew until he stopped suddenly.

"Beg. On your knees."

She couldn't quite believe what he was asking, but he forcibly motioned for her to get off the mattress, so she dutifully did, kneeling on the floor. He coached her with what to say and waited insistently until she complied. "Please, I beg you; please, I need it. I'll do anything you say. I'll be your slave. Please, I'm begging." Her voice was a reluctant monotone, but he seemed to relish that. He yanked her back on the bed and began licking her again, round and round in circles until she moaned and screamed out loud. She was shocked at the noise emanating out of her and understood then what an orgasm was.

Spencer kissed his way up her still-pulsating body until he got to her mouth. "Taste yourself, Martha, you amazing creature." She tasted the salty, pungent stickiness in Spencer's mouth, amazed that he didn't want to wash it off. It was confirmation: he loved her.

After they had sex, Spencer often fell asleep, giving Marti a chance to study his face. Although his hair was dark, his skin was pale, and she'd run her hand over his cheek, touching the line where his dimple lay at rest. If he hadn't shaved, his skin felt like sandpaper. Sometimes he'd grind his teeth in his sleep. The first time she heard this, it alarmed her and she woke him. "Oh, yes, I do that," he answered nonchalantly before falling back asleep. Now she liked listening, mesmerized by the sound. To Marti, this grinding was a sign of how deep and passionate he was.

When it was time for her to leave, she tried waking him to say goodbye, but he'd only mumble and stir slightly. She learned to let herself out, lonely as it was.

After a snowstorm, Marti arrived at his house and found Spencer setting logs into a hole he'd dug in his backyard. He lit a fire, and they sat on a blanket in the snow watching the flames. The fire bounced shadows on the snow, and Marti nestled against Spencer, breathing in the toasty smell of a campfire. Occasional flakes were still falling. "Close your eyes and hold out your hand," he said.

She was astonished that Spencer suggested exactly the thing she'd done walking home after their first kiss. "Beautiful, isn't it?" Spencer said as the flakes dissolving on her palm tickled her ever so lightly. "The softest landing in the entire world," he whispered into her ear, his breath a tender breeze. Marti thought this must be the most romantic moment of her whole life.

They smoked a joint in silence, watching and listening to the crackling fire. She was cold, so cold, and yet she wanted time to stand still, so she snuggled closer.

"Take your clothes off, Martha."

"What? Here?"

"You're shivering. The snow will warm you, don't you know? That's why people build igloos." The fire was dying down, and instead of adding more logs, Spencer stood up and kicked snow onto it. "Well?" His tone was suddenly rough, harsh. "Don't you believe me?"

Warily, Marti removed her clothes.

"Get off the blanket and sit in the snow."

"But—"

"I'm telling you, the snow will warm you. You must be *in* it." Spencer removed a camera from his coat pocket. He took several photos of her and then asked her to lie down. He arranged the snow around her and carefully dotted some on her naked body.

He circled around her, clicking. He told her to make a snow angel.

"Perfect," he said, when her arms and legs were outstretched. "Don't move." He took several shots looming over her. Next, he knelt and told her to lift her knees and rest them on his shoulders while he clicked away. He pushed her legs wider apart, and her feet fell to the ground. He placed the camera closer between her legs, clicking, clicking, and clicking.

"Turn over." She flinched as he drizzled snow on her back and legs, and she tried to keep her face out of the snow until he forcefully pushed it down. After photographing her face down, he abruptly went into the house without an explanation. Marti sat up, shivering. She wrapped the blanket around her body, but it was soaking wet and every part of her hurt now with a sharp, stinging pain. She grabbed her wet clothes and ran to the door. It was locked. She knocked, pounding louder and harder. She put her wet clothes on and heaved her body against the door. Why wouldn't he open it? She started blubbering, moaning. She'd walk home, but her book bag with her keys was inside.

Spencer opened the door. "A beggar at my door! So much noise, is that necessary?"

"You locked me out. I'm freezing."

"I told you I'd run a hot bath for you, silly goose." Marti was confused; he hadn't said that, had he? He led her to the bathroom, removed her clothes, and rested them on the radiator. Her legs began itching unbearably from the contrast of warmth against her cold skin. "Get in," he commanded.

She dipped her foot in and quickly pulled it out. "Too hot," she whimpered.

"Nonsense. Your body will adjust. Go on." She gingerly stepped in the stinging water and saw her legs were covered with hives. She bent down and started scratching, hard enough that she began bleeding. "Stop. That's disgusting. Sit down. You need to calm down and stop fighting it." In time, she got used to the water. Spencer picked up a washcloth, lathered soap on it, and washed her back, arms, and breasts. Bizarrely, despite everything, it felt good, bewildering her even more as it reminded her of both sex and being a small child.

Finished lathering her, Spencer turned the overhead shower on. Cold water blasted out, shocking Marti, and she shouted that it was too cold. He turned the tap fully the other direction, and suddenly it was burning hot. She reached for the knob, but Spencer blocked her from moving it.

Marti jumped out of the tub, crying, "Too hot! Stop! It hurts!"

Spencer laughed. "Can't make up your mind, can you?" He left the room without turning it off, muttering as he closed the door, "Never too hot, never too hot. Now you know how I feel." She turned the water off and sat on the edge of the tub, shivering while other parts of her body still stung from the scalding water. Covered in soap, Marti put her still-wet clothes on.

He was sitting at his desk with his back to her when she emerged and didn't turn around. He mumbled that he'd see her later. Walking home, Marti realized it was the only time they hadn't had sex, and yet she felt more degraded than ever, filthy while covered in a film of pungent Dr. Bronner's peppermint soap.

The next day, Marti feigned illness so she could stay home from school. Maybe she was ill—she still felt both the chills and hot water—which was which? Did Spencer love her or hate her? Did she feel love or hate?

She stayed home again the next day, and on Friday there was a blizzard big enough to close school—something that almost never happened. *We Vermonters are used to snow.* Marti rejoiced in it.

On Saturday she persuaded her mother she was better. It wasn't difficult because she'd looked terrible and now didn't, so her mother let her out. She went across the street to Peter's, where they played in his backyard with the younger kids. Nancy asked her to make snow angels. Instead of responding, Marti pelted Richie with snowballs, leading to a big battle. When cold, they all tramped inside where Mr. Colgan lit a fire in the fireplace. Mrs. Colgan brought them hot chocolate—hot chocolate in the living room, Marti's mother would never. They sat watching the fire, listening to Mr. Colgan tell ghost stories. Mr. Colgan had a way about him where he could thrill them and in the next breath completely calm them with his steadying presence. On Sunday Marti waited for the Colgans to return from Mass and went over again. She'd like to keep doing this, day after day after day.

Monday came and that meant Spencer. It continued just as before.

One day, after they were done having sex, Spencer casually asked, "You're on the pill, right?" She nodded, scared to say otherwise.

Scanning the aisles in the drugstore, she was pretty sure none of the pills were *the* pill. She debated what to do next; she certainly couldn't go to her pediatrician. She decided to ask Brooke casually, pretending she just wanted to be ready. Brooke didn't question her and agreed to take her to Planned Parenthood but warned her they might not give her the pill as Brooke's mom was with her the first time she went.

Debra, a counselor, led her to an office and sat behind a desk, motioning for her to sit in one of the two chairs facing the desk. Marti looked at the books propped on the windowsill, including *Our Bodies, Ourselves*, which Jan had brought home from college last summer. Marti used to sneak the book out of Jan's room and read it and was glad she had because not everything Spencer did came as a surprise. She wondered if Jan were home, would she have asked Jan? No, anything she told Jan went straight to Mom.

There was a poster on the wall showing a couple holding a

baby together. It said: *A Wanted Baby Is A Happy Baby.* A baby she had with Spencer would be wanted, wouldn't it? She pictured the three of them: Spencer wearing a backpack and Marti with the baby strapped to her body. Marti's dress, a white peasant one with embroidery around the yoke, while the baby, a girl, wore a matching one.

"So you're interested in birth control. How old are you?"

"The pill," Marti responded, dejected by the daydream interruption. Debra waited and Marti understood she wanted an answer. "Fourteen," Marti mumbled, instantly regretting this. She should have said fifteen or even sixteen.

"And you're sexually active now?" Debra's tone was neutral. Marti hesitated; how many questions would there be? She shook her head. "Do you have a boyfriend?"

"No."

"Have you been sexually active in the past?"

Again, she shook her head. "In case I become sexually, uh, in case I get a boyfriend."

"Just to be prepared?" Marti nodded vigorously. "Smart girl. I wish everyone who came in here were that careful. You wouldn't believe the sad stories . . . Never mind. That won't be you. Why the pill?"

"My friend Brooke has it. She likes it."

"It doesn't make sense for a girl like you who isn't active. Does your mother know you're here?" Marti shook her head, deflated. "There can be side effects from the pill, and taking it every day can be hard to remember, especially if you're hiding it from your parents. And it isn't effective if even one day is missed. A diaphragm might be best for now. Later you can come back and explore other options. In any case, you'll need to be refitted, as your diaphragm size can change." Debra gave Marti a bag with pamphlets and a tube of cream and told her to wait outside for the doctor. "He'll size you, and make sure everything is okay. You'll be lying on a table with your feet up. It will feel awkward, but every woman has these exams. It might pinch a little, but it's over quick." Debra squeezed Marti's arm.

Marti worried that the doctor would know she'd had sex; she needn't have worried as he barely spoke or looked at her. With her feet in stirrups and the speculum inside her, she had an unsettled, familiar feeling. When Spencer encouraged Marti to talk about the accident, she thought he cared, but they never talked about that—or anything about her—anymore. She yearned for that tender attention, not understanding where it went. Now, as the doctor's fingers probed her, she was beginning to comprehend: Marti was a specimen, and Spencer had finished his examination. She'd mistaken his fascination for caring.

At home she practiced putting in the diaphragm. She couldn't remember which side of the lip should be up, and did the cream go on the top or bottom? The easy instructions eluded her now. The cream was messy, dripping out of her for hours. She needed to use the diaphragm without Spencer knowing, and it wouldn't be possible with cream oozing out. She decided to put only a drop in. She'd been safe so far, and she'd just had her period.

The next time at Spencer's, he was thrusting into her when he halted suddenly. "What's this?" He reached his fingers inside her, pulling it out by the rim. "A diaphragm? What for? You're on the pill, aren't you?" It lay between them, an ugly round rubber useless thing. Marti hadn't realized he'd feel it and was afraid to answer. "Are you especially worried for some reason?" She looked away. Spencer propped up on one elbow and turned her face toward him. "Did you forget to take your pill?" Marti nodded. "One day won't make a difference; was it more than one?"

"A couple. I forgot."

"Don't look so nervous. I'm not going to bite your head off, but I don't like the diaphragm; I feel it as I move." He sat up, lit a joint, and said, "You've ruined the mood." Smoking silently for a few minutes, he didn't offer Marti any. She lay curled in a tight ball, her back to him. "All right, just use it till it's safe again. Besides, the cream will make it unpleasant for me to eat you. And you do love that, don't you, Martha? You *need* that, don't you?" he said, nuzzling her until she unwound herself and turned around. Just at the mention of it, Marti felt herself throbbing as if there were a frightening power controlling her.

Walking home, she stepped carefully around the mixture of mud and melting snow. Winter was ending and mud season beginning, just a few weeks' wait for the muddy mess to leave and crocuses to sprout, welcoming in the new season of hope and rebirth. But all Marti could see was the soggy, slimy dirt. She wanted what she thought she'd had with Spencer, understanding now that it had never really existed. And yet, just like the melting snow, she was clinging on and disappearing at the same time. Compelled and unable to stop, she'd keep going to Spencer's.

9

Tess persuaded a reluctant Marti to go to the public beach. The scenery struck Marti as so altered from what she remembered; the large pine trees that once surrounded the beach were gone, replaced by houses peeking out behind groomed bushes. The beach now had amenities they'd never even imagined: a snack bar with picnic tables, a children's playground, and even an enclosed room with pinball machines and video games. Marti wistfully observed the young families of frolicking children and chattering parents, thinking how happy they seemed. She turned toward Tess, but Tess had already fled, having found her friends. Marti opened her beach chair, sat, and picked up her book, a biography of Diane Arbus, whose photography she'd long admired.

After a few moments, she glanced up. Tess was in the water where she and a boy were splashing each other, their heads close, forming a triangle of light on the water, the distance between where their almost adjoined heads met the water. They weren't touching each other, yet something struck Marti as deeply intimate. She turned away, but now was unable to concentrate on reading.

"Marti! You've finally come. Isn't it great?" Linda was holding several beach bags with shovels and buckets spilling out.

How many shovels do two kids need?

"May we join you?" Not waiting for an answer, Linda spread

96

her blanket out and patted the sand, inviting Rose. "Sweetie, over here, build us a castle. Marti, been catching up with old friends? Did you see that neighbor?"

"No—she—" Marti hesitated. "I've just been relaxing, enjoying vacation."

"Don't I wish! If it was only Emily I could, but with Rose and Matthew, forget it! At least Matthew's off with his father today."

How many shovels does one kid need?

"Rose keeps me jumping, never a break. You don't have to worry about that." *There it was: the superiority of parents of multiple children. Did it keep multiplying? Did parents of nine feel superior to parents of eight?*

"What are you reading?"

"A biography."

"Studious on vacation! Who's she?" Linda pointed to the cover photo.

"A photographer."

Linda lifted the book off Marti's lap. "Oh, I remember. From college. She's the one who took photos of freaks, right? That wouldn't be politically correct now, would it? Still, they *were* creepy, weren't they? I suppose you need to know about things like that in your work. Those kids must have some weird diseases."

Marti watched Tess come out of the water. Waving her hand behind her, Tess beckoned and the boy followed. She pointed to the snack bar before running to Marti and asking for money.

"I'll give you enough for the day. I'm leaving."

"You just got here, Mom."

"I have things to do."

"Like what?" Tess demanded.

"My mosaic." Marti held out the money.

"You *need* to do that?"

Linda turned her eyes away.

"No, Tess, I don't. I want to. Are you taking it or not?" She waved the bills up and down until Tess snatched them. Really, Marti couldn't understand—what teenager wanted their mother around? Marti quickly gathered her things, retrieving her book from Linda, who looked all too eager to give it back. "Nice to see you, Linda."

"Marti, wait. Why don't you and Tess come over tomorrow evening? Art is grilling steak. We'd love to have you."

"Sorry, I can't."

"Mom—"

"Can Tess come alone?" Marti asked.

"Sure, but you need to eat too. Art does a mean job with steak."

The Grilling family ought to be their name.

When she got back to the cabin, she worked methodically attaching her sketch to the mosaic board and playing with the color scheme. Unsettled, she pushed the tiles away, unable to get the image of Tess and the boy out of her mind.

The following afternoon, Tess rushed in, dropped her bag and spoke rapidly. "I'll be ready quick for the barbeque, you ready?"

"I'm not going."

Tess was bent over, brushing her wet hair forward. She lifted her head, her hair cascading downward. "It'll be fun, a party. They invited other people." Marti walked over to the table where she'd been working on her mosaic, picked up her sketch and held it off at a distance, studying it.

"You're staying here to do that stupid thing?"

"Thanks for calling it stupid."

"It is, when you won't do anything else." Tess was brushing her hair furiously now. "What's your problem?"

"I just don't want to sit around with the Grilling family."

"The what?"

"The Grilling family, that's how I think of them. The *we-are-so-perfect-with-our-three-children-and-our-grill* family."

"God, Mom, stop! I'm the teenager, the one who's supposed to be cynical, but it's you thinking you're so above everybody." Tess banged the table, and some tiles flipped to the floor.

"Oh, that's really mature!"

"Yeah, mock me, like always. Can you ever be real?" Tess went into her room and slammed the door. Marti was stooped over picking up the tiles when Tess emerged a moment later and hurried out. She caught a glimpse of Tess all dressed up in a sundress with her hair whooshing behind her before the door closed. Marti felt a wistful ache of loneliness. *Above everybody? Hardly.* She just couldn't find common ground. Linda thought Diane Arbus was weird; what would she say about Marti if she knew?

She ate dinner and felt empty. She supposed it would be all right to go to bed before Tess came in. Linda's cabin was right down the road, and Art would walk her home. Marti pushed thoughts of Spencer and Brooke's dad out of her mind; not everyone was sordid. She kept reminding herself: *Tess is not me. My history is not her story.*

Awaking in the night, she realized Tess wasn't home and looked at the clock: one thirty. Where was she? Would Linda really let her kids stay up this late? She'd have to go to their cottage. She could hear Linda now: *The kids are having such fun. The steak was divine! Come in, have a drink.* Marti hadn't given Tess a curfew but never dreamed she'd be this late. She was throwing on her clothes when she heard noise.

"Tess? I was worried." Marti opened her door, but Tess was already closing hers.

"Sorry. I lost track of time. Good night."

She stood outside Tess's room, debating: *Should I check if she's been drinking or...?*

In the morning, Marti straightened up the cottage and sorted clothes for the laundromat, gathering some off Tess's floor, hoping this would wake her. Frustrated, Marti tried working on her mosaic. There were so many shades of color she wanted to fold into the sky, but she couldn't focus. Feeling a presence behind her, she turned to see Tess roll her eyes. "Busy, Mom? Is this what you did last night?"

She knew this technique—the proverbial strike. "No, Tess, what I did was lose sleep worrying where you were."

"You were asleep when I got in."

"No, I was getting dressed to come find you. We talked, remember? I left it alone because I didn't want to argue in the middle of the night."

"It wasn't the middle of the night." Tess sunk down in a chair.

"What time do you think it was?"

"Around twelve, maybe a little later."

"It was one-thirty."

"If you know, why ask? What is this? Nag me into answering a trick question? Such bull." Tess went into the kitchen and rustled loudly in the refrigerator. "Don't we have any more English muffins?"

"No, and it's not okay to come home when you did, Tess."

"All right, all right."

"Eleven o'clock is late enough. Did Art walk you home?"

"Uh, yeah. Where's the granola?"

"On the counter where it always is."

"You don't have to say it like I'm stupid. We don't always live here."

Marti sighed. "That's where it's kept at home too."

"Touché." Tess sat down with her bowl and grinned. Her moods changed so quickly; Marti didn't know what it meant. Was she agreeing to an eleven o'clock curfew? Was Marti's job done?

"How was it, anyway?"

"What?"

"The party, the whatever."

"What do you care?"

"I like to know you had a good time."

"Oh, fine. I'm going to the beach now." Tess stood up and carried her bowl to the kitchen.

"I'll come."

"You don't have to. I know you don't want to, and I'm over it. See you later."

"Wait, I have to do laundry anyway, so I might as well drive you and stop by for a bit first."

"I'm ready now, are you?" Tess stood impatiently at the door.

Marti sat in her beach chair determined to relax, telling herself if Spencer still lived here, he wouldn't recognize her after all this time. But touching the side of her face, she knew he would. She closed her eyes, trying not to think and just appreciate the warm sun, when she felt a pat on her arm.

"Remember me?"

Marti opened her eyes to see Pearl, dripping wet. "Of course I remember you, Pearl!"

"I'm gonna build a sandcastle. Wanna help?" Pearl grasped Marti's hand and led her over to Peter. It felt gratifying having her hand held. How long had it been? Of course the kids at work held her hand, but that was different; their hands pulsed: *need, need, need*, whereas this was just affection. "Daddy, look, it's the lady I thought was the reality lady!"

"*Realty* lady, Pearl." The adults both laughed at this and Peter ruffled Pearl's hair, giving Marti a flash of memory of that easy way Mrs. Colgan had with her kids. Peter looked handsome standing in his bathing trunks, lean yet solid.

"Let's build the castle." Pearl nudged her.

"Pearl, don't bother Marti."

"No bother, I love sandcastles." Marti smiled at Pearl, and Pearl ran to get her sand toys. Peter began walking away. "Wait"—Marti touched him lightly on the arm—"I want to ask you something." His face tightened and he looked away. She hesitated before blurting out, "Do you know what became of Spencer?"

Peter whirled around, staring at her. "Why would you want to know that? Don't you just want to forget him?" Pearl ran back with shovels and buckets and started scooping the sand. "He was gone by the time I was in college."

Oddly disappointed, she felt the scrutiny of Peter's gaze. "I—I'd like to talk with you more. Can we get together sometime?"

"To talk about this? I can't see why you'd want to. God, Marti, you're not—"

"Of course not," she snapped, angry. *How could he think that?*

Pearl tugged on Marti's leg. "Marti, you said you'd help."

"I will, just a minute, Pearl." She turned back to Peter, but he'd left. Marti bent down and ran her fingers through the sand. Pearl, true to her name, smiled with teeth like little seed pearls. "I'll get some water," Marti said, grabbing a bucket and heading toward the water's edge where Peter was. She stood next to him.

"Look," he whispered, looking down, "I'm sorrier than you'll ever know, but I don't want to dredge it up." He shook his head. "The accident—"

"I thought we passed that years ago."

"I didn't."

"I'm the sorry one," Marti spoke carefully, "for dragging you and your family into my mess with Spencer. I came here to talk to your mother, ask her forgiveness."

"Ma loved you."

"That only makes it worse."

"I know." Peter sighed. "We hurt a lot of people. And we let the bastard get away with it. But it's done, Marti." Before she could respond, he splashed through the water to where Ned was playing and scooped him up in his arms.

She filled her bucket and walked back to Pearl. Together they worked diligently on their castle and Marti got lost in its creation, teaching Pearl all the tricks she knew: how to make a staircase, a bridge, a moat, and even a gargoyle. Marti felt almost as excited as Pearl. She could never make it up to Mrs. Colgan, but at least she could be kind to her granddaughter.

"Mom?" Tess stood, looking amused.

"Oh, hi," Marti said. "Tess, this is my friend Pearl."

"Can you help us make the castle bigger?" Pearl asked.

"Sure." Tess knelt and started smoothing a wall.

Ned ran up. "Don't!" Pearl shouted, holding out her arms to guard the castle. "Marti, don't let him wreck it!"

"I won't," Ned said. "I'll just build," he added, looking at Tess. They all worked together, Marti conscious of Tess trying to figure it out.

Peter came over and said, "Guys, we have to go." He turned to Marti. "If they don't get a nap, they're beasts out of the wild—" He stopped, noticing Tess. "Oh, wow, you must be Marti's daughter; you look *so* much like her. I knew your mom years ago. I'm, I'm . . . Peter." He said his name softly, shamefully, and Marti winced with understanding.

A look of comprehension crossed Tess's face, and she stood and smiled broadly. "I'm Tess. You've got great kids. I could babysit for you sometime." Peter didn't respond. Tess spoke rapidly. "Maybe you and my mom could go out to catch up or something."

"I'd like to take you to dinner," Marti blurted out.

Peter said he was busy on the weekend. After hesitating a moment, he added, "I could go next Tuesday." He let out a trace of a smile. The gap between his front teeth was oddly appealing; it was so subtle Marti had to look closely to be sure she wasn't imagining it.

After they left, Tess smiled, victorious. "Good work, Mom. He's cute."

"It's not what you think." *But was it?*

Marti was trying to concentrate on her book when Tess ran over, saying, "Mom, let's go. I'll come help with the laundry."

"You will?" Marti chuckled.

"Yeah, I wouldn't mind looking around town. Come on." Tess quickly stuffed things into the beach bag. Marti noticed Linda walking across the parking lot, Rose and Matthew in tow.

"Wait, there's Linda," Marti said.

"Like you want to talk to her?"

"I should thank her for last night," Marti said, thinking what she really wanted to say was: *Why the hell did you let them hang out so late?* Spotting them, Linda waved.

"Mom," Tess whispered, tugging on Marti's shirt, "let's go before she bogs you down."

"Hang on." She walked in Linda's direction. "Linda, I want to thank—"

"Mom, the laundromat might close early here."

"You!" Linda affectionately tweaked Tess's hair. "We missed you last night. Emily was all mopey that you weren't there."

Marti froze. "You mean, last ni—"

"Mom, you've got to go, but I've changed my mind. Linda, can you show me where Emily is?" Tess now pulled at Linda's hand.

"She'll be here later. She's trying fishing."

Tess began heading to the lake, but Marti grabbed her arm, holding tight, not releasing. She steadied her gaze on Linda. "Tess wasn't at your house last night?"

"No." Linda looked from one to the other.

"Let's go." Marti pulled Tess's arm.

"Hey, off of me!"

Marti stood still, not letting go, waiting until they started to move as a unit.

"This is embarrassing," Tess hissed, glancing back at Linda. "It's not a big deal. I can explain."

"Stop." Marti held her hand up like a traffic cop. "Don't speak. Get into the car."

10

Spencer rarely glanced at the mural Marti was working on, and she convinced herself he was just being cautious. Some other kids had gone to the principal complaining that they wanted to work on the mural, so now it was officially called Art Club and Spencer had to open up the afternoons to any interested students, not just the chosen ones. No joints were passed and he didn't play music for this group, but he continued to pontificate about art. Marti looked up artists he discussed and mentioned them in their talks, hoping to impress him, although now she was beginning to comprehend that it wasn't Marti Spencer was impressed by but rather himself: how much *he* had influenced her or how smart *he* was to single her out.

It distressed her always being in limbo, guessing at what would please him. She'd stopped wearing a bra, wore her hair down, and did everything he asked, and yet he criticized her more and more, almost as if her compliance antagonized him.

Brooke had started hanging around the health food store in town and took Marti. They both admired the owner, Penny, who lived outside of town on a farm. She had one thick braid that hung forward over her right shoulder, braided into it were strands of bright ribbons, and her earrings were long wires with a marble-like ball on the end, each one a different color. Her floor-length dresses were always either yellow or orange; her look never varied. Penny gave them each a bottle of patchouli oil. "Smell, it's really groovy."

Marti dabbed some on before seeing Spencer, eager for his reaction. He kissed her neck and groaned, "God, Marti, why that awful smell? Don't you know your natural scent is much more appealing?"

The lack of attention Spencer paid to her work freed her to take it in the direction she wanted. She'd finished sketching sunlight illuminating the dollhouse. A little girl was arranging furniture in the dollhouse rooms while the doll family hung precariously on the roof. The girl sat serene, oblivious to their fate. Marti was going to stop there but now was carefully drawing a figure of an older girl sitting behind the younger one. She covered the older girl's face with hair but left one anxious eye peeking out at the panicked doll family pleading for help. Half of the girl was detailed clearly, while the rest of her Marti sketched lighter and lighter until the figure dissolved into the space around her.

Having never worked this hard on anything before, she showed her mother the sketches. "These are lovely, Marti, I'll have to see the mural when it's done. Did I tell you I met your art teacher? Mr. Douglas, right?"

Marti froze, the sketches hanging limp in her hand.

"Don't look so alarmed. I ran into him at the college. We were in a forum together, and I realized who he was and introduced myself. I wasn't checking up on you."

"Uh, did he say anything?"

"Of course. We chatted." Marti frantically fanned the sketches up and down. "Relax, Marti. He said you're quite talented. I could've told him that!" She squeezed Marti's cheek. "I can see for myself that your art class means a great deal to you, but you still need to concentrate on other subjects."

The next day, Marti asked Spencer about this. "I met her," he answered nonchalantly while rolling a joint. "Some stupid meeting the school had me go to."

"Why didn't you tell me?"

"Take a hit of this. You need it more than I. Trust me, you don't want to hear about those stupid meetings." Smiling, he handed her the joint. "Oh, what do you think I said? *Hello, Mrs. Farrell. I enjoy fucking your daughter's brains out.*"

"No, I don't think that." Feeling fuzzy already, she put the joint in the ashtray.

"Ah, I see, you're fishing for compliments."

Fishing for compliments, isn't that what Spencer does? Marti was realizing how hollow his compliments were; they were self-praise, a way of using her to stroke his own ego.

"What's to tell? Your mother is insipid like most middle-aged women but not stupid. I see a bit of your intelligence in her. Now, shall I try to fuck your brains out, Miss Martha? Hmm, shall I try?" He tweaked her nipples and they stood upright, good little soldiers.

Marti had stopped using the diaphragm and developed a new routine where she'd push a little of the spermicidal cream into her vagina upon returning home. She'd been safe so far. Her period continued, although last month she worried because it was late, and when it came, it was barely anything, just a few streaks. But that was good as she always felt embarrassed being with Spencer when she had it, although he never seemed to mind (one of the few things he didn't mind). "Don't hide your blood. I want to possess every part of you and please you, unlike those stupid teasing kids. I'll fuck you until you can't remember them."

Spring was moving along, and Marti wondered what their relationship would be like when school ended. Would they see more of each other? She didn't ask because she knew Spencer didn't like questions, and in truth, she didn't know what she wanted. He talked of traveling and of places he'd show her. "Wait until you see the Greek isles and meet some Greek women, Marti. Their vivaciousness is something you could learn."

Even when he wasn't directly criticizing, every comment felt like a put-down. So maybe he'd end it and she could forget it ever happened. She didn't really think he was traveling anywhere as she saw no preparations: she'd learned he liked to talk, but it wasn't necessarily followed by action.

She was having trouble translating her sketches to paint on the wall and wanted technical help with how to get the figure of the older girl to gradually disappear into the canvas. In junior high, Miss Jarvis would demonstrate useful techniques. Spencer never did. When she tried asking for advice, he started kissing her mid-sentence.

Spencer might have been growing bored with her mind, but not her body. He insisted she come to his house more often, and when she arrived, he'd pull her straight into the bedroom. He didn't even bother with wine, no longer concerned with her mood. "Martha," he said one day, pausing from sucking on her nipples, "your breasts are growing bigger. You're becoming more of a woman, so compellingly sexy. I told you you'd grow with my help." He was rougher that day, biting her nipples intensely. He sat up and straddled her, rubbing his penis between her breasts and squeezing them so hard it hurt. No longer did Spencer ask what she liked; it was all commands now.

At school they were finishing the mural. Marti managed to solve her technical problems on her own. Now she worked on infusing the background with light and shadow, contrasting the mood of the happy young girl with the somber older girl who watched the frightened doll family, helpless to save them. Marti felt proud of her work, thinking it was the finest she'd done.

She was curious that Spencer didn't comment on it, as he criticized other students' work incessantly. "That ignorant Alison Quint, all she paints are those quaint landscapes, not an original idea in her whole head. And Brandon, he thinks he's some groovy genius. All he knows is what I've taught him, the little parrot chirping my ideas." Brandon always appeared to be Spencer's favorite. If this was what he thought of Brandon, what did he think of her?

At the end of May, Spencer still hadn't said what would happen in the summer. Marti worried because once again, she hadn't gotten her period. Maybe being late was what happened when you started to have sex? She wanted to tell Spencer and have him reassure her. *Silly girl. Of course you're not pregnant. Ah, but if you were . . .*

Spencer said it was their last day to complete the mural. He urged them, "Let your inhibitions go, make the paint come alive and free yourselves!" Energized by the ending of the school year, the kids painted in great swirls, letting paint drip down the walls with Spencer's encouragement. "Just think," he said, "it's your chance to leave your mark."

Marti was concentrating on the final details of her painting, wanting the expressions on the girls' faces to convey the distinction between them, one girl unaware of the dolls' danger and the other paralyzed by it.

Trey and Bobby were painting wildly beside her, and they splattered paint on each other, laughing. A bit of it spilled onto her picture. "Sorry, Marti," Trey mumbled, moving away. Marti worked methodically to fix it; it was only a small smear.

Other kids began painting themselves and each other. They stuck their handprints on the wall. Brandon used his brush to lob paint across his painting. "Now it's a Jackson Pollock painting! Here I go, freeing this work. *Way* too uptight before!" He continued flinging blotches.

Everyone stood poised waiting for a cue telling them how to respond until Spencer clapped his hands. "Brandon, that's wonderful! You've taken a risk, and art is all about risk." The students all started covering their work except Marti, who continued her careful painting.

Bobby walked up to her and said, "Marti, you're way too precious." He threw a tray of bright orange paint across her painting. The orange spread quickly; the dolls were completely covered, and the two girls had streaks running down their faces. Marti froze. The other students looked to Spencer for a reaction.

"Bobby, you're a moron!" Peter said, rushing over to Marti's painting with a rag.

"You can't fix it, Peter! It's ruined! It's ruined! Ruined!" Marti's voice grew shriller with each word.

Brooke tugged on Spencer's arm. "Can we put paint thinner or something on it?" Spencer bent down, picked up a clean rag, and dipped it in water. He dapped away at the paint smear Brooke's green hand had made on his blue work shirt.

Marti picked up a can of paint and heaved it against the wall. "Fuck! You've destroyed me!" The can clattered to the floor. A stream of putrid olive green oozed out, surrounding her feet.

She turned and ran down the stairs. She could hear Bobby saying, "I destroyed her? Sorry, I didn't know she was a picture on a wall."

And Brooke responding, "Shut up, asshole." Marti opened the outside door, and a breeze of fresh air assaulted her senses.

At home she was crying in her room when the doorbell rang. Was it Spencer? Would he come to her house? Had he found a way to clean her painting? Maybe he hadn't answered Brooke because he was *thinking* about what to do, and later, without the distraction of students, he cautiously took his time restoring it. Surely, if he'd done this, he wouldn't wait until tomorrow to tell her. He was probably explaining it to her mother. *The kids got a little wild with the paint today, Mrs. Farrell. You know kids. Paint splattered on Marti's work, and she was upset. I want to reassure her I fixed it.*

"Come down, Marti. You have a visitor." Her mother's voice sounded oddly formal. Of course it would be if a teacher came over!

She ran down the stairs, dismayed to find Peter. That's why her mother was stiff; Peter never came over. Her mother hadn't invited him in, and neither did Marti. She stood in the doorway while he spoke. "I'm sorry about what happened."

"You didn't do it."

"Everyone was upset. Everybody's mad at Bobby."

"Thanks. For telling me." She chewed her lip. "Did Spencer say anything?"

"Not specifically. I know it seemed weird that he didn't do anything, but of course he was upset."

"You think?" Her voice was thick with scorn.

"Sure he was. Here—you forgot your sketches." He held out the roll of paper. "Maybe you can do your picture again."

"I don't think so." She accepted the sketches. "Thanks anyway."

"I bet you can, you're so talented . . . Hey, that dollhouse was from my den, right?"

She nodded. "The idea came to me after I gave Marybeth the circus set."

"My mother would've loved to see that painting. She hung that birthday card up and goes on about it. Who were the girls? I didn't recognize either of them. Did you mean them to be Marybeth and you, or someone else?"

"I don't know, Peter. I don't know if I knew the girls at all."

The next day was previously arranged for Marti to go to Spencer's. She'd planned to tell him she might be pregnant, fantasizing that Spencer would ask her to go away with him. *We'll travel the world, we three . . .* She'd even dreamed up names for a baby, Amelia Charlotte for a girl, and Byron Spencer for a boy. Now, she couldn't believe her stupidity. Spencer would never go away with her, and the truth was, she didn't want that. She wanted to go back in time before Spencer. But that dream was as useless as the one of them together. The best scenario would be that Spencer would take her for a pregnancy test and it would be negative. *Silly girl.*

If she were pregnant, she'd need Spencer's help in making it go away. It was the last and final thing she wanted of him.

Yet she didn't go to Spencer's house at the appointed hour, the first time she hadn't done what he asked. When she was leaving class the next day, he touched her arm and spoke. "Marti," he began while students were still in the room, "Peter tells me you have sketches of your picture. I'd like to see them, and we'll see what we can do. Meet me at school tomorrow morning, seven a.m." He whispered this last part.

She woke early and carefully packed her sketches. She felt easier meeting him at school as they wouldn't have sex. They'd talk about the sketches; maybe he did care. She could tell him her worry, and he'd fix it so there'd be no baby.

"Come in, Marti." Spencer closed and locked the door and pulled the curtain down on the door window. "Sit at your desk." She sat in her usual seat and unrolled the sketches. "Never mind that," he said, approaching and unzipping his pants. "Suck me off."

"What?"

"Don't act shocked, not like you haven't done it before. Don't worry, no one can enter, except me entering you." He laughed at his pun and held his swollen penis expectantly in front of her face. She clamped her mouth shut tight. "Come on now, you can do this for me. It's a fantasy I've had all year—you and me with you at your desk. Too bad you don't have a Catholic schoolgirl uniform.

"Martha, baby, please?" He stroked her hair while his penis nuzzled her cheek. She closed her eyes and began sucking him, feeling suffocated in a deep dark cave. The sketches were crumbling and cracking as Spencer thrust back and forth. To her relief, Spencer pulled back a moment later. "Ah, baby, I see your heart isn't in it. Besides, your face is such a turnoff. Don't be scared. I would never force you. I'd never do that; I care for you.

"Come into the closet and just lean against the wall. You won't have to do anything."

"No, please, please. I don't think, think . . . I don't want to—"

"Oh, yes, Martha, yes, you do. I always know what you want. Hmm, don't I?" Spencer took her arm; Marti pulled back.

"No games. Stop the spoiled brat routine. It's trite and boring." He looked sternly at her and she followed him. It was a long coat closet with peeling yellow wallpaper; hooks along the wall held a few forgotten stray sweaters. Dust and bits of paper lay on the floor. Spencer shoved the sliding door closed. It bounced back and remained cracked open. Spencer pulled her pants down and turned her around so she faced the wall. He began entering her from behind; he knew she disliked this position. It made her feel like a dog.

"Please, I don't want—" He pushed hard into her, and her head slapped against the wall. "Stop. Please—" Her voice was muffled as her mouth was pressed into the corner. A coat hook dug into her shoulder, and she felt the wallpaper imprinting its pattern on her cheek. She tried to concentrate on the bit of light filtering in through the door crack and listened as the door rattled rhythmically back and forth. She didn't try to speak again as there was no language inside her, just a void where her voice once emanated from. He pulled her buttocks closer to him and pushed down on her back until she bent forward like a Barbie doll; the only resistance was her fingers clawing their way slowly down the yellow wallpaper. Looking at the floor now, she felt she was less than nothing, less than the dust balls rolling around her feet. She breathed in the musty odor, vaguely aware of a sensation of pain, as if each thrust were breaking her fragile cocoon.

No longer as strong as a Barbie, she went limp and released her hands from the wall, letting her arms swing back and forth.

It seemed like it must be happening to someone else because she was numb in the center of her being.

No bones, no bones.

"Put your hands on the wall, Marti. Your head is banging. I can't hold you up." He was curt, impatient.

No bones, no bones. I'm a rag doll.

"Martha, do what you're told."

No bones. No bones. Nothing inside. No guts.

A rag doll waving free.

Limp as can be. No bones, no bones.

Rag doll.

"Okay then," Spencer said, thrusting so hard there was a loud thud when her head hit the wall. Her neck jerked, and she felt as if her head might snap off. *She lost her head!* Mercy in that. Spencer lifted her arms and placed her hands on the wall. "Baby, c'mon now, stop hurting yourself." Obediently, she left her hands where he placed them.

"Oh, Martha," he muttered, "I'm in you, in your body, in your head. You'll always remember me." She closed her eyes and watched her body slither through the gap in the door imagining it sliding out the window. *Up, up and away!* Her body parts, severed from each other now, floated in unison all around the endless sky, twisting, twirling through clouds until they were effortlessly engulfed into the white wilderness.

When she and Peter were small, they lay on the grass not next to each other but top of head to top of head, staring up at clouds and debating if there was anything in the world softer than a cloud. *Pillows? No. Wonder Bread? No. Cotton candy? Almost, but no. Water or snow? Which was softer? No matter, a cloud was still softer.*

Mrs. Colgan tried cajoling them to have lunch. "How about you two scientists come inside and have a soft Wonder Bread sandwich on Ma's lap?" Marti could think of nothing better than

Mrs. Colgan's lap—maybe that was even softer than a cloud— but Peter was not interested in eating, insisting they first pick a cloud to be their home. *Home.*

The last time she tried sitting on her mother's lap, Peg had brushed her off, saying, "You're too old for that." Afterward, Marti went to her room and cried on Papa Bear's soft belly. Now, mercifully absent from her body, she recognized the truth her mother had spoken: she was too old, and she'd always be too old for everything.

A cloud can be a home. Marti pictured that broken body nestled safely inside. Home at last. Would the body fall, landing hard on this unforgiving earth? *No bones, no bones.* Freedom in that. The cloud dissolved into sky, a pale creamy sky, so you couldn't tell cloud from sky. Everything was the most beautiful sameness as if it had always been so, and would always be so, everything disappearing into everything, everything disappearing into nothing.

Spencer finished, pulled up his pants, and walked out of the closet shaking the dust off his clothes. Marti continued leaning against the closet wall. *I'll be an old coat, left behind, full of moth holes.* This thought was comforting, and she understood now what she needed. Slowly she slid down the wall and sat on the floor of the closet, hugging her knees tight and closing her eyes.

Stay.

Spencer looked down on her from the doorway, disdain in his gaze as he spoke brusquely. "Get up."

The light blinded her as she tried looking up. "I'll stay here."

"What? Of course not. School will be starting soon."

"I'll be quiet. Quiet as a little bird. You always said I was a bird. Please. I need to stay here. Stay with you. Stay in the closet."

"That good, eh? You can come over this afternoon, but now you've got to go." He chuckled, reaching down to caress her face. She captured his hand with both of hers.

"I'll make no noise, not even chirp, a quiet little bird am I. No one will know I'm here. I won't exist." He pulled her up. "No, no, I can't leave. I need to stay with you." Wrapping her arms around his neck, she clung tightly while keeping her body rooted in the closet. "Please, please," she murmured in his ear, a seduction.

He removed her arms and slid the door open with a bang. *Too bright.* He yanked her out of the closet.

"Fix your clothes." Marti looked down at the jeans bunching around her ankles. Bewildered, her fingers picked uselessly at the fabric. "I'll help you." His tone was one of indulging a child. He reached for her pants and she backed away. "You can't go out in the hallway like that." She continued backing away, her legs twisting in her jeans until she stumbled and he caught her before she fell. He pulled her pants up, zipped and snapped them closed. "There, there," he said soothingly.

She wrapped herself around him again, kissing his face, his neck, his chest, his clothes, over and over. "Please keep me. Keep me. Keep me."

"Martha, my dear, stop. You're being silly. Don't worry, we can be together this afternoon." He pried her off his body and handed her the crumbled sketches. "We'll look at your work and have more kisses, yes? School ends tomorrow and I'm leaving the day after, but we have this afternoon. Until then," he whispered, directing her toward the door.

She stumbled out of the classroom. She stayed at school all day dutifully finding her way to each classroom where she'd sit staring down at her tightly clasped hands. She noticed bits of the yellow wallpaper stuck under her fingernails, the tips of her nails now the color of vomit. She wanted to go home and crawl under the covers. Or better yet, go inside the hospital tent. Wasn't that her real home?

Get up, she told herself after each class, *walk down the hall.* Her underwear hadn't been properly straightened and it coiled uncomfortably, but she made no attempt to fix it. She could feel Spencer's sperm seeping out of her body. She didn't look down, afraid there would be a big puddle pooling beneath her desk. She didn't have the cream to put inside and kill it. What if she hadn't been pregnant and now was?

When she was finally home, she went into the bathroom, praying before pulling her pants down. *Please be blood. Make it go away. Go away. Go away. Please. Please. I'm begging. Mercy.*

11

Linda watched as Marti drove away. "Mom, the laundromat's the other way."

"Obviously not going now."

"Don't be so dramatic, making this a big deal, just—"

"Stop"—Marti put her hand over Tess's mouth—"talking." Tess squirmed as far away from her mother as she could get, her shoulder pressed against the car door. Driving slowly, Marti concentrated on the empty road.

As soon as she opened the cabin door, both animals vied for attention, the cat meowing loudly and Caliban wagging his long tail, ever hopeful. "Sit down," Marti said, lifting her mosaic sketches off a chair.

"Precious needs to eat. You never feed her because you only care about Caliban." Marti opened her mouth to object but stifled this as it wasn't the argument she wanted, and besides, it was true. Rob and his wife, Lisa, had given Tess the cat, intending for Precious to live with them until they abruptly changed plans after their first child, Adriana was born and they then asked Marti to take the cat. Later Marti realized why: Precious was a hostile creature, a cat only Tess, a child, could love.

Seven years later, the cat was *still* more attached to Lisa than Marti. Well, why not? Self-assured Lisa was generous and calm with her two children, her husband, her stepdaughter, and appeared content with her own soul. But Marti wouldn't think about that now, her failed marriage and Rob's happy second marriage—further proof of her failure. She needed to focus on Tess.

"You do that then," Marti said scornfully, watching as Tess carefully measured out the food and gave both animals fresh water—tasks Tess rarely performed.

Finally, Tess sat across from Marti at the kitchen table, fiddling with the napkin holder as she spoke. "Like I said, it doesn't have to be a big deal, unless you make it one."

"If I make it one? You stay out till two—"

"One," Tess corrected.

"Whatever. *Where were you?*"

"With friends on the beach. You didn't want to go to Linda's, and I didn't want to go without you. It's embarrassing always having to explain where you are. Which, by the way, is nowhere."

"This isn't about me. It's about you, Tess. About lying, not obeying."

Tess pushed the napkin holder away, and the paper napkins fluttered to the floor. "*Obeying?* God, it's not the Stone Age, Mother."

"Okay, wrong choice of words. The point is you lied."

"I didn't lie. I didn't exactly say I was at Emily's."

Marti hated how Tess trivialized it all into a game of semantics. "That's rich. I ask, *How was the barbeque?* And you say *fine.*"

"It probably was fine and would've been great if you'd gone with me."

Was it Marti's fault for refusing to go? No, no, she wouldn't get sidetracked. "You weren't truthful, Tess. Who were you with? Is it that boy?"

"What boy?"

"I saw you in the water talking. There was this triangle of light between you and him, a small space. It, well, implied a kind of closeness . . ." Marti trailed off, realizing how absurd she sounded.

Tess leaned back in her chair, laughing. "A triangle? Get a grip, Mom. You're so disconnected, you don't even see people—you see triangles."

"All right, you've had your fun. The point is I saw you and this boy, and then you stay out late and lie. What should I think?"

"Of course you think that!" Tess stood and turned to leave. Marti reached over, attempting to pull Tess back down but Tess pushed her chair farther away before sitting down hard. "It has to be a boy, right? You dragged me up here because you thought I *might* have a boyfriend. And now that I've made friends here—and you haven't—you can't stand it and want to lock me up. Gee, Mom, for someone who doesn't have sex, you sure have a dirty mind. Funny, considering Dad told me you were frigid. You act like some martyr, like Dad abandoned us, but he didn't leave *me*. Only you. He had to leave you. Dad wanted a life, just like I do! What ended your marriage wasn't Lisa, it was you." Tess leaned her face toward Marti and pointed her finger. "Frigid you."

Marti swatted Tess's hand away, and the force felt good. Next, a loud slap reverberated in the air; Marti knew she'd done it upon hearing the sound.

Precious climbed atop the refrigerator and glared down at them with her back arched, yowling loudly. Caliban jumped and barked before leaping between them. Tess pushed him away and Caliban ran into Marti's bedroom, cowering.

Tess looked stunned, but before she could place her hand on her reddened cheek, Marti did it again, relishing not just the sound but the sting she felt pulsating in her hand and the power that sprung from that. Tess caught Marti's arm and pushed her against the table. A glass fell to the floor. It bounced back up, gushing water before falling again and shattering.

Tess ran to the doorway of her room, her hands covering her face. "God, you're crazy! Sick! Hitting me because I went out with friends, because I *have* friends, because I don't want to stay cooped up in this stupid cabin with you and your stupid mosaic. Hit me—that solves *your* problems, right?"

She slammed her bedroom door. Marti could tell she was leaning against it, holding it closed. Was that for effect? Or was she frightened? Marti could barely absorb the words Tess continued venting. "And don't give me the lecture about birth control. You've had me in a chastity belt since I was eight, before I even knew or *wanted* to know what sex was. I'm not having sex, Mom. I'm fourteen! And most fourteen-year-olds aren't having sex, despite what some stupid magazines say. God, what do you take me for?"

She momentarily opened her door and stuck her head out. "But if I were having sex, it would be *your* fault."

Marti slumped over the table, her arms propping up her head. "Were you drinking last night?" she called out feebly as she stared down at the worn plastic tablecloth.

"Drinking? Oh, yeah, I was shooting heroin, sniffing glue, and doing meth. Satisfied? Enough info for you? Leave me alone!" Tess slammed her door again.

Had Rob really said she was frigid? Used that word to Tess? When? How old was Tess? Marti had been so conscious to never, ever undermine Rob to Tess. She never talked about the problems in their marriage. *Rob* had the affair. He betrayed Marti and left. By choosing a new family, he betrayed Tess too, didn't he? Yet Marti never said a word against him or Lisa. Just the opposite: she *encouraged* Tess to have a good relationship with Lisa. She did this despite how deeply it hurt. Now she felt betrayed all over again; he'd confided in Tess what he never said to Marti.

And yet: Rob named it. She was cold, wasn't she? Cold, like her moth—no, cold like cold. But she had her reasons and he knew this Why couldn't he have understood? Couldn't she be forgiven? Marti tapped her hands lightly on the table. She sat a long time with salty tears stinging down her face. Tess was right;

not every fourteen-year-old had sex. She knocked gently on Tess's door. "May I come in?"

"Can I stop you?"

Marti opened the door halfway. Tess was lying on her bed, turned toward the wall, hugging her pillow. *She looks*, Marti thought, *like a little girl who's been slapped by her mother. A mother who got a charge out of it and did it again, and maybe would have kept on had the little girl not shoved her.*

"Tess, I'm sorry and ashamed. I never should have—"

"Whatever." Tess's body was unbending.

"—hit you. It was wrong. I know saying this doesn't make it better. I did it, but, but . . ." Marti's voice was faltering. What could she say? She gritted her teeth in an effort to stop crying; she shouldn't saddle Tess with her emotions. Hadn't she done enough of that already? "I'm your mother and I worry about you."

"You worry about me by *hitting* me? Gee, good one. You know how pathetic that is?" Tess rolled over and faced Marti. Upon seeing Marti's teary face, she said, "Oh, forget it. You don't have to start sobbing. You hit me. Big deal. Get over it." Tess's tone was harsh. Still, Marti could see she'd been crying. Abruptly, Tess sat up. "It's hot in here; I can't breathe, no air flowing. Can I go to the lake?" Marti stared, incredulous. "Please, Mom, I don't want to be stuck here. Tell me when to come back, and I will. I will. I'm going to swim, hang with Emily."

"Like you hung with Emily last night?"

"I said sorry. You *hit* me, remember? Haven't I been punished enough?"

Actually, Tess hadn't said she was sorry; Marti was the one groveling with *guilt, guilt, guilt.* But Tess was right: it was suffocating being together in the hot cabin. "Fine, go," Marti snapped. Tess jumped off the bed and hurriedly grabbed her things. "Be back at five, I mean it, five o'clock," Marti called out as the door shut. *She couldn't get away fast enough.* Marti lay on Tess's bed and pulled the blanket over her head, shrouding herself in darkness. Eventually, she unwound herself, went into the bathroom, and splashed water on her face, trying to gain strength. How dare Rob say that to Tess? He thought he got away with it, but he hadn't, had he? Tess *told* Marti, even if it was within the context of an argument.

Sure, before the divorce, their sex life had diminished, but Rob said he understood—until he left, abruptly and absolutely. There'd be no working on their problems, no trying to save the marriage. He was simply done. And so he told Tess what he never said to Marti, his wife. Did he want Tess to tell her?

Looking in the mirror at her blotchy face, she realized it was obvious why Rob left: no one wants to be married to the walking dead.

She went into the kitchen and sat down, looking around. Why had she thought this cabin was wonderful? It was dark inside and shabby with its worn, mildewed furniture. *Vacationing* here, how ironic, revisiting the happy childhood. What kind of masochistic idea was that? She wouldn't even be paid for the time off work. How much of her savings was she wasting on this trip? She felt unsteady, teetering near quicksand just waiting to swallow her whole and there was no one to throw her a rope. She'd come all this way to see Mrs. Colgan. *What did you do this summer, Marti? I went to visit a dead woman. Because I'm dead.*

Could she talk to Peter? She sensed how reluctant he was. In Brooklyn, a few friends knew her past (some of it, anyway) and would listen if she confided, but it was just a story to them. Peter was her only witness, and he wouldn't even look at her. How lonely was that? She thought of all the young families on the beach and remembered that time in her life: husband, baby, new beginning. Oh, how she grasped at that brass ring! Amazed to think she'd actually caught it.

How could Rob understand? When she met him in grad

school, Marti was busy pretending her past never happened—had almost convinced herself—and was elated at finding a seemingly uncomplicated boyfriend. She didn't really let him in—why wreck her fresh start? The facade they erected together was never very stable; secrets were already cracking the foundation when they plunged into a wedding with all the trimmings, feigning great confidence. The facade crumbled bit by bit until it fell upon them as irrefutably as a house of cards collapses. All that remained was Tess, a child wandering amongst the ruins.

Parenthood was like navigating a minefield. Being cautious didn't help because the bombs were never where you expected; they were hidden, lying in wait, steadily ticking. Marti felt alone in this minefield, and that loneliness was familiar ground.

She began picking the strewn napkins off the floor, deciding she'd deal with the glass later. She heard a knock and cracked the door open. "May I come in?" Linda asked. Marti shrugged, opened the door fully and gestured for her to enter. Linda spotted the napkins and stooped to pick them up.

"Don't," Marti practically hissed, placing her hand on Linda's arm. She noticed Linda's gleaming diamond engagement ring soldered with the wedding ring; both were contoured and nested neatly together, obviously purchased as a pair. *Perfect.* "Would you like some coffee, water, anything?" Her tone swung between a monotone and aggravation.

Linda shook her head. "No, I just wanted to say I didn't mean to cause any trouble." She started to sit.

"Don't sit there," Marti said, gesturing, "there's glass."

"Glass?" Linda looked around. "Oh my, broken! Let me help you. Where's a broom?"

"Never mind it." Marti moved to the couch on the other side of the cabin, and Linda reluctantly followed, gaping back at the shards.

"I didn't know Tess hadn't told you. Emily tells me you and

Tess have some problems . . ." Her voice trailed off as she looked into Marti's stony face.

Confide in anyone other than me. Just like your father.

Linda laughed nervously before trying again. "Well, all mothers and daughters have problems."

"Yes, they do," Marti agreed loudly. "Like you and Emily, I'm *so* sure. And that sweet little Rose, all in due time." She knew she was being mean (wasn't that a wicked witch line?).

"Emily's mad at me for telling you. But"—Linda smiled with a look of collusion now—"where *was* Tess? What was she doing last night?"

"I wouldn't know. Tess's problem, not mine."

"Aren't our children's problems our problems? After all?"

Later Marti thought about the truth of what Linda said. This was the reason parenthood was so claustrophobic. It was as if your child walked into your life, waved a mirror at you, and plopped down all your dirty laundry into one enormous pile. The pile was so large it covered the doors and windows of your home, allowing no escape. There it was: your weaknesses, your mistakes, every cruel and dishonest thing you'd ever done, every stupid thing. The child was like a dog digging for a bone; they wouldn't rest until they'd dug it all up, baggage you didn't even know you had. Ironic, given the impetus for having a child was a chance to leave the past behind and begin anew. A baby dangled a false promise of rebirth.

She thought back to her mother's will and how she'd bristled upon seeing her name listed as *Martha*. It was the name she never, ever used after Spencer claimed it, but of course, her mother didn't know that. Surprisingly, Jan and Marti were left everything equally; Peg didn't favor the good daughter. She took care to mention mementos she wanted Marti to have. It was loving and selfless given all the ways she'd hurt Peg—the mother Marti never gave herself the chance to truly know. She understood now why Peg hadn't fully forgiven her. How could she? She blamed herself for Marti's problems, and Marti abandoned her mother by not trusting her with the truth. Peg was dead, so there would be no release for either of them.

Caliban crept out of the bedroom, cowering almost, anxiously averting his eyes. "Here, boy," she called to him. He came and sat obediently. Marti ruffled his head and he licked her arm. "I'll bet you want your swim, don't you? Let's go." She grabbed their towels and headed out the door. Precious was mewing. *Not my cat. It belongs to Tess, and Rob, Lisa, Adriana, and Nathan—their problem, not mine. I'm not a member of that picture-perfect family.*

Marti ran down onto the dock and hesitated, remembering the broken glass. Why hadn't she cleaned it up? Both Precious and Caliban could have stepped on it. But Caliban was safe. She dived in with a loud splash, and Caliban, ever faithful, followed.

12

M arti arrived at Spencer's clutching the sketches, not because she expected or wanted him to look but they were an appendage to her body now. He gestured for her to sit and he reached for the sketches. She sat on the lone chair by his desk. Reluctantly, she released the sketches. "They're breathtaking," he said, unwinding the roll and fixing his eyes on each of them. "You shouldn't be upset. After all I've taught you, all the reading you've done—I see *Siddhartha* sticking out of your bag—you must understand, nothing is permanent, nothing lasts. Reality exists only in this moment. This here. Right now." He gestured widely with his hands. "No past, no future. Art is the process, the creating, not the keeping and holding. You understand?"

Marti readied herself to say: *I'm pregnant.*

"You created that picture and now it's gone, but you'll create more. The imagination that dreamed that wondrous creation is still present, actually freer and more alive without the stagnant past on a canvas. *Be here now.*" He reached out and took her hand.

She jerked it away.

"Ah, you're upset. There's much you don't comprehend, although, sex, you have felt the power of that. And do you know why it's so powerful?"

Tell him. Tell him.

"Because when you have an orgasm you exist only in that moment, fully present. Alive. There's both beauty and terror in that. It's one of the most spiritual experiences you can have." He reached over and started unbuttoning her blouse. She flinched. Holding her blouse closed, she scraped her chair along the floor in a feeble effort to move away.

Tell him.

"I had my fun this morning and now I'll please you, Martha, only you, and you'll live in this moment."

Tell him.

"I'll serve you." He got on his knees, crawling on all fours. Marti continued backing her chair away until he grabbed the front chair legs. She swung her legs over his head and stood up, moving toward the door. Spencer was still crawling. Cornering her against the door, he grabbed her firmly by the buttocks and lowered her pants. She was still wearing the same underwear. *I smell like your sperm. That's what you like.* He started to lick her, reminding her of Brooke's dog sniffing her crotch doggedly, and the humiliation she'd felt as Mr. and Mrs. Davies sniggered watching the dog pursue her. She looked down at Spencer, on all fours, his mouth incessantly noshing her. *Who's the dog now?* She could feel his tongue moving precisely. Against her will, her body stirred.

"There, there, let go. You know you can't resist me, Martha. You're a sensual being. I'll do only what pleases you. I'm your slave." Marti looked down at the top of his head and grabbed at his hair to release him, but he reached up and pulled her arms, yanking her to the ground.

She was sitting now with her back against the door, her legs spread only as far as the bunched jeans at her feet would allow. Spencer lay prone on top of her legs, his arms holding them down as he licked her, his tongue flicking, cobra like. Occasionally he'd bob his head up, a smile or sneer curling on his lips. He removed her jeans, slid her flat on the floor, pulled off his pants, and began entering her.

She moved to resist until she had the thought: Surely this couldn't be good for the baby? Weren't you *not* supposed to have sex if you were pregnant? Couldn't it cause a miscarriage? She pulled him into her, wrapping her legs tight around his back. She pushed hard against him, closing her eyes and picturing Spencer's penis ramming against a baby's head, blood oozing out the head until the baby dissolved into blood.

"Baby, you want me bad, don't you? Just like I want you, baby," Spencer moaned.

Baby? No. No baby. No.

She pushed against him, chanting rhythmically in her mind, *Kill it, kill it, kill it.* He thrust harder in response. This rhythm pulsated inside of her, and she spewed the venom of hate with each push. *Kill it. Kill it. Kill it.* Harder and harder, faster and faster. *Kill it, kill it.* The rhythm beating, thumping, throbbing, vibrating, becoming everything.

And then she felt that familiar gush of warmth and release. She screamed out loud, louder than she ever had, every fiber of her pounding, pulsing. Her body had a life of its own and it betrayed her; it wasn't even hers anymore. She waited for the body to still, reminded of the jerking of an animal's limbs at the moment of death.

"Oh, Martha, so good, so good," Spencer said, rolling off her. "Oh baby, oh baby." *No baby, no baby.* She pulled her pants on, went into the bathroom, and vomited. On her way back through the hall she noticed a large painting hanging, the one Spencer declared his best work, his favorite. She discerned a date next to his signature: 1966, six years ago.

Nothing lasts. Don't try to hold on. Live in the present. She could do him this one last favor, after all he did for her.

She reached in her pocket and found a pen. *It'll do.* She jabbed at the red-and-black circle in the heart of the canvas. Unable to puncture it, she punched harder and harder and was about to give up when it yielded to her, the sides of the canvas recoiling away from each other. *There, there, you've wanted this. I'm freeing you.* She sliced an *X* across the canvas. Displeased by the symmetry of that, she carved a jagged line throughout, and listened to the satisfying sound the slashing made. Hacking more, she pulled bits of canvas off with her fingers and shredded these into little pieces of black, red, and orange confetti. She threw them in the air: a celebration.

Spencer was at his desk rolling a joint when she returned to the kitchen. "I have packing to do. You can come tomorrow, Martha. I leave the next day."

After closing the door, Marti realized she'd left her sketches on his desk. Wanting them, and not wanting Spencer to possess them, she wavered, gripping the doorknob. But of course, she couldn't. She ran down the street, and once she turned the corner, she began to breathe easier. *The sketches are gone, but it's one less reminder.*

She remembered a George Harrison song she'd listened to many times at Spencer's: "All Things Must Pass." Was it true? Would it all pass? Were all those teachings Spencer foisted upon her correct? Did only this moment exist? And if so, then what just happened between them no longer existed? A mirage even. Maybe none of it had been real. Reaching her block, she skipped, euphoric, thinking someday, someday, this would be over. Over and done, she wouldn't even remember. She only had to try hard enough to will it away.

Of course, first there was the pregnancy, that roadblock to her future that she couldn't get around. She didn't know if she'd killed the baby. She must have. Everything inside her was decaying; she was disintegrating bit by bit. Surely no baby could be alive inside that wreckage? All she had was hope.

Still, there was one certainty: she'd never, ever enter Spencer's house again.

Part III

TEETH

13

Summer 2000

Tess dutifully returned at five and headed straight to her room while Marti made an elaborate dinner of Tess's favorite foods: lasagna, garlic bread, corn on the cob, and a green salad with all the extras Tess liked—avocado, cheese, and a creamy dressing. Their conversation was polite and inconsequential, and Marti felt embarrassed looking at the overly plentiful rich food, with chocolate chip cookies still to come. Definite overkill, and it couldn't change what happened. After dinner Marti suggested a game of Sorry.

"Sorry, ha. You've got to be kidding," Tess responded. Marti insisted it would be fun. They each tried to let the other win, just to make the game end sooner. Marti felt tempted to take the TV out of the closet, anything to break the stifling atmosphere. Too obvious, and besides, they'd be watching while wallowing in their discomfort. Instead, Marti retreated by taking a swim with Caliban.

When she returned, Tess was lying on the couch, all scrunched up, and the sight filled Marti with terrible remorse. *She's a little girl and I hit her.* Yet she wasn't little anymore and that was Marti's problem. She sat tentatively on the edge of the sofa. "I'm sorry I overreacted." Still troubled by Tess's lie, she understood her actions invalidated her ability to reprimand that. "Regardless of what you did, I should never have responded with violence."

Tess rolled her eyes. "Oh gee, Mom, you think it was a bad idea? Duh." Tess swung her body to face the back of the couch.

Marti stood up. "I wanted you to know how sorry I am."

"Don't expect me to say *okay*, because it isn't." Marti inwardly smiled; Tess had used Marti's phrasing back at her.

Marti went into her room and lay next to Caliban, petting him. Precious climbed on the bed and snarled at Caliban. He jumped off and the cat rolled around, purring victoriously. Marti shoved her off the bed. Precious turned and gave Marti one last defiant hiss before sashaying out the door. Caliban, insecure now, couldn't be coaxed off the floor.

The next day, Marti went with Tess to the beach where there was a large group of teenagers including the boy, Ethan (Marti had pried his name out of Tess). In Marti's dark imagination, Ethan was at least twenty years old, but looking at him now, she realized he couldn't be much older than Tess. He was tall, yet his face, dotted with pimples, held a baby look. His blond hair reached his shoulders, and it hung in soft curls. He and Tess could be twins.

Linda arrived with Elaine, her new friend, and sat next to Marti. Thankfully, Linda didn't bring up the subject of Tess's evening, and instead, made small talk. Marti wanted to read her book but didn't know how to disentangle herself. Truly, she'd rather be at the cabin or on her own dock yet felt compelled to keep an eye on Tess. Their conversation turned to the election.

"I'm not sure, think we're voting for Gore," Linda said.

We? Marti inwardly scoffed.

"Oh, I can't," Elaine said. "I can't vote for him after Clinton and that Monica affair."

"He cheated on his wife. That's the only person he did a wrong to. What do you think, Marti?" Linda asked.

Marti was taken aback, not wanting this conversation. "I'm voting for Gore."

"What about the Monica thing?" persisted Elaine.

"It has nothing to do with Gore."

"Right." Linda nodded. "Besides, Clinton is cute. If I were Monica, I might have done it too. She went looking for it."

"Definitely agree there," Elaine said.

"No," Marti interjected forcefully. Both women turned to look at her. "It doesn't matter whether she wanted it. They weren't equals, and that makes it wrong. He held power. It's abuse." For two years Marti had listened to endless discussions about the scandal but never articulated these thoughts even to herself.

She was working hard on her mosaic. She loved this lake, the beauty of blue water merging into blue sky, blues of different tones and textures, and the band of green forest surrounding it all, holding it together. If she looked long enough, other colors worked their way in, purple in the water, red in the hills, and a soft, calming yellow gray in the sky.

When she finished, she took the mosaic to the store and showed Anna, the store owner. Anna studied it closely, saying, "You can have a discount on materials for your next mosaic if you'll give me the privilege of displaying this gorgeous piece in the window." Encouraged, Marti chose a long rectangular board. She would make a strip of just sky and clouds.

Rob called, wanting to take Tess for the weekend to his parents' house on the Cape; his siblings and their children would be there. "You know what a kick Tess gets out of the cousins." *Yes, rub it in*, Marti thought, *big, happy family*. She hadn't any reason to say no, and really, it would be a relief. The polite truce with Tess was deadening.

She wished she could see Peter on the weekend. It would be easier without Tess around. What was he busy with? His wife must be coming. Was she Asian, or were the kids adopted? Did it matter? No, of course not. She was just curious about the wife. Marti felt a twinge—jealousy? No. It was the mystery. Why didn't he simply say, *My wife will be here?*

Rob was picking Tess up Saturday, so Marti had only Friday to get through. She loosened the reins on Tess, allowing her to go alone to the beach in the morning, and Marti came later in the afternoon. A crowd of kids were playing volleyball. It amazed her how easily Tess joined in; it was a social skill Marti had never mastered, and she felt proud, not because it was her accomplishment but rather because Tess had achieved this despite her mother.

She spotted Linda with a group of women and decided to ignore them, dropping her stuff in a remote corner and then going in the water, swimming backstroke, looking up at the sky and thinking about her next mosaic. It was easy to believe in infinity when she looked at the layers of purple and blue in the cloudless sky, comforting and powerful in their monotony, steady as an open prairie. She didn't think she could achieve those layers of depth on a flat board but wanted to try.

After swimming, she walked over to Tess who was standing by the snack bar with her friends and told her she was leaving.

"You just got here."

Marti shrugged. "Be home at five." Tess nodded without looking at her. Noticing Ethan, Marti smiled and stuck her hand out, introducing herself. Ethan looked surprised yet friendly as he returned her handshake. Taking in Tess's red, scowling face, Marti regretted how obvious she'd been. There was a whole group of kids, yet she'd introduced herself only to Ethan.

At the cabin she sketched her new mosaic, taped it to the board, and began arranging tiles on top of the paper. When she checked the time, it was six. She took Caliban on a long walk, hoping to see Tess on her way home. Returning, she found Precious sitting on top of her mosaic board, purring and licking her paws, tiles scattered across the floor, and the sketch lay shredded in a ball on the table. Marti toppled the cat, picked up the tiles, and carefully unfolded the sketch. She tried futilely to tape it back together before giving up, throwing it away and heading to the beach.

She found only a couple of families with young children having picnic dinners, and this made her wistful. *Tess and I should do a picnic dinner. Would Tess even be interested? Did I appreciate her while I had her?*

Back home, she flitted about, watching the clock: after seven. She walked to Linda's. "Marti! A nice surprise! Come in, have a glass. You've met Elaine; this is her husband, Jack." A table was set with wine and appetizers. She could smell barbeque. She asked if Tess was there, feeling foolish, as obviously she wasn't.

"Maybe she's still at the lake," Linda suggested. "There was a really big group of kids today. We practically had to drag our kids away, didn't we, Elaine?"

"Couldn't blame them, beautiful day," Elaine said, sipping her wine.

Marti asked for Emily. Linda called down the stairs, and two girls came. "Girls, say hi to Mrs. Farrell. Marti, you know Sarah." Did she know Sarah? She'd seen her face but hadn't paid any attention to the other kids at the lake. Was that the problem? Should she have been getting to know all the kids instead of being so hyper-focused on Tess?

"She was at the lake when we left," Emily said.

"I told you," Linda interjected, "we had to *drag* them out." Marti asked if the girls knew where Ethan lived, and they both shook their heads.

Art walked her out. "Marti," he began, touching her on the shoulder, "I don't think you need to worry; Tess seems like a solid kid to me. Let us know if you don't find her. Of course you will. If we can help in any way . . ."

The sun cast its red light on the water at the empty beach, yet the moon was already up, almost as orange as the sun, glowing with pride as if pushing the sun away: *My turn.*

She returned to the cabin; it was now eight-thirty. How could Tess do this again? Marti picked up the phone, placed it down. After pausing a moment, she lifted it again; she wasn't in this alone. "Rob, about tomorrow. Yes, noon will be fine. The thing is, I need to talk with you, so don't bring anyone."

"I was going to bring the kids. They're looking forward to seeing Tess, and it would give Lisa a break."

Like I care? "I need to talk with you about Tess. And . . . and other things."

"What about Tess?"

He's not interested in other things. "She's out when she isn't supposed to be."

"Where?"

"Obviously, I don't know."

"Marti, just tell me what's happening."

"She met a boy." He didn't respond. "I told her to be home at five."

"I'll see you in the morning." His tone was dismissive.

"Rob—"

"Five isn't reasonable."

"She was out until two a.m. the other night. Five was a consequence for that."

"Oh, you didn't say that. Still, she's angry at being there, which I sympathize with. Call if she isn't in by midnight." Marti seethed—had she always felt this undermined?

Tess came in at eleven.

She dreamed of Tess, her arms outstretched, walking along the brink of a cliff above rushing murky water while Marti called her to come back. *It's fine, Mom, I can balance, and even if I fall, I can swim. You taught me.* Marti ran toward her, the ground crumbling beneath her feet. Tess was skipping along the edge, humming a little tune.

Down will come baby, cradle and all.

Tess receded from view, and Marti began falling. The fall made her sit upright in bed.

14

M arti was sore when she awoke in the morning. This made her hopeful, and she checked her underwear. *Still, maybe it takes time for a miscarriage.* She rode her bicycle to school, speeding toward each bump in the road—*Can't hurt, I mean, hopefully can hurt.* She laughed to herself, enjoying the breeze the speed created on this hot last day of school. She wasn't worried about seeing Spencer, predicting he'd ignore her completely and the destroyed painting would not be addressed. At last, she understood.

"Class, there's a form of art we haven't discussed," Spencer spoke, threading his way back and forth through the desks. The students, a bit dismayed they weren't having parties like the other classes, nonetheless, obligingly shifted their heads to follow him. "Mixed media. I want you to realize anything—be it sculpture, photography, painting, or drawing—can be combined together. I have an example of this to show you, a new piece I created last night." He held up a canvas, pieces of a painting glued onto it.

"Aren't those from one of your paintings, Spencer?" Peter asked.

"Astute, Peter, yes. I cut up my favorite painting to do this." Students gasped and Spencer continued. "Next, I mixed it with some inferior sketches lying around my house." Marti recognized the missing pieces of her work. "The point being, they are bound together, enslaved, opposite though they may be. Hate and love being one and the same."

"What about that headless photo in the corner?" Brooke asked. "Weird. Who'd be crazy enough to lie naked in snow?"

When the bell rang, Marti tried to rush out the door, but Spencer squeezed her arm. "Miss Martha, I need to speak with you."

As soon as he released her arm, she bolted quickly down the hall, avoiding looking at the mural mess on the wall. She had a sensation of being followed and began running down the stairs. "Marti, wait!" Relief flooded through her as she realized it was Peter. She paused, mid-staircase. "Why," Peter asked as he caught up to her, "wouldn't you talk to Spencer?"

"Because I don't want to be late to my next—" She stopped, seeing Peter wasn't buying this. "I'm angry about the mural."

"Did you ask Spencer about it?"

Students were pushing past them on the stairs as they were clearly in everyone's way; Marti didn't want to prolong the conversation by moving to a less awkward spot. "He said it's no big deal. Life changes, you know?"

"I guess he didn't want to get Bobby in trouble and—"

"Right," Marti snapped, abruptly, continuing down the stairs.

Peter trailed behind her. "Aren't you coming to Spencer's room today, the last day?"

"I have plans," Marti said. "I'm . . . I'm going horseback riding."

"Really? I thought only Jan rode." It was true; like most of the athletic pursuits in their family, only Jan had the gumption to ride. Yet the more Marti thought about it, horseback riding seemed like a good idea. Wasn't that how women had miscarriages in movies?

She received her report card. Her grades had dropped in almost every subject. This was partly because of the time she'd spent at Spencer's but also because of his influence; he'd sniped whenever she mentioned homework and belittled all her other teachers. Her only good grade was in art. Previously he'd given her an A- in art, but now it was an A+. Under "comments," he wrote: *Marti has superlative talents.* Reluctantly, she showed her mother the report card.

"I don't understand. How could your grades slip so badly? You must bring these up next year. Well, at least your art grade is wonderful. Which reminds me, I've got to see your mural."

"I didn't finish."

"Didn't finish? Whatever did you get an A+ for?"

It dawned on Marti just what her superlative talents were.

"Don't look sulky, Marti. Obviously, he saw something in you, and you'll just have to work that hard in every subject."

Sleep with all my teachers?

Marti couldn't think of next year as she was staring down a dark tunnel, uncertain whether there even was an opening at the end. If only it were last year and she could do it all over by never, ever meeting Spencer.

She spent most of her time in her room. Tired, she went to bed early, slept late, and sometimes napped in the afternoon. One day, trying to relive an old comfort, she sucked her thumb. Her thumb no longer fit; it was big, awkward, and slimy, reminding her of . . . She jumped off the bed, washed her hands, and gargled with mouthwash. Grabbing Papa Bear off his chair, his head still sagging back, she took him into the bed and yanked the covers tight over her head. It didn't matter that it was summer; this hot, dark cave was where she wanted to be.

After a few days, her mother admonished her to get out of the house. "Why don't you call a friend, go play tennis or something?" Marti snorted at this; tennis was another sport Jan did, whereas all Marti did was swim. She went to the lake, hoping to avoid running into anyone. She needn't have worried; her friends would be sitting in Brooke's incense-smelling basement, getting stoned and listening to music, music their guru, Spencer, endorsed. They'd be down there all day, vampires ignoring the daylight, only coming up to Brooke's kitchen for food. Mr. Davies would find his way next to one of the girls and roam his hand across her ass. Marti remembered her shock the first time it happened to her and the certain conviction that she'd imagined it—or worse, caused it to happen—until she saw his hand slide under Alison's leather belt. She watched as his fingers twisted until Alison squirmed away, never to return to Brooke's house again; no wonder Brooke's crowd was mostly boys.

At the lake Marti jumped off the high dive repeatedly, each time getting the most bounce out of the board, spreading her legs wide before hitting the water, imagining water surging in and drowning the baby—if there was a baby.

When her period still wouldn't come, she asked her mother about horseback riding. Pleased, her mother signed Marti up for lessons. The instructor, Henry, a kind older man, encouraged Marti, telling her she was a natural, just like her sister. She hid her terror and took the soreness in her loins as a good sign.

One day her regular horse was injured, and Henry gave her a different one. This horse, Brown Bell, was harder to control. The ride went slowly at first with Brown Bell stopping constantly to eat grass. "Give the reins a tug. You've got to show him you're the boss," Henry said.

Marti thought, *Why shouldn't he eat?* Brown Bell stopped at each patch to nibble while the group got farther and farther ahead. Finally, she tried jerking the horse up, but he just ignored her. She tugged harder and he pulled his head back down, determined to eat. She was frustrated and embarrassed; the other riders were barely even glancing back now. What if she *never* got the horse to move? Where was Henry? Should she try to get off? She'd never done that without help.

She yanked as hard as she could and held the reins tight. Brown Bell lifted his head and began running. He veered off path. Marti had to duck and sway to avoid tree branches lashing her face, and this shifting made the horse accelerate faster. Brown Bell quickly overran the group, and Henry shouted at her to pull back on the reins, but she couldn't as she was too scared to sit up. "Pull!" Henry yelled.

Marti pulled as hard as she could from a crouching position, and finally Brown Bell yielded. He bent his head to drink from a mud puddle while Marti prayed, waiting for Henry. "I have to get off," she said when he reached her.

Henry moved next to her. "The horses aren't used to dismounting here. It's okay, give me the reins." Henry led the horse while she shook with panic, loathing herself for this, and for so much more.

Looking down, she felt terror at the long distance to the ground, suddenly recalling why she was taking these lessons in the first place. She stood, swung her leg over, and dived off, making sure to land belly first. Brown Bell took off, and there was much commotion as Henry first secured the horse and then came to assist her. She tried to say Brown Bell threw her. Henry, not buying it, was trying hard to conceal his anger.

She was bruised and sore, but had no broken bones. Her mother worried most about the cuts on her face. "You'll have to put the scar cream on. It isn't good to have those cuts on top of your skin grafts. You should've been more careful and listened to the instructor."

"I did. I told you, I had the bad horse. I'm not going back anymore." *Why does Mom make me think everything is my fault?*

"Haven't you heard of getting back on the horse?" Her mother smiled at her own joke; Marti, still fuming, didn't.

"The horse could have fallen on me, like the one did on Brooke. I could have been maimed." She said this with an almost wistful air.

"Fall on you? My dear, I don't think you'd survive that. A horse never fell on Brooke."

"Yes, it did. You said so yourself, her handicap."

"Brooke has mild cerebral palsy, something that happens at birth, a lack of oxygen to the brain. That's why she limps, and it's why her speech is a bit slurred."

Marti looked the word *cerebral* up in the dictionary. *Intellectual rather than emotional or physical . . . use of intellect rather than intuition or instinct.* This seemed the opposite of who Brooke was. She looked up *palsy*: *any variety of atonal muscular conditions characterized by tremors of the body.* She never, ever saw Brooke tremble; she was as confident as could be. Confused by these definitions, Marti concluded that maybe this was what her mother meant when she said Brooke overcame her handicap.

The jump off Brown Bell *must* have caused a miscarriage; she only needed to wait. After that, she could start anew. Her belly was bruised and she used her fists to beat on it, pushing it with her hands and tightening her muscles until it was a concave bowl. Even at rest, her stomach was flat. How could there be a baby inside? She wasn't pregnant. No, she couldn't be.

At dinner she pushed her food around her plate, taking a few bites and then spitting into her napkin. *I'll starve it.* She had no appetite and sometimes threw up. *Not morning sickness, life sickness.*

She sat on the front porch, rocking in the double rocker. She read her old *Archie* comics, only now they infuriated her. Why did Betty even *like* Archie? When she was little, she dreamed of sitting in this rocker with her first boyfriend. *What a stupid fantasy. There won't be any first boyfriend.* It grew too dark to read, and still she sat. The June bugs were out in force this summer. She rocked back and forth, listening to their fragile bodies cracking beneath the rocker.

One morning she noticed Marybeth and Nancy playing hopscotch across the street. Marti put down her stack of comics, walked over, and asked to play.

"Sure!" Nancy responded enthusiastically.

Marybeth looked baffled. "Don't you have . . . teenage stuff to do?"

"Absolutely not." Marti picked up a stone and threw it on the number one. She'd always enjoyed this game with its simple, well-defined rules. It was easy to jump in the boxes, turn around, go back, and start again. Nancy threw her stone, but it bounced and rolled away.

"You lose!" Marybeth crowed. "My turn."

"No, she gets a do-over," Marti said. "You should always get a do-over." She picked up the stone and handed it to Nancy. Marybeth shrugged while Nancy threw again, landing in the center of number one.

They played for hours, and the next morning she took a walk with the girls in the meadow at the end of the street. Marti taught them how to make dandelion chains and braid them into their hair, after which they pretended to be fairies. They hunted for four-leaf clovers, and when they couldn't find any, they picked dandelion parachute balls.

"You make a wish and blow," Marti instructed.

"What are you wishing for?" Nancy asked.

"She's probably wishing for a boyfriend," Marybeth whispered to Nancy, "Peter." Both girls giggled.

Marti blew the seeds. *No baby. No baby.*

Each day she played with the girls while being careful to avoid Peter. He called twice inviting her to Brooke's, and she made excuses. Brooke, who never called anyone (they called her), called. "Where have you been? Is everything cool?"

Touched by the concern in Brooke's voice, she hesitated: *Should I tell her?*

I'm pregnant.

Wow. Who'd you fuck?

Spencer.

She couldn't say it but realized she could go to Planned Parenthood without Brooke, and this made her hopeful. They'd tell her she wasn't pregnant.

Debra wasn't working, and instead it was a woman named Annie. Marti waited in her office. The posters on the wall seemed to mock her now: *The best place to be is part of a loving family.* The Colgans, they were a loving family. Marti remembered watching Mrs. Colgan carefully tuck her rosary beads in her purse before leaving for Mass. If only Marti could go with her and confess; she'd say some Hail Marys and all would be okay.

Annie returned, reading the file. "You're using a diaphragm. How's that working? Perhaps you need to be resized?"

"No. Maybe, but . . . but I'm here because, well, um . . ." Marti slowly looked up. Annie put the file down and fixed her eyes on Marti. *She knows, so say it.* "I don't think I used it right."

"We can go over it again."

"I, um, I think . . ." She looked down and twisted her fingers together. *If I say it, it's true. Don't say it.* "I'm pregnant," she mumbled. The words sounded as if they were echoing off the walls. The time until Annie spoke seemed endless.

"It's good you came. How long has it been since you had your period?"

"I don't know, more than a month, or maybe two months. Last time I had only a few streaks."

"Okay. We don't know for sure, so I'm going to do a blood test. Stay here while I get everything set."

Marti crossed her fingers, her last chance. She prayed, *Please God, please. I'll be good. I'll do better in school for Mommy.* Useless, given her mother didn't believe in God. *Please God, I'll make Mrs. Colgan happy. I'll go to Mass with her.* She thought of her father. *Daddy, Daddy, where are you? Don't be so dead.* Tears rolled down her face. She closed her eyes tight and was startled when Annie gently touched her. "One little prick and it's over."

Over. Forgotten. Done.

She told Marti three days for the results, and to bring some-one. "Your mother, perhaps?" Marti shook her head. "Your boyfriend or a friend, maybe? It'd be a good idea."

"No."

She waited while Annie studied her. "Marti, who did you have sex with?"

"Uh, my boyfriend. He's from another town."

"How did you meet?"

"He was here on vacation."

"Two months ago? Kind of an odd time to vacation with school winding down. Is he older?"

Marti stood. "I'll be back Thursday."

"Wait." Annie touched her arm. "Did someone hurt you?"

"No, I just don't want to be. I can't be."

"I know you're scared, Marti, but sit tight and don't assume the worst. Young girls are often irregular."

Waiting seemed intolerable now that it was real. She lay in bed hugging Papa Bear, wondering if the bear's belly was still big enough for all her tears. *How big will my belly get?* Years ago, she used to stuff a pillow under her shirt, trying to imagine that far-off future, an image that was never this. She jumped off the bed and put a record on, playing one song over and over, lifting the needle up and wearing the grooves down. The song was about trying to be free, and she thought it would give her comfort. But instead she zeroed in on one phrase: *a worm on a hook.* Oh, that had been her, all right, dangling on a line Spencer held, squirming, even writhing with ecstasy sometimes. Such a stupid, disgusting, worthless worm, she deserved her fate, didn't she? Repulsed, she pulled the needle off the record and stuffed the album on the bottom of the pile.

She reread her comic books and despite not enjoying them, she went to the store and bought new ones. Time moved slowly. Her mother prodded her to go out and so she rode her bike to the lake and jumped off the high dive several times, although she no longer believed it would help. Now that she'd taken a test, her thinking had shifted. Any efforts to cause a miscarriage seemed childish.

Peter, Marybeth, and Nancy arrived. Marybeth shouted her name as she splashed toward Marti with Nancy tagging along behind. Marti played with the girls for a long time, pretending to be mermaids, swimming while keeping their legs joined. *Should have kept mine like that.* Marti watched Peter dive, confident and smooth. He wore cutoff jeans. There used to be a rule about proper bathing suits, but after some hippies were caught skinny-dipping, no one cared what kind of clothes you wore, so long as you wore them.

Nancy begged Peter to give her a ride on his back. Marti recognized in Nancy's face that sure sense of safety and love, and she choked back tears of longing. Peter stood up to take a breath with Nancy still clinging to his back. Looking at Marti, he asked if she was okay.

"Of course!" Marti splashed him with water. "Give your sister a ride."

She rummaged through the top drawer of her mother's bureau. Maybe she could find her father's rosary beads and she'd take them with her tomorrow. There was a stack of papers from her accident, hospital reports and pamphlets on burn care. Marti spotted a series of letters from a lawyer and realized what they were: her mother had considered suing the Colgans. Marti slammed the bureau shut.

On Thursday morning there were bright blue skies, and a warm sun. Looking at the mountains surrounding town as she walked to the clinic, she hoped the perfect day was a good omen. *I can't be pregnant. I won't be.*

Annie was talking to another woman behind the desk. She told Marti she'd be with her in a minute and smiled before returning to her conversation. *Must be good news or she wouldn't have smiled.* Marti felt lighter already, thinking of how her life could begin again. She'd be just an ordinary girl going to an ordinary high school, planning an ordinary future. Suddenly, all things ordinary were magical.

She sat and picked up a magazine, thumbing until she got to a column called *Can This Marriage Be Saved?* She'd always loved reading those, imagining her father alive and her mother writing in: *My husband loves our youngest daughter more than me.*

She began reading. *I want children and my husband doesn't. He says our life is perfect as it is, but I'm afraid I'll never feel fulfilled if I don't have a child.* The column went on to describe the woman's nieces and nephews and her desire for her own. Marti tried conjuring that feeling, remembering her fantasy of a baby with Spencer, but all she felt was horror. She jumped when Annie tapped her shoulder.

Inside the office, Annie pulled her chair close to Marti's and looked directly at her. "Your results came back positive. You're pregnant." Her voice was both soft and firm. Marti struggled to comprehend: *Positive, didn't that mean good? But she said* pregnant.

"Marti," Annie continued, "what do your parents know?" Marti looked down at her hands twisting in her lap. "You're fourteen, correct?"

"My birthday's soon."

"This is too big to face alone. You live at home, right? Your parents need to know. I can help you tell them."

"I'm pregnant?"

"Yes. Here. A copy of your test." She held it out, and Marti shoved the paper in her bag without looking at it. She folded her arms across her chest. "I don't want it."

"Do you want to consider adoption?" Annie rested her hand gently on Marti's knee.

"No. I don't want to *have* it." She shook her legs as if shaking off a fly. Annie removed her hand.

"Are you talking about abortion, Marti?" She nodded. "Abortion isn't legal in Vermont."

"But I know someone—" She broke off, trying to remember something Brooke had told her once about a girl at school.

"It recently became legal in some other states, like New York."

"Where can I go in New York?"

"These are things we can explore. Are you afraid of your parents' reaction?"

"No," Marti answered, realizing in a way, this was true. Her mother wouldn't beat her or lock her up, nor would she make her keep it. But she'd want to know *how*. Telling would be like being in the closet with Spencer all over again. If no one ever knew, she could forget. That was the only way.

Marti was given an appointment for the next day to bring her parents. Walking home, she decided to tell Brooke; she'd call and ask to see her alone. Marti contemplated explanations for the father: a college friend of Jan's or the vacation story. Concentrating deeply on her plan, she hadn't realized she'd reached home until she heard someone behind her, calling. She bolted up the steps.

"Hey, wait!"

Marti opened her door.

Peter caught up and touched her arm. "Hang on, you look upset. What's wrong?"

The only sound was the door creaking as Marti swung it in and out, deciding whether to let Peter in. *What the hell? He has those older sisters. Maybe he can help.* She waved him in. *I can count on him to be discreet, something I can't be sure of with Brooke.*

"I'm pregnant." She let it drop, watching it register on his face. He slid into a chair, and annoyed her with childish words like: *you're kidding, gosh.*

"Are you sure?"

Marti raised both her arms in a gesture of obvious vexation.

"Who—who?"

He sounds like an owl. She intended to tell the story of the vacation boy until the image of Peter with his puppy love for Spencer floated through her mind—Peter, the little gopher boy. She could hear Spencer now: *Do this, Sweetie Petey.* She wanted to crush that adoration, wanting Peter to feel the ravage she felt.

"Spencer."

Peter's face contorted into several expressions as it wavered between shock and disbelief. It finally stilled into mystified acknowledgment. "Wow," he said.

"*Wow?*"

"Spencer? As in Spencer Douglas? You slept with him?"

"Yes, Peter, Spencer. Our teacher. We were—he was fucking me for months."

"Does he know?"

"He's in Timbuktu, remember?"

"You just found out?"

Marti nodded.

"You have to contact him."

This concern for Spencer enraged her. "Think he cares?"

"Of course he cares, I'm sure—"

"He *fucked* me; I didn't say he loved me. They're not the same thing."

"But—"

"He's not to know! Do you understand?" Her voice grew

shrill, and she was sorry she'd told Peter; his loyalty was to Spencer, not her. "You can't tell."

"Yeah, he could get in trouble. Still, he has a right to know."

"He has no right. None! Get out!" She pushed Peter toward the door. *What a mistake! I'll get rid of him and call Brooke.*

"Marti, stop!" Peter elbowed his way back in and stood stubbornly in the middle of the room. "I want to help."

"How? Do you know where I can go to get rid of it?"

"Get rid? God, no! But you told me for a reason. I have an idea."

"What?"

Peter sat down and picked up a tin silver coaster from the table and studied it carefully, turning the rim around in his hand. The coaster had a picture of a flying goose pressed into the silver, and he traced the image with his index finger before speaking. "People will want to know who the father is. I'll say it's me."

"You would say that? Why?" She sat on the edge of her chair.

"Don't you think it'd work? Everyone knows we hang out together."

"But why?"

Peter spun the coaster on his hand. It fell and rolled on the floor and he watched it wobble, scooping to catch it at its last moment of movement. He clenched it in his hand as he looked at her. "Because I'd be helping two friends, you and Spencer."

Marti felt sick in her stomach, but ignored this. She needed him, even if his goal was helping Spencer. "You'll really do this?"

"Yeah."

"I think Brooke knows a place I can go. We'll go see her and you'll say—"

"I said I would," Peter interjected curtly, "but what kind of place?"

"For an abortion."

"That's illegal."

"Not everywhere."

"Marti, you can't! It's a sin! You can put it up for adoption."

"I'm not doing that."

They argued back and forth, each resolute in their position until Marti shouted at him, "I'm not having it. I can't have this baby! No! Get out!" She tried to shove Peter out the door again. Again, he resisted. After more heated discussion, he eventually agreed to help her with what she wanted. *Why help with something he's so clearly horrified by?* This thought nagged at her, yet she brushed it aside.

On the walk over to Brooke's, Peter tried to get Marti to talk about Spencer; she cut him off, and they walked in silence. They found Brooke alone in her house. It was unusual for her to be without her posse, yet with her parents not at home, Brooke seemed altogether freer and lighter. They followed her down into her basement cave. Brooke had redecorated since Marti was here last. Purple tie-dyed sheets hung from the ceiling, and there was a new poster hanging of a little boy and girl walking into the woods holding hands. It read: *Today Is the First Day of the Rest of Your Life.* This poster, like the ones at Planned Parenthood, seemed to ridicule Marti. *Is that supposed to be Peter and me? Hansel and Gretel?*

She noticed the pictures of Brooke's brother and sister were gone. Marti felt sad, surmising that Brooke had been defeated and given in to her parents' decree to forget.

Brooke lit some candles, and they sat on the shag rug. She took an album from a pile, Jimi Hendrix, *Are You Experienced.* The needle skipped, as this record, like all Brooke's albums, was heavily scratched.

"Wow, it sounds bad," Peter said.

"I know, isn't he heavy?" Brooke answered, deliberately misconstruing his meaning. She removed a cigarette from her silver case. Marti spoke while Brooke was leaning into a candle to light her cigarette, her hair dangerously close.

"I'm pregnant."

Peter jumped in, "I'm the father." Marti thought she heard glee in his voice.

Brooke swung her head up; her hair flew back as she stared at them, not speaking. Eventually, she started to chuckle. Marti pulled firmly on the rug strands. They were hard to break, but she managed a few and clenched them in her hands. "You two? *Please!*" Brooke's lips twitched slightly as she spoke. Peter nodded. Brooke inhaled deeply on her cigarette. She blew a perfect smoke ring around Marti's face, then turned and blew another around Peter's.

Peter moved closer to Marti, placing his arm around her. "It's true, we're together."

"Peter, you dog!" Brooke slapped his knee. "I didn't know you had it in you! I thought you were, kind of, you know . . . Oh, never mind what I thought." Peter shook his head. Brooke began laughing. "Joke's on me! I tell you everything," she said, pointing her cigarette at Marti, "but you were holding out!"

After recovering from her laughter, Brooke agreed to help. She knew a girl who'd gone to New York City to have an abortion, but she thought there was another girl who went somewhere closer, Troy, New York, only a few hours away. "I think the youth minister at her church told her where to go. I'll find out."

Over the next few days, Marti collected all the money she could. She guessed the abortion might be about seventy dollars. She had twelve dollars. She asked her mother for money for a tennis racket. That was no problem, so she went back and asked for more to take riding lessons again, further pleasing her mother. In her room she found the two Kennedy half-dollars her mother gave her when they were first minted, and she pried the pennies out of her blue penny album; 1903 was the oldest. She fingered a silver dollar that her mother gave Marti on her tenth birthday, saying it was one of her father's favorite possessions. Dated 1870, it had an image of a horse on the front. She passed the dollar back and forth between her palms; she'd always considered it her good luck charm. *Maybe I won't have to use it. I'll take it for luck. Probably they won't even make me pay.*

She rummaged for change in her mother's bureau, taking care to bury the lawsuit letters on the bottom. Next, she went through Jan's room, sweeping up loose change. *If Jan were home, would I tell her? No point thinking about it.* She opened Jan's jewelry box and the ballerina popped up, twirling to the music. She took Jan's two Kennedy half-dollars and a pile of Indian Head nickels. There was a silver charm bracelet in the box with a horse, a tennis racket, and a violin on it. Marti put the bracelet on, remembering how she'd always coveted it. She closed the lid on the ballerina and pictured the ballerina lying there, trapped in the dark, waiting for light and music to spring her back alive. *I'd stay in the box.*

Altogether now she had forty-two dollars. Peter told her he had eight dollars. She was surprised he'd use his money, yet Marti never considered refusing. He said he'd ask Betty to lend him five and that he could empty out Marybeth's piggy bank. Marti winced, pausing before nodding in agreement, vowing silently to replace it later. She couldn't feel guilty now.

Brooke gave them the address. They'd hitch there early the next morning. Peter had a map of New York showing the route to Troy; the clinic was on Utica Avenue. Since it was an avenue, they figured it would be easy to find. Before going to bed, she snuck a ten out of her mother's purse.

She lay in bed with the lights out and ran her hands along her abdomen. When she suspected she might be pregnant, she'd felt her stomach constantly. Since the test result, not once had she touched it. Her hips protruded out in a kind of denial, but now she could feel a little round hill that hadn't been there before. Or was she imagining it? Still, it was so small the baby could only be the size of a marble, or at most a golf ball. She pictured it lying like an egg in a bird's nest. *Womb.* She said the word aloud, thinking it sounded like the most comforting place there could be. *I'd stay in the womb if I were you.* Perhaps it was a tiny matryoshka doll nesting inside another and another and another, much too vulnerable on its own. *Grow a thick skin. Hide.*

15

Peter tried making small talk as they walked to the end of town, but Marti could only hear a voice in her head chanting: *Get this day over. Done.* They crossed the covered bridge that led out of town. The road soon diverged into two, and they knew which one to take. Thumbs out, they quickly got a ride from a hippie couple that lived on a farm outside of town. Next was a middle-aged man who was going halfway. He said he hated to see them hitchhike. Didn't they understand how dangerous it was? "You could be my kids," he told them. "Please don't do this again." The third ride was a truck that dropped them at an exit for downtown Troy.

They walked half a mile before seeing any streets. Finally past the outskirts of town, they began asking for Utica Avenue. Everyone seemed to have heard of it; no one could point the way. "What are you looking for? Maybe I'll know the place," an older woman said.

"My uncle's candy store, it's very small," Marti replied. They headed in the vague direction where people had indicated Utica Avenue might be. The town was much larger than Chatham with little greenery, and the sun was unrelentingly hot. They felt encouraged when they finally found the street. The address of the clinic was 3510, and they were at 900.

"Shouldn't take long now," Peter said. They walked and walked into the 2000s, where the road ended.

"It can't stop. We have the address; it has to be here." Marti's voice was shaky. There weren't many people on the street now. Eventually, they found a man to ask. The road continued over a canal a few blocks away.

"What do you want over there? Nothing but empty factories."

He was right. Most of the buildings were boarded up. Signs on the outside showed what the warehouses once were, but windows were broken, paint was peeling, and dust was everywhere. A pack of stray dogs hovered nearby. Noticing Marti and Peter, the dogs headed in their direction. They seemed to signal each other before encircling the pair and fixing their gaze upon them. The sound of machinery was grinding in the distance but Marti and Peter couldn't tell where that life might be and so they stood frozen, casting their eyes downward. In time, the dogs grew disinterested and ambled off.

They walked another twenty minutes into the 3000s. A few buildings were open. Some old men sat inside a barbershop. Marti and Peter passed a large building: *City Department of Social Services.* Women and children milled outside, including a girl about their age, her pregnant belly protruding as she carried another baby in her arms. Marti stared until the girl growled, "What ya looking at?"

Several blocks later, they spotted a small sign: *Troy Women's Clinic.* After such desolation, they were surprised to find it bustling inside with a long counter, several women behind it talking on phones while more phones rang. Two men wearing white coats were deep in conversation, their heads bowed over a chart. Marti walked over to the first woman who seemed unoccupied and stood several minutes before being acknowledged. "I'm here for, uh . . . uh, an abortion."

"Your name?"

"Marti Farrell."

The woman scanned a list.

"I'm not there."

The woman looked up and raised her eyebrows. "Abortions are by appointment. The cost is two hundred dollars, upfront, and we don't begin the process until you've had counseling."

"I had counseling at Planned Parenthood."

"Nonetheless, you need it here. And how"—the woman leaned over the counter, looking fully at Marti and glancing at Peter—"old are you?"

"Sixteen," Marti said, feigning confidence.

"You don't look—never mind. Do you want an appointment to speak to someone tomorrow?"

"*Tomorrow?* No, today. I've come a long way, I—"

Another woman behind the counter turned toward them. "I'll speak with you." She reached her hand out. "I'm Janet." The first woman shrugged and turned away.

"Marti," she mumbled, tentatively returning the handshake.

Janet reached her hand out to Peter as well. "I have a few things to take care of. Have a seat." She gestured at the waiting room and began walking away but turned back, looking closely at Marti. "Don't leave. Promise?"

The waiting room was sparsely decorated with a few chairs and a table displaying pamphlets on birth control. *Too late*, Marti scoffed. A middle-aged woman wearing a stained white turtleneck sat in the corner twisting a gold ring around her finger.

A younger woman sat huddled with a young man, talking in low tones, occasionally laughing. Marti sat near, straining to hear what they were saying—anything to distract her mind. Eventually, the guy reached into his backpack and took out a book, *Journey to Ixland*. Marti recognized the book as one Spencer had foisted upon her. He began reading and the woman slouched back in her chair, staring up at the ceiling and thrusting her legs straight out, tapping the points of her cowboy boots together. *No place like home.*

A touch on her shoulder startled Marti. "Come," Janet said. She turned to Peter. "I'd like to talk with Marti alone." Peter nodded, although it hadn't been a question.

Marti followed Janet to a small office. The room was empty except for two chairs, no happy posters on the wall. "Sit," Janet said, gesturing to one of the chairs while she sat in the other. "Are you sure you're pregnant?"

Marti nodded. "I had a test at Planned Parenthood." She produced the crumbled paper, and Janet scanned it.

"It's unclear how far along you are. How far do you—"

"I live across town." Marti worried Janet would detect that she was from Vermont where abortion was illegal. Could she be arrested?

"No, no. How pregnant are you?"

"Um, about two months, I think."

"You think?" Janet shook her head and sighed. "Is that really the father out there?" Marti gave a small nod and looked at the floor's brown linoleum dotted with speckles of gold. "Do your parents know?"

"My father is dead." She hoped this might elicit sympathy.

"Does your mother know you're pregnant?"

"No." Marti stumbled her way through several more questions. Janet told her she would have to return with her mother.

"I'm sorry you're in this trouble, but listen, okay?" Janet set her eyes on Marti. "You really can't go through this alone. You need your mother." Marti shook her head vehemently. Janet paused before asking whether her mother had a boyfriend. Stumped by this question, Marti didn't respond. Janet gently asked if anyone was bothering her, and it dawned on Marti what she meant: there could be worse things than Spencer. "Bring your mom, and we'll all talk and figure things out." She stood, handing Marti several papers.

She stuffed them in her bag and walked out. Peter looked

questioningly at Marti, but she didn't speak until they were on the street. "They won't do it."

"What are you going to do?"

"I don't know. I don't know." She hurled her bag on the ground. After trying so hard, she was completely, utterly defeated. "Fuck! Fuck!"

Although they suspected there must be a shorter way to the highway, neither wanted to ask. They were thirsty, hungry, and drained as they retraced their steps. They knew the route as if they'd dropped breadcrumbs along it. Reaching the highway, they stood for an hour with their thumbs out.

A cop car stopped. He rolled his window down and leaned over, surveying them a long moment before speaking. "Don't you kids know I could arrest you?" They didn't answer. "I'm not going to, but you kids sure are dumb. Hitchhiking's not safe. I want you to walk off this ramp, forget wherever you were going, and call your mamas."

They walked back into town and stopped at a diner; they might as well spend some of the money now. In her efforts to starve the baby, Marti had been eating very little. She was suddenly ravenous. She ordered a cheeseburger, fries, and a Coke. She'd given up drinking soda, as Spencer said it was poison; none of that mattered now, and the Coke seemed a small comfort.

After eating she felt nauseous and sluggish from the weight of the food in her stomach. In the bathroom she tried unsuccessfully to make herself sick and then sat on the toilet seat, leaning her head against the stall. There were all those tales of miscarriages in airplane bathrooms. She'd read a newspaper story once about a girl who gave birth in a bathroom stall at her prom, leaving the baby to drown in the toilet while she danced. Marti raised up and put her head between her legs, looking into the bowl, somehow expecting something.

A woman came in and after a time, sighed, and shuffled around, making her impatience obvious. Marti continued sitting. *You can just wait.* The woman finally knocked on the stall and asked if she was okay. She didn't answer and the woman left. Marti closed her eyes. *I'll just stay.* The woman might get a manager, and there'd be lots of commotion. She'd say she was having a miscarriage. Could that make it so? They'd take her to a hospital, and maybe she could get an abortion when she told them she was losing the baby anyway. Hearing noise outside the door, she bolted past the hostess, brushing off her concern. She put down more than enough money and, ignoring Peter's questioning look, ushered him outside.

They walked back to the road, keeping an anxious eye out for cops. It was almost dark now and growing colder. Marti wished she hadn't worn shorts. Finally, a truck stopped. They squeezed in, flanked by the driver and another man. The gearshift was between Marti's legs. The men didn't talk much at first, but when they said they were going to New Hampshire, Marti and Peter expressed relief. "Yup, we're turning north on Route 7. That work for you?"

Deflated, as Route 7 cut off before Chatham, Peter said, "We're going to Chatham. It's farther on this road."

"I know where it is." The driver paused. "Maybe we could stay on this and take the cutoff at Route 58 instead. What do you think, Mike?" He leaned across Marti as he spoke.

"I suppose we could," Mike replied, "though it's longer that way."

"We'd be really grateful," Peter said.

"Would you now?" Mike smiled at Marti. His gums showed, and his teeth were bright and perfect.

"Yes, we've had a long day," she answered.

"The lady's grateful," Mike said. "I want to know how grateful."

After a moment's silence, he repeated, "How grateful?"

"Very," she answered, and Peter nodded.

"Well, maybe you could show it."

"What?" Peter asked warily.

"Not you, pal. Your girlfriend. We had a long day too. Heck, a long week. We started in St. Louis with pickups and drop-offs up to Chicago and so on, with a lot more before we head home. That's a lot of lonesome driving."

"You don't have to take us—"

"I'm talking to your girlfriend. What do you say? Care to express your gratitude?" She stared out the windshield. A pair of red dice and a silver cross hung from the rearview mirror. "We've been on the road a long time with no lovemaking," Mike said.

"Let us out." Peter waved his arms for emphasis.

Lovemaking. Making love. Once I thought of it that way.

"Let us out," Peter repeated.

"Now hold on. We could do that, but I want to hear what the pretty one says. She's had a long day. Maybe she likes the idea." Mike flashed his wide smile at Marti. "You wouldn't have to do intercourse, and nothing rough. How about going down on us? Two friendly BJs?" Marti didn't answer. She noticed the dice were snake eyes any way you looked.

The driver slowed. "Forget it, Mike. Let's let them out and keep on the way we were headed." He unlocked the doors.

Peter whispered, "It's okay now."

"I'll do it."

"No way, Marti! He's letting us out. We'll get another ride."

Ignoring Peter, Marti looked at the driver. "I'll do it. And you'll drive us to Chatham."

The driver shifted uncomfortably in his seat. "Mike, look at her. She's just a kid. We'll take you to Chatham anyway."

"I want to."

"She answered us," Mike said, rubbing his palms together.

"Are you sure?" the driver asked. Marti rested her hand in his lap, near his groin.

"What the hell? Cut it out, Marti!" Peter yanked her arm.

"You shut up." Mike slammed his elbow into Peter's face. "She's got a right to make her own decision. Leave her alone."

Marti placed her hand back in the driver's lap, and he started the truck up. His hand grazed the inside of Marti's leg as he shifted gears. She stared stonily out at the dark sky.

"Told you we could find some action, and she's a slick one at that." Mike grinned at the driver. "Pull over when you see a good spot."

"And we'll get out," Peter said.

"I told you to shut up. You ain't going nowhere. The lady would like some privacy with us, wouldn't you, Marcie? That's your name, right—Marcie?"

"It's Martha."

"Well, Martha, nice to meet you." Mike leaned across Peter, reached for Marti's hand, and kissed it. "I believe we'll all have a good time, excepting your friend here. He's kind of a drip, isn't he? Should we just ditch him?"

"No, but I'll—you'll—have a good time. I give a good blow job. I had an expert teacher."

"Woo," Mike chuckled. "Your teacher wasn't him, now, was it?" He jabbed his finger at Peter's chest, and she shook her head. "You're lonesome for action yourself, aren't you, Martha?"

She nodded. *Lonesome.*

"Check that? She's cool as a cucumber and hot as a tomato."

The driver exited, turned onto a dirt road, and parked by an empty field. "Ready, steady, go!" Mike said, hopping out of the truck. Peter tried following, but Mike pushed his head against the dashboard and closed the door. "Remember? You ain't going nowhere." The driver got out on his side and gestured to Marti.

Tugging her arm, Peter whispered, "No, Marti, no." Marti shrugged him off and climbed out. Mike leaned in, opened the cargo hold, and pointed for Peter to get in. Peter shook his head and continued trying to exit. Mike gestured threateningly. Peter inched into the back and the driver locked him in, leaving the interior lights on.

Mike, his pants already down, called to Marti from the field. The moon was full or almost full; Marti could never judge a moon with certainty. Once when she was little, she'd spotted a glorious moon and shouted to her family that it was full. Her father told her to run and catch it, and she ran across the wide-open field, leaping to try and grasp that creamy glowing brilliant ball until her mother remarked, "It's not full. It's almost full." Marti stopped running, stopped reaching, and ever since doubted her own eyes. Was it three-quarters, or full, or was it never full? Was there no such thing as full?

Either way, tonight was a beautiful moon, and it was quiet except for crickets chirping. She knelt in front of Mike. Holding his penis, he shoved her head close with his other hand. Tall weeds brushed against her face as she moved back and forth, Jan's charm bracelet jingled musically on her wrist: *ping, ping, ping.* The truck shone like a spaceship; she could hear Peter shouting and banging on a small round window, a porthole. It sounded far away, and she closed her eyes so she wouldn't see him—or anything. Just then Mike pulled away from her and moved toward the truck.

Perplexed, Marti opened her eyes. Mike was laughing, jerking his penis up and down at Peter's face, pressed against the window. Turning back to Marti, Mike pulled on her braids, as if they were reins, directing her face back into his groin. "C'mon, baby."

She felt the contents of her stomach backing up, a taste of bile, hamburger, and Coke swirling up into her mouth before receding to her stomach. It rose up and fell again.

Back and forth.
Rise and fall.

Ebb and flow.

In and out.

She rocked in a steady rhythm, sucking the hard penis while remembering sucking Spencer off that morning in the classroom. *It's no big deal. After all, how many times did I want to suck Spencer? I liked it, didn't I? What's the difference now? It's all the same. I could do it again and again. Back and forth. In and out. No big deal. I could do it all the time, every day, any day. A vocation.* She closed her eyes and pictured an assembly line of men waiting, Spencer at the front calling: *Next!*

Mike pulled out as he began to climax, and Marti reached her gaping mouth toward his penis like a fish bobbing for food. "You want it, huh?" He pushed one final thrust and she swallowed, the salty semen mixing with hamburger, Coke, and bile. Mike turned to the other man. "Your turn, Danny. She's good!"

Danny. I know your name now. As she crawled toward him, Marti's knee sank into a piece of paper with something warm and mushy on it; she didn't stop to see what it was. She opened Danny's pants, and his penis sprang out like a jack-in-the-box. *This will be easy, Danny. You got a thrill just watching, didn't you?*

A mild breeze was in the air. Peter wasn't banging or shouting anymore; Marti didn't know when he'd stopped. A lone frog was added to the cadence of crickets. *Why only one? Who's he croaking for?* Hair on Danny's stomach poked out between two shirt buttons and tickled Marti's forehead. The paper on her knee made a crackling noise as she rocked.

Chug, chug, chug.

I'm the little engine that could.

Chug, chug, chug.

I'm the little engine that did.

Chug, chug, chug.

"Nice," Danny murmured, kissing her forehead. "Can I do something for you now?"

"You already have." Marti smiled, semen dripping out the sides of her mouth like vampire blood. She wiped it with her hand.

Back in the truck, Peter whispered through the metal wall, "Are you okay?" Marti looked down and saw what was stuck to her knee, a Milky Way wrapper. *My favorite candy.* She clasped her sticky semen hands together, alternating between staring out at the night sky and looking at the wrapper, wondering why it was named after the galaxy, an endless expansive eternity, while the candy bar was something so deliberately finite, a brief burst of pleasure that ended too soon.

The truck pulled over at the Chatham exit. Mike hopped out and waved his arm for Marti to follow. "Should we let him out?" Danny asked.

"Hell yeah! What do we want with that useless piece of crap?" After letting Peter out, Danny sat back down, leaning his arms across the steering wheel, staring down, not looking at any of them.

Mike bowed to Marti. "Thanks for the good time. You're right, you give a mean BJ." He shook his head at Peter. "Your dumb luck you got a hot girlfriend and don't know what to do." He climbed back in and the truck sped away, Mike's laughter mixing with crunching gravel.

Once they were truly gone, Peter turned toward her. "Are you all right? I'm sorry, Marti, I couldn't—"

"Don't," she interrupted, speaking sharply. "Don't. Not your fault, okay? I did it. *I did it.* Never, ever mention it again. Not your fault, not your problem. It never happened." Walking quickly away, she crossed the covered bridge, turned, and walked down the stairs to the river walkway below. She didn't stop hurrying until she was sure Peter wasn't following.

The moon loomed over her like a wrecking ball as she stood looking at the shimmering, swirling river. Reaching into her pocket, she took out her father's silver dollar. The image of the horse gleamed in the moonlight, and she imagined mounting that silver horse, holding onto its strong, solid back and galloping unafraid to somewhere, anywhere. She'd traverse across fields, down endless roads, splashing through rivers until she reached that magical divide: the place where land falls away and ocean becomes everything.

The edge of the world.

She'd climb off the horse and walk along the shore, letting the waves engulf her feet and mourning them as they receded. *Please don't leave.* Again and again.

How many miles is the world?

Descending into water, cold as a womb, she'd swim and swim until she knew the answer, and the answer wouldn't even matter because she herself would be liquid.

She clenched the silver dollar tightly before flinging it with her wrist the way Peter's father had taught them years ago. It skipped buoyantly across the river before vanishing with a soft, protesting splash. Her eyes fixed on the water until not even a ripple remained to say the coin had ever been.

16

"Mom had plans for Lisa and her to go antiquing. I figured the kids could watch TV or something." Rob said as he arrived with Adriana and Nathan in tow.

Antiquing? Rob's mother had never asked *her* to go antiquing in the years she was a member of that family. Of course, Marti couldn't think of anything that interested her less, but that was beside the point. It was useful now as ammunition to add to her present irritation and anger.

Tess looked puzzled. "I'm packed. Ready."

Rob gave Tess a hug, and the children crowded around her. "What time did you get in last night, kiddo?"

"Uh, around ten or so."

Marti rolled her eyes at the lie, but stayed silent.

"You should've let Mom know you'd be late."

"I didn't have a phone, and I came home before everyone else, Dad."

"Good girl, but try to come home when Marti tells you."

Marti interpreted this as: *Try to accommodate your neurotic mother.* He wasn't addressing the fact that she'd stayed out till 2:00 a.m. Avoidance always worked for Rob. She turned to Tess. "Why don't you take Adriana and Nathan to the lake? I think they'd enjoy it."

"Mom . . ." Tess looked questioningly at Rob.

"We got time, Tess. Good for them to get their jollies out after the car ride."

"You don't need to worry," he began as soon as they left. "She's a good kid."

You don't need to worry about a good kid? Does he really believe that?

Rob was forty-three, same as Marti, yet he always seemed younger. She'd attributed it to the young kids and younger wife, but now looking at his open, unlined face, she credited his uncomplicated life: easy parents, happy childhood, and a career that satisfied without overly challenging him (and didn't burden him with other people's pain). The biggest test Rob had faced was their marriage and divorce; her presence in his life gave him weight. She smiled at this. Still, he'd gotten what he wanted, both going in and coming out of the marriage.

"Rob, she was out till two the other night and practically admitted she was alone with a boy that whole time." That wasn't quite true; Tess still hadn't explained anything about that night, but Marti thought, *Close enough.*

"If she admitted that, then surely nothing was going on."

"How can you say that?"

He walked over to the refrigerator, opened it, and rummaged around. He took out a bag of baby carrots and crunched one. This familiarity annoyed Marti, yet she understood it was a marriage leftover, same as when they'd casually touch each other, forgetting. "Hungry, Rob?"

"This is good. Don't need anything else." He'd mistaken her sardonic remark for an offer. *Nice to be confident of your privilege in the world.* "Although, is that some of your banana bread? I'll have a piece."

Marti cut a large piece. "Coffee?"

"Yeah, great. Anyway, five o'clock's too early to expect her home. She's on vacation."

"I told you, it was a consequence for coming in at two."

"Well, that's too late."

"Duh, Rob. That's my point. I know it's not the Stone Age. I'm not"—she wanted to say *frigid*—"out of touch."

He paused, searching for the right words. "Why are you here?"

"Why am I here in the kitchen? I'm making you coffee. Here on this planet? That's a big question." She spread her arms wide.

"In this town."

Marti lit the kettle and began scooping coffee into a filter. "It's *Vermont*, the most beautiful place."

"I thought summer vacations were limited at your job."

"I've been there a long time now, seniority."

"Tess said they made you take it. Something going on?"

"Oh, am I losing my job? Or better yet—my mind? A forced mental health break. Is that what you think?" Marti whirled around, glaring at him. "I had to take it, as in, too much accumulated time I'd lose otherwise."

"Seven weeks, I'd think you'd want to really travel with that opportunity. Haven't you been wanting to take Tess to Europe?"

"Don't you think this is a nice place?"

"Not for you. What do you hope to accomplish?"

"Accomplish? As in running a certain speed in a marathon?"

"Don't be flip. I'm thinking maybe you're having a hard time with Tess because . . . because of your own stuff. And that makes me wonder, you're not . . . not looking up that teacher, are you?"

How crazy does he think I am? "What's it to you?"

"Not a good idea."

"Not your problem."

"I care about you."

"Do you, Rob?"

"Sure."

Hearing his casual tone, her anger rose. "Care, as in cared

when we were married? Cared what I'd been through? No. You dismissed it."

"I never—"

"Not in so many words, but you did, all the time. *Get over it, Marti. Everyone has teenage angst, Marti. No big deal.*" She said the last part in a singsong voice, dancing about the room and waving her arms. The kettle whistled, and she stopped suddenly and made the coffee. Placing the cup in front of Rob, she leaned into his face. "It was a big deal. It affected everything: you, me, our marriage, my relationship with my family. You wouldn't help me, not one bit. You couldn't listen because it made *you* uncomfortable. Yeah, gee, well, sorry it was hard to hear about. I don't know what that's like; I only had to *live* through it."

"I didn't—"

"What you did, Rob, was judge me."

"Never judged you."

Marti turned her back, unable to look at him while she spoke. "Oh no, telling Tess I was cold—*frigid* is the precise word I believe you used."

"I, I was trying to explain to her."

"Justify yourself, that's what you were doing. But you know what? You were right: I was cold and yes, at times, even frigid. Did you ever wonder why? My god, it was awful . . ." Marti felt tears extinguishing her voice, and she didn't want to cry; she needed him to hear her. "I wanted your help. I'd been through . . . a lot."

Rob stood, touched her arm lightly, and turned her body toward him. She kept her arms folded stiffly in front of her, and he put his arms awkwardly around her, lowering her head to his chest. "I'm sorry, Marti. I was young, you know? I couldn't handle it."

Astonishing herself, she melted into him, sobbing.

"I might do better now, but—" He removed his arms and separated from her. "I'm not the person you should come to. I'm married to someone else."

"I know that," Marti retorted, moving away, furious at herself for being so vulnerable. "When I needed you most, you shut me out and went elsewhere to fill *your* needs."

"I don't think you should be dwelling on these things; it's not good for you. Or Tess."

"I'm doing what I need. Just like you did."

"It's not that simple, Marti. Remember our first weeks? We barely knew each other's names, but you—*you* were eager. You *wanted* me. My god, it was glorious! And slowly over time, you told me about that teacher and giving blow jobs hitchhiking. It wasn't easy to hear my wife talk about her prior sex life, but I listened and sympathized, yet the more you confided in me, the more you didn't want me."

"Oh, so the real thing wasn't as good as the preview? Gee, I'm sorry it couldn't be nirvana every time."

"Shut up and listen! I didn't understand what was happening, why you shut me out. I understand more now, but I wasn't psychologically astute back then and I thought, *Those creeps turned her on; why not me?* Do you know what that was like for me?"

"You think they turned me on? You were *jealous*? God, how clueless! It's all about you, isn't it? Fuck you and fuck all of them!" Marti balled her hands into fists and beat them against her own legs.

"No, it was all about *you*. You didn't want a husband. You wanted a goddamn shrink. And now here you are, ready for round two. Hoping to run into that teacher? Is he the only one who turns you on?"

Marti backed away. "How dare you."

"Think I couldn't see it?" Rob said, leaning toward her. "We'd be having sex, you always with your eyes, not just closed but squeezed tight, enduring it. Sometimes I could feel you counting the minutes until I was done. Touch me? No, you couldn't do that. It was like there was a line of demarcation across my waist, police tape ordering: Never go south of that line!"

"How can you—"

"You weren't just a cold fish. You were a dead fish."

"Stop. Oh, god, stop, stop," she moaned.

Rob sat back down, turned his chair away, and slumped forward, his eyes on the ground. The only sounds were Marti's stifled whimpers until he whispered, "I'm sorry," without lifting his head. "We shouldn't be talking about this. You hurt me a lot, and now here I go hurting you back."

"Hurt *you*? You left me."

"I left a sinking ship."

"That's not very noble. The captain's supposed to stay with the ship."

"Captain? *Hardly*. I wasn't anything to you anymore."

Marti turned back around to the counter, shaking. The kids would be back soon. "You told our daughter I was the problem. It was both of us."

"I know that. Look, Tess is very protective of you. I'm her father and don't want her thinking I'm a total shit, the jerk who left her mother. I needed her to see my side. She shouldn't have told you. Sorry it hurt your feelings."

"Hurt my feelings? For Christ's sake, that's not what this is about!" Marti slammed a heavy cookbook down on the counter and faced him. "It wasn't appropriate. You don't discuss your sex life with your child."

"I wasn't really—"

"I've never said a bad word against you. I told her it was both our faults the marriage failed."

"You've been great, but you underestimate Tess and how loyal she is to you. *She* thinks it's my fault. *She* blames me." Marti poured herself coffee and sat down, savoring a sip; she couldn't help but be pleased. "Give her a chance, Marti. I'll talk with her this weekend. You need to recognize she's going to have boyfriends; it doesn't mean they're bad guys. Get to know them a little."

Marti understood this was good advice yet couldn't dispel how terrified she was for Tess, knowing she couldn't share that with Rob as it would only reinforce what he already thought. They sat silently drinking their coffee. Precious jumped up on the table and hissed when Marti pushed her off. "Another thing, Rob, the cat. I don't want her anymore."

"You mean for the summer?"

"No. Forever."

"She's Tess's cat."

"Actually, she's the cat *you* got Tess. Your kids are older now. I don't think the cat can be any more abusive to them than she is to me."

"Tess is with you most of the time. She'll miss the cat."

Marti curled her lips. "Give her a chance, Rob. She's growing up. She'll cope."

He agreed to take the cat after the weekend and then tried returning to the subject of her visit to Chatham. Marti cut him off. "We're not married, Rob. You said I shouldn't look to you for support."

"I didn't mean—"

"Yes, you did." Rob didn't try again. He sat silently, gazing out the window. She knew he considered himself a kind, supportive man who'd tried to help his ex-wife. *Fair enough*, Marti thought, *we all have myths we hold onto.* And she understood his view held a partial truth: she'd spent years covertly ramming her memories down into a deep crevice, stifling any impulse to raise them to the surface. This resurfacing was not her doing; the past carries a life of its own, and she couldn't take credit any more than she could blame Rob.

The kids returned from the lake, and Marti made them lunch. Tess, sensing tension, pretended to concentrate on packing, despite being fully packed, while Rob followed her, acting like a caricature of a stern father, admonishing her to respect her mother.

Nathan sat at the kitchen table fumbling with a plastic superhero, making five-year-old role play chatter. His face was so like Tess's at that age and Marti felt great tenderness for him, as if they were somehow connected by blood. She found herself ruffling his hair, touching him lightly on the shoulder as she placed a sandwich in front of him. It was harder with nine-year-old Adriana; they'd always been guarded with each other, polite and careful, whereas Nathan was uncomplicated, pure innocence in Marti's eyes.

As they were walking out the door, Tess suddenly pulled Marti aside. Marti expected this might be an apology. "I know I'm supposed to babysit Tuesday night, but Mom—"

"What? You're bailing?" Marti fumed at the buildup to a non-apology.

"No. But I saw Peter at the lake and well, uh, Mom, don't get your hopes up." Marti could see Rob intently listening. It was maddening that Tess kept misconstruing her relationship with Peter, and even more infuriating that she'd do so in front of Rob.

"Tess, go already." Marti pushed her out the door.

"When I saw Peter, he was with—"

"Bye, Tess." Marti gave Nathan a last wave and closed the door.

What was Tess trying to say? Peter had a wife? Marti assumed that already. She *told* Tess this. So why did Tess make this announcement? It didn't matter to Marti; it wasn't important, was it?

17

Summer 1972

Her mother was dozing on the couch when Marti came in, and they passed a few inconsequential words about the lateness of the hour before Marti escaped to her bedroom. She craved a shower yet didn't even take her clothes off, crawling under the covers seeking darkness.

In the morning she listened for her mother, not wanting to encounter her on the way to the bathroom. When she heard coffee percolating downstairs she crept into the bathroom, peeled her clothes off, and stuffed them in the hamper, vowing to throw them away later. Full blast, she let the hot water drum hard and steady on her body. She washed her hair twice, scrubbed her skin raw. Eventually the water turned cold, really cold, but the coldness felt like a cleansing. Turning the faucet off, she stared at the drain expecting to see dirt, blood, and guts swishing around and felt an odd disappointment at only seeing suds. She watched as the last bits of water and soap were sucked under, lingering to be sure. She brushed her teeth vigorously, threw the toothbrush away, and swirled cups of mouthwash around her mouth and gargled with it. For a final touch, she swallowed some. The medicinal taste made her gag, and she was glad to feel that slight stinging burn go down her throat.

She took her time dressing, choosing a never-worn flowered blouse her mother gave her last Christmas. It had a Peter Pan collar and little pearl buttons on the front. She folded the sleeves up carefully, the way Jan did, and put on her least-worn pair of jeans, neatly tucking in the shirt. She pulled her hair into a tight bun.

She checked her underwear, hoping for a last-minute reprieve. *I should have let them fuck me.* She carefully folded the pregnancy test slip in her pocket. The phone rang when she was midway down the stairs and she paused, listening. "I'm a little shocked. It's hard to comprehend. I'll talk with Marti." Who could have told? The clinic—had she given them her phone number? Planned Parenthood? She turned in retreat but wasn't fast enough; her mother was at the foot of the stairs, saying, "We need to talk." Marti followed her into the kitchen, slinking down into a seat.

"That was Henry at the stables. Do you have something to tell me?"

"Henry? Oh, I—"

"I know you weren't riding. Where have you been going? Where's that money?"

"I'll get it." Marti dashed off and returned with the bills. Her mother took them, saying the money wasn't the point. Marti tried justifying herself by saying she was scared.

"Nobody said you had to ride again. Frankly, I never thought you would. *You* asked to go. Why lie? It baffles me and yes, makes me angry." She paused, looking at Marti. "Nothing to say?"

Marti shook her head.

Her mother sighed. "I guess maybe you were trying to work up the courage. Anyway, you look nice today; that blouse is pretty on you." She turned away, pouring herself coffee.

Marti felt a certain relief, understanding it was a fleeting feeling. She closed her eyes and waited until the inevitable words finally fell from her mouth. "I'm pregnant."

Her mother swung around, coffee pot in hand. "What did you say?"

"I said I'm pregnant."

Her mother put the pot down and stared. "You've been with a boy?"

Nodding, Marti looked at the spider plant hanging in the window with several baby plants sprouting off it. She noticed the plant was resting in a macramé hanger she made for her mom as a Christmas present. How long had it hung there? She'd assumed her gift had been discarded or stuffed in a drawer.

Her mother poured her coffee; the cup and saucer rattled slightly as she carried them to the table. She sat, gripping her cup tightly. It seemed like a long time before she spoke. "Being with a boy doesn't necessarily make you pregnant. You're scared is what you are. We need to see a doctor."

"I did."

Her mother released her hands from the cup and held them in the air as if to ward off Marti's words. "What doctor? You must be mistaken."

"I'm not mistaken!" Marti's voice was piercing; after carrying this for so long, she wouldn't give her mother time to catch up. "You think I'd be telling you if I wasn't sure? I haven't had my period for over two months!"

"That could be any number of reasons. It could—"

"I had a test at Planned Parenthood." Marti pulled the paper out of her pocket and started opening it. Her mother grabbed it from her hands and held it off at a distance, unfolding it gingerly. After taking a prolonged time reading, she finally put it on the table, turning it over to the blank side. She rested her elbows on it and looked down, propping her head in her hands. Marti shifted in her seat, waiting.

Without looking up, Peg finally spoke. "Who's the boy?"

Marti hesitated.

"I asked—"

"Peter," Marti said in a rush.

"Peter Colgan? I should have known!" She sat up straight and looked at Marti. "How long have you and he—how long? You're just a girl, Jesus, not even fifteen! My god!" She stood up and moved unsteadily toward the sink. She turned the water on, looking down at the sink, and let out a strange, strangling cry.

"Mom . . ." Marti stopped, not knowing what to say. This crying was a sound she didn't recognize.

"Give me a few minutes alone, please. Go to your room." Peg gestured without turning around.

Upstairs, Marti left her door cracked open and listened while her mother called her job. "Water all through my basement . . . sorry for the short notice . . . major leak I need to take care of . . . no, no classes today, just the office hours . . ." Her mother rarely took days off from work, and the lying seemed alien. She made another call but all Marti could hear were muffled voices, and she didn't dare go downstairs. Instead, she lay in her bed, pulling the blanket over her head, clutching Papa Bear.

There was a knock, and her mother carried a tray in and sat on Marti's bed. "I brought you some toast and milk." She pulled on the covers until Marti lowered them, revealing Papa Bear.

"Papa Bear, oh my, you've gotten a lot of use out of him over the years." Peg propped him up next to Marti. "His head sags so. We could fix that."

"I will," Marti said.

Her mother released a sad smile. "It's a sign he's been well loved. Love. Marti, you may think you're in love, but you're too young to have a baby." She spoke gently. "Planned Parenthood told me about a place—"

"I know. In New York." Marti got up and went into her bag and found the crumpled papers, smoothing them before handing them over, feeling a surge of relief. *This is it. Live through this and it's done. Mom will take care of it. We'll never have to speak of it again.* "Here."

Her mother stared at her. "Whoa, you think you have this all figured out? Not so simple, not something to be taken lightly."

Marti started trembling, and her mother took her hand. "Look at me. We'll get through this, I'll arrange it, but . . . well, for one thing, you're not to see Peter anymore. I never should have let you slip back into contact with him, and I won't make—"

"Fine."

"*Fine?* What did having sex mean to you? Is he the only one?"

"Of course!"

"And you don't care if you never see him?"

"No, I understand . . . we shouldn't have . . ." Her voice trailed off.

"Well, I can't understand any of this, Marti," Peg said, shaking her head. She stood to leave. "You stay here now and eat your breakfast."

Marti ate the toast and drank the milk, relieved. There would be no long discussions; they never had those. Her mother was pragmatic, always going for the practical solution quickly. She should have just told her in the first place. Marti snuck downstairs and slipped the stolen ten back into her mother's purse. She heard her mother scheduling an appointment: Monday. Marti counted: *Four days and it's over. Only a memory.*

She sat on the stairs, listening to her mother's next call, her job again. "Can you get a sub for Monday? I'll be in tomorrow . . . yes, plumber's here now . . . but I have a funeral to go to, an aunt I haven't seen in years . . . when it rains, it pours. Sorry to inconvenience the department."

A funeral. Marti leaned her head against the stair railing. *It is in a way. But it's my chance to live.*

Her mother dialed again. "Hi, Betty, it's Mrs. Farrell. Can your mother come to the phone?"

Marti ran into the kitchen. "Mom, no—stop! You can't tell them!"

Her mother cupped her hand over the receiver and pointed to the door.

"No, Mom, no, wait!" She grabbed her mother's arm, wrestling for the phone.

Her mother pushed her off. "Get in your room!"

Marti retreated to the stairs.

"Hi, Connie, I need to meet with you and Richard tonight. It's important. No, can't talk about it over the phone. It's about Marti and Peter. Have Peter there too. Seven o'clock is fine. We'll come to you."

Marti ran into the kitchen. "Please don't. It will kill them."

"And it's not killing me, Marti? Nice to be concerned about someone else at this late juncture."

"It's nothing to do with them. They don't need to know."

"*Nothing to do with them?*" She paused and peered closely at Marti. "Ah. You haven't told Peter."

"I did," she answered, aware that they'd never discussed telling his parents.

"Do you know how much this will cost? I'm not bearing this burden alone."

"I'll pay you back with my allowance. Please, Mom, they're Catholics."

"We're Catholic too. Have you forgotten?"

Marti snorted at this but her mother had already left the room, letting the kitchen door swing behind her until she poked her head back in, saying, "You're coming. You need to take responsibility for your own mess."

Mrs. Colgan gave Marti a quick hug before turning to her mother. "Marti's been wonderful, entertaining the girls this summer. I so appreciate—"

"Peg, come in," Mr. Colgan interrupted, looking apprehensive. He led them to the living room. A pile of folded laundry sat in a basket in the corner. Peter was slumped down in a rocking chair; purple bruises from Mike visible on his face. He was rocking very slowly and didn't look up. Marti's mother sat on one of the worn couches, and Mr. and Mrs. Colgan sat on the other. Marti started toward an armchair on the other side of the room until her mother directed her to sit next to her.

Mr. Colgan began, "Is this about whatever scrape Peter got into yesterday? He hasn't explained it."

"It's not like Peter to get into a fight," Mrs. Colgan added.

Her mother looked at Peter's face and then questioningly at Marti before shaking her head. "I don't know anything about that. I'm here about something else."

"Do Peter and Marti really need to be here?" Mr. Colgan asked.

"Yes, they do." Sounds of laughter came from the den. "But I'm sure you don't want your other children to hear. I didn't think of that; maybe we should go to my house."

"Not necessary." Mr. Colgan had a self-confident manner. When Marti was small, she confused his strength for sternness. Since then she had grown to recognize his kindness. She was counting on that now. He stood up and called into the den, "Betty, come here."

Betty looked curiously around the room. Mrs. Colgan said to Marti's mother, "We're so proud of Betty; she's finished college now and is doing reception work at the church while she applies for social work jobs."

"Congratulations, Betty," Marti's mother responded listlessly.

Mr. Colgan handed Betty money to take the younger ones for ice cream and to the playground. She asked if they wanted some too. Everyone gestured no, except Peter; he was rocking harder now, his elbows resting on the chair arms and his hands cradling his bent head. Walking over, Betty gently nudged him. "Peter? Do you want—"

"That's okay, Betty, just take the little ones," Mr. Colgan commanded.

No one spoke until the door closed and the excited chatter of the children died down. Peg began, "It seems Peter and Marti are more than friends."

"I'm glad they have found friendship again, particularly in light of . . ." Mrs. Colgan twisted her hands on her lap. "We're still so deeply sorry. Not a day goes by I don't think of—"

"*More* than friends, I said. I didn't come here to talk about the accident. No easy way to say this." Peg's voice waned, but she strengthened it. "Peter has gotten my daughter pregnant."

Mrs. Colgan gasped and the sound seemed to echo through the room, followed by a slow rumbling silence.

"Are you certain of this?" Mr. Colgan asked. Marti's mother produced the blood test. Mr. Colgan turned to Peter, asking if this was true. He didn't respond. Marti began trembling and Jan's charm bracelet, still on her wrist, rattled against the wooden sofa arm. Peter looked not at Marti but at the bracelet. "I'm waiting for an answer," his father said.

Without lifting his head, Peter nodded slowly and then stood as if to leave. Mr. Colgan gave him a penetrating look, and Peter sat, closing himself off again. After several minutes, Mr. Colgan spoke slowly. "We'll do the right thing, Peg. Whatever Marti and you think best. They're so young. Maybe adoption would be the better answer?"

"Better for whom?" Peg's voice was sharp and Marti rattled the bracelet louder, competing for noise. Her mother reached over, stilling her hand. "Marti's been through enough. She's faced ridicule because of the burns, and now, going around town pregnant at fourteen? No, no. Too much."

"If you think it's best for her to go away, we'll help with the expenses—"

"No, of course not," Mrs. Colgan interrupted, placing her hand on top of her husband's. "You don't want her going away; they'll marry, when they're of age." Both Peter and Marti contorted into separate looks of astonishment while still managing to avoid eye contact with each other.

Her mother shook her head. "Or," Mrs. Colgan said, sitting up tall, "we could take the baby and raise it as our own."

Peter paused his rocking and looked at his mother. "Ma, no, not—" he began, but stopped as soon as everyone turned to him. He bowed his head, hunching deeper, rocking furiously now.

Mr. Colgan spoke to Peter. "You will accept your responsibility."

"We can do it together," Mrs. Colgan said, laughing nervously. "What's one more for us? And you can be sure"—she looked carefully at Marti's mother—"we'd love him or her as our own. He *is* our own. Peg, you could have as much involvement as you like, and Marti"—she reached out, touching Marti's knee—"it will always be *your* baby. We'd honor that. Goodness, you're already like a daughter to me!" Marti heard her mother subtly scoff. "And when you're older, Marti, if you wish to take the child, we'd accept, respect that."

Marti pictured herself living with the Colgans, everyone cooing over her baby, wrapped snug in a cozy blanket Mrs. Colgan and Marti had knitted together. Her baby, part of her, would belong to the Colgans, and she would belong—why, she already did, didn't she? Mrs. Colgan said *daughter*.

The we of me.

"Constance." Mr. Colgan took his wife's hand, entwining their fingers and closing his eyes.

Peg broke into the quiet, speaking gently but firmly. "Connie, Richard, I don't think you understand. I've—we've already decided what we're doing. An appointment has been made, an appointment for an abortion."

Mr. Colgan spoke. "Abortion? They aren't even legal. Surely you don't mean to put Marti through—"

Peg cut in, "Of course not. They're legal in New York."

The Colgans pleaded with her mother for several minutes,

and Mrs. Colgan began crying, almost like a faint whimper. Peter shuddered in response to the sound. Mr. Colgan looked directly at Marti. His eyes were steady. "Is this what you want, Marti?"

She looked over at the big fireplace, envisioning a warm fire with Colgans cheerfully gathered round, Marti and baby center stage. *Home at last.* However, neither Peter nor her mother figured into this idyllic image, and as she recognized this incongruity, the tableau dissolved into blankness as if conjured by one of Dickens's ghosts to taunt her.

"Yes," she whispered into the void. Then in a stronger voice, "It's what I need to do." This truth turned Marti into stone, numb, dense, impervious to the pain surrounding her.

Mr. Colgan looked at Peter. He nodded his bruised head without looking up.

Peg asked for a check for half the amount and was given one for the full amount. On her way out the door, she added, "There's to be no further contact between our children." It seemed a moot point, as Marti and Peter couldn't even look at each other. Mr. Colgan nodded in agreement, yet her mother continued, "After all, nothing good has ever come of it. Marti's been burned, been impregnated—"

"Enough." Mr. Colgan held up his hand. "Not necessary."

Peg absorbed the strength of his voice, stopped, and sincerely apologized.

In bed that night, Marti laid her hands gently on her belly. If the baby had truly been Peter's, *a Colgan baby*, what would her answer have been? It didn't matter, as it was a sad, desperate lie and that's what she would have birthed: not a baby but a sad, desperate lie. *Not your time, baby. Not mine either.*

The next day, Marti stayed inside until taking a walk in the evening. She heard someone running behind, calling her. It was

Betty. After catching her breath, Betty said, "Ma saw you from the window and sent me to give you this." She held up a set of rosary beads. "To take with you."

Marti stared down at the beads.

"They were my grandma's. Ma wants you to have them. She asked if they could be buried with"—Betty's voice wavered—"the baby . . . whatever they do with the baby—"

Betty stopped. "Oh, Marti, sorry. We're all sorry. Take them to give you comfort. Really, that's all we want." She took Marti's hand and opened it carefully, placing the beads in her palm. "Ma wants you to know you're in her prayers. Always. She thinks only good thoughts for you."

Marti closed her palm tightly around the beads and put her closed fist in her pocket.

18

On the near-silent ride back to the abortion clinic in Troy, Marti peered masochistically at the road, searching for the turnoff the truckers took her down. The roads all looked alike with no telltale signs, which seemed wrong somehow. Wouldn't she know where, surely?

A brief counseling session occurred, first with both Marti and her mother and then with just Marti. She convinced them of her clarity on the matter, not difficult for a stone.

She fingered the rosary beads in her pocket, planning on placing them with *it* when they did whatever they did to *it*. But she had to remove her clothes and put on a gown, and so she clutched the beads one last time before lowering them into a garbage can, the garbage being as close as she could come to fulfilling Mrs. Colgan's wish.

An IV was put in her arm, and it brought the accident whirling back. She assumed they'd immobilize her arm, but they didn't. *Right. I'm not a child anymore. Not by a long shot.* She lay on the table with her feet in stirrups, conscious of a nurse shining a light and a doctor examining her. *I'm a fossil they're excavating. You won't find anything. Spencer and the truckers already gutted me.* Suddenly, it struck her as funny, because it was all so unnecessary: *nothing alive in this hollow shell.*

Staring up at the panels in the ceiling, she noticed water stains in the corners of two of them. She started counting the little holes in each panel, far too many to count, a pointless task, a waste of time, and that was what made it so worthwhile.

She slept the whole car ride home and then got into bed and slept more. Periodically her mother entered her room, bringing food and drink and checking for bleeding. Marti had incredible thirst, just like after the accident, only now she needed no prodding; she drank whatever she was given as if it were the magic elixir of life. Her mother's kindness transformed into impatience after a day or two. Marti could sense her mother holding back from saying: *Snap out of it.* And she understood: Peg wanted it over, just like Marti did, and that couldn't happen until Marti left the bed.

When she finally did, she asked her mother to take her for a haircut. Marti insisted the hairdresser cut off the braids without unraveling them. She looked at them lying on the floor, satisfied that the harness was off, and asked for more hair to be cut. The hairdresser was surprised, as the style all the teenagers wanted was long hair. *Even the boys*, she cackled in an aside to Peg. Marti left with a short bob and bangs. It looked like the haircut she'd had as a child, when her father teasingly called her Buster Brown. Her mother was pleased, and Marti was glad to please her.

She began to reenter the world with her mother monitoring and restricting her activities. She was allowed to go to Brooke's. Her mother dropped her off and picked her up, checking that Peter wasn't there. Her mother's attitude to Brooke had always been mixed; clearly, she didn't approve of her and considered her a bad influence, yet in another way, she admired Brooke's outgoing personality and popularity. To Marti, this admiration translated as disappointment in her own daughter.

Brooke was solicitous of Marti, asking lots of questions about the abortion, treating her with new respect. She offered to pass messages to Peter. "Why not?" Brooke persisted. "Don't let your mom break you up." She convinced Brooke they'd broken up before her mother found out. Believing that Marti was devastated, Brooke offered to drop Peter as a friend. "He was low for ditching you when you needed him."

Brooke's misplaced support reinforced Marti's alienation and she half hoped Brooke would probe for the truth, yet Brooke believed the story. Marti felt a shift between them: Brooke was now the naïve one.

The summer passed with visits to Brooke, trips to the lake, and more comic books. She'd longingly watch Marybeth and Nancy playing out front. Sometimes they'd give Marti a tentative half wave; evidently they knew not to approach her. Marti didn't just want to play with them; she wanted to *be* them.

Jan came home and Marti braced for a lecture. Instead Jan said she was sorry.

"Sorry?"

"Because I wasn't here for you and you didn't feel close enough to write and tell me what was going on." Contemplating Jan's misplaced guilt only made Marti feel worse, and she couldn't burden Jan now.

She expected her mother to discuss birth control with her, but it was Jan who took her to Planned Parenthood where Marti was fitted for a new diaphragm. Afterward they went out for lunch. Jan gave Marti a copy of *Our Bodies, Ourselves*. "I already read yours," Marti said, grinning, and they both laughed, a rare bit of levity.

Jan asked Marti if she missed Peter. Marti didn't answer. "I'm sure you do. I know first love can hurt, but you were too young. Mom's right. You shouldn't see each other. There can't be much left after the abortion, anyway. Someday you'll be older and ready for a boyfriend. Just wait."

Marti dreaded returning to school in September and was hoping that Spencer wouldn't return. He did. She decided she'd ask for a change from art to music, but it wasn't necessary. Because of the popularity of Spencer's class, they'd added a second art teacher. The new teacher wasn't really an art teacher; she'd been a sub for all subjects. No one wanted to be in her class. Spencer handpicked his students, and the other class consisted of Spencer's rejects, including Marti.

Brooke was shocked. "I can't believe it, Marti. You were the best in the class. Brandon says a mistake must have happened. Surely, Spencer wanted you—"

"Never mind," Marti said. "I'm happy where I am." She was finding it easy to avoid Spencer, as he averted his eyes every time they passed in the hall. The rumor was that he was dating a new teacher, Miss Markus, Marti's English teacher. Miss Markus seemed easily swayed by students, too eager to be liked. Or maybe it was Marti, seeing everything with a new cynical eye. *He would go for a weak one. That's what I was.*

Her friends continued going to Spencer's room after school; Brooke assumed Marti wasn't going because of Peter. Once she invited Marti and turned to Peter, dismissing him in front of a large group. Peter's face turned red and he left. "Come now?" Brooke beamed at Marti.

"You shouldn't have. It isn't Peter."

"Marti," Brandon said, "Spencer's been telling us all about Morocco, the people he met and the insights he attained from the hash he smoked."

"Sometimes," Trey added, "Miss Markus stops by. She's your English teacher, right? She's cool."

Marti kept her tone nonchalant, explaining she had to go home. "Your mom's a drag," Brooke said, and Marti let it go at that.

After a while people stopped asking, and Brooke's group of friends shifted after she replaced Brandon with a new boyfriend, a senior named Keith, while Trey continued doggedly tagging behind Brooke. There were a couple of new girls in the group.

My replacements, Marti thought, acutely aware of how isolated she was becoming. Of course, that was a familiar feeling. *Home again.*

She wondered how Peter, knowing what he knew, could still be one of Spencer's admirers, yet Peter seemed happier than ever. He walked with a confident swagger, and all of a sudden he had a girlfriend, Laurie, a freshman. They walked through the school with their arms wrapped around each other. Marti felt betrayed; she knew she wasn't entitled to this feeling, but other people didn't know, and Marti had to endure their sympathetic looks.

Every year at Chatham High they put on a play. None of Brooke's crowd was interested, and Marti thought this might be a chance to find new friends. She signed up to do scenic design and build sets with the shop teacher, Mr. Powell, a much-beloved, grandfatherly teacher. Girls weren't allowed to take shop (they had to take home economics), and so this created an opportunity to learn from Mr. Powell.

The play was *West Side Story*. Mr. Powell came to each classroom, telling the students to read the play and envision what the sets should be. Marti pictured a background of stacked wooden boxes representing apartment windows, a different scene in each window showing life in the city. She thought the dress shop would be fun to do with colorful fabrics draped across rods, and as Maria sang "I Feel Pretty" she'd throw on fabrics and dance, a whirl of color.

Her mother eagerly approved, saying it was perfect for Marti and expressing relief that Marti was getting on with things.

Interested students gathered in the auditorium while the drama teacher introduced each teacher and group. When it came time for set design, she said, "You might have noticed this play needs a lot of sets. I'm pleased to announce that in addition to Mr. Powell, we'll have the skills of our art teacher, Mr. Douglas."

Spencer walked on stage to loud cheers and waited for the auditorium to quiet down before speaking. "This play's been done many times and usually people design elaborate sets of a cityscape, but my students and I have been talking about the themes of the play: characters trapped in constricted lives, stifled by the prejudices of the crowded city. We think the most compelling set should be stark black fabric enveloping the stage. I'm sure there are many seamstresses out there who can help."

Marti left as soon as they broke into groups.

One day on the school lawn, Denise approached her. "Can I talk to you?" Marti was surprised as they didn't really know one another, yet she was pleased, thinking maybe this was a chance for a new friendship. Denise asked Marti where to get birth control.

"Me? Why ask me?"

"Because you know. After all, you, you and Peter . . ." Marti stepped back, looking around. Students were sitting on benches eating lunch, and Bobby was on the grass strumming a guitar, a crowd around him. Denise leaned toward Marti. "You were having sex."

Marti shook her head and stood straight. "We've been neighbors and friends since we were babies, cousins almost." She feigned a laugh. "The idea of us as boyfriend and girlfriend—"

"Come off it, Marti, I know about the abortion. Everybody does. Fine, don't help. But quit the virgin act."

"Who—" Marti paused, stunned. Denise started walking away; Marti caught sight of Brooke dancing to Bobbie's guitar, all the eyes on Brooke as she reached her hand out inviting Laurie, Peter's girlfriend. The two of them laughed as they whipped their long skirts at each other. Realizing then, Marti called out to Denise's retreating back, "Go ask Brooke. She's told you everything else."

Brooke was the one friend she thought she had. Now it was clear Brooke considered Marti just another someone to blather about. She wondered whether Peter had heard the gossip and thought to warn him, knowing how upset his Catholic family would be. Spotting him alone in the hall, she approached him, "People know about the abortion. Brooke must have told. I'm sorry." He looked away. *Embarrassed to be seen with me.*

"Uh, yeah. Well, sorry too," he mumbled. At that moment Laurie walked over, looking apprehensive. "Oh good, I've been waiting for you." He put his arm around Laurie, and they sauntered off.

Marti became aware of boys checking out her body and jeering, just like elementary school all over again. She couldn't concentrate, and her grades were plummeting.

Her biology teacher, Mr. Logan, spoke to her after class, asking if she knew she was failing. She simply nodded. "You know this class is a requirement. I have peer tutoring sessions after school; why don't you come and let the seniors help you?" With no ability to concentrate, she knew this was useless, yet she dutifully went, dreading each session. It was as if they were speaking a foreign language. The benevolent students tried, and this made Marti wish she'd made a different choice in friends at the very start. *Too late now.* The thought of three more years of high school was intolerable, and college—what would that be like? *Full of girls like Brooke, teachers like Spencer.*

Angry as she was, Marti didn't confront Brooke. She was the stray puppy starved for any crumbs that Brooke might deign to drop, loathing herself for this. And so she eagerly answered the door when Brooke came to visit. Brooke said she had something important to tell her.

They went and sat on Marti's bed; Marti waited anxiously for Brooke to finish rolling her cigarette. Was Brooke going to confess to talking about the abortion? Or had she guessed about Spencer? Brooke took a few deep drags before speaking.

"I'm leaving. Can't take my parents anymore." She flicked her ashes onto the floor before continuing. "Actually, never mind my parents. Remember Penny from the health food store?" She knew Brooke was still hanging out at the store. Marti didn't; she was embarrassed by the talk of healthy food since she mostly ate the fish sticks and Kraft Macaroni and Cheese her mother made for dinner, and when home alone, she'd open a can of Spaghetti O's.

"She told me about a commune in Canada full of lots of cool people. Penny understands why I need to leave, and she's arranging for me to go there." Brooke never complained to Marti about her parents. Marti thought about the drinking, the groping, and the absent, never-to-be-mentioned siblings. What was that like for Brooke? What could she confide in Penny that she couldn't tell Marti?

Brooke hugged a pillow to her chest. "I'm leaving in two weeks." Marti asked about Keith. "Aw, Marti, you should know—look at you and Peter—relationships are bullshit, meaningless." Did she want Marti to change her mind or encourage her? Neither response was what Marti felt, only sorrow at the trap both their lives were.

Marti continued going to tutoring where students earnestly taught, yet she wasn't learning. Mr. Logan spoke to her at the end of one session. "I appreciate that you're coming, but here's your latest test." He handed Marti a paper, thirty percent. "How are you doing in your other classes?" She looked down without answering and he resumed, "That's what I thought. Marti, you're a bright girl. Something's wrong here, and I won't presume to know what. Have you ever spoken to Mrs. Reade, the guidance counselor?" She shook her head. "Nothing to be afraid of; she's easy to talk with. I'll call your mother, and we can all have a conversation. Your mother needs to know you're failing. With grades like this, you'll have to repeat tenth grade, and you're too smart for that. Give Mrs. Reade a chance."

Her mother had no idea how badly Marti was doing in school. When Marti attended tutoring, her mother thought she was working on the play. Marti walked slowly down the hall, trying to think of a way out. Walking past the mural wall, she turned her head to avoid it and glimpsed Spencer and Denise in the far corner, Denise leaning against the wall, one leg propped up behind her. Spencer loomed over her with his face obscured by his hair hanging down. He twirled a lock of Denise's hair, intertwining it with his. They separated at the sound of Marti's footsteps, and she hurried from the building.

Later, she was angry at her cowardice. She should have let them see her; she wasn't the guilty one. A wave of nausea hit her as she remembered both Denise's request and Spencer's nickname: Desirée.

The next day after French class, she waited for Denise. Marti was taken aback by the hostility visible on Denise's face. She spoke anyway. "I saw you outside Spencer's room. Don't make the same mistake I made."

Denise laughed. "What would that be? Are we talking about losing your boyfriend and your friends? Or maybe we're talking about getting pregnant?" Denise was loud; students passing by glanced over, listening.

Marti spoke quietly. "I know what's going on because it happened to me."

"What are you talking about?"

"Spencer."

"Yes, Spencer admires my artwork. Are you jealous that you're not in his class?"

"You asked me about birth control."

Denise shifted her books, looking away. "I'm seeing a boy from a different town."

Now Marti was the one to laugh, a bitter laugh of recognition. "Oh, Denise, that's the same story I told. I understand—"

"You're pathetic with your dirty mind! Spencer's helping me with my art because he sees promise in me, which galls you because he didn't see that in you. You want me to think he was *with* you? Probably you deliberately got pregnant by Peter so Spencer would think you're easy and give you a whirl. Now even Peter's moved on. We all saw you swooning over Spencer. That's why he didn't want you in his class. I feel sorry for you, Marti, I really do."

"No," Marti whispered, "don't feel sorry for me. It's over. But you—it's just the beginning. Don't do it." Denise was already walking away.

Leaving school, she bumped into Peter and Laurie, giggling away; they didn't even acknowledge Marti.

Her mother was pleased to be home early enough to make a nice dinner, and she roasted a chicken. Marti watched uneasily as her mother cut the meat off the headless carcass. Half-carved, it lay on the table, a ruined thing. Her mother chatted while they ate, not noticing Marti moving the food around her plate and covertly spitting the meat into her napkin.

That night Marti dreamed of a female body floating in space, its lower torso a chicken carcass, absent wings and legs. Pulled bits of meat created a tufted pattern much like pubic hair. The bottom opening was a huge gaping hole, jagged edges leading to a hollow cavern. It reminded her of something you might stumble across in the wilderness or find on the side of a highway, something so ravaged it was almost unrecognizable.

Getting out of bed, Marti quickly sketched this naked woman, making the carcass an exaggerated rendition of her pubic area while everything else about her body was perfectly proportioned and ordinary, though her eyes held a disquieting vacant look.

She continued perfecting it for several days until she was fully satisfied and then handed it in for an art assignment. The teacher returned it with red writing scrawled across it: *Unacceptable. Do not hand in disgusting, filthy things in MY class.* She knew what the emphasized *MY* meant, and this was ironically fitting: Spencer's impact had led Marti here. She took the sketch home, lit it with a match, and held it until the fire singed her finger. She dropped it in the kitchen sink and watched it burn until it dissolved into bare slivers of ash. She turned the faucet on, waiting until the water sucked it all away.

Not wanting to encounter Denise, she'd begun skipping French class. She received more failing tests. Report cards and parent-teacher conferences were next week, and she was sure Mr. Logan would discuss counseling with her mother.

Brooke came by and Marti started talking about flunking, but Brooke, with a faraway look on her face, wasn't really listening. She interrupted, "Next Tuesday, I'm leaving, supposedly for school as usual, my book bag full of stuff I'm taking to the commune. Penny has a friend who will drive me there. It's on the outskirts of Montreal, but they're mostly Americans. Some of the guys are draft dodgers. They earn a living farming and making crafts, leather stuff, pottery—"

"Can I come?" Marti surprised herself with the question but latched onto this as soon as she said it, a solution.

"God, I can't believe you're asking! Maybe I can get in touch later and you can visit—"

"Not visit. Live there."

"Don't be crazy because you're flunking."

"Same as you, I need to leave."

Brooke walked around Marti's room, looking at the shelves. She randomly picked up one of Marti's miniature creations, a lamp, the base of it made from an empty wooden thread spool with an unbent paper clip running up the center, propping up a thimble as a lampshade. "I always loved these so much, you know? That's why I wanted to be your friend." She beamed at Marti but couldn't hide the melancholy underneath. She put the lamp down and began fidgeting with members of the forest family. "What were their names? Oh I remember some. Twig and Acorn, is that right?" Marti nodded. "I could be . . . Hey, I don't need a different name. Brooke would fit right in, wouldn't she? I just need to drop the stupid pretentious *e*. We could live together happily with the forest family. Maybe the commune will be like that." Her tone was doubtful. "You could be Stream. Remember when Spencer called you that? Better than Martha Washington—never did get that one—Betsy Ross, more like it with your talents. I'm gonna take my tie skirt with me and lots of clothes you sewed. To remember.

"Ah, Marti, you don't have to leave. You're smart and talented. God, how I've admired that! You have other choices."

Marti shook her head. "I don't."

"I didn't know you took the breakup with Peter that hard. If you come, there's no turning back, no changing your mind. It would get Penny in trouble."

"I'm not coming back, not ever."

"Why—"

Marti shook her head resolutely.

"Okay, okay, I don't get it, but I'll ask Penny."

Over the next few days, Marti vacillated between hoping the answer was yes and hoping for no. If she left, she would never have to face her failing grades, her mother, people at school, the Colgans or Spencer.

And yet: What was she going toward? She felt queasy, as if it were out of her control. If she stayed, she'd keep failing and her mother would find out. Counseling? Keeping the secret was so hard. Could counseling be a release? But what would her mother do? Go to school and tell the principal? Demand Spencer be fired? She'd tell the Colgans and they'd know Marti tortured them with a lie.

She went to the health food store, intending to talk to Penny herself, yet upon spying her in the window, she lost her nerve and ducked next door into the Country General Store, a favorite childhood destination. The store was crowded with tourists, foliage season being at peak. She fiddled with boxes of maple candies, remembering how she'd always had a hard time choosing which one to buy. Now she had plenty of money in her pocket—weeks' worth of unspent allowance, as she'd lost the desire to buy records or clothes, the trimmings of a discarded life. Did she want the big maple leaf or the box with tiny leaves or the old-fashioned girl or boy? She got them all.

At home, she looked carefully at the maple boy and girl, excited to see the girl holding something. Was it a violin or some other clue to a hidden talent? Peering closer, Marti was disappointed to see a purse. What would an old-fashioned farm girl carry in a purse? They were working too hard to waste time impressing someone with patchouli oil. *Maybe it's for rosary beads.* She noticed then that the girl had a demure expression on her face and her body was constricted, whereas the boy was grinning confidently, his hands jauntily holding his coat lapels while his legs were kicking.

Pressed into their boxes, lying flat on the table, they looked encased in coffins, coffins with see-through lids—see-through, so they wouldn't miss anything in death. Marti slid them out of the coffins and walked them across the table, zombie style. When she was little, she used to have them bow to each other and dance, picturing the girl's long skirt twirling around. She'd always been deliberate about which part to eat first, nibbling their shoes and hats, the outside of their clothes, saving their smiling faces for last. Today she ate the boy's head first, devouring it in one gulp of oozing sweetness. She took the girl and sliced her in half the long way, rearranging her. What if half of her body faced backward or was upside down? She tried to put the girl back together the right way, but she was melting in Marti's hands. She ate the girl, startled at how quickly she melted into nothing. She got up and put the other candy boxes in her room. Returning to the kitchen, she drank a glass of water, purging the sticky sugar taste from her mouth. She noticed the headless man lying forgotten on the table and scooped him into the garbage.

Brooke gave her the news that she'd been okayed to come. "They'll meet us at Dunkin' Donuts tomorrow, nine a.m. sharp." Marti had an impulse to say, *I've changed my mind*, but she felt propelled forward, a kind of fate.

She packed her clothes and the two boxes of maple leaf candy; they might be the only treats she'd have for a while. Brooke said to destroy any recent photos of herself so cops couldn't use them for identification. Looking through family albums, Marti found her school picture from the beginning of last year, hair falling on her face, head cocked at an unnatural angle, nervous smile as if anticipating something unfathomable. She ripped it up. There was a picture of Marti, Jan, and her mother standing in front of the house, springtime with rhododendrons blooming behind them. Taken before the accident—the family pictures dwindled after that—Marti was smiling, unscarred and unafraid. Was she never seeing her family again? Was she vanishing? She tucked the picture into her knapsack.

That evening Peg suggested they play a game of cards. "We can play Spit, your favorite because you always win." Marti wanted to be just an ordinary girl playing cards with her mother, having an ordinary evening. She wanted that mood to last and last, and so she made deliberate mistakes, slowing the game from reaching its conclusion. Finally, Peg won.

"I should be glad, but it isn't like you. Are you feeling all right?"

Marti stifled an impulse. "I'm fine. Can we play again?"

"Again? But you hardly even tried. Something's wrong, I can tell. Sometimes, Marti, I feel I've been too busy with grad school and work and if I'd been paying more attention, well, what happened last year wouldn't have happened. You needed more guidance. I'm sorry. Sorry I let you down."

"You didn't, Mom."

"Anyway, I'll be graduating in a few months and we'll have more time together. Just think, you and Jan can come watch your old mom in a cap and gown! That'll be a sight, eh? And before you know it, Jan will graduate college and you high school. It all goes so fast.

"Not another game tonight, but how about some warm milk before bed? I wish I had a little treat to go with."

"Hold on." Marti ran into her room and returned with the box of little candy maple leaves.

"How sweet!"

Marti ate a small maple leaf and sipped the warm milk. This combination reminded her of when they'd bring buckets of fresh snow into the Colgan kitchen and Mrs. Colgan would scoop the snow into smaller bowls, adding a dollop of hot maple syrup on top and giving them each a mug of warm milk to wash it down. As the taste seeped its way into Marti's senses, she felt a wave of sorrowful longing. *Graduating high school? I'd rather be six years old.*

Peg scrutinized her with a worried look. "Maybe you're worn out from working on *West Side Story*." She squeezed Marti's arm. "I can't wait to see your sets! You know what? I won't wake you in the morning until just before I go. Let you sleep a little longer, catch a few extra winks."

She wasn't asleep when her mother woke her but pretended, waiting to rise until the house was empty. She found a note in the kitchen: *Have a good day. Here's a little money for a snack after school.* Marti carefully tucked both the note and money in her pocket. Brooke had said to sneak all the money she could, but

Marti wouldn't steal from her mother again; she had what she had. She reached into her knapsack and took out the large maple leaf, placing it where the note had been.

Backpack on her shoulder, she took a last look around the familiar house. It was approaching nine. She spotted the little red rocker from her bedroom, resting in a corner, seeming forlorn and abandoned. How odd of her unsentimental mother to keep a childhood relic after Marti had discarded it. She put her bag down, ran upstairs, and retrieved Papa Bear and placed him in the red chair.

She again swung her knapsack on her shoulder and turned to leave, noticing then Papa Bear's head sagging from its own weight. She regretted all the times she promised she'd fix him. She ran back upstairs for her sewing kit. Sitting on the living room floor, she cut a small opening in his neck and stuffed cotton balls into his head. Carefully, she sewed him back together. Now Papa Bear sat perky in his red rocking chair. Satisfied, she was enjoying the sight of a revived Papa Bear.

Glancing at her watch, she realized she'd lost track of time. She'd need to hurry as it was after nine and Dunkin' Donuts was twelve blocks away. She lingered no longer.

Part IV

BONE

19

S itting at the table, Marti played with the remains of the kids' sandwiches, stacking the rejected crusts like Lincoln Logs, turning them up to make a teepee and waiting for them to fall. She drank her barely sipped coffee, cold now. Rob's cup was drained and his banana bread eaten. *Of course he'd gotten what he needed.* Filling the sink with soapy water, she lowered the dishes in, watching them bob, a brief respite before surrendering. Rob's words were echoing in her head: *I left a sinking ship.*

At least—at last—she'd had her say. Yet she didn't feel triumphant. Even being free of the cat felt like a hollow victory. And there was Tess, always pushing buttons, pushing and pushing. Obviously, she'd seen Peter with his wife. What of it? Tess was acting as if Marti had some schoolgirl crush, and in front of Rob for further humiliation. Peter's marriage was irrelevant; she'd assumed he was married. Wondering where his wife was didn't mean it *mattered* to her, did it? What she wanted from Peter was something else entirely, wasn't it?

She tried concentrating on the soothing feel of the warm soapy water in an effort to quell her nagging, troubling thoughts. She'd rearranged her summer to see Mrs. Colgan, and now that focus was channeled into Peter. If she wanted to rehash the past, couldn't she have saved all this trouble and just gone to a therapist in New York?

She worked on a new sketch for her mosaic, trying to capture a moment, one solitary, fleeting play of light in the sky. She soon gave up, realizing the absurdity: if Marti were looking at the perfect sky, she'd miss it. All the disquiet churning in her head prevented her from experiencing such a moment. How could she focus on something beautiful when an ugly past loomed over her? Instead, she started cutting tiles into smaller and smaller pieces, finding comfort in the sharp sound and the feel of the jagged edges, the wrenching separation. *No wonder I'm doing mosaics. I understand brokenness. I seek it in my job, my art. Can something good come from the wreckage?*

Tess's words kept orbiting. She abruptly headed for the beach, hoping Peter was still there. A Saturday, it was crowded with kids zooming around while parents chatted together. She scanned the children building sandcastles near the water. No Pearl or Ned, they must have left. Should she go to Peter's house? It would be bold, as he'd said he was busy until Tuesday. Defeated, she turned to leave when she caught a glimpse of Pearl on a swing, pushed by a man other than Peter. Was it one of his brothers? Richie? Tom? No, the man was tall, broad, and dark, nothing like the slight, fair-haired Colgans. Marti noticed Peter waiting at the bottom of a slide for Ned. She took a deep breath and was heading that way when Pearl spotted her.

"Papa, I want to get off. Stop the swing—that's Marti! Remember, I told you about her?" Peter walked over, tentatively muttering hello while keeping his head down. Pearl ran, trailed by the man she called Papa; what Tess meant was dawning on Marti.

"Marti," Peter said, awkwardly shuffling back and forth, "I'd like you to meet Roger, my partner." Roger held out his hand, and Marti shook it a little too heartily. He had a firm handshake, but it wasn't necessarily friendly. She felt his eyes assessing her. Did he think she was interested in Peter? Did Peter? Was she? She looked from one to the other, reading nervousness on Peter's hunched back and suspicion on Roger's face.

"Nice to meet you." She tried for a dazzling smile.

Roger nodded in response. *He's not glad to meet me.* Roger looked older than Peter, with graying hair and a weathered face. The overwhelming impression he gave was of strength: his jaw jutted out, and his nose was unapologetically large. He reminded her of Peter's father. Was there a similar kindness underneath? She wasn't sure.

"Hi, Pearl, Ned. Tess told me you were here. You must be having fun, been here a long time." Again, she smiled at Roger. "You have lovely kids."

"Thanks, and you're right. We've been here quite a while. Guys, come pack up your stuff. Time to go."

"Aw . . ." Ned looked at Peter, but Roger firmly propelled both children forward. The kids said goodbye to Marti, while Roger didn't even glance back at her.

Peter started following until Marti pulled his arm. "Wait. I want to talk to you." He looked down at the sand. *He looks like a dog that peed on the rug. Like he looked in the months after my accident. Why?* Seeing this, she could only say, "I want to be sure we're on for dinner."

"If you want."

She noticed Roger scrutinizing them. "Of course! See you then." She waved cheerily at Roger.

He didn't wave back.

She thought about this encounter the rest of the evening. Peter had endured so much for her. Was that why he was distant and why Roger was suspicious? Peter wasn't in the closet. He had children with Roger. Why hide this from her? Sure, they hadn't seen each other in years, but didn't he know her well enough? And why would he care about her reaction? But no, they'd been kids—he wouldn't know her reaction, and she felt regretful thinking of how they could have supported each other over the years. What baffled Marti most was that *it did matter.* She felt deceived and couldn't understand why. She remembered those buttons people wore in the seventies: *Don't presume I'm heterosexual.* She usually didn't make that mistake; nonetheless, she had. Was it because she was interested in him? Or was it something else? A glimmer of something kept gnawing in the back of her mind. *He hid it from me.*

She tried again, fruitlessly, to work on her mosaic, finally deciding to abandon the project altogether. She read the week's newspapers, engrossing herself in articles about a rapist on the loose in Vermont, a white male in his early twenties. He'd already raped three women. He could have years of raping ahead if he wasn't caught. The first two victims hadn't gotten much attention, one was a drug addict and one a stripper. But now, the third was a college student at Middlebury; she'd been followed home from the library. It was front-page news.

The greater attention the college student received angered Marti, as if it were okay for a drug addict and a stripper to be assaulted. The newspaper coverage was rape of another kind. Marti focused on several quotes in the paper.

The first woman said: *I didn't come forward because who wants to believe a drug addict? I probably deserved it.*

The stripper was giving lots of interviews. *Use my name. Why not? Why should the raped have no name? I have a name. Even if I'm a stripper, I am someone. Stripping is a job, not a license to rape.*

The college student wasn't talking, but her mother said: *I can't believe this happened to her. She's such a good girl.*

Marti ripped the articles out of the paper and found herself cutting the quotes into careful strips, rearranging the order of them:

I am someone.
Even if I am a stripper.
She's such a good girl.

I have a name.
Why should the raped have no name?
I probably deserved it.
She's such a good girl.
I didn't come forward.
I probably deserved it.
Use my name.
Stripping is a job, not a license to rape.
Why should the raped have no name?

It was early when she rang the doorbell, not caring if she woke them. More awake than she'd felt in a long time, the glimmer was now a glaring headlight illuminating some of the murky past.

Peter stood reluctantly at the door. "Let me in," Marti said, pushing past him into the living room. The room was remarkably unchanged since that miserable evening thirty years ago, except for piles of Mrs. Colgan's clothes lying on the sofa, dresses from a bygone era waiting expectantly on their hangers.

"Roger home?" She could hear TV coming from the den.

"No, he left for Boston early. He has a big case."

"A case?"

"He's a lawyer."

"Funny, I didn't know that. Or anything."

"Marti, look, I was in the middle of—"

"Roger wasn't eager to meet me."

"It's just, well, he's protective of me."

"You need protection from me?"

"No, it's . . ." Peter fidgeted with his hands and eventually mumbled, "complicated."

"How so?" Marti sat in the rocking chair and raised her arms, fanning them behind her head, keeping her head high while her eyes focused on Peter. "Do you think I never saw a gay person before?"

"It's not that."

"Right. It isn't that." Marti rocked the chair. "But it changes the past, doesn't it? For me, anyway. All this time I've felt grateful, overcome with guilt concerning you, your family, and what I put you through. After the abortion, I could barely look at you, the remorse eating away at me." Peter turned away. "Like you feel now." Marti stood and grabbed his arm. "Sit down. You can't avoid me. You're the reason I'm in this fucking town!" She shouted this last part before plopping down hard into the rocker.

Peter sat next to his mother's clothes on the couch. "What? Marti, I'm sorry if—"

"Oh, don't be an ass. It's not for your body." She laughed and crossed her legs, swinging the top leg up and down. "Your parents, I hadn't anticipated my mother telling them. I'm here this summer because I wanted to apologize to your mother. What she must've thought of me once you told her."

"Ma never thought badly of you."

"Well, she's extraordinary that way. Was, I mean." Marti shook her head before continuing. "I didn't expect her to absolve me; I just wanted her to know I regret the pain I caused."

They sat silently until Peter moved to speak, but Marti cut him off. "And I thought, *If I can't tell Mrs. Colgan, I'll tell Peter.*" She leaned forward, looking solidly at him. "Tell you how sorry I am for hurting you and your family, for exploiting you."

"Exploiting me?"

"That's it!" Marti slapped her knee. "We both exploited each other! I thought you helped me because of your guilt about the accident, and I felt like shit for using that."

"I did feel guilty. Still do."

"There's more, though, isn't there? That's why you can't look at me."

Peter stared down at his hands. "The accident, it's always there."

Marti's leg began swinging again, an angry movement that caused Peter to stop speaking. "I was your beard."

"You could say that, but I didn't fully comprehend it at the time."

"Well, neither did I! And even now, you *still* don't want me to connect the dots. That's why Roger and your life was a big fucking mystery." She quieted her leg, concentrating on clarifying her thoughts. "You sat in this chair, Peter, the night my mother told your parents. Rocking and rocking."

He picked up a baby-blue sweater from the clothes pile, crocheted with a lacy shell pattern. He poked his fingers through the holes. "I remember every detail of that night, who sat where, who said what. You kept clanging your bracelet against the couch arm each time your mom spoke, and she'd place her hand on the bracelet to silence it—or you."

"Really?" Marti shook her head. "Wow, that detail I don't remember." She paused before speaking again. "God, Peter, your mother wanting to adopt our baby"—she whispered the last part—"was awful."

Peter suddenly stopped fidgeting with the sweater and cradled it in his arms. Neither spoke for a moment.

"Must be so hard, going through her things. She had a stroke, correct?"

Peter motioned to the staircase. "She was carrying laundry down the stairs. We'd been here the weekend before, Nancy and me with our kids. Nancy started to strip the beds; she was going to wash the sheets before we left, but Ma said no, we had more important things to do, take care of our children and get them home. Besides, it would give her something to keep busy with after we were gone." Peter's voice faltered; he cleared his throat before continuing. "She fell down the stairs. We don't know which happened first, the fall or the stroke. Either way, she couldn't move. The next morning, she didn't show up for Mass. Usually after Mass she went with her friend Maureen to visit shut-ins. You know, old people . . ." Marti nodded. "Ironic, isn't it? They should have been visiting her. Maureen called Ann; she lives closest. Ann found her with the laundry basket tucked under her body. We try to think Ma didn't lie there and suffer, but you can't be sure, can you?"

After a few moments, Marti stood and looked at the clothes. "She had such old-fashioned dresses. Even back then they were old-fashioned. She never wore pants, did she?"

"Sometimes, in later years."

Sifting through the dresses, she said, "They're beautiful. Simple and understated, like her." She smiled at Peter.

"You could take some if you wanted. My sisters already took what they wanted, and I took a few. Not for me, don't worry, I won't be doing a Norman Bates masquerading in my mother's clothes. They're for the twins, if they want them someday. I, I hope they remember her."

"I remember my father, and I was around their age."

"You do? I don't. My older siblings told me he was a fun guy, always doing tricks."

Marti felt that burning hunger, an insatiability that materialized whenever someone provided new knowledge of her father. "I remember Daddy vaguely yet strongly, if that makes sense, like an impressionist painting. Pearl and Ned will have that; she'll be a positive force for them."

Peter nodded, gesturing to the clothes again. "These are what's left to be donated."

"I couldn't take . . . not after . . . Please tell me you told your parents the truth."

Peter stood up abruptly. "I don't want to go into that." He shook his head wearily. "Marti, what do you want from me?"

"I need you."

He stepped back.

"Stop. Already told you, I'm not interested in you that way. I was taken aback to learn you're gay because it sheds a new light on our past. And I'm still digesting what that means.

"I need to deal with what happened to me; I never really have. Instead, I've tried hiding it, stuffing it down, and it hasn't worked. Thirty fucking years later, it isn't working. Impossible to bury it deep enough."

"I can understand that." Peter sat down. "But what does it have to do with me?"

Ned ran in the room, oblivious to Marti's presence. "Daddy, Pearl says we can't watch another show." He flung himself onto Peter's lap. "But I want to."

"Hi, Ned," Marti said.

Caught off guard, he didn't leave his father's lap. Pearl came into the room. "Daddy, I told him—" Upon seeing Marti, she let out a squeal and hugged her. "You've come to play with us!" It wasn't a question; Marti admired this confidence—how different her childhood could have been with a dose of this.

"I was just leaving, but I'm glad to see you, Pearl, Ned. We'll play another time." She smiled at them. "Peter, see you Tuesday?"

He nodded. As she walked to her car, she saw the front door open a crack before firmly closing.

After leaving Peter's she stopped at the art store, walking up and down the aisles filling her cart with various materials—canvas boards, paint, another larger mosaic board, more tiles, fabric to embroider on, embroidery threads, yarn, and glue. As she was going through the last aisle, Anna came over. "Wow. That's a lot of materials. You embroider also?"

Marti nodded and laughed. "At least I hope I remember."

"I'm sure it'll come back to you. You're doing amazing with the mosaics. What are you going to make?"

"I've no idea," Marti said, reaching for a spool of lace.

After placing the purchases in her trunk, she went across the street and bought the day's newspapers. There were more articles about the rapes.

Intimidated by the overflowing bags, she left the art supplies in the car but brought the newspapers in. A police detective was talking about the rapes: *I'm not even sure if you could call it rape, what happened to the stripper. Kind of a gray area.* In another section, the stripper responded: *Nothing gray about it.*

Marti carefully cut out the articles, letting the rest of the newspaper fall to the floor. She added these quotes to her pile, ignoring the scattered papers.

20

The next morning, the phone rang, startling Marti. It was Marisol, her friend from work. "Sorry to bother you. I know you're busy with your aunt. How is she?" It no longer seemed an easy lie. "Well, I left you a message yesterday, so I know you want to know why I called. It's bad news. Jeremy died. His little heart finally gave out." Marti listened to the details: *in his sleep, painless, inevitable.* After hanging up, she cried for the boy she'd known, funny, cheerful—*living,* despite his odds. How did people do that?

She wrote a letter to the family. She'd had lots of experience with these letters. The important thing was to tell them stories of their child, as they'd want to know he'd be remembered. It was easy with Jeremy, and she promised to send artwork he'd done upon her return.

Return. This made her think: time was running out. Would she have gotten what she wanted out of this trip? What *did* she want?

Impulsively, she drove to the high school. People were going in and out, as summer school was in session. She sat in her car, staring at the building. She thought about the mural and wondered when the school painted over it. As soon as they could, she was sure.

She remembered the smell of the stagnant dusty air in Spencer's closet and could feel her nails digging into the wallpaper. She lived with nightmares of a voice inside her head shouting: *No, no, no!* Yet as the voice left her mouth, it was only a whimper: *Please, please, please.* Please—how pathetic was that?

Inside, the halls were painted a cheerful blue. Everything seemed remarkably familiar yet distant, and a of kind of nostalgia enveloped her. Why? Was it merely because she was younger then and therefore further from death? Yearning for that time would be crazy, masochistic. Or was it a longing for something she'd never had?

Making her way to the office, she asked the secretary if they kept records on former teachers. "Records?"

Records, Marti thought, *as in police records.* Realizing her choice of words sounded odd, she changed her tone. "I was a student here eons ago and . . . and a teacher inspired me. I'd like to get in touch, thank him, Spencer Douglas."

"No one here by that name."

"Do you keep information on where teachers go when they leave?"

"That would be confidential."

"He's been such an influence. If you had an address . . ." Learning it was more than twenty-five years ago, the secretary chortled, yet Marti continued pressing to no avail, hoping to hear he'd been fired and forbidden to teach.

Sitting outside on a school bench, she felt ghosts approaching, creeping stealthily, waiting for their moment to claw at her. The one whose presence she felt most acutely was a quiet one, that scared and scarred girl who'd entered this new school, clinging tight to her friend Brooke. What did that little girl want of Marti?

And Brooke—oh, Brooke with her toxic parents—Mrs. Davies tugging at Brandon's jeans and peeking inside. "Let me see, boxers or briefs?" she'd asked, pulling on his underwear before releasing them with a snap. "Briefs, how swell," she purred. Everyone laughed except Marti. At the time, she'd thought this was her failing.

She hadn't heard much from Brooke over the years; she knew

she'd had three children by three different men, drifting between a farm in Tennessee, a commune in California, somewhere in Baja, and the list went on and on. Marti last saw her fourteen years ago when Brooke called out of the blue, saying she was in New York traveling with a band and would come over.

Tess was less than a week old, and it was Rob's first day back at work. Marti wasn't really up for visitors but wouldn't miss a chance to see Brooke, and it felt serendipitous that she called at such an important moment in Marti's life. Rousing herself from her sleepy stupor, she straightened up the apartment, took a shower, and dressed Tess in her cutest outfit. She was contemplating what food she could offer when the doorbell rang.

Brooke sauntered in with two sullen kids and four guys trailing her (she hadn't said she was bringing the band). "Hey! Awesome to see you!" Brooke gave her a hug. "Here's Organic Rage, you've heard of them, right? Harry, Rogue, Pip, and Bernie."

Marti held her hand out to each of the band members, and they returned disinterested half shakes. Peering behind them, she smiled at the preteen girl, pale and freckled with a wide face, looking nothing like her mother. The younger boy had Brooke's almond eyes and angular features.

"Oh, right," Brooke said, "this is Clementine and Zeke. Say hi. Marti's an old friend." Marti noticed the girl was carrying a small cage. She peered inside at the animal; it looked like a guinea pig, only Marti was used to them being plump and this one looked streamlined, more like a ferret. "That's Karma. Dragging that thing around is Clem's destiny."

"It's not Karma." Clementine scowled at her mother. "It's Caramel, my guinea pig. See her coloring?"

"Caramel is a good name," Marti agreed.

Brooke sprawled out on the floor, leaning back against one of the guys, Pip, who sat on a chair. She shook her long hair onto his lap, and he began playing with it. When he moved his arm at a certain angle, Marti noticed track marks. She instantly checked Brooke, but Brooke was wearing a long-sleeve billowy peasant blouse in the style they'd worn in high school. Marti looked again at Pip's arm, reassuring herself that the marks weren't fresh but quite faded. Tess was stirring. "I'll get my daughter so you can meet her."

"Cool, Marti. But first, we're hungry." Brooke giggled.

She put out cheese, bread, and strawberries and started a pot of coffee. By the time that was ready, all the food had been devoured. After rummaging around again, she offered cookies to the children first, as she had a hunch that they hadn't gotten much the first round. She noticed Clementine feeding a strawberry to Caramel through the cage bars and offered her a bunch of lettuce. Caramel devoured the lettuce as fast as Clementine could stuff it in. Marti told Clementine she could let her out of the cage. Caramel hopped in circles around Clementine before settling on her lap to finish the lettuce remains.

Tess was wailing when Marti finally got to her, her dress soaking, so Marti changed her into a nondescript onesie. "She's cute," Brooke said, looking at Tess. "They're all cute at that age. Tess—that's the book we read in high school, right? The milkmaid?" Marti didn't answer, swaying back and forth, quieting Tess.

"Both of us mothers, who'd have thought?" Brooke laughed.

"When you think how messed-up we were," Marti said slowly, wanting it to lead to a real conversation, but Brooke only stared blankly at her. She asked Brooke about her other child and Brooke explained that Jesse, her two-year-old, was in Tennessee with his dad; he was *way, way too needy*. She said this last part looking behind her for confirmation. Pip and Zeke both rolled their eyes in agreement. It was the first time Marti saw Zeke show any emotion; she hadn't succeeded in getting the boy to make eye contact.

Clementine put Caramel back in the cage when they were getting ready to leave. Marti offered for her to come look in the refrigerator and take whatever else Caramel might eat. Clementine took a bunch of spinach, paused, and then added zucchini, saying, "I don't know if she'll eat these, but Caramel's always hungry."

After everyone was halfway down the stairs, Brooke paused and climbed back up. She said, "You seem good, Marti. God, I'm . . . I'm sorry, I really am." She stammered awkwardly; Marti had never seen Brooke uncertain.

"What do you mean?"

"What you said before—you weren't a mess. I should never have taken you with me. I had no options, but you, you could have stayed, finished high school. You'd have gotten over Peter. You didn't need to go down the losing road." Brooke said the last sentence softly. Marti opened her mouth to protest that she wasn't losing but realized that would be tactless, as one of them was.

Looking around the disheveled apartment left in their wake, Marti sat holding Tess close, thinking of Brooke and her forlorn children. She'd always been so enthralled by Brooke's charisma, too dazzled to recognize the damage. Each of them floundering in their own way, so they could be of no help to the other.

She noticed turds of Caramel's dotting the floor. Something about the sight moved Marti, and she was careful not to disturb them. Later when Rob asked what they were, she shrugged and swept them behind the couch, leaving them to fester.

Glancing at her watch, Marti suddenly remembered Tess was returning today. She should have been back an hour ago. She drove quickly. Tess and Rob were sitting on the porch steps, locked out. "Where were you?" Tess demanded before Marti was out of the car.

"Sorry, I forgot what time you were coming."

"We've been here like an hour!"

"You okay?" Rob asked.

"Of course. I meant to leave the door unlocked." She hugged an unresponsive Tess and bent to pick up Tess's bag, but Tess snatched it.

"Forgot? Great, Mom, you watch me like a hawk and then leave me outside for hours, jeez."

"Tess." Rob touched her arm. "Chill. Give your mom a break. Anyone can forget something."

"Her own daughter?"

"Take it easy." Rob touched her more firmly now.

Tess pushed into the cottage where the newspaper clippings were strewn about. "Wow, Precious do this?"

"No." Marti scooped the articles quickly into a big pile, some falling to the floor. Tess and Rob both stooped to pick them up. "Don't," Marti hissed, spreading her arms across the pile. "I've got them." Rob continued reaching. "Leave it, Rob, leave it."

"Okay, okay." He backed away, looked at Tess, and shrugged.

"I've got them in the order I want."

"What are they, Mom?"

She weighed down the pile with a book. "Are you guys hungry? I could make lunch. Coffee, Rob?"

"We ate," Tess said.

"Coffee sounds good before I hit the road," Rob said.

Tess went into her room and came out a minute later. Her bathing suit straps showed underneath her tank top. "I'm going to go to the lake. Bye, Daddy." She gave him a hug.

"Hang on," Marti said. "Your dad might need help with the cat." Tess looked confused. Marti looked at Rob. "You told her, didn't you?"

"No, I—"

"Your father's taking the cat. Precious is going to live with him."

"What? Why?"

"Because it was never my responsibility to begin with. And she's mean to Caliban." Caliban cocked his head at the sound of his name. Marti leaned over, petting him.

"That's not fair! She's my cat."

"She'll still be your cat. Your dad's house is your home too."

"Now? Today?" Tess looked from one to the other.

"I should have told you," Rob said.

"You got that right," Marti muttered.

Ignoring this, he said, "Maybe we should wait till after the summer, give her time to adjust."

Marti shook her head. Tess picked up the cat and went into her room. Marti debated whether to follow but didn't. Tess came out a few minutes later with red eyes. *It's too abrupt*, Marti knew, yet she remained unmoved. Without speaking, Tess put the cat in the crate. Precious began shrieking in protest; Tess turned away, her face set tight.

"Be back by five-thirty."

"That early?"

"I haven't seen you. I want to have a nice dinner and hear about your weekend."

Marti watched out the window while Rob tried soothing Tess's rigid body. She heard Rob say Tess would see both Precious and him in a few weeks in Brooklyn. Again, it hit Marti how little time was left.

Marti made Rob coffee. The cat's shrieks were audible from outside. "Maybe we should let her out until I leave?" Rob asked.

"She's impossible to get in the crate. Only Tess can do it. She'll stop . . . eventually. Here's the cat's stuff." Marti held up the packed bag until Rob reluctantly took it.

"I talked with Tess. She knows she overstepped her boundaries, but you've got to—" Marti gave Rob a hard look. He shifted in his chair. "Lisa talked with her too. She's not . . . Marti, she's not having sex."

"I know that," she snapped. *Do I know that?* She tightened her grip on her coffee cup, pressing her palms against the warmth.

"She really likes this guy, and they both know they're not ready. They're not physical at all. In fact, that's part of why she likes him."

Marti inwardly scoffed. How naïve was Rob?

"Lisa did talk to her about birth control. I hope that's okay with you."

"Okay with me?" Marti shook her head, incredulous. "Gee, Rob, what the fuck do you think? I *want* her pregnant at fourteen?" Her voice grew loud, as did the wails from Precious.

"You don't have to be hostile. Look, sometimes Tess has an easier time with Lisa precisely because she's *not* her mother. I'm sure you've talked to her about birth control, but another voice can't hurt. We didn't know if Tess knew where to buy condoms, so Lisa showed her them in the drugstore and talked about STDs and the importance of using condoms even if she uses other birth control."

Marti had talked to Tess but never showed her condoms. It was the logical next step that she hadn't taken because she wasn't ready. She understood she should be grateful to Lisa. Thinking sadly of her own mother, she wondered if it hadn't been all up to Peg, if there'd been other adults to help, maybe things might have been different.

She watched Rob drive off. The cat was standing in the crate, staring back at Marti. Caliban looked bewildered. Marti petted his head. *You're not the only one confused, boy.*

Rummaging through the art materials in the car, she thought about women throughout history communing together in sewing circles; even Louise Bourgeois got her start helping her parents repair tapestries. She drove to the library, wanting to look further at traditional forms of women's crafts. She pored over books of quilts, tapestries, and samplers.

On her way out of the library, she noticed stacks of phone books and picked up the Vermont one, looking under *Douglas*. No Spencer Douglas. *Maybe he's dead? Would that give me peace?*

She felt a tap on her arm. "Marti, it is you, isn't it?" She looked up into a vaguely familiar face. "It's Alison, Alison Quint. Remember me? I can't believe I recognized you! You look the same, wonderful."

Marti instinctively reached her hand to her face, betting she knew what was recognizable. "Sure, I remember you, Alison. How are you?"

"Good, good. I still live here in town."

"I'm just passing through. Are these your children?" she asked, noticing a girl and a boy behind Alison. She smiled at the children, and they said hello before running off to the bookshelves. After chatting a bit, Marti asked if Alison knew anything about Spencer's whereabouts.

"I don't. Is that who you're looking for in the phone book?"

Caught, Marti changed the subject. "What about Miss Jarvis? Is she still at the middle school?"

"She *is*. My oldest has her for art. He loves her. She's still fabulous."

"She was great," Marti agreed, wishing she'd been looking up Miss Jarvis or Miss Anton—anyone who treated her well. *What am I doing?* Remembering Spencer's nastiness directed at Alison—*Another nauseating sunrise from Wonderland Alice. How quaint the Quint is.*—she said, "Your artwork was beautiful, Alison. Do you do any now?"

"Me? No, I stopped after high school. Frankly, Spencer squashed that in me." She shook her head. "Probably a good thing. I didn't have real talent like you and Brandon. Tragic about Brandon."

"What?"

"You never heard? He crashed his car into a tree one night on Route 7. He died about twenty years ago."

"That's awful." After a pause, she said, "Alison, you were talented. I admired your work. Miss Jarvis loved it. Spencer was wrong."

"Thanks. I never liked Spencer. Don't know why you'd want to find him." Alison looked closely at Marti. "I'm glad to see you're okay. I thought about you often after you ran away." She wavered before continuing. "Maybe I shouldn't say this . . . but I know leaving must have been hard and I understood—the abortion, a sad thing."

"Brooke told you, huh?"

"Brooke? No. She was really angry at Peter for talking, but Peter needed to talk. He was devastated."

Marti sat in her car piecing it together. *Peter. Not Brooke.* She slammed the steering wheel. *Why didn't I realize? He was using me to hide, so of course he told people. That was the whole point after all.* She remembered him strutting arm and arm with his so-called girlfriend and his reluctance to talk. *Now* it made sense. *How angry I was at Brooke! Brooke with her sad lost life, I gave up on her.*

In the car she headed toward his house until noticing the time: six. *Damn! I told Tess five thirty and promised dinner.* She stopped to pick up pizza; it took a long time, but she had no choice as the kitchen was bare. Marti hurried into the cabin waving the box. Tess was sitting at the table with the newspaper articles in front of her.

"That's the special dinner you thought we should have?"

"You like pizza."

"Yeah, and I eat it all the time in Brooklyn. I don't need Vermont pizza. There's nothing in the fridge, nada. Some home-cooked meal."

"Since when don't you like takeout?"

"You wanted me home and I came home. Where were you?"

Marti gathered plates and glasses of water. "The library, if you must know." She tried to move the newspapers, but Tess's arms were folded on top of the pile, not budging.

"Not at Peter's?"

"Why would you think that?" Marti continued tugging at the papers.

"You know he's gay, right?"

"So?"

"He *was* your boyfriend."

"Already told you he wasn't."

"Why did Aunt Jan say he was?"

"Can you move, please? So I can put the newspapers away?"

"Don't answer my question. Everything has to be a mystery with you. Like why"—Tess waved the newspapers back and forth—"are you saving articles about some maniac raping women? Is it to scare me into staying home?"

"Not everything is about you." She reached her hand out for the papers. Tess dropped them quickly. Marti caught some of them and had to stoop to retrieve the ones that sailed across the floor.

"Gee, Mom, how's that aunt of yours?" Tess said, tapping the answering machine. *I left you a message.*

Marti kept her eyes on the papers she was straightening. "Oh. Marisol was confused. I told her about Mrs. Colgan and she misunderstood, thought she was a relative."

"Bullshit! Is a fake aunt how you got all this time off work? Did you lie to come here and chase Peter? You make me sick!" Tess grabbed some pizza and went to her room, slamming the door.

Marti read through that day's papers, cutting out more articles and organizing them. She liked what the drug addict said today: *I know I said I deserved it, but my family didn't. I'm still somebody's daughter.*

Marti ate the pizza cold, standing up. As soon as she was sure Tess was asleep, she drove to Peter's.

"I'm the bad penny that keeps showing up. Kids asleep?"

"Yes, but—"

"Good. I'm coming in." She pushed past him and sat down on the couch. Mrs. Colgan's dresses sloped toward the weight of her body. She moved to the rocker. "Ever wonder about me after I ran away?"

"I worried about you." He sat in the armchair on the other side of the room.

"You did?" She laughed. "Must have thought I was crazy to leave with Brooke!"

He shrugged. "I understood why you left."

"With Brooke?"

"She was your friend."

"You think? She blabbed to everyone about my abortion, remember? And then I ran away with her. Talk about codependent!" She slapped her forehead, enjoying teasing this out.

"Marti . . ."

She waited, leaning forward, her hands on her knees. "Aw, spit it out, you can do it."

"I'm the one who told, but you know that. Brooke told you years ago."

"No, Peter. Not Brooke. I've blamed her all this time. I just found out it was you. *Today.* I ran into Alison Quint, a good thing too, because *you* weren't going to tell me. I remember warning you that Brooke was gossiping because I felt terrible that you'd suffer even more for my problems. How deluded I was! And no, you didn't enlighten me."

"Marti—"

"I know, ancient history. But see, I'm just playing catch-up. And you're *still* determined to keep me in the dark. Why?"

"I tried—"

"Bullshit, Peter! How could you do that to me? Do you know what it was like? People leering, laughing, pointing—like the accident all over again." She saw him cringe at the word *accident*, and maybe it wasn't fair, but she wanted him to cringe. "And you strutting around with that girl, looking like you dumped me, like I was the slutty throwaway. You, the poor Catholic boy whose tramp of a girlfriend insisted on an abortion. Oh, you were so distraught you had to tell *everyone*. Poor you!" Her voice was loud and heated. She was clenching her teeth so hard, they throbbed.

"I was afraid." He looked at the ground, his voice low. "I was looking for any way to hide. It didn't matter who I hurt in the process."

"Didn't matter? That's classy, Peter. *What about now?*" She began to shout. "Damn you! This is hard enough without you stonewalling me!"

A sound came from behind her. Pearl stood at the foot of the stairs, crying. "Daddy!" She ran onto his lap, curling into him. Her face was buried in Peter's chest as she stuck her arm out behind her, pointing her finger at Marti. "She's yelling at you!"

"I'm sorry, Pearl," she said. Pearl covered her ears. "I didn't mean to scare you."

"Marti," Peter said, motioning for her to stop. He rose with Pearl in his arms, gently swaying and rubbing her back. Watching them, Marti felt a strange stirring of melancholy. "I'm going to settle Pearl. I'll see you tomorrow for dinner. We'll talk it all through."

Marti left. Guilt, humiliation, rage, she couldn't tell which emotion possessed her at any moment; they all held her tightly in their grip.

21

Ned greeted Marti and Tess with enthusiasm while Pearl hung back, holding onto her father's leg. Assuming Pearl was simply feeling shy, Tess tried talking to Pearl while Ned chattered to Marti, showing off a toy. ". . . turns into a robot. Wanna see?"

"What! I don't believe a car can be a robot. Do you, Pearl?"

Pearl latched even tighter to her father's leg. Peter picked her up. "It's okay, Pearl. Marti and I are friends."

"Told you. You dreamed it," Ned said.

"Dreamed what?" Tess asked.

"It wasn't a dream. She was shouting at Daddy last night." Pearl pointed at Marti. Evading Tess's astonished expression, Marti bent down, trying to soothe Pearl by explaining she was sorry for scaring her and wasn't mad anymore. And it was true: that boiling cauldron of anger had evaporated.

Pearl continued clinging to her father and Peter picked her up, speaking softly, eventually coaxing her into the idea of the fun she'd have with Tess. "Oh, wait," Peter said, putting her down and slapping his head. "Did I say *fun*? I forgot our number one rule! What is it, Ned?"

"No fun allowed!"

"That's right. Got that, Tess? They can't have any fun." Ned and Pearl giggled behind their father's back.

"Ah, I caught you!" Peter grabbed them both. "No fun!" He involved Tess in the game until everyone was laughing and relaxed. He showed Tess the dinner waiting in the oven and the kids' laid-out pajamas, explaining the bedtime ritual. "One story you make up with all kinds of interesting characters, dinosaurs, dragons, and of course, two brilliant children named Ned and Pearl. And two books, no more. Right, Pearl?"

"If they're short—"

Peter cupped Pearl's mouth with his hand. "Don't listen to her. Con artist! Two books. Period. End of story. Catch the pun?"

Outside Peter told Marti about an Italian restaurant in walking distance, explaining it was the old five-and-dime store that used to give them free sodas when they brought school supplies. Reminiscing about the store's rows of candy bars and comic books, they teased each other back and forth about who liked what. Marti knew the banter was avoidance, yet she was enjoying it because despite everything, there was still something so comfortable about being with Peter, like putting on that cozy worn sweater when you finally reached home.

Once they were inside the restaurant, the banter dwindled and they sat in uncomfortable silence, neither knowing where to begin. They ordered a bottle of wine, and Marti drank her first glass quickly while they discussed the menu. Peter was knowledgeable about food and mentioned he'd been a chef "in another life." Marti started playing with the candle in an effort to pace her drinking. Peter gestured at her hand. "You always did that. All those candles in Brooke's basement, you messed with them constantly."

"Just a way of fidgeting," she said, enjoying the feel of the warm wax on her fingers.

"Well, I thought, *She's been burned. Why would she play with fire?*" Marti pushed the candle away and poured more wine. She dipped some bread in the olive oil but didn't eat it.

"Poor Brooke," she said, "I blamed her." She asked if he ever heard anything from Brooke. As she expected, the answer was no. "I tried to see her one time when I was home. I'd seen in the paper that her father died, and I went to the wake. She wasn't there. Her mother hung all over me, crying about how glad she was to see me. She was pretty messed up. Oh, and I met her brother. A nice guy, dressed in his naval uniform. He seemed like he was itching till he could leave."

"Do you remember that photo of her sister? Because of my work and all, I've figured out her story—fetal alcohol syndrome—those beady eyes so close together and no name for what was wrong."

"Huh," Peter said, taking it in.

"Did you know Brooke had CP? Mildly."

"Only 'cause Ma told me," Peter replied. "I'd always believed the horse story." Marti mentioned what she'd learned about Brandon. Peter told her by senior year he was totally messed up on drugs.

"Could have been any of us," she said, "we were all train wrecks."

Peter took a sip of wine. "I am truly sorry. You ought to know, Brooke gave me hell for telling."

"Good," Marti said, glad to see the conversation shift to what remained unfinished between them. "It's high school bullshit, I know, and I'm the one who dragged you into my mess. But what I don't get is, why so evasive this summer?"

Peter refilled their wine glasses, emptying the bottle. The food hadn't arrived. "I wonder what's taking so long." He looked around for the waiter.

"It hasn't been long, Peter. And you're doing it again—evasion."

He sighed. "Guys were starting to say shit, and so I latched onto it: I'd gotten a girl pregnant. I told lots of people. I didn't think about the consequences." The food arrived. Looking down, Peter twirled linguine on his fork and spoon over and over. "I almost *believed* I'd gotten you pregnant. I wanted it to be true. It wasn't until you ran away that I realized how destructive my self-delusion was. Seeing you this summer, it brought everything back and I shut down."

He lifted his eyes, and Marti could see a mirror of herself: shame. "Peter, that's not why I left, not really. It was—"

"Spencer," they said in near unison.

"Let's get another bottle of wine, and I'll tell you what he did to me." Peter motioned for the waiter.

"Oh fuck, he fucked you too?"

"No. Clever pun, though. He knew I was gay."

"You told him?"

"He figured it out, probably by the way I mooned over him."

"Ugh."

"Hey, you shouldn't talk."

"Touché," Marti agreed, shaking her head. "God, what morons we were!"

"Spencer knew it and used it. He had me do so much crap for him. Did you know I graded student work? And filled in his grade book, went to the store, the library, whatever. He practically had me cleaning his toilet. He told me not to be ashamed of being gay, to embrace it. He said it in such a tender way that I thought he was getting ready to make a pass at me, and when he didn't, I loved him even more. I thought he was brave and selfless."

"A knight of valor." Marti laughed.

"Exactly what *he* thought. He used it to control me. I thought he was helping me accept myself until I noticed him making these inside jokes to others, little innuendos. *Peter will prance downstairs and get us more paper. Fly like a good little fairy.* Everyone knew what he meant, and when I finally worked up the courage to confront him, Spencer said he'd done me a favor. Outing me for my own good."

"Calling you a fairy built your self-esteem, I'm sure."

The second bottle arrived and their plates sat uneaten, except for the few bites they took to please the waiter who'd asked if

something was wrong with the food. "Do you know, Marti—I'm
sure you don't—after you left, Spencer said to me, 'Thank you for
taking care of that little problem'. He didn't say your name, but
it was clear. He'd heard the gossip, and my part, and was pleased
with the sham."

"My god! Remember Denise? *Desirée*. I know he had a thing
with her. Any others?"

"Hell, I didn't know about you and that happened right under
my nose. I was so naïve that when you told me, I thought it was
cool. That day—the truck drivers—I should have realized."

"How could you when I didn't understand it myself? That day
must have been awful for you."

"It was." He looked at her like a kid forcing a brave smile.

Marti stood up and felt a rush of warmth flood her face.
*Thanks to alcohol, such a great release. I feel lovely in spite of—all
this.* In the bathroom she splashed water on her face and leaned
against the sink, savoring the wine swirling through her. Returning to the table, she took a long, steady drink of water before
speaking. "I need to find him."

"*Spencer?*"

Marti nodded. She noticed the restaurant had filled. Tourists or locals? She couldn't decide, and which was she? Peter was
studying her. She drank more wine. She asked Peter if he had a
computer that she could use to locate Spencer. He said he did but
told her it was crazy.

"I know and I hope he's dead. But imagine if he's still teaching. We've got to blow him out of the water. Tell his school, smash
his car, bomb his house. What about sugar in his gas tank?"

"That would work."

"It's not enough!" Marti shouted, suddenly passionate. "We've
got to *ruin* him. What goes around comes back, or goes . . . whatever the saying is."

Peter motioned for the check, saying they'd had enough. She

stood unsteadily, throwing some bills on the table. She stuffed a piece of bread in her mouth, instantly regretting this. The bread was hard and soggy at the same time, and she wanted to spit it out. Instead, she swallowed it almost whole before speaking. "C'mon, you've got to come. You owe me." She winced, wanting to take those words back, but they reverberated in the air.

Stumbling outside, she discovered the fresh air was as intoxicating as the wine. Peter followed a few minutes later, and she quickly said, "You don't owe me anything, Peter. I shouldn't have said that."

"I'll help you look. That's all—for now." On the walk home, Peter pointed out more changes to the town.

"If only we could erase Spencer as easily as a town erases its past. And we will. We'll find him tomorrow. *Tomorrow, tomorrow*—" Marti sang, until Peter cupped his hand over her mouth.

"You," he said as they reached the block, "are not driving."

"Agreed, agreed."

"You could spend the night. Plenty of bedrooms."

"I couldn't possibly sleep in Mrs. Colgan's house! That bun in her hair, she was like someone from another century! Did you know I worshipped her? Maybe I should sleep in my old house." She giggled. "I could ring the doorbell and introduce myself. Do you know them?"

"No. Ma said they're nice."

"Your mother thought everyone was nice because she was the nicest of the nice."

Having momentarily forgotten Tess would be there, Marti startled at the sight of her sitting, watching TV. Peter asked about the kids and told Tess he was going to make Marti tea and call a cab. Tess looked at Marti. "Something wrong with the car?"

"No, it's just—you know, I've told you, don't drink and drive. Here's your firsthand lesson."

"Mom—" Tess stood up.

"Finish your TV show." Marti flung her hand dismissively.

Peter shoved Marti into the kitchen, reassuring Tess. Marti slumped down in the booth while Peter made tea. "Next!" She shouted remembering the old game. She pretended to fall out of the booth until she almost did fall; Peter caught her in time. Tess called from the living room, "Roger called. He said to call no matter how late."

"And that's an order," Marti mumbled.

Peter shook his head. "It's not like that; we've got a good thing. Roger just wants to be sure I keep it together."

"Keep it together?"

"Yes," Peter said, facing the stove, "I used to get anxiety attacks. That's why I'm not a chef anymore, too high-octane stress for me. Staying home with the kids has been great. Roger worries, with Ma dying, and now, seeing you, that it might stir things up." Marti didn't know what to say and thought it best if she didn't say anything in her current state.

Tess quickly left for the beach in the morning, after first grumbling annoyance at the empty refrigerator. Surprisingly, much to Marti's relief, she made no mention of Marti's late-night visit to Peter or her drinking, or Marisol's message. Marti gave her money for food, an extra amount. *Pay her off.* Tess promised to be home by eight. *She wants to avoid me as much as I want to avoid her. Good.*

She took a cab back to Peter's and found him with the kids in the backyard, the kids running through the sprinkler. *We played with water that day.* Peter waved his cup of coffee, offering her some. "God, yes!" Marti groaned. "Of all the times not to have coffee in the house. And you should've heard Tess complaining about the lack of food."

"She's like Roger, wants you to keep it together."

Marti nodded emphatically. "Shouldn't she just be the child?"

Peter went inside and returned with coffee. "I promised the kids I'd play this game with the sprinkler. I set it a certain way so they can sit on it and pretend it's a rocket ship zooming to the moon."

"Sounds like fun."

"A blast." He grinned. "Let me show you the computer if you still want to look."

"I've had no sober reflection."

Marti searched the sites she was most familiar with. There was no Spencer Douglas in Vermont, but several nationwide popped up. She clicked on two in California but the ages were wrong, and she ruled out ones in Texas and North Dakota, as they seemed like improbable places for him to live. There were two in New York, one even in Brooklyn. Marti clenched her teeth as she searched that one, even in the same neighborhood. Could it be? Had she sat near him at the movies? Drank coffee next to him? Did they have children in school together? She felt violated by these thoughts and relaxed when she saw that this Spencer Douglas was twenty-three years old. Marti scanned the list looking to see where to go next, and then she saw it: Spencer Douglas in Bantree, New Hampshire. Maybe he wasn't in Vermont but hadn't gone far. She clicked on it and the age was right, fifty-seven.

"Peter," she called excitedly, following their voices into the den. All three were sitting on the floor, each holding a stuffed animal around a tray with play food. "I think I found him, but I need to know more. Could you try looking?"

"Sure, take over here. Monkey was about to place his food order. Don't give him any more bananas; they make him bananas!"

Pearl looked uncomfortable, and Marti was determined to win her trust back. She fed the animals and made a playground for them. Next, they played a game of Candy Land, marching their gingerbread people around the board gobbling treats. So engrossed was Marti that she startled when Peter called her to check what he'd found. Walking down the hall, she hesitated: Did she really want to know?

"He's still an art teacher. At a boys' juvenile hall."

"Poor boys."

"Totally. The place is a pit." Peter went on to explain what he already knew about the place from an exposé in the news on these for-profit treatment centers popping up all over New England with shoddy conditions, substandard care, and low-paid employees.

"That part's good—for him, anyway. He's married. Wife's name is Susan. She's thirty."

"Figures. Kids?"

"A boy and girl, ages four and two." Peter paused, then started laughing, barely getting his next words out. "Names are—Frida and Horatio."

"Oh, my god, it's him!" Marti jumped up and gave Peter a high five.

"Yeah, Frida Kahlo, a favorite of his."

"And who else would saddle a child with a name like Horatio? Oh, this is fun!" Marti said, laughing. Peter printed the information and told her where Bantree was, about four hours away.

"We have to go there." Peter offered no response. Marti spoke again. "I don't want to go alone. Tess could watch the kids for the day—"

"Marti, it's crazy; he won't willingly see you, and what would you do?"

"Don't know. I've got to do something. He wronged you too. Okay, let's take a few days. I'll drop Tess at my sister's, and you could get one of your siblings to watch your kids. Or bring them. They're adorable, Peter. You're such a good dad." She spoke rapidly.

"Flattering me?"

"No, it's true, but please come. I . . . I need you."

"It would be fun to bust his world open—that's not a yes. I'll call you tomorrow."

Tess returned home on time and continued keeping her distance. She played with Caliban a long time, throwing a ball for him. Marti wondered if this was because she missed Precious. She knew they should talk more about that—and everything else— but all she could concentrate on was Peter's answer.

He called the next day. Roger would take the kids home after the weekend, and he could meet her in Bantree on Monday. "It might take a few days. We can get a motel and do our surprise attack or whatever. If you still want."

Did she? All her doubts came into focus, and she felt that same passivity she'd always shown: *Spencer wants me, so I guess I want it. Brooke said I could come, so I'm going. It's Rob's choice, so I won't make a scene. Peter can go, so we're going. Let fate decide.*

Neither of them talked about slashing Spencer's tires or bombing his house. Now that the plan was materializing into something real, they'd lost their bravado. It was as if, once again, Spencer held power over them.

Originally, Marti had planned to visit Jan when their time at the cabin was up. Marti called and asked if they could come now. Jan explained that her daughter, Meg, wasn't home from her summer camp job and would be disappointed to miss Marti and Tess. Marti continued as if she hadn't heard Jan's objection and next asked if she could leave Tess there.

"Where will you be?"

"Montreal. At an art show."

"I'm sure Tess would love Montreal, and then you could come when Meg will be back. Perfect."

"No, she'd be bored, and I won't have time for her."

"This wasn't the plan. I'm confused here," Jan said.

Just say yes.

"Of course, I'll be thrilled to have Tess."

When Marti told Tess that evening, Tess objected, given that Meg wouldn't be there. "Here's the thing, the art show is only on next week." The lies came easy now.

Tess said she could stay with Emily's family. Marti hadn't considered that possibility but didn't want to change plans for fear of disrupting what was already set in motion. "Tess, it's our only chance to see Jan. I'm not driving north twice, and we'll be back by next weekend, before even."

"God, Mom, I don't believe you. You're doing it *again*. Where you gonna drag me next? Boys are everywhere, you know."

Marti got up to leave and Tess followed, pulling on her arm. "Ethan's my friend, Mom, that's all. This isn't fair. I've been following curfew—not like you'd notice, since *you're* the one sneaking out at night drinking and lying."

"Enough." Marti had wondered when Tess would finally come out with it. She turned around. "Let go of my arm." She was wrangling Tess's hand away when Tess shoved her against the wall. Caliban barked and lunged between them. Tess retreated to her room, and Marti went outside and walked in circles to calm herself. She didn't come inside until she was certain Tess was sleeping.

The next day, they barely spoke to each other. Tess came in at eleven and Friday night at midnight. Marti couldn't focus on that now.

She rose early Saturday morning and finished packing, wanting to be ready as soon as Tess awoke. The sooner they got on the road, the less opportunity for drama. Hearing a knock, she expected Emily; instead, it was Roger. He said he needed to talk to her. She led him to the dock where they sat on two Adirondack chairs. Roger's large frame filled the chair. He was well over six feet tall with broad shoulders and a powerful build. She looked at his face, understanding the meaning of the cliché *prominent features*. Roger's exuded confidence.

"I'll get to the point. I don't think this trip is a good idea, although I won't stop Peter."

That's good, Marti thought, *because neither Peter nor I are any match for you.*

"What do you hope to gain from this trip?" Marti was flustered by the question. "Are you thinking to somehow prosecute that teacher for statutory rape?"

"No, no."

"Good. Because I'll tell you, in Boston I've worked with some of the altar boys accusing priests, and it's a tough road. They get notice because it's priests and because of homophobia. A girl ten or fifteen years younger than her teacher? Why, back then it was practically acceptable."

"I know that."

Roger sat back, crossed his legs. It wasn't relaxation, rather, self-assurance. "Why involve Peter? Payback?"

"*Payback?* No. Because . . . because he's my friend. I want support, that's all."

"You sure? I know you've had an axe to grind with Peter, and I've got to say, your timing stinks. Peter's lived most of his life feeling guilty about your accident and sees everything that happened to you as a direct result of that."

"It wasn't. He shouldn't blame himself. They were my mistakes, and I dragged him in when I shouldn't have."

"Aren't you doing that again?" She stared down at a beetle crawling across the deck. The beetle frantically changed directions several times. "Look, you need to be certain of your motives. Peter's fragile. His mother just died, remember?"

"I don't want to hurt Peter."

Roger continued as if he hadn't heard her. "He had a rough

time coming out to his family. When we got together, I was clear, commitment meant being open. His dad was gone by then, but Connie handled it. Sure, it rocked her, being old-school Catholic, but she loved her son. And when we went to Vietnam to get the twins, she couldn't have been happier. Now she's gone, and Peter is thinking of all the years he squandered with dishonesty."

"That's hard," Marti responded. "I'm glad you told me."

"Talk to him yourself. Coming here and culling through his mother's life is taking a toll on him. One of his siblings would be done in a week or two, but Peter, he's dragging it out and raking himself over the coals." He looked at Marti; his eyes were a deep and steady gray. "And then you show up."

"Sorry."

"Oh, don't be sorry; it is what it is. I'm not the ogre you think I am."

"You were pretty hostile when we met." She released a tentative smile.

"Can you blame me? Maybe I'm wrong and this trip will be good for Peter. At least he'll be away from his mother's house." Roger stood up. "I'll be going now."

Walking Roger to his car, Marti repeated, "I don't want to hurt Peter. I said some things I didn't mean, but it's all been a revelation."

"I'll say. I hope you give it good to that creep. He deserves it. Just don't do anything crazy. Stay away from the deep end."

She nodded, yet as much as she was starting to like Roger, she wasn't sure she could keep that promise. Turning back to the house, she saw Tess at the window.

22

Marti braced for Tess's questions, but all Tess said was that she was packed, ready, and wanted to say goodbye to Emily, running out the door before Marti could respond. She watched Tess's figure recede as she hurried down the road, knapsack still on—she hadn't stopped to drop it at the car—her loose hair waving like a handkerchief before the ship sails.

Putting the last things in the trunk, Marti added the newspaper clippings to the art supply bag. She'd pick up today's papers when they stopped on the road. Nothing left to be done—no cat to chase—she put Caliban in the car and drove to Linda's. Picking Tess up would speed things along.

Linda greeted her by saying. "Sorry we couldn't help you, Marti. Art's friends are coming to stay and don't you think three kids is enough to inflict upon them? Actually, it will be *five* kids with their two. Not that Tess would be a bother; we love her, just, well, the numbers—"

Marti didn't know what Linda was prattling on about and she felt annoyed at having to endure this chatter; why hadn't Tess come straight back? She knew Marti was ready. She cut in before Linda could continue. "I'm here to pick Tess up."

"She's not here."

"Not here? Did I miss her? Did she go out a back way?" Marti looked at the back door trying to imagine what different route Tess could have walked, maybe a shortcut through the woods?

"Marti, she hasn't been here."

"But I saw her—" Marti stopped, trying to remember what

Linda had said when she first came in. "What were you saying before? Tess and I are going away for the week."

"Emily told us you were going away but that Tess needed somewhere to stay."

"No. That's not right. She's coming with me." It was beginning to dawn on Marti that something was amiss, but she kept pestering Linda as if she could change this reality. "She came here a few minutes ago to say goodbye."

"I didn't see—I'll get Emily and she can sort this out. Sit down." Linda gestured to a chair.

Marti waited at the kitchen table, listening to hushed tones that threatened loudness in the other room. She traced her fingers along the outline of embroidered flowers on the cotton tablecloth. Linda had replaced the cottage's plastic tablecloth with this one. *Why didn't I make our cabin nice?*

Emily looked reluctantly from Marti to Linda as she revealed Tess was at Ethan's. "He was finding a place for her."

"A place?" Marti's voice faltered. "Why would she—"

"To stay, in case" — Emily looked at the floor and mumbled— "you were looking for her. She hoped you'd just go anyway."

How preoccupied have I been? Just like my mother. "Leave without her? Where is she?" Marti's tone was demanding and Emily shrank back from her.

Art came in and Emily ran to him. Linda explained what was going on and Art took Emily outside. Marti couldn't hear the conversation as their voices rose and fell. They came back inside and Art said Tess was at Ethan's, and Emily was going to show him where that was. "Marti, we'll bring Tess back here."

"I'll go," Marti said.

Art exchanged a glance with his wife, and Linda said, "I'll make tea. You can pull yourself together. They'll be back in no time."

"I need to come." Upon standing, Marti realized she was trembling, and tried to hide this.

Looking out the car window while Art drove, Marti remembered another ride, Brooke and the driver up front chattering, while Marti, silent in the back, stared out the van window.

Did someone drive Mom to search for me? No, she'd have driven herself. How alone she must have felt! Marti had never faced thinking about her mother's moment of anguished discovery—or the months and years that followed. She didn't contact her mother for over three years, waiting until she was eighteen. *Three long years I let her dangle. Until I wanted something from her. The gall of that!*

She was living in Berkeley, California, when she finally called. A parade had gone down Telegraph Avenue celebrating the end of the Vietnam War. Still muddled about that murky war— thinking it had already ended—she watched the cheering, the jubilation, and felt a sudden, familiar ache for home and family. She was tired of living in limbo, belonging nowhere. She wanted that sense of an ending with a new chapter beginning. Three long years. Yet she was shocked to find her mother's phone number changed; the new number had a Massachusetts area code. A man answered. Marti mumbled, "I must have the wrong number; I'm looking for Peg Farrell."

"She's here, hold on. Peggy, come to the phone." There was urgency in his voice.

Peggy?

Marti considered hanging up when she heard her mother's anxious hello. She sounded vulnerable in a way Marti had never heard before. "Mom—" she began, but was interrupted by Peg's sobbing into the phone. This irritated Marti. (*Irritated! My god!*) "Are you okay? Where are you? Can I come get you? Is something wrong?" Peg's words were said in a rush. Marti waited for a break before answering.

"California. I live here now." Across the phone wire she could feel her mother deflate yet Marti pressed on, chattering happy details of her life, leaving out anything that might alarm her mother. She didn't want to hear that fragile voice again. She shared an apartment with three other women, worked odd jobs, and sometimes sold crafts she made. She gave the reason for the call: she'd found a craft college she wanted to attend and needed money for it. "I'm taking my GED next month."

"Honey, that's great. I'll help with school, but first I must see you. I'm in Northampton, Massachusetts, now. Come home."

Northampton wasn't home. Her mother hadn't said who answered the phone. Peg sent a plane ticket; Marti made sure it was a round-trip.

She learned home was an ephemeral place. Not only had Peg moved, she'd remarried. A stranger lived with her mother. Avery had recently retired as an English professor at the college. He was older than Peg, a widower with no children. Jan was living with her fiancé in Burlington (another stranger to meet), and they came down to see Marti. She told Jan how weird she found all the changes.

"You selfish bitch! You wanted the world to stop because you left?"

Marti was taken aback by Jan's anger; she hadn't considered them at all.

"Well, it did stop—for a while. Mom got her dream job, yet she wouldn't move. She commuted all the way from Chatham and slept in motels. Even after she met Avery and they wanted to marry, she wouldn't move, needing to be sure you could find her."

"I'm sorry," Marti stammered.

Jan continued as if she hadn't heard. "Finally, we persuaded her, only after she had assurance from the new owners of the house that when—if—you condescended to show up, they'd tell you where Mom was, and even try to keep you there till Mom arrived. They promised to notify Mom if they moved because she didn't know how many years it might be, how many homeowners she'd have to recruit. She's been paying the phone company not to give away our old number—to keep providing a forwarding number.

"Look at this room." They were sitting on twin beds in a room in her mother's house. "It's a freaking shrine to you." Papa Bear was sitting in his rocker in the corner, old clothes of Marti's were in the closet, and her sketchbooks sat on the desk. Even her gum wrapper chain was draped around a mirror. (Later, she tore it apart, having a perverse need to see if *Spencer and Marti* was still written on the eighth wrapper.)

And that's how it remained over the years. She never explained or apologized. Consequently, Peg and Jan never truly forgave her; it was all just pushed aside. Even after becoming a mother, Marti didn't fix it.

They pulled into a long dirt driveway. A woman, older than Marti, answered the door. She led the three of them into a spacious room with exposed beams on a vaulted ceiling and large windows overlooking a vegetable garden. Tess and Ethan were sitting looking at photos, laughing.

"They've been helping me sort these out. I'm putting together a book for my oldest, Daniel, who leaves for college soon. Tess has been having a good laugh at the ones of Ethan in diapers."

This peaceful domestic scene took Marti aback. Tess jumped to her feet and looked questioningly at Emily, who shrugged and looked at the floor. Marti said they needed to leave, betting Tess wouldn't argue as she'd want to keep up a pretense in front of Ethan's mother. Marti didn't disturb that, saying a gracious goodbye, explaining about the long drive ahead.

Art tried to make conversation on the ride, but getting little response, he gave up, and they rode in silence. Even Emily and Tess didn't look at each other.

Peter and I know that feeling.

When they returned, Linda repeatedly asked if Marti was

okay. "You left your keys here and it's a good thing too, because you left the dog in the car. He was really hot. I took him home and gave him water." Marti was embarrassed, thinking of Linda having to round up the kids to do this. Ignoring Tess's contemptuous looks—she felt enough guilt as it was (*did I even leave a window cracked?*), she thanked Linda and they left.

Caliban, yelping frantically, had ripped up newspapers and peed on the floor. "Poor baby," Marti said, stroking him.

"Mom, this is stupid. I can stay here with Caliban. What if he pees on Aunt Jan's rugs?"

Cleaning it up, Marti kept her eyes on the floor. "Were you running away?" Her voice broke.

"No, Mom, *you're* the one doing that. I wanted to stay home this summer, remember? And now I want to stay here. But oh no, once I'm happy, you want to sabotage it."

"Let's go," Marti said tersely. "We'll talk later."

"Or not," Tess muttered.

Jan lived in a small town outside of Burlington in a saltbox house remarkably like the one they grew up in. Marti hadn't visited for several years, though Jan faithfully came to Brooklyn every year. "Either you're getting smaller or I'm getting bigger," Brian, Jan's husband, said, releasing her from a hug. "Don't answer that. And you," he said, turning to Tess, "are an Amazon. I believe you're taller than Meg." Marti liked Brian, the history between them was less complicated.

"Thought you'd be here sooner," Jan remarked, briefly hugging Marti. "Come in the kitchen. Tess, I'm making your favorite, eggplant parmesan." She gave Tess an affectionate squeeze. "Josh should be home soon." Marti followed Jan while Brian and Tess took Caliban on a walk.

Marti looked at the wall of family photos behind the kitchen table, a jumble of different sizes and frames that somehow seemed coherent. *Just like Jan*, she thought with admiration. *She makes it work.* There was a rare post-accident picture of Marti, Jan, and her mother, Marti looking at the ground. There were photos of Jan, Brian, and the kids sitting on mountaintops or horses. She noticed one of Jan's college graduation with Jan standing between Peg and Avery. She studied Avery's face. He remained a pleasant stranger, having died a few years after Marti's brief reappearance. She felt like a time traveler peering into a past she'd missed. A small picture tucked in a corner caught her eye: her father with Jan on his lap. Jan looked like him, brown hair and a square face. In the photo she was holding his tie, laughing while his mouth was open.

"You've hung a picture of Daddy—Ed."

Jan turned around. "Oh, that, yes, I ran across it in a box of Mom's things. Do you remember that game we always played with Ed's ties? We'd pull on his tie and he'd honk."

Marti felt an image float vaguely into her consciousness. Had she heard this story before? *No, it's a real memory.* She could recall the giggling suspense as she'd pull his tie. This unexpected gift unleashed her desire for more memories. However, it was a fleeting gift: as quickly as it rose to the surface, it sank back down. Irretrievable.

Jan walked over and stood by the picture. "He had another tie joke he played to get me out of bed for school. He'd come into my room holding one, saying, 'Jan, honey, time to get dressed. Put your tie on.' I'd say, 'Daddy, don't be silly. I don't wear a tie.'" Marti had never heard Jan refer to him as Daddy. "And it worked; suddenly I'd be wide-awake, laughing, ready to get dressed."

"That's a sweet story," Marti said softly.

"I missed that game. About a year after he died, Mom came in one morning with one of his ties and tried the joke. I hadn't seen any of Ed's clothes in all that time. The tie hung limp in her hand. It looked dead. It frightened me. How messed-up an idea was that?" Jan shook her head.

Marti felt sad for Peg. "She was trying."

"You don't have to tell *me* that."

They stood in silence for a few minutes until Jan asked, "Marti, those skirts you used to sew out of ties, were any of them Dad's?"

"No, I got the ties at thrift shops. Besides, I don't have any of those skirts anymore."

"Too bad, they were great. I never hung a picture of Ed before, yet when I found this one"—Jan carefully straightened the picture, although it didn't need straightening—"I decided to make peace with Ed. He wasn't nice to Mom, but he was good to me. Maybe I took on too many of her battles." Jan turned away from the pictures. "So if I can decide not to be hard on Ed, maybe you can go easier on Mom."

"I just defended her, didn't I? I'm not hard on Mom."

"Aren't you?"

"Aren't you still taking up her battles?"

Jan went to the counter and started shredding cheese. The kitchen door swung open and there stood Josh, grown taller and broader, with his father's shoulders. He grinned at Marti, and she gave him a hug.

"Where's Tess?" he asked.

"Out walking the dog."

"Caliban's here? Cool."

"Hey," Jan said, turning around. "Where's the cat?"

"Rob has her."

"I thought you had her?"

"Precious didn't like country living, so Rob took her temporarily."

Marti directed her attention at Josh, asking him about colleges he planned to apply to, the job he'd worked for the summer, any subject she could think of. He talked about the pressure of figuring out college while keeping his grades up. "You remember that, I'm sure," he said, and Marti vaguely concurred, not looking at Jan.

Brian and Tess returned with Caliban who poked his nose into every corner of the house. Marti asked Jan if she was really okay with keeping him. "Sure. I can't imagine you'd find a hotel room in Montreal that allowed dogs. I hope you have a reservation. Busy in summer. And your passport? You know you might need it even for Canada."

Marti felt a moment of panic—before remembering she wasn't really going to Canada. "Got it." Marti inquired about sleeping arrangements and asked Tess to help carry the bags up. Tess dropped their bags on the twin beds in Meg's room and turned to leave. Saying they needed to talk, Marti gently touched her arm.

Tess flailed as if shaking off a fly. "What's there to say? You wanted me to come and I'm here. Case closed."

"Where were you going?" Marti sat on one of the beds, motioning for Tess to sit on the other.

Tess didn't, her hand still on the doorknob. "Going? I wasn't going anywhere. That's the point; I wanted to *stay* in Chatham. I was gonna stay with Rachel, a friend of Ethan's—my friend now too."

"Did you think I'd leave without you?"

"You *really* want to see that art show. Besides, I'm old enough. After all, you left me alone in the middle of the night."

"It wasn't—" Marti stopped. "You're not old enough. You scared me."

"Scared you? You're so over the top! I'm at a friend's, and you say I'm running away. *Cra-zy.*" Tess shook her head. "Well, you scare me by controlling every detail of my life, yet shutting me out of yours. I'm here. Isn't that enough? You said it was important for me to see my aunt—my real aunt, not like your fake one—so let me do that." Tess left the room, closing the door.

When Marti came downstairs, she found Brian, Josh, and Tess playing basketball in the driveway. Despite her insecurity around competitive sports, Marti joined them, thinking, *This will take until dinner, and then I'll claim to be tired. Day one over.*

The next morning, Marti offered to cook dinner. "You'll be feeding Tess for a few days, so let me shop and do dinner." Jan said she'd go with her but Marti nixed this, insisting she wanted to have a wander in town. Brian suggested she might want to check out the new art store near the antique shops.

After the art store, she went into one of the antique shops, noticing a wall covered with old practice samplers, the ones young girls routinely worked in the past, embroidering the alphabet or a Bible verse, over and over, each successive line growing smaller and smaller, as they perfected their craft. *Another way to be invisible.*

She bought ingredients for a vegetable stir-fry and a fruit salad, figuring all the chopping would eat up time. When she returned, Tess and Josh were watching a movie. Josh said hello while Tess, tightly hugging her knees, barely nodded. Jan was about to take Caliban for a walk. "Come with me," she said, her tone commanding.

Jan walked a brisk pace with the dog until stopping abruptly, impatiently waiting for Marti to catch up. As soon as Marti did, Jan said, "Tess is upset. She feels her whole summer has been you dragging her away from friends, first Brooklyn, now Chatham."

Marti hadn't expected this. She tried some light mother banter. "Yes, what teenager doesn't think it's all about them?"

"She said you made up a sick relative to leave work."

"Oh, she's confused. I had vacation time I was about to lose and, well, they don't normally let you use it in the summer."

"So you lied?"

"Wouldn't be fair to lose time I earned, would it?" She was annoyed with Jan giving her an ethics lesson. *Always the bad one.*

"To visit Chatham?"

"Can't I be nostalgic?"

"Nostalgic for a childhood you ran away from? Tess thinks there's more to the story. She thinks you're going to Montreal with Peter."

"Peter? I guess Tess didn't tell you he has a family."

"She did. And also told me you've been seeing a lot of him, even going over there at night, arguing so loud you wake his children. Tess heard his partner say he didn't want you and Peter going away."

"She misconstrued. Heard wrong."

"Why would you want to get your heart broken again?"

Marti shook her head. "You don't understand."

"Understand what? You were devastated when you broke up with Peter, so devastated you ran away and almost ruined your life."

"Is that what you think? Is that what Mom thought?" Marti's voice was suddenly loud and belligerent. Caliban started to whine and she bent down, reassuring him.

"What else is there to think? You hurt Mom deeply and came back into our lives all *la-di-da*. No explanation. Most kids run away because they're abused, beaten. Mom didn't do any of that."

"She wasn't perfect, Jan."

"Well she didn't deserve what you dished out, all because of some boy."

"I didn't run away because of Peter!" Marti shouted, causing Caliban to bark this time. Jan gripped the leash tighter, pulling him closer to her. "I'm tired of being cast as the ungrateful child. There are things you never understood."

"What things? That Mom broke up this great love you had? Excuse me if I don't care."

"There was no love affair with Peter." She said this quietly.

"So it was casual sex and that's supposed to make it better?

You ran away because you didn't have enough freedom? *Please.* And here you go keeping a tighter rein on your kid than Mom ever kept on you." Marti snatched the leash from Jan and walked quickly away, pulling Caliban. "Go on, run away, you're good at that. Tess told me about the cat. You better start paying as much attention to your child as you do that dog."

Marti started to run.

"Wait! Marti, sorry! Please, can't we talk? I'm worried." Jan ran to catch up. Marti stopped but didn't turn in Jan's direction.

"Will you watch Tess or not?"

"Of course. I love my niece. But she doesn't understand what's going on, and neither do I."

Marti went inside and asked Josh to help her in the kitchen.

23

ager to leave in the morning, Marti tolerated awkward small talk for only as long as necessary. She drove with speed, as there was no one and nothing she wanted responsibility for, especially not Tess. Rolling down the windows, she let the wind rip through her hair.

Peter hadn't yet checked into their adjoining motel rooms when she arrived. If he didn't show, she'd follow through, and it struck her now as both cowardly and selfish to have involved him. She unpacked her few things, placing Spencer's information carefully by the phone before sprawling across the king-size bed and riffling through the newspapers, scanning for articles on the rapes. The headline was from a radio talking head: *She's a stripper, not a candy striper.* She pushed the papers off the bed and crawled inside, loving the crisp hotel sheets with their tight hospital corners. She cocooned under the covers. *Home.* She quickly fell asleep.

Awakening to a knocking sound, she was dreaming that it was Jan knocking, saying, "Time!" while holding out a tie. Marti stood up, slowly recognizing where she was, and went to the door, but no one was there. Deciding it was part of her dream, she lay down again until another knock made her realize it was the adjoining door.

"I was about to give up," Peter said. "Oh, you're sleeping. I'll come back later."

"No, come in. What time is it?"

"Six o'clock."

"Wow, I slept a long time." Marti sat on the bed, and Peter sat in the armchair by the round table in the corner.

"I have two beds in my room," he bragged, grinning.

"So? Bet they're not king-size."

"No, I'm a queen anyway."

"Ha ha. The puns never stop, do they? Just like Spencer."

"I think I picked it up from him, and I'd give it up except it drives Roger crazy and that's my job."

"A difficult job?"

"*Yes.* I have to use all my wits to knock him off-kilter. It only takes real life to upset me. Hey, so I've driven around town. Not much here, kind of a run-down stop off the highway. I found Spencer's house. It looks like where he lived in Chatham only worse, if you can believe it. You'd never think a family lives there. The porch is falling apart, and the yard is totally bare except for garbage strewn about. And yet oddly, there's an amazing garden on the side. I drove by where he works, ugly—"

"Let's go to his house," Marti interrupted before going into the bathroom and splashing water on her face.

"Marti, he has kids. Call him."

Calling somehow seemed harder than just showing up, but she agreed to this. "I'll need a drink first."

Peter said he had to call Roger and would meet her in a few minutes at the bar across the street. Grudgingly, she called Jan and Tess. *Oh, I must run because there's a gallery I want to catch before it closes.*

There were a few others sitting at the bar and one or two families eating at tables. Peter ordered a beer and Marti, a martini, which she drank quickly. Peter asked if she wanted to get a table for dinner. "No. Phone call. But another drink for fortification." She drank this one a little slower, contemplating how to begin. She sucked the olives like they were ambrosia she was extracting courage from.

Spencer, hi. (Would she say hi? No, of course not.)
Spencer, this is Marti. (Did she need to say Marti Farrell?)
Spencer, this is fourteen-year-old Martha whom you fucked.

"Peter, let's go." She gulped the last of her drink, yet unfortunately wasn't feeling the alcohol. It would take a gallon to reach her in this heightened state. "Never mind." She put her hand up. "You stay, finish your beer. When I get back, we'll order dinner, unless . . . unless we're seeing him tonight. It would be great to get it over with."

In her motel room, she sat on the edge of the bed, fiddling with the phone. *Just do it.*

"Is Spencer there?" she asked. *The wife. Susan.*

"Who's calling, please?"

"An old student of his."

There was a long pause, and then she said carefully, "I'll get him." Marti wondered at the tension in her voice. *Had others called? Denise?* Maybe she should have contacted Denise, and they could have done it together.

"Spencer, this is Marti."

"Who?"

"Marti Farrell."

There was silence, except for his breathing, until he said, "I'm sorry, I don't know who you are."

"Yes, you do. Cut the crap."

"No, sorry. Don't remember you."

Marti heard that familiar self-satisfied tone and twisted the phone cord tightly around her fingers, squeezing hard, trying to contain the fury rising inside her. "Maybe you remember me more as Martha. That's what you called me when you fucked me. You remember. I remember. It festers inside me like a spreading tumor. I'm here in Bantree to see you."

"What? Not possible."

"You have to meet me."

"I don't know you. Therefore, I'm not meeting you."

"I know where you live, where you work. You will see—"
She was talking to a dial tone. Dialing again, she listened to it
ring and ring. Realizing what a losing move that was, she quickly
returned to the bar.

"Another martini, please," she said to the bartender before
turning to Peter. "He hung up on me, so *now* we go to his house."

"Whoa . . . slow down, Marti. It's nighttime, the kids. We can
go to his job tomorrow." She shook her head, dissatisfied. "He's
not going to answer the door. He'll be watching for you. At work
we can catch him off guard. C'mon." Peter stood up and took her
arm. "Let's eat." Slowly, she unclenched her teeth and followed
him, clutching her drink. This was why she needed Peter.

Marti shoved her unopened menu away. She couldn't think
about food and didn't want to think about Spencer anymore
tonight. Peter was chattering about the menu, how the only thing
he'd trust was a sandwich. She could care less and would order
whatever he did. Searching for a topic of conversation, she asked
Peter, "What kind of chef, what kind of cooking did you do?"

He looked uneasy. "How did you know I was a chef?"

"You told me, remember?"

"Right, sorry. I thought maybe Roger . . . Never mind." Peter
waved the waitress over, and she took their order. Marti waited
for Peter to return to the topic. He didn't.

"Why would Roger—"

"Roger worries too much."

"He loves you," she spoke softly. "That's worth everything."

"But sometimes it makes me feel weak."

Marti nodded. "I can relate to that, people expecting you to
fail, but Roger doesn't think you're weak."

"You would know that how?"

"I wouldn't really. Sorry if I'm overstepping. I just think, well,
it's obvious Roger loves you and he's a good guy."

"One conversation and you're his fan?"

"I'm your fan," Marti answered, recognizing this as true.

Peter drained the last of his beer. "All right, guess I can't joke it away with you. I was pretty shaky when I met Roger. My boyfriend had died, and Dad right after. And now, Roger thinks—another death."

"I'm sorry. What did your boyfriend die of?"

"AIDS. Logical, right? He was fine, and then suddenly, he was HIV positive. Supposedly didn't have AIDS, just the virus— or maybe ARC—remember when they called it ARC? A month later he went in the hospital with pneumonia and never came out. People tell me I'm lucky it was quick, not the slow-motion horror AIDS often is. Randy was his name, Randy Torres. He could dance like nobody's business." Peter looked up and smiled. "He taught me to dance, or rather untaught me, helped me feel the music, relax enough to move without thinking about who's watching. Just become part of the music, easy as a curl of smoke, and—wow—that rhythm with your partner, that intimacy, you know?"

"I don't," Marti said.

Peter looked puzzled. "When the music—"

"I get what you're saying," Marti cut in. "I just haven't felt it, have never been able to relax dancing."

They looked silently at each other until Peter mumbled, "The accident. It made you self-conscious." He turned his empty beer mug round and round in a circle.

"No," Marti answered firmly. "Not the accident. Spencer. He ruined me for intimacy."

"Permanently?"

"I hope not." Marti smiled faintly. "Back to Randy, unless you don't want to talk about it."

Peter ordered another beer. "I wasn't out to my family. A couple of my siblings knew, but not my parents. Randy was just my roommate. When he got ill, I said he had leukemia. My brother Richie asked if it was AIDS. I got all indignant on him. *Why does it have to be AIDS? We can't get sick like everybody else?* I vented all this outrage at him. Such a champion of the homosexual, I wouldn't let us be stereotyped! Randy was dying, and all the while, I was crouched down in the closet. Lucky me, I wasn't even HIV positive."

The bitter ring of self-loathing was familiar to Marti.

"A year later, Anne called because her good friend was diagnosed with leukemia. She was frightened, especially because of how quickly Randy died. She wanted to know all this treatment info. I just bullshitted her. Lord knows, I hope her friend didn't follow any of my lame advice! Even when I finally came out, I *still* didn't come clean about Randy's illness. I was—still am—ashamed."

They ate in silence for a few minutes, Peter mostly just moving his sandwich around. "Cleaning out the house, I keep discovering things. I learned that, after I came out, Ma started making donations to the Leukemia Society in Randy's name. Imagine that? She could only piece bits of truth together, so naïve in her way."

"It shows a real acceptance on her part, doesn't it?"

"Being gay didn't jive with her religion, yet she never missed a beat of loving me and was never unkind to Roger."

"Your mother was incapable of being unkind. Your father would have been okay too."

"I think he suspected. He was savvier than Ma. He gave me openings to tell him. I never did, and then it was too late." He paused. "There's something else I recently found. You might not want to know. It concerns you."

"Go on."

"After your abortion, Ma never brought it up again. Dad talked to me about birth control, handed me a pack of condoms—like one pack ought to do it!" Peter laughed loudly before continuing. "Said he'd rather I waited until marriage but didn't want any unwanted children conceived by me ever again. That was it. I figured if my parents put it out of their minds, so should I. But I never knew . . ." His unsteady voice petered out. He looked away while Marti waited.

"I found these prayer cards, donations to the church." He paused and looked remorsefully at Marti. "In the name of Baby Farrell."

"Oh, my god!" Marti moved back from the table and turned her head away, feeling the vermouth whiz inside.

"It seems she paid the church to say a private prayer every month, including her last month, right up until she died. A prayer for Baby Farrell's soul. She gave money to a Catholic adoption agency too, in Baby's Farrell's name."

"You never told her." Marti's voice was less than a whisper.

"What would it have cost me to tell her? Even before I was out of the closet, I could have said, *Marti didn't want to name the real father.* She'd have thought I was noble, a hero. A lot better than what I am. You can imagine how confused she was when I finally came out. *Peter, you've had girlfriends. You've made a baby with a girl. Is that why? Did that scare you off? How can you be sure you're gay?*

"I *still* didn't tell her. Fucking coward!" He took the final swig of his beer and suddenly began laughing. "Remember Laurie, that girlfriend I had? I ran into her years later at—get this—a gay pride march. We had a good laugh. That was such a great relationship, both of us closeted, not suspecting the other. *Do you want to kiss? Uh, no. Me neither. Let's just say we did.*" Peter was cackling at the irony.

Marti couldn't join in, her mind still on the prayer cards. "I made such a mess of it for so many people, Peter. It keeps reverberating. I never told my mother either, and she's gone too. I came to Chatham to apologize to your mother, yet I didn't even realize the extent—" Her voice broke.

"I know. That's why I'm here. Tomorrow, we'll put his ass to the wall."

"The motel has coffee?" Marti asked the next morning, grateful for the cup Peter handed her.

"I'm not drinking that shit. I made this myself."

"Wow, it's good." Marti savored the first life-affirming sip. "How did you get the milk to froth?"

"A frothy thing." Peter smiled.

"I guess, being a chef and all—hey, I never did learn about that."

"Don't you think we covered enough ground last night? Sorry to have laid it on you."

"I needed to know. Why should you carry that alone?"

It was a bright day, so they sat out on her small balcony overlooking the parking lot. Marti wanted the rich coffee and sunshine to be positive omens. "Have you figured out what you'll say to Spencer?" she asked.

"I think it's best to ad-lib."

"Maybe. I keep trying to plan it, but it makes me tense. Right now he still has power over me because when I think of Spencer, I'm fourteen. I'm hoping it will be different, adult to adult."

Peter scoffed, "Still one child present."

Marti took her time getting dressed. She wanted a certain look, strong and female. She chose black dress pants and a white sleeveless blouse with a red cardigan over it, as fall was creeping into the air.

The concrete building was grim and institutional. "Didn't I tell you?" Peter whispered. "It's a shitty facility; these boys don't get treatment, more like prison." Marti showed her work ID, saying she had a résumé to drop off, and told herself this was why she'd dressed up. The security guard pointed toward the office. The secretary told her there were no openings. Marti hadn't expected that—a place like this must have a lot of turnover. She stood, uncertain.

"Is there something else?" The secretary was clearly annoyed by Marti continuing to loom over her desk with Peter standing behind her.

Marti couldn't think—what now? And then she knew. "My old friend, Spencer Douglas works here. I'd like to say hi."

"Not working today." The secretary spoke without looking up.

Marti nodded and retreated to the hallway. She felt a momentary reprieve. Seeing Peter look to her for a cue as to their next move, she pushed that coward's relief aside, and said to Peter, "I can't wait until tomorrow. How do I—"

"Make an offer he can't refuse. Advise him you'll talk to his job."

"Shouldn't we do that anyway?" Marti looked around the desolate hallway with locks on every door, the sadness of the place overwhelming. "Peter, these kids have nothing and then they get Spencer." She thought of Brooke, Brandon, Peter, and herself. Lost souls, they too had gotten Spencer.

"I suspect the administration already knows about him. I've checked through his job history, and it's pretty spotty. He's definitely been asked to leave jobs. This place is either a starting job or the end of the road."

"Let's talk to the director." Marti pulled him back into the office.

The secretary barely glanced up. "I already told you that we have no jobs."

"I need to see the director. It will only take a minute."

Sighing, the woman pointed to a door. Marti knocked and entered. A man looked up from some papers and removed his glasses.

"We need to talk with you regarding one of your employees,

Spencer Douglas. Are you aware of his job history? His reasons for leaving jobs?" Marti spoke in a rush.

"Who are you, reporters? I can't discuss our employees."

"You can listen. Spencer Douglas was let go from schools for sleeping with students—"

"You need to leave. I've no time for this hearsay," he said, shuffling through papers for emphasis.

"Make time," Peter said, placing his hand on top of the papers. "Your students' well-being depends on it."

The man stood and moved to the door. "Wendy, call security. Leave now." The man backed out of his office, gesturing for them to go.

"It's not hearsay, please listen," Marti implored. "When I was fourteen, Spencer Douglas, my teacher, had sex with me."

"No concern of mine." He continued moving away.

Peter and Marti followed. "It is your concern!" she said. "And I can tell those reporters. I'm not the only one; there were others."

A security guard arrived. "Escort these two out." The director waved his hand and went back into his office, closing the door. The guard ushered them down the hall.

Marti shouted at the people milling in the hallway. "Spencer Douglas sleeps with students! He needs to be watched. He shouldn't work with children!"

A woman tried to propel some laughing boys into a classroom while more students and teachers spilled out of rooms to see the commotion. The guard gripped Marti's arm tightly. "Be quiet and walk out."

Peter yelled, "It'll be on your heads if Spencer Douglas ruins any more lives. Child molester! You've been warned!" He circled around, his hands pointing at each group of bystanders until the guard swung toward him, pulling his arm roughly. "Okay, okay. We're going. Your responsibility now. It's on your watch!" Peter shouted as he was tossed out the door.

They were getting into the car when they heard a voice. "Wait!" A young man, his tie swaying back and forth, ran toward them. Catching his breath, he said, "Spencer's a creep. I knew that but didn't know this."

"It's true. It happened to me," Marti said.

"What about boys?" He looked at Peter.

"Don't think so. He just treated them like dog shit on his shoes."

"Doesn't he treat everyone that way? Not trying to pry, I'm asking because I never suspected Spencer of molesting our boys. He barely knows their names, punches the clock and bolts when the day's over."

"That's a good thing," Peter said, "less damage."

"I heard you in there; a lot of us did. And . . . and I'm sorry," he said, making eye contact with Marti. "My name is Evan McGill; I teach science here." He held out his hand, and they introduced themselves. "We, myself and other teachers, we'll keep an eye on Spencer. You'll never get a response from the administration, but I'll let Spencer know we know." He smiled. "Honestly, I'll enjoy that." He handed Marti a card with his phone number, and this struck Marti as an incredibly thoughtful thing to do.

As they drove off, Peter said, "I think he'll take your call now." He held up his hand, and Marti slapped him five. They were giddy with what they'd done, shouting, "Attica! Attica!" as they pumped their fists out the car windows.

"Not yet, though," Peter said, seeing Marti eye the phone as they entered his motel room. "Give it time for the news to spread." He flopped down on one bed, and Marti lay on the other.

"You're an art therapist, is that right?" Peter asked.

"I work with kids in a hospital."

"Like Spencer." He smirked, and she threw a pillow at him. "You like your job, Marti?"

"I love my work, although I can get overly involved. This break is good."

Peter leaned up on one elbow. "You call this a break? Girl, you need a life!"

"True, true."

"You have a college degree?"

"A master's."

"How'd you manage that?"

Marti wondered if Peter's questions were because he wanted to find a new career; he still hadn't told her what had gone wrong. "I first went to a craft college in California. A portfolio got me in."

"California? I thought you and Brooke went to Canada."

"Not forever. In fact, Brooke left shortly after we got there. She was sleeping with two guys, and there was friction between them."

"Duh."

"The commune held meetings, concluding Brooke was free to live as she wished and the guys needed to suck it up." Marti laughed. "So to speak. A week after the meeting, Brooke left with a third guy."

"And you?"

"I left some time later . . . with a guy too, named Coyote."

"*Coyote?* Oh, spare me! Was it his animal magnetism that grabbed you?" Peter turned over onto his hands and knees and lifted his head high. "Ooowoo!"

"Shut up!" Marti was laughing so hard she barely got the words out. She stood up and hit him with a pillow.

"A real howl. And if you go for biting, all the better." Peter pulled the pillow from her, and as she tried to wrestle it back, he yanked her onto the bed, pretending to bite her. She gave up in a fit of laughter, and they lay together until their laughter subsided.

Marti sat up and stretched her arms over her head as she spoke. "I'll have you know, it was very romantic." She fell back on the bed. "Except that he was headed west to be with his girlfriend, and I didn't realize that until we were on the road. Fortunately, he believed in *love the one you're with*."

"Didn't we all back then? And you were eager to oblige because of those animal teeth of his—" Peter held her arms down, mimicking biting again.

Hysterically laughing now, she pushed him off. "It was exciting. We hopped freight trains."

"Hey, now that *is* cool." Peter sat up and grinned. "You win. We should all do it with a coyote."

"Meeting him was a lucky break."

"How so?"

"For all their peace and love, the commune was a bunch of self-righteous bastards. The only ones I felt in commune with were the little kids. They were so neglected; some barely knew who their parents were."

"I bet they loved you."

"Latched on is more like it. The children were just supposed to run around carefree, never asking for anything. The attention I paid them shone a light on their needs, so the parents hated me."

"Coyote to the rescue."

"He got me out of there and gave me an address of some friends of his in San Francisco, these three great women who took me in and helped me start building a life." Marti paused, smiling. "Although as you pointed out, I'm still working on the life thing."

"Aren't we all? Except Roger, he's already there, born there, emotionally healthy. What a concept."

"Refreshing."

"Exactly. He was a burst of fresh air wafting into all my sealed-up rooms. Speaking of fresh air . . ." Peter stood up. "I'm off for a drive, maybe find somewhere nice to take a walk. Wanna come?"

"No thanks, I'll go for a swim in the pool."

Marti lay on a plastic float in the middle of the empty pool with her eyes closed, thinking about Coyote and his intoxicating way of being erotic and tender in equal measure. Making love with him under the open night sky remained vivid in her mind; it could arouse her even now. The beguiling sex made it seem as if Spencer's mark on her was, at last, not only being erased, but replaced by something miraculous. Coyote's deft hands touching her ever so lightly yet completely was a memory she held dear. She could still evoke the sensation of their entwined bodies moving in harmony. She felt herself melting into the water's weightlessness, startled each time the float hit the side of the pool, having forgotten she wasn't in an open, endless sea.

Rob was wrong: she wasn't frigid. Further proof was this summer. She *had* been attracted to Peter; she could admit this now. It didn't matter that it was futile. Experiencing the feeling was good in and of itself.

Still, there was truth to what Rob said. The sex was wonderful when they met. But over time, when she realized that Rob wanted a real relationship and wasn't leaving, terror lodged in Marti. All of the men she'd dated previously were temporary, passing through awaiting their next adventure, a given at the start. Once, much to her shame, she'd even been involved with a married man (she rationalized it at the time by knowing she was one of many).

And the only man she'd been with since the divorce was from Australia, in New York for just a year, and he wasn't the commitment type: *No one's ever snared me.* It was so casual that they never even said a goodbye—*see you later*—just the way she wanted it. How hollow and sad all those relationships were.

She'd opened herself up to Coyote because he was on his way to someone else.

Rob was part of a dream she chased, her face pressed against the window glass, gazing longingly at those elusive, seemingly happy, normal families. It wasn't love but rather a safety net she was grasping. She sealed herself tight inside that false bubble and couldn't let anyone in—especially not Rob—for fear something so fragile would break. He was just a symbol to her. It wasn't fair, and that was why the marriage failed.

Peter wasn't back when she returned to the room. She called Spencer anyway. He answered on the third ring.

"It's Marti."

"I know you went to my job and made a spectacle of yourself," he said. Clenching her teeth, she refused to feel belittled. "Who was with you?"

"Not your business. There will be more of the same or worse if you don't see me."

"Tut-tut."

She shook her head firmly as if he could see through the telephone wire. She let her silence speak.

"Fine, have it your way," he said. "I'll meet you in the parking lot of CVS at seven-thirty. It's off Route 12, north of town."

Peter returned and she told him. "Marti, I've been thinking, I won't go if that's okay with you. I don't want to see him."

"Thought you did?"

"No, well, maybe I half convinced myself, but it's your battle. I came to help you through it."

"You pretended you needed to see him to help me?"

"Something like that, but not so gallant. I deluded myself. I'm good at self-delusion, haven't you noticed? It was a diversion from everything else. Yeah, he was a shit to me—easy to do to someone in the closet. I don't need to give him more importance.

"It's different for you. You need to do this. You *should* do it, and you don't need me. You're strong enough. It'll carry more weight if you go alone." Peter paused, scrutinizing her. "Okay with that?"

"I am." She truly was.

24

Marti left early to locate the store. Panicking when she couldn't find it, she drove back and forth along the same stretch. There was a strip mall with another drugstore, not a CVS. Was that what he meant? Or did he, with no intention of meeting her, make up a phony place? Finally, she pulled into a gas station and learned CVS was farther down the road. Fearing lateness, she drove quickly. It wasn't even seven, plenty of time; she was just latching onto little things to feel uneasy about. Cars were in the parking lot and the store was open, but for how long? She didn't want an empty parking lot, not because she was worried what Spencer would do but rather because she wanted some kind of check on herself. Driving past the front, she read the sign: open until nine. Her nerves were too taut to feel any relief.

Debating where to park, she desired neither a deserted corner nor an area full of cars, and parked in a spot off to the side. She spotted a dog waiting with his head thrust out the car window and felt an ache; Caliban could make her feel safe. Watching customers move about, she got out and stood, rubbing the scars on the side of her face; their familiarity was a comfort to her now. It was 7:40, ten minutes past their meeting time, and the cars were thinning. There was a crispness in the air that signaled summer's end. It wasn't dark yet but soon would be. That was fitting, wasn't it? Their encounters had always been in a terrible kind of shrouded darkness and so should this . . . Reunion? Confrontation? Reckoning? What was the word? No, no, Marti wanted bright sunlight because only light could kill it. Yet here it was, neither dark nor light with the increasing chill signaling the threat of nightfall.

One car came in, and Marti looked closely as some laughing teenagers got out. It was a while until another car arrived, a woman driving with children in the back seat.

He's not coming. What do I do now?

The woman with the kids parked at a distant corner of the parking lot, and Marti noticed then that there was a man with them. He was turned toward the back, pushing a toy train along the top of his seat. He made the train dip up and down while the children laughed, a girl and a boy. He handed the train to the boy, kissed the woman, and got out of the car. His back was to Marti, but the hunch of his shoulders was familiar.

That morning she'd been deliberate about her clothes but tonight had paid no attention. She was dressed in a pair of gray sweats with a long-sleeved purple T-shirt, and her hair, still wet from swimming, hung unkempt. Looks didn't matter to Marti now; they were irrelevant as a barometer of self-respect.

Leaning against her car, she watched while he scanned the parking lot. It was incongruous—he looked the same but so much older, his gray hair tied in a thin ponytail. He was dressed much as he would have been back then, worn jeans and a black T-shirt, only the shoes were of a new era, no longer work boots but a pair of brown suede Merrells. He was slender still, yet somehow he sagged, as if carrying an impossible weight. She felt a tinge of pity, thinking his baggage was harder to manage than hers. Her eyes straight ahead, she walked in his direction.

His face telegraphed recognition and he stopped, his hands in his pockets, deliberately not looking at her, waiting for her to approach.

"You brought your family to hear this?" she said, gesturing at his car and standing a few feet from him.

"To hear what? I don't know what this is about. I don't know you." He didn't look at her.

She had a moment of doubt: Had he done what he did so often to so many girls that he truly couldn't keep track? Was it possible that those seven months were just a blur in a long line of blurs? Extraneous, as it didn't matter. He still owned it. She could barely contain the rage threatening to engulf her. "You remember the girls you raped in closets." Her voice was loud and piercing. She noticed a woman hurrying a child into a car. A man leaned against his open car, studying the scene with his keys in hand.

"Raped?" Spencer said. He raised his eyebrows, scraggly now, but still with that distinctive arch. "I'd never hurt a woman. I saved a woman from rape once in college; walking past a fraternity party, I saw some jock jerks hassling this girl, so I—"

"Stop. I don't want to hear your fantasy." The man with the keys got in his car and was driving off. "Never hurt a woman? You think fucking a fourteen-year-old—"

"You weren't fourteen."

"Oh, you remember me now?" Marti laughed. "That was quick! Was it the closet or my age that clued you in?"

Spencer looked back at his car. Marti could see the kids tussling in the back seat. Frida's hair was dark and her skin pale, like her father's. Horatio had thick brown curls. Susan, his wife, was not looking in Spencer's direction nor at her children, but down at her hand where she was concentrating on picking at her index finger.

"I was fourteen, lonely and insecure."

"Yes, I knew that." Spencer nodded in eager agreement. "I saw how those kids treated you. It was painful to watch, and I wanted to help."

"Help?"

"I tried to. I encouraged your artwork."

"Fucking me was *so* helpful."

Spencer shrugged and started to turn away. Marti regretted the sarcasm, as it wouldn't give her what she wanted. She noticed the sky with colors of orange and gray merging together; it wouldn't be long until sunset finished. What did she want from him? She tried again. "You're right, I had problems. My father died; that's an endless wound, but he didn't hurt me. He died. I had an accident and that's what it was, accidental. And yes, there were kids who teased me, *children*. You, Spencer—you were different."

He smiled at that.

"You weren't an accident. You weren't ignorant. You were calculated. You saw my vulnerability and used it. You fed off my pain. It excited you. It turned you on. Again and again, you used me. A parasite, you sucked everything you wanted, and when you were done, you spit my carcass out."

"I tried to boost your self-esteem."

"Posing me naked like your fucking doll in the snow? That was helping me? No. No."

"Oh, you liked it plenty."

It came to her suddenly, as if for the first time. "It doesn't matter what I liked; I was fourteen. You were more than ten years older. *My teacher*. Fourteen-year-olds think they like a lot of things that are harmful to them."

"Loved it, in fact. Begged for it." He leaned closer, whispering the last part with his familiar smirk, his head cocked to one side, revealing that perfect crescent-shaped dimple. She reached out and hit him with her arm. Balling her fist, she hit him again.

Her blows were ineffective and he laughed gleefully, not even backing away. His wife had gotten out of the car now, watching. "Look, you'd better stop or my wife will call the cops."

"Good. Tell them your sad story. Coward, hiding behind your wife. How could you bring your children here? No, don't answer;

I know how. Whoever you can exploit to your gain, that's okay by you. It's all about you. You're a narcissist."

"Big word, Marti."

She wouldn't fall for the bait. "Helped me? You took everything from me: my childhood, my artwork, my family, even my name. It almost destroyed me. I'm not the only one. Denise. And others. You've had to leave schools. I know your history, and now your job knows."

"Going to my job, and now this—harassment." Spencer glanced over at a couple watching in the parking lot and straightened up. "I won't stand here and be abused by you. You're stalking me, and I *will* call the police. You had no right to go to my job." He turned away.

Marti grabbed his arm. "You'll stay until I say go." He snatched his arm back and stood, half-turned away from her. "No right to contact your job? I had every right. You had no right to violate me. There are laws that you broke over and over."

"Oh, going to arrest me, are you?" He held his arms out as if ready to be cuffed. He leaned in closer and whispered, "Cuff me already, I know you like it rough."

His wife got back in the car.

Marti drew back in repulsion. She took a steadying breath. "It won't work. You can't control me with humiliation. Oh, it worked easily back then; I was a sad, stupid child who inhaled all the degradation you dished out. Of course I did! And you *knew* I would. I'd never tell on you! So easy to manipulate, wasn't I? You chose your mark well.

"Have you any idea what it did to me? I was fourteen and pregnant. What could I do?"

"You had an abortion. Sweetie Petey to the rescue."

"You think? Really? You think Peter and I would know where to get an abortion? As you well know, I knew *nothing*. I ran away, remember? Kind of a drastic thing to do, unless . . . unless there's a reason. Ever wonder what happened to the baby? Not a baby anymore, a grown man, turned twenty-eight last December. Just a bit younger than your wife." She paused, relishing the moment. "And that's why I'm here. Are you ready to be introduced?"

She hadn't planned this; it came to her impulsively and seemed fitting, a logical conclusion to the wreckage he'd caused. She was enjoying watching the shock and suspicion register on his face. Their positions had flipped: she was the puppet master now, and he the hanging marionette.

"You had an abortion, I'm sure of it."

She shook her head. "I ran away and couldn't come back. But you're right, I did ask Peter to help me. I asked him to spread rumors so you wouldn't try to find me. I knew you suspected I was pregnant. Your quick exit that summer was so convenient."

"God, Marti—no—you can't be sure he's mine."

"Can't be sure! Wasn't that the point? Fucking a virgin?"

He looked around the parking lot. "He's here? Now?"

"He's already met your work colleagues. I didn't want to tell you on the phone and ruin the surprise. What will you say to him, Spencer?"

Spencer repeatedly ran his hands through his hair, looking frantically around him. "That I never knew. I never knew. I'd have been there for him. You kept him from me. You're the one he'll be angry at! He and I, we can have a relationship."

"No. No, you can't. Your poison will never touch my child."

"Hardly a child anymore."

Marti paused, savoring the moment. Should she leave him dangling, doubting, questioning? That would be a kind of revenge, wouldn't it? She'd haunt him the way he'd haunted her all these years. On his deathbed, he'd still be wondering.

But what if he searched? She had to keep him away, had to protect Tess. And herself. She wanted nothing between them, and this lie would be a heavy chain, binding them together.

"No, not a child. Not anything except some random dust in the universe. I had to kill your baby to survive." Watching the relief spread across his face, she didn't react. Any reaction would be too light for the rage and revulsion weighing on her, that boulder of shame, disgust, and terror that she'd hauled uphill all these years. She wanted to hurl it at him and watch it crush him so he'd never be able to get out from under its weight.

"You let someone else take the rap for it. You think that was good for Peter? For his family? Mrs. Colgan, a kind and honorable woman, went to her grave praying for what she thought was her grandchild. That's on your head."

"You said you were using birth control. You lied. How was I to know?"

"No, Spencer, not a lie, ignorance. It's why you chose me. You fucked me for months before mentioning birth control. You couldn't have cared less. You really think a child virgin will 'take care of things'? Really? Picture Frida in my position. Let that image keep you awake at night."

"Leave my daughter out of it!"

"Gladly. And I pray you'll leave her alone."

"You're disgusting!"

"Me? God, Spencer, are you so insane you don't know what you did? How many times have you done it? All those job changes?"

"I see you've been checking on me. For how many years? Can't get me out of your head? Still obsessed? That's how much you liked it, craved it. I was so good that you can't forget."

Marti drew back, every fiber in her being taut, and yet she was shaking.

"I'm leaving now if you're done with your sanctimonious crap," Spencer said.

"No. Not until I'm finished. You have no power over me. I'm not a child you can manipulate. I understand it all now. You knew exactly what you were doing back then, but I didn't. I couldn't even function afterward; I had to leave home—"

"Aha! I figured it out. Peter is who was with you. God, Marti, how perfect! Playing house again? One disaster after another with that savior of yours—will you never learn? You could have been arrested today. Peter is the reason you left home. He burned your face, and if that wasn't enough, went blabbering all over school about getting you pregnant with his big cock—"

"No, Spencer, *you*."

"I never told anyone!"

"Of course not. You were good at protecting yourself, only yourself. Did you really think I could pick up my childhood again like nothing happened?"

"Pining for me, were you?" He twirled his hand in the air. "Well sorry, you should have let me know. We could have carried on."

"Your self-delusion is incredible. It's how you sleep at night! I loathe the very air you breathe. I had to leave home to survive what you did to me. My mother, my sister, I can't begin to fathom how much I hurt them. That's on your head. *Helped me?* You shattered my self-respect, my dignity. I couldn't have a healthy marriage—"

"Oh, blame me for everything, your whole life. There's that hangnail you had once too, isn't there?"

"I've had to claw my way out from your squalor. But I did it. I'm here. I've put it all back together—"

"Humpty Dumpty," he muttered, "you know your nursery rhymes."

"I lived, in spite of you. I survived. I'm here to warn you: I'll be watching. Those poor boys you work with—"

"Hardly poor boys—"

"Shut up, I'm talking. Everyone will know what you did. If you ever damage anyone again the way you damaged me, I'll find out. I'll hunt you down. Now get in your car and leave."

"Marti—"

"Don't say my name. I'm not a weak, pathetic girl anymore. I can't hear you."

He started walking away before turning back. "I did care, Martha. I saw something in you, something special—"

"You can't seduce me. You have no power here. You can't speak. Get in your car and let her drive you away. Not one more word." She said the last bit slowly, emphasizing each word, and pointing her arm straight at his car. "Go."

His hands in his pockets, shoulders hunched, eyes on the ground, he turned and walked away. As he got into his car, Marti could see his wife frantically questioning him and Spencer shaking his head, motioning for her to drive. The boy leaned forward, and Spencer ignored him until he sat back down. After a pause he turned and ruffled the boy's hair, taking a last peek at Marti. She stood watching as the car began to move. The wife gawked at her but immediately stopped when Marti tried to make eye contact. Spencer's head was bent down. The children turned and pressed their faces against the back window, staring intently at Marti. She returned their gazes until the children vanished from view.

25

"How does it feel?" Peter asked as they sat for dinner across the street again.

Marti pumped her fist in victory. The waitress came over. "Oh, sorry, I wasn't waving for you," Marti said, giggling, "but I am ready to order." They ordered the same sandwiches as the previous evening and a beer for Peter. Marti, intoxicated with retribution, didn't order a drink.

"I can't believe he brought his children," Peter said, shaking his head.

"It makes perfect sense. He's using them, same as he used us, a buffer between himself and reality." The waitress put bread on the table, cold and stale; Marti, ravenous, enjoyed it.

"I taunted him with the image of a grown son. Said I'd never had an abortion." She laughed. "He thought that's who came to his job."

"Wow, that must have freaked him. Good fun."

"Oh, yeah, it was great. I couldn't keep it up, though, not another lie to carry, and so then he figured out you were the one with me."

"Too bad, I didn't want to give Spencer the pleasure of thinking he mattered. He didn't ruin my life."

"Mine either. If I didn't know that before, I know it now. Spencer's still swimming in his poison. He'll never pay for his crimes, justice being arbitrary at best, but at least he'll be stuck in his own hell forever. You and I—we made it out, Peter."

"Hallelujah!" He tipped his beer.

Over dinner Marti encouraged Peter to talk about himself. He sighed. "You're fishing, Marti. Again."

"Don't be evasive. We're past that."

"You don't need the burden."

"Burden?" Marti put her sandwich down. "I'm insulted; I thought we were headed for real friendship."

He nodded and took a deep breath. "In college I couldn't figure out what I wanted to do. I didn't hop freight trains or live in a commune, but I had my seventies experience too, working at a health food restaurant. Baked a lot of bread and grew sprouts. I ended up at culinary school and worked my way up to sous-chef at a high-end restaurant in Boston. I thought I was top of the world until Randy got sick and the work became a lot of pressure. One night, busier than expected, I asked one of the line cooks to hurry up with what he was prepping." Peter paused, taking a long swig of beer. "He did what I told him; I was his boss after all, and in speeding up, he cut his hand. Everyone rushed around, getting bandages, putting pressure on the wound, while I just stood there watching the blood spurt out. It was bad. He severed a nerve. I didn't do a damn thing except *cringe*."

Peter called the waitress over and ordered another beer, waiting until it was safely in his hands before speaking again. "After he went to the ER, things quieted down in the kitchen except I couldn't calm down. I felt the walls closing in on me and had to get out of there. Full-fledged panic attack. I went back to work the next night thinking I was okay. And then I saw it."

"What?"

"A big fucking pot of boiling water. The lid rattled up and down, challenging me, and the panic started all over again. I'd been boiling water for years, but it was as if . . . well, you know."

Marti reached across the table to take his hand, but before she could, he leaned back in the booth, folding his arms across his chest. "Pablo's hand got better, but I couldn't do the work anymore." He lifted his head and looked up at her. "Marti, I'd give anything to have never thrown that stupid pot of water."

"Oh, Peter—"

"Don't *Oh, Peter* me! I've heard that before from my family, my friends, my shrink, and every fool who'd listen. *Oh, Peter, it was an accident. You didn't know. Oh, Peter.* The truth is, I did know. The pot was heavy. I had to hold it with both hands. It was hot in my hands, and I thought, *So what?* I didn't want you, a girl, beating me in a water gun fight and having my brothers tease me. I got a small burn on my finger. I wanted to show Ma, jealous of you getting her attention. *Me too, look at my finger!* Your skin—it was awful. And even though I could see that, all I felt was: *Poor me.*"

The last words were whispered to the floor. They sat in silence until Peter spoke again. "You never would have gotten involved with Spencer if it weren't for the accident."

Marti leaned across the table. "I wouldn't change what happened to me, Peter."

"*What?*"

"I told Spencer he didn't destroy me; I survived. And if he didn't destroy me, then you certainly didn't. I learned something today: I'm no victim. I played my own part. You and I were both being bratty kids that day, end of story. Spencer? Well, I wanted him."

"Marti—"

"Oh, I know Spencer's guilty; nothing absolves him. But he couldn't have seduced just any girl. Some would've been smarter and stronger. The pregnancy's on him. The lie? I was wrong. I should have gone to my mother from the start. It was cowardly and selfish. And mixed with a little self-delusion."

Peter looked baffled. "What do you mean?"

She took a sip of water. "There was more than one reason for making you the father, subconscious maybe—like you claiming fatherhood—but there, nonetheless. Quite a pair, you and I were, two kids with large ids! Do you know when I first suspected I was pregnant I thought Spencer and I would raise the baby together in some little cabin in the woods? That's how naïve I was. When Mom told your parents, and your mother wanted . . . well, my fantasy crystallized into the secret one I'd nurtured my whole life. I pictured me, a Colgan at last, living in your house, your mom helping raise the baby. Why, she'd almost *be* my mother! And my, how I longed for that!"

"Marti, we weren't a perfect family."

"Still, you were happier than most."

Peter shook his head. "Eight kids, that's a lot of chaos. Tom could be a sadistic bastard at times and always got away with it. Total blind spot, on Ma's part: *Kids will be kids.* Ma would go to Mass each day, and it didn't matter who was around to watch the little ones or what ensued while she was out. God was what mattered. Not us. Once when Betty was out, Ma left a too-young Ann in charge when she went to Mass. Ann had a bag of potato chips that Andy was pestering for. Ann and Tom went into the hall closet to eat them, closing the door, unknowingly locking themselves in. Andy banged on the door, breaking the outside mirror, and Richie cut his foot wandering through the glass. Marybeth was howling in her crib. I was the oldest with Ann and Tom locked up. Of course, I had no idea what to do, couldn't even get the door open. I didn't stop Richie from walking on the glass or attempt to clean it up. Hell, we were all too little.

"And you know what? Ma came home totally unfazed. The next day, she left us again. They replaced the mirror yet never removed the closet lock to make it safe. Maybe your mom was right."

"What do you mean?"

"What was Ma thinking, taking a nap and leaving a bunch of kids with a big pot on the front of the stove? Not even moving it to the back? And Ma *did* leave the stove on. You lay there scream-ing for a while. I was bawling. Ann heard, ran and got Ma. I don't know, maybe it wasn't such a long time, but it was the bloody longest five minutes of my life." Peter stopped himself. "Sorry, I shouldn't do this—not my mother's fault. Mine, all mine."

Marti told him about the time she was walking home from the park, Tess in the stroller while Marti chatted with another mom when Tess suddenly popped out of the stroller, unnoticed by Marti, and ran into the street. A car screeched to a halt and the driver yelled, rightfully so. The startling awareness of what almost happened remained imprinted upon Marti.

She'd been eager to walk from the playground with this other mother, not because she necessarily liked her but rather because she coveted acceptance in the group of playground moms with their sometimes tedious, often competitive, always judgmental conversations. The other mom asked: *Didn't you strap her in?* Of course Marti hadn't; she'd been hurrying to walk with this pop-ular mom, wanting to belong, afraid of being left behind by the cool kids. Now seeing the look this mom gave her, Marti knew the jig was up. She'd been exposed as a fraud, not worthy of mem-bership in the perfect mom club.

Ah, and then there was Tess, her lower lip stuck out in defiance, while her upper lip curled into a defiant smile. Her eyebrows knitted together in concentration, taking in the yelling man and the other mommy questioning her mommy. It was as if she deduced that Marti was at fault, twice over, first for not strap-ping her in and now for doing so, thereby ruining all the fun. And quite unnecessary, given that the horse had already left the barn.

From the beginning Marti and Tess were alien to each other. She'd always try to soothe baby Tess by nursing her only to have Tess flail about until Rob rescued her. "You need to read her cues; she doesn't always want to feed. Sometimes she wants to rock or be in a different position." And sure enough, Tess would calm right down in Rob's arms, content that someone knew what they were doing.

Marti gave Tess paints, assuming she'd be like her mother, interested in art, but Tess wasn't—unless she was smearing paint on herself. Once Tess painted her feet to make footprints and ignored Marti's command to put her feet only on the paper, wriggling out of her mother's clutches and stomping on the new rug Rob's parents had just given them. Marti had disliked the rug with its pale, impractical, too cheerful colors, knowing it was a bossy gift, implying that Marti's decorating skills were inadequate. But Tess ruining it was not a triumph but rather a repudiation of both Marti's parenting skills and artistic interests.

Tess always wanted to be outside, away from her, running, playing with other kids. She was athletic and participated in all sports: soccer, basketball, softball, even water polo, which somehow Tess discovered on her own, maneuvering her way onto a private school's team. These social and athletic abilities—skills that eluded Marti—made Tess seem at an even further distance.

But had those skills always been out of Marti's reach? Sometimes she liked to think Tess was her redo: Marti without the trauma. She knew this thinking was amiss—too symbiotic, too controlling. And besides, everyone has their own trauma. Yet the cord that had attached mother and daughter loomed as a powerful metaphor, and Marti hoped she had passed on only her best self.

Before the accident, playing with the Colgan and neighborhood kids, Marti was full of gusto and bravado, a very different girl. But once that protective skin was ripped away, it exposed a fragile Marti, and the introspection and artwork were the aftermath; maybe she'd have been someone entirely different with a different history.

A neighbor gave her a present when she returned home from the hospital, a board with the shape of a fish, ready to be filled in with bits of colored rice. Marti hadn't been much interested in art or crafts before, but with nothing else to do, she deliberated over the design, making her own color choices and working laboriously to get it just so. She was pleased at having something to immerse herself in, something private and only hers. She completed the fish—a dazzling display of purple, green, and yellow stripes. She hung it on her wall with great pride, instantly hungering for more projects, the black fish eye staring out, encouraging her.

"I know accidents happen. But some are worse than others," Peter said, in response to her tale about Tess and the car.

"It's random, it's chance. That's why they're called accidents. And a good thing came out of mine," Marti said, thinking still of that discovery of art. "The kids I work with, sick kids, some with burns—they're like me, and I'm damn good at my job because I've been where they are."

"It's not because you were burned; you were always good with kids."

"Well." Marti smiled. "I learned a lot from hanging around you Colgans."

Peter left for Boston right after their coffee the next morning. Marti could see how eager he was to get back to Roger and the twins, and she felt happy for him.

However, she had more to do. She called the school and asked for Spencer. "He's teaching now. Can I take a message?" Marti hung up.

She drove to Spencer's house and walked across the dirt lawn onto the porch. The porch reminded her of the one she'd stood on so many years earlier with its sagging steps and peeling paint; the only difference was the blue tricycle resting against the porch railing. She knocked on the battered door; there was no bell.

The door opened. Upon seeing Marti, Susan began closing it. "Spencer isn't here."

Marti pushed her hand against the door. "I know. I'm here to see you." Susan shook her head but stood passively. "First of all, I'm sorry your kids had to see that last night." Marti was struck by the similarities in their looks, both blonde and slight, and Susan's depressed affect was familiar. She moved again to close the door, but Marti didn't relinquish her arm. "I'm not done."

"It has nothing to do with me."

"Ah, but it does. You're married to him, and you need to know."

"Know what? That you're someone he had an affair with eons ago and it ended badly? So what?"

"I was fourteen. He was my teacher."

Susan looked away. "I don't need to hear this. It's another lifetime."

"Is it? Are you sure? I wasn't the only one."

"No, you weren't." Susan's lips twitched slightly and she lifted her head, looking at Marti as if expecting disappointment. Her eyes were a pale blue, so pale they were almost translucent. "He lost a job for sleeping with a student. That's when I met him. It's in the past now. We're a family and he's a good father."

"What makes you think that would stop him?"

"Because I know." Susan folded her arms across her chest.

"No one should endure what I went through. I'm going to be watching, and you should too."

Susan sighed and shook her head. "Did you look at him? Stop thinking of yourself and really look at him? Obviously not, because if you had, you'd see he's no threat to anyone, except maybe himself. He's beaten down. He can barely get out of bed in the morning. If it weren't for the kids, he'd probably be dead."

Marti understood Spencer had his demons, yet she remained unmoved. Susan continued, "An old man before his time, he's harmless."

"Spencer is never harmless. I could see that last night. He doesn't even feel remorse."

"How do you know? Because he didn't show *you* any?" Susan released a caustic smile. "You expected him to grovel?"

"No, but—" Marti began, but then stopped. She didn't want to argue with Susan; she wasn't the enemy. "Look, I'll go now. I wanted you to know because I don't want what happened to me to ever happen again."

"It won't."

"I am sorry your kids witnessed last night."

Turning to leave, she noticed the side garden Peter had mentioned. It was such a contrast to the squalor of the front yard and facade of the house. The garden was a big square, with successive squares of flowers each getting smaller and leading to the next inward square, like the patterns kids drew on Etch A Sketches. Purple framed the outside and next came orange, then yellow. In the center was a brilliant square of bright pink with one lone red flower like a bull's-eye in the middle. She noticed then that the red flower was subtly repeated at each corner of the other rows, creating a vertical line. Each row had white flowers placed into the mix at two points, forming a luminous white circle all the way around. Marti was mesmerized by the carefully curated quilt-like design of shapes and lines. She'd never seen a private garden this intricately designed, balanced, and carefully tended. She couldn't begin to fathom the effort it took. The flowers weren't even recognizable varieties to her; it was as if they'd been created to bloom just for this unique garden.

Susan watched her reaction.

"Your garden is breathtaking. You did this?"

Susan nodded proudly.

"It's astonishing. Beautiful. I've never seen . . ." Marti reluctantly pulled her eyes away from the garden and looked at Susan. "You deserve better than Spencer. Your kids deserve better. We all do."

"Spencer helped design the garden." Susan looked at her with her pale eyes that could disappear a person, revealing nothing.

The elation Marti felt last night was beginning to fade, and in its place was a new uncertain discontent. She couldn't comprehend why the elation left. As she drove along, she tried focusing on the landscape, the trees beginning their magnificent foliage, yet somehow to her they seemed dull, lifeless. *Well, duh, the leaves are dying.*

It's over. Isn't it? Why don't I feel it?

Not over, of course not. She wouldn't really know if Spencer hurt anyone again, and would that even matter? There were thousands of other Spencers. She'd carry it, a heavy stone. It was different than her scars; they were a faded reminder of an injury long healed, but this one never would. Not completely. It lodged deep inside her, not a smooth stone but a rough one whose jagged edges could wound her when she least expected it. She'd just have to live her life—not an easy feat.

Still, she was longing for Tess, the kind of ache she'd had when Tess was an infant, a physical sensation, a missing limb. She drove fast in eager anticipation.

Tess didn't stir from the computer game she was playing with Josh and hooted when Josh asked how the art show was. Caliban yelped joyfully in greeting, twirling in circles, his tail slapping against her leg. Marti nuzzled against his warmth, whispering to him. Jan said, "Caliban needs a walk, come with me."

This again?

Jan walked rapidly, not looking at her. "How's the visit been?" Marti asked, trying to keep up with Jan's pace.

"Gee, not so good."

"What's wrong?"

"You have to ask? And you call *once* with: *I've got a gallery to run to.* Same shit you pulled as a kid."

"Stop." Marti touched her arm. "Slow down."

"Tess has been scouring the Internet. No big art show in Montreal, and she's called the Colgan house in Chatham." Jan pulled up on Caliban's leash and looked harshly at Marti. "You already know no one answered."

"I was with Peter but not in that way."

"He disappointed you, huh?"

Listening to Jan, Marti recognized how demeaning her own sarcasm must be. *A familial trait learned from Mom.* "Mrs. Colgan died."

"Tess told me. Sorry, I know you really liked her."

"Loved her. I came to Chatham to see her to tell her—" Marti stopped. Shifting gears, she told Jan she was leaving, not even spending the night. Jan stared at her, incredulous. Marti told her she had a lot she needed to tell her, could she come for another visit soon—some weekend in the fall?

"Of course. But I'm worried about you. And worried for Tess."

"Thanks for everything. For caring." Marti paused. "I owe you the truth, and I owed Mommy the truth. But Tess comes first; I have to talk to her before I can explain to you."

Tess was surprised they were leaving but didn't resist. She slumped down in the car and played her music so loud it filtered through the headphones. Unpacking the car, Marti lifted the bags with the art supplies and took them into the cabin.

"I thought you wanted that to stay in the car for your job."

"Changed my mind."

"Whatever." Tess dropped her bags inside. "I'm going to Emily's."

"Not yet. We need to talk."

"You said we were coming back here so I could see my friends. Was that a lie? So many lies. Wanna tell me about the art show? *Pathetic.*"

"You know I wasn't at a show."

"That's all you can say?" Tess gestured with her arms.

"I have a lot to say. Sit down. The story starts when I was your age." Marti poured herself a glass of water before sitting at the table.

"I know, I know." Tess sat and swung her legs up over the chair arm, pumping them up and down. She turned her face away from Marti and began speaking in a singsong voice. "La, la, Peter was your true lost love. And now you meet again. Voilà!" She twirled her arms in the air and kicked her legs higher for emphasis. "Happily ever after—for *you*."

"That's not it."

"Mom, I'm not stupid!" Tess swung her feet to the floor. "I'm sick of your shit! You drag me here. You lie to your job—do you still *have* a job? Are we even going back home?"

"Yes, Tess, yes—"

"You tell Dad I'm a problem, take away my cat, my friends. Meanwhile, you're getting drunk, chasing a gay guy—"

"Whoa—" Marti reached her hand out and laid it on Tess's arm; Tess pushed it off.

"—upsetting his kids—"

"You've got it wrong. I was with Peter, not—"

"Finally, you admit—"

"—not because we're having an affair. We were *never* boyfriend and girlfriend. We pretended we were."

Tess paused and then shook her head. "I could believe that a gay guy might fake he had a girlfriend in high school. But now?"

"In high school, I had an affair with a teacher. I got pregnant."

Tess sat up straighter. "God, Mom. Is he my . . . my father?"

"No, Tess, do the math. I was fourteen. I'm not twenty-eight now. Your father is your father. I'm your mother. Nice fantasy if I weren't—" She started to laugh and couldn't stop. Tess watched as Marti took a sip of water and had to spit it out, the explosion of nervous laughter continuing, a great release. She wiped her face.

Tess waited on the edge of her chair. "I have a brother or sister?"

"I had an abortion. I was young and stupid with no idea what to do. And I was ashamed of my relationship with the teacher. I turned to Peter for help, and he pretended to be the father. That's what I told my mother."

"That's why Aunt Jan thinks—"

Marti nodded. Tess turned away, petting Caliban. She couldn't place Caliban on her lap the way she could the cat. Tess obviously missed Precious. Still, Marti wasn't going to change her mind. "We didn't come here this summer because of you. We came because of me and mistakes I made. I never told my mother the truth. After the abortion, being at school with Spen—the teacher, well it was intolerable. Kids were gossiping about me, and I couldn't do my schoolwork. I couldn't face my mother or the Colgans. I was completely falling apart. I was scared and didn't know where to turn. I ran away from home. That's why I panicked the day you were missing."

"I wasn't running away."

"I'm learning you're not me, but I'm a slow learner." Marti revealed a faint smile.

"What did you do, um, become a prostitute or something?"

Marti laughed. "You told me not to believe everything I read in magazines. I found okay places to live and it worked out, more or less. I was lucky. Really lucky. But I never made it right with Grandma. We came here because I wanted to tell Mrs. Colgan the truth."

"Why go away with Peter?"

"I went to see the teacher."

Tess stood up, a look of revulsion on her face. "God, Mom! You're in love with—him? The teacher?"

"No, Tess, no. No love story here. Sit down. He demeaned and abused me. That's been with me lurking in the background ever since, hovering like an evil monkey on my back, tethering me to him. I needed that to end. And I wanted to try to make sure he'll never do again what he did to me. I couldn't stand up for myself back then. Now I can."

"Is he in jail?"

"No. He's married with little kids."

"Gross."

"Yeah, that's what I say. I told his job about him, and his wife. Most importantly, I told him."

They sat in silence until Tess whispered, "I was scared, Mom. I didn't know what was happening." She started to cry and Marti reached out to hug her, but Tess shrunk back, shook the tears off, and looked away. She sat up straight and began drumming her fingers on the plastic tablecloth.

Marti handed her a tissue. "God, that ugly tablecloth! Linda made their cabin nice." Tess nodded, wiping her face. "I bet sometimes you wish Emily's family were your family."

"I-I don't—" Tess squirmed uncomfortably.

"Maybe not Emily's family but some other family. Ethan's perhaps—they seem lovely. Or Aunt Jan. I'm glad you could go to her. I used to pretend the Colgans were my family. It's a normal desire.

"I'm so sorry." Marti choked out the broken words. "I know I was awful this summer. I know it must have frightened you. I wish I could have handled things differently." Tess didn't look at her.

"Sometimes you end up making things worse before you make them better. It's like the chaos you create cleaning out a closet, you know? This summer I was making a mess by emptying out the dark corners of a closet I hadn't opened in years, and if I stopped to explain, I'd lose my nerve. I always understood that I owed you the truth. I'm overprotective at times because I know firsthand fourteen-year-olds can have big troubles."

"Well, I don't. I know you didn't like Lucas and he was a little rude. Ethan's great. We're not having sex, not even close. You're crazy if you think we were. I needed someone to talk to. He listens."

Marti nodded. "I'm glad you had someone."

"We barely kissed. Maybe he's gay." Tess giggled.

"Hey, a gay boyfriend is a great thing to have. Take it from me."

26

Marti got to work. First, she went to the newspaper office, gathering up all the issues she could. She contemplated whether to research newspaper accounts of other rape incidents or maybe keep it specific to these. Next, she scoured the thrift stores and antique shops, buying up old handmade linens. Noticing a man in the back of one store laboriously cleaning old books, she asked him how to preserve newspaper, explaining that she wanted them to be not easily torn but still flexible, with the qualities of paper. He asked her many questions, giving serious thought in a craftsman-like way that Marti appreciated. Eventually, he decided on the right product, a spray that a hobby shop two towns away would have. She went and procured it.

Using the biggest cloth she'd found, a long table runner with a tatted border all the way around, she began embroidering the long way on it: *Why should the raped have no name?* She planned to embroider several lines of it, getting smaller and smaller like a traditional sampler; once they were as small as she could manage to stitch, she'd continue in reverse, embroidering larger and larger until the loudness of the question dominated the table runner.

She'd found a set of tea towels, named for the days of the week, specific activities tied to each day with Sunbonnet Sues performing them. She began thinking about which quote to put on each day; Sunday, church day, could be: *She's such a good girl*, or Monday, cleaning day, might be: *I'm a stripper. Stripping is a job, not a license to rape.* Thursday's chore was ironing, the perky Sunbonnet Sue leaning over the board with an iron in hand. Marti remembered a poem titled: *Language, like an ironing board, being one of the many tools of oppression.* She would choose carefully, highlighting the symbolism of each day's chore.

Among her purchases were several tatted handkerchiefs, including a half-finished one with the tatting needle and bobbin still attached. She'd use that somewhere, leaving the bobbin and needle, and maybe embroider: *A woman's work is never done.*

The word *please*, small and meek, would hide in a corner, like a signature. *Please* sometimes being the closest word a woman had for no. *She's such a good girl.*

Unsure how she'd put it all together, she purchased the largest canvas the store had. Clearly, it still couldn't contain all her ideas. She could create different pieces for different women, reflecting the AIDS quilt (she thought then of Randy, wondering whether he had a square, and if not, perhaps she could help Peter make one). Or maybe she'd make this piece triangular, mimicking Judy Chicago's *The Dinner Party.* Perhaps it wouldn't be just one work but a series. Whatever she ultimately decided, it was going to be a long process until she honed it into a complete work. She wouldn't stop until it expressed exactly what she wanted.

After swimming one day, Marti noticed the rowboat attached to their dock, and was struck that they'd never used it. She mentioned this to Tess who responded that she thought Marti would be too scared to enjoy it, and it was okay because she'd used Emily's canoe many times.

Afraid of water? Marti marveled at how little they knew one another. She suggested Tess ask her friends over the next day and they'd go for a "floating lunch". Marti packed several sandwiches, lemonade, cookies, and fruit. Emily and Matthew rowed over in their canoe, and Ethan came as well. Marti was surprised and pleased when Tess invited her along. They rowed to the middle of the lake, stopped, and ate. The sun was warm, not too warm, and a good time was had. Marti considered it an accomplishment.

The next day, Tess invited them again, minus Matthew, and including Sarah. Marti made more sandwiches and gave them two bags of chips. They didn't invite her this time, and she was fine with that as she wanted to work. Her materials were spread all over the cabin. The spray had worked on the newspaper just like the man said it would, and now she was weaving them with the jute, making sure the quotes fanned out, readable. She smiled thinking of all the time she'd spent teaching kids to make those endless, tedious lanyard ropes, and how that skill was paying off now.

Engrossed in this, she suddenly heard commotion, and went on the dock to investigate. The four kids, two in each boat, were standing and throwing potato chips at each other. Marti shouted at them to stop, but they ignored her. Next, pieces of sandwiches went flying. She yelled again, but they couldn't hear as they were ramming the boats, laughing and pulling on each other until the canoe tipped over. Tess and Ethan fell in with all the picnic gear including Marti's beloved picnic basket. Irretrievable, it sank to the bottom.

When they returned to the dock, Marti began scolding them. "How could you be so careless? What a waste, and now my basket is gone."

Emily, Sarah, and Ethan instantly apologized and looked at the ground. Ethan offered to swim out and try to see if he could reach the bottom. "You can't. It's too deep." Marti snapped. She wasn't ready to let them off the hook.

Tess hadn't spoken and Marti looked at her, "Well? What do you have to say?"

Tess mumbled, "Sorry," in a sulky tone that didn't communicate regret, only embarrassment at her mother disciplining her friends.

Tess didn't bring her friends over again, and Marti was glad. She wanted quiet for her work.

Marti understood that her dream of a large family like the Colgans was never based in reality. She'd be awful at it, and miserable too. She couldn't choose the kind of mother she wanted to be; she could only work with who she was. And of course, Peter was right: the Colgans hadn't been a perfect family. Mrs. Colgan was never who Marti thought she was. She'd absorbed what Peter said about the stove still being on and it gave Marti more sympathy for Peg's position. Still, everyone wants a hero—she'd keep Mrs. Colgan on her pedestal while forgiving herself for not being like her.

She retrieved her mosaic from the art store and went to see Peter. He opened the door and music filtered out, Glenn Miller, big swing band. "Wow, that's a blast from the past," Marti said.

"Great, isn't it?" Peter gestured for her to come in. "I'm finding all my parents' old records. Wanna dance?"

"I can't, remember?"

Peter took her hand, swinging her back and forth and all around. "It's impossible not to dance to this."

Marti was enjoying herself. "They had fun in that era, didn't they?"

"Didn't we?" Peter asked.

"Well, Dylan and the Doors weren't exactly dance music. We were too busy nurturing our angst." She paused, thinking for a moment before continuing. "We weren't dying in a world war. And maybe that's the difference; they were clinging to life."

"Oh, shut up and dance."

A slow song came on next, and they moved together. "Close your eyes," Peter commanded, "and stop all that . . . *whatever*. Just feel." Marti swayed back and forth, following Peter's warm body moving perfectly in rhythm. Opening her eyes, she smiled at him and he kissed her on the lips, a gentle kiss. She responded. After a moment, they separated, awkwardly.

"Now I've done it," Peter said.

"Done what?" Marti asked.

"Kissed the ice princess. I can cross it off my list of impossible accomplishments. On to Everest."

"Fuck you!" Marti said, laughing as she pushed him away.

"No, sorry, I won't go that far. However, I did always want to kiss you, but you weren't interested."

"Actually, this summer I was."

"Too late. But good to know."

He motioned for her to sit and pulled the needle off the record. It had been a while since she'd seen a record player, and being in this house sent her childlike perceptions in motion, imagining the needle to be a bird beak, like on *The Flintstones*. Feeling an absence, she scanned the living room for Mrs. Colgan's clothes. There were several suitcases in the hall.

"Where are the kids?" she asked.

"Home. I left them in Boston because I'm leaving tomorrow. Glad you came by."

"You're done?" She gestured around the room.

"Ann is coming to finish. I can't do it. I need to get home to my life."

Marti pulled the mosaic out of a bag and held it out to him. "For you, a gift. It's the lake and mountains."

He studied it carefully. "You did this? When?"

"This summer. I've started working again."

"That's great, although you never gave up your art. You use it in your job."

"True, but as far as doing my own, it was lost to me like a lot of things, post-Spencer."

"Now you're post-post Spencer." He slapped her five.

"My kids don't start school full-time for another year, so I won't think about my career till then." Peter paused. "I could keep on doing this."

"You're great at it."

"Yeah, maybe we'll adopt again; it's hard, though—adoption agencies are suspicious of gay parents. But Roger is a lawyer, so maybe it will work out."

"No one could refuse Roger."

"Oh, look. I'm taking Fancy-Fancy to add to my collection of plastic gay icons."

"Plastic gay icons?"

"Yeah, don't you think Fancy's one? Too bad I didn't realize, back then, I'd have let you have Top Cat. I've had my collection for years on a big shelf in the kitchen. I've got a Liberace, Bert, and Ernie all nestled in their beds, Tinky-Winky—though the kids keep nabbing that one. I'm proudest of my Oscar Wilde. I just found a Rock Hudson—how obscure is that? Someone else must collect these things."

"This must drive Roger crazy."

"Yeah, that's half the fun. When he's mad, he threatens to buy me a Roy Cohn. Wait." He left the room and returned holding out his closed hand. "Surprise! For you." Top Cat lay in his palm.

"Oh, Jeez Louise! I *finally* get a turn with Top Cat."

"Hey, feel lucky I didn't give you chewed-up Spook. Oh, and check this out." He took a basket off a shelf; inside were the troll dolls.

"Wow, our favorite, favorite toys!"

"Yeah, the twins have been playing with them. We're taking them, but you could pick one."

"Not if they are using them—"

"Not like they'll miss one. There are dozens."

"Okay, you know which one—"

"Natty-Bratty Baby." Peter laughed. "We loved her best because we were bratty babies. Hang on, something else." He handed her a picture of the two of them, age six, covered in mud. "We had a hell of a lot of fun. Here's another." It was a picture of Marti playing hopscotch with Marybeth and Nancy.

"I never knew anyone took this picture."

"Ma was good at sneaking around. Hundreds of pictures in this house."

Marti studied it closely. "I'm pregnant here."

"Maybe you don't want it."

"I do; playing with your sisters was a bright spot in a dark summer. I wonder, do you think your mother realized?"

Peter winced slightly. "She did. It was in an envelope in her night table, along with . . . those prayer cards."

Standing in the doorway saying goodbye, Peter touched her scars. "That's the other reason I never tried to kiss you. I was scared of these."

"Me too. Not so scary after all."

"Come visit us in Boston. The kids adore you and Tess."

"Pearl?" Marti scoffed.

"Okay, Pearl adores Tess. She'll get there with you. You can be another aunty."

"Don't they have enough?"

"You know us Colgans—never enough."

She stopped across the street, and seeing no car in the driveway, crept around back to visit her forest family tree. She knew children lived in this house; she'd seen the bicycle and now there was more evidence: a doll carriage and some stray balls. She wanted to entice them to come play at the tree and discover its magic. Reaching in her pocket, she took out Top Cat and wedged him between two tree roots. The tree roots still looked like dinosaur feet to Marti. Top Cat's head cocked with attitude as he jauntily tipped his hat in greeting. She took Natty-Bratty Baby and stood him in the valley between the dinosaur feet facing a large toadstool. She placed some acorns and leaves on top of the toadstool table. *Dinner.* Next, she took a stick and fashioned a kind of fork and tied it to Natty-Bratty Baby's hand with a weed stem. As if in on the joke, the troll grinned his foolish grin.

Marti stood back, looking at the tableau, satisfied. She felt like Boo Radley hiding presents in a tree, and this was fitting, because in those lonely years, she'd been a kind of Boo Radley. She could credit Brooke for rescuing her from her friendless state and for getting her out when she needed.

Marti went to the lake one afternoon, seeking out Linda and thanking her for helping with Tess. She invited Emily to come to Brooklyn to spend a weekend. She considered extending the invitation to the whole family, but didn't as it wasn't what she wanted. Worried about transporting her new artwork, she purchased a hard rooftop carrier for the car, a good solution. After she finished packing and cleaning, she took Caliban for a final swim. The trees were in vivid color, and the water was getting colder. Marti, a Vermonter, liked the water cold.

They stopped for lunch at a diner before crossing the state border. Tess fidgeted with things on the table. "Look, Mom, they have honey sticks. Can I take some?"

"One."

"Only one?"

"All right, two." *Did she ever stop negotiating?* "Pass me one," Marti said, reaching out her hand.

"You never use honey."

Marti twirled the stick with her fingers and tore the plastic with her teeth, smelling the honey before sucking up its sweetness. She closed her eyes and was instantly transported: Mommy making little Marti tea, more milk and honey than tea. Daddy spooning in still more honey, lifting his finger to his lips, and mouthing *Shh* with a wink. Thinking about it now, Marti was sure her mother knew; it was part of the game.

She remembered sitting in the Colgan kitchen while Mrs. Colgan passed the children a seemingly endless supply of warm honey cakes. She'd walk around the table and put a dollop of soft honey butter on top of each one, the butter slowly oozing down the sides. Marti could taste the sweet treat melting in her mouth and hear Mrs. Colgan's murmur: *Are you sure you wouldn't want another, Marti, thin as you are, child?*

And then there was Rob, calling her to come marvel at young Tess, standing in their back garden. Tess's head was bent back, wisps of golden curls dancing behind her, one arm clutching the honey jar to her chest while her other hand, suspended high in the air, dangled the wooden dipper dripping with luminescent swirls of amber honey. The honey rippled ever so slowly into Tess's wide-open, expectant mouth. The gazing, adoring parents mirrored the delight on their daughter's face. Spotting them, Tess gave a sheepish shrug. Marti responded with: *Who are you, Winnie the Pooh?* inviting squeals of joyous laughter.

Marti opened her eyes.

"Where were you?" Tess asked.

"Right here."

Waiting to pay, Marti fiddled with the maple candy at the register, picking out the carefree, confident boy for Tess and the maple leaf for herself. She paid by card, scrawling *Martha Farrell* across the slip.

Turning to Tess, she said, "Let's go. No time like the present." Before they reached the car, Caliban stuck his head out the rear window, and Marti could hear his tail thumping against the seat with anticipation.

ACKNOWLEDGMENTS

t's a sign of a rich life when you have many people to feel grateful for:

Much gratitude to Brooke Warner and She Writes Press for helping me realize my vision.

Students and faculty at the City College of New York guided this fledgling book in its tentative early flight. In particular, I am indebted to Professors Linsey Abrams and Emily Raboteau. Linsey Abrams had a unique gift of steering students' novels in the direction they wanted. I'll never forget a meeting with her when she said, "You know on page sixty-two when she answers the question? Don't have her answer. That's all." How incredibly illuminating and profound this simple advice was. Kudos to fellow student Amy Veach, who spent days with me in libraries and coffee shops across New York City where we carried each other on our long slog to fruition.

To friends and family members, too many to name here, who read multiple drafts, came to readings, and boosted me in numerous ways. Your support was everything. And always, thanks to Josephine for enriching my life, and to Jean and Jay Meinhardt for the lifelong friendship.

Friends in particular: Lizzie Olesker for her clear vision and steady encouragement. Lois Terry for cheering me on from across an ocean. Karen Ritter for brilliantly commiserating with me whenever I needed it. Lynn Steger Strong for steering me back to the beginning when I was lost in the weeds.

I owe a huge debt to Lenore Los Kamp. She traveled this journey all the way with me, offering me space to write, printing pages, reading drafts over and over and over. Lenore, my biggest champion, I can never fully express how much it's meant.

Gratitude to my parents for fostering a hunger to soak up all the world has to offer, and for providing me with a love of literature as a road map. My mother managed to read an early draft of this novel in her difficult final year, even putting her wise copy-editing skills to use.

Most of all, thanks to my sons, Timothy and Ian Holloway, who never expressed resentment for all the times I overlooked them while immersed in this book over many years. They advised me patiently in the minutiae of finding just the right words or phrases. Tim and Ian offered me such steady love and reassurance— parenting me—while they were growing into wise adults. You are the greatest gifts of my life.

ABOUT THE AUTHOR

Melissa Connelly dropped out of high school at age fifteen. In spite of this, she went on to receive a BSN in nursing, an MA in special education, and an MFA in creative writing. She's had a long career working with children in a variety of roles in schools, hospitals, psychiatric clinics, and day cares. Her work has been published in *American Heritage Magazine*, *Ruminate Magazine* and the anthology *It's All About Shoes*, and she was a finalist for the 2019 Montana Prize. Connelly has a home in the mountains of Western North Carolina but lives most of the year in Brooklyn, New York.

Looking for your next great read?

We can help!

Visit www.shewritespress.com/next-read
or scan the QR code below for a list
of our recommended titles.

She Writes Press is an award-winning
independent publishing company founded to
serve women writers everywhere.